SOME OF US ARE LOOKING

Books by Carlene O'Connor

Irish Village Mysteries

MURDER IN AN IRISH VILLAGE

MURDER AT AN IRISH WEDDING

MURDER IN AN IRISH CHURCHYARD

MURDER IN AN IRISH PUB

MURDER IN AN IRISH COTTAGE

MURDER AT AN IRISH CHRISTMAS

MURDER IN AN IRISH BOOKSHOP

MURDER ON AN IRISH FARM

MURDER AT AN IRISH BAKERY

CHRISTMAS COCOA MURDER
(with Maddie Day and Alex Erickson)

CHRISTMAS SCARF MURDER
(with Maddie Day and Peggy Ehrhart)

A Home to Ireland Mystery

MURDER IN GALWAY

MURDER IN CONNEMARA

HALLOWEEN CUPCAKE MURDER
(with Liz Ireland and Carol J. Perry)

A County Kerry Mystery

NO STRANGERS HERE

SOME OF US ARE LOOKING

Published by Kensington Publishing Corp.

A County Kerry Novel

SOME OF US ARE LOOKING

CARLENE O'CONNOR

KENSINGTON
PUBLISHING CORP.

www.kensingtonbooks.com

KENSINGTON BOOKS are published by

Kensington Publishing Corp.
119 West 40th Street
New York, NY 10018

All Kensington titles, imprints, and distributed lines are available at special quantity discounts for bulk purchases for sales promotion, premiums, fund-raising, educational, or institutional use. Special book excerpts or customized printings can also be created to fit specific needs. For details, write or phone the office of the Kensington Special Sales Manager: Attn. Special Sales Department. Kensington Publishing Corp, 119 West 40th Street, New York, NY 10018. Phone: 1-800-221-2647.

The K with book logo Reg US Pat. & TM Off.

ISBN: 978-1-4967-3755-7
First Kensington Hardcover Edition: November 2023
First Kensington Trade Edition: October 2023

ISBN: 978-1-4967-5113-3 (trade)
ISBN: 978-1-4967-3757-1 (e-book)

10 9 8 7 6 5 4 3 2 1

Printed in the United States of America

"We are all in the gutter, but some of us are looking at the stars."
—Oscar Wilde

CHAPTER 1

Tonight would be a spectacular night for her to die. A glorious send-off. The Perseid meteor showers would attract quite a bit of attention, and if there was ever a night to "go to the light," this was it. One hundred meteors per hour streaking from the Irish skies while the Atlantic Ocean thrashed in the background. What a way to go! It was possible, knowing her, that even *that* wouldn't be enough to coax the vixen to heaven. She may very well sink into the dark abyss. *Goodnight, angel.* She was a stunner, a head turner; that was just an objective fact. She was the one who chose to exploit it, used her beauty to destroy men, not to mention a few women. She had mastered the art of humiliation, but she would not have the last laugh.

She was visible now, just through the trees, a flash of dark hair, a glimpse of a royal blue dress lifting in the summer wind. Those shapely thighs and heart-shaped calves, that skin which defied their pale-skinned people and actually tanned, that long dark hair cascading down her back, that youthful laugh. She had so many people fooled. Was there anything more ignorant than assuming a beautiful face came with a beautiful soul?

She was laughing now, twirling for an audience in front of the silver caravan. The location, in close proximity to the

Camp-to-Annascaul section of the Dingle Way hiking trail, was ideally situated for preying on gullible tourists. Grown men throwing away euros on a lucky rabbit's foot just to have a close-up gawk at her. *You reap what you sow.* A nearby patch of trees beckoned. From the cocoon of the woods, the sounds of Tralee Bay were amplified, as if fanned in by the leaves. Trees. What fascinating plants. Oak, birch, ash, Sitka spruces. Sharing information and nutrition through their root systems. A secret underground society. Hidden in plain sight. The trees knew what was coming. What an appropriate grave for the little nymph.

One could see what she was doing. One could see it all.

She, on the other hand, had no idea what was coming. What a pity. *Blindsided.* That had a certain ring to it, although it would also be satisfying to whisper the news into her ear, watch her eyes widen with fear, see a shiver run down her perfect spine. *To everything there is a season.* "Turn, turn, turn." . . . Hunting season. Her beauty would not save her this time. It was tempting to stay and watch her some more. Her last full day on earth. But time was of the essence, and essential things were needed. A list had to be made. The hand that held the biro trembled with anticipation as the four essential ingredients were penned:

Twine
Rope
Rabbit's foot
Butcher's knife

CHAPTER 2

Chris Henderson barged past the reception desk at the Tralee Garda Station, and before anyone could stop him, he'd flung open Sergeant Barbara Neely's very flimsy door. "I caught a pervert," he announced. It was his third visit this week, but his first time making this particular pronouncement. He stood with one hand behind his back, the other resting atop his cane.

Inspector Cormac O'Brien, who still hadn't spilled whatever he'd come to spill, was making her mental by standing behind the chair across from her desk instead of sitting down like a normal human being. He was gripping it so tightly his knuckles were turning white. In this job, there was no such thing as enough cups of tea. She'd wanted a quiet morning, had been hoping to squeeze in a workout during lunch, yearning for some calm before the meteor storm. She glanced at her mug of lukewarm tea and imagined pouring a shot of whiskey into it. Neely stood. "You do know that I can arrest you for barging in here." She probably couldn't. But she could certainly threaten it. Being elderly was no excuse for storming into her station like his arse was on fire and she was the only one with a water hose. Neely was a fool. At sixty-three years of age, instead of retiring, she'd transferred to the Tralee Garda Station from

Dingle. And ever since, she'd dealt with complaints like this one. *Eejit.*

Chris Henderson pounded his cane, and his dark eyes flashed with anger. "You are the guardians of the peace, and there is no peace in the village of Camp with that caravan!" He whipped his hand out from behind his back, revealing a massive pair of binoculars.

Cormac O'Brien turned and took in the binoculars. "For the meteor shower?" he asked. "Nice pair."

Neely flicked him a look, and Cormac grinned. The detective inspector had loosened up since his move to the Dingle Peninsula a few months back, and Neely wasn't sure she liked it. She suspected his eternal grin had something to do with his crush on the local veterinarian, Dr. Dimpna Wilde, but given that they'd done nothing but dance around each other at trad sessions, funneling their lust through a fiddle and a squeeze-box, she was going to keep her nose and her gob out of it.

Mr. Henderson shook the binoculars. "They belong to a pervert. Caught him creeping around that caravan in his black Audi. I said it before, and I'll say it again. Only perverts drive German cars!"

"It's not against the law to drive a German car, Mr. Henderson," Neely said, lowering herself back into her seat. "And I've seen no evidence to suggest that those who drive them are perverts."

"But have you studied it?" Cormac asked her, keeping a straight face. "Properly?"

She seared him with a look. "Maybe I *should* conduct a study," she said. "What do you drive again, Detective Inspector?"

"A Toyota that's nearly as old as me," Cormac said. "But she's steady as she goes." He winked.

Neely rolled her eyes. She'd been afraid the Perseid meteor showers would bring forth a bit of insanity; she just hadn't expected it from within the ranks.

Chris Henderson frowned, eyes bouncing between them as they bantered. "Now, what are you going to do about this pervert?"

Neely gestured to the door. "Please see our receptionist in the front. She'll give you an incident form to fill out."

Henderson banged his cane on the floor. "I'm not filling out another bloody form. I'm telling you now. He was *perving*. Looking at that girl in the caravan with these yokes." He waved the binoculars again. "What caravan, you ask? The one I keep telling you to do something about!" He jabbed his cane at Neely.

"Hold your horses," Neely said. "I sent an *inspector* there yesterday to lay down the law." She gestured to Cormac. His jaw tightened. He didn't like the spotlight.

"And?" Henderson said, his gaze sliding to Cormac. "Did you boot them out?"

Cormac shook his head. "I only talked to one of them, but from what I could see, they weren't breaking any laws."

It wasn't Cormac's words that startled Neely; it was his tone. *Meek.* The detective inspector she knew was anything but. Humble at times, albeit mostly pushy. He had his weird little ways about him. Whenever they went to lunch, he had to sit facing the door, and he always wiped the table before the server arrived, even when it was spotless. He was fidgety. Allergic to everything. But other than that, he was bright. She'd rather have him on her side than against her. He was handsome, but somewhat scruffy, which was odd for a perfectionist with a boatload of quirks. But she'd never met an inspector sharper or more determined to seek out the truth. He was an enigma, that was for sure.

Henderson pursed his lips. "I told you I saw a pervert—a creeper—lurking across from the caravan in his German car, with these things aimed directly at that bonnie girl." He lifted the binoculars and peered through, then took the binoculars from the ground to the ceiling, as if reenacting the scene. Neely half-expected his eyes to pop out of their sockets, like some kind of cartoon character.

"How did you get your hands on the binoculars?" Cormac asked. He stepped back from the chair and crossed his arms.

"I approached his car, yelling, 'Hey! Pervert! I see you!'" Chris said. "Your one dropped them out the window and screeched away like a bat out of hell."

"Are you telling me that you picked those binoculars up with your bare hands, perhaps ruining any chance of us getting fingerprints off them?" Neely asked, staring him down.

Mr. Henderson let out a yelp, and the binoculars clattered to the floor. "Take me prints," he said, wriggling his hand like it was a fish he caught. "You can take me prints and separate out his, can't ye?"

"Alright, alright, let's all calm down," Neely said. She was only messing about the fingerprints; she had no intention of following through with that, but she rose and yelled out the door for a guard. A moment later, Garda Lennon stuck his head in the door.

"I was just headed your way." Barry Lennon, the youngest addition to the station, had yet to wipe that eager-to-please look off his face. With his platinum-blond curls and blue eyes, she had no doubt he was mercilessly teased in garda college. But given that he completed any task asked of him with nary a complaint, she was beginning to think he was a grown man after all. But really. Twenty-two? One day he'd be running the place, and she'd be nothing more than a dusty plaque on the hallway wall. *Depressing.*

"Can you grab some gloves and an evidence bag for these binoculars?" Sometimes it was best to go along to get along.

"Sure thing." Garda Lennon lingered in the doorway.

Neely frowned. "Something on your mind?"

Lennon nodded to Cormac. "Just got a call from the Dingle Garda Station asking for you, Detective Inspector."

Neely glanced at Cormac. "Don't you have a mobile?"

Cormac tilted his head. "Turned it off. Was hoping for a private chat." He didn't look in Henderson's direction, but the connotation hung in the air.

Neely threw open her arms. "Best-laid plans."

"Is there a message?" Cormac asked.

"There's been some kind of vandalism at the shops in Dingle."

Cormac groaned. "More than one shop?"

Lennon nodded, then scratched his head. "They said something about writing on the wall."

"Can you give them a bell, tell them I'm on my way to the harbor?"

"Absolutely." Lennon hurried out of the room.

"You're leaving?" Mr. Henderson shook his fist. "I didn't even get to talk about me foxes."

Neely couldn't help it, she audibly groaned. Again with the foxes. Had she known Henderson was coming, she would have made a bet with Cormac. *How many minutes until he mentions a fox?*

"You're in good hands," Cormac said, grinning at Neely. Before she could reply, he slipped out the door. She turned to Henderson. "I know someone who might be able to help with your fox dilemma."

"Oh?" Chris Henderson arched a bushy white eyebrow.

"The clerk at the reception desk has a calling card for a man from ISPCA." He'd been called out to the caravan to check on the well-being of the dogs. The caravaners had a giant pair of drooling mastiffs that had been breaking their chains and chasing after cars. He hadn't seen any signs of abuse, but he dropped his calling card off at the station. Maybe it was fate. "You're welcome to take his card, give him a bell."

"And he can help, can he?" From the tone of Chris Henderson's voice, he was doubtful.

"I hope so. They are the Irish Society for Prevention of Cruelty to Animals, are they not?"

She prayed that would be the end of the discussion, that he'd scurry out to fetch the card.

"People drive too fast," Henderson said. "One thousand, three hundred and seventy-seven of these stunning creatures are killed every year on Irish roadways." He pounded his cane. "*Every year.*"

"Good on you for leading the brigade," Neely said. "But you can't wander the roadside wagging your finger at drivers, or you'll be the next stunning creature to get knocked down." Neely came around from behind her desk. She'd have to leave the office to get him to follow suit.

"What about Brigid Sweeney?" Henderson asked.

"What about her?" The caravaners were no longer breaking any laws. There was nothing they could do.

"She dances in broad daylight!" Henderson said. "Charges hikers and tourists to pose with her for photos. She's twirling around and showing off her assets!" He slid a look to his feet. "They're considerable," he added under his breath.

Neely groaned. Respecting the elderly was a virtue she held dear, but it was way too early for his misogyny and stereotyping. She imagined taping his mouth shut, another indicator she might be approaching career burnout. "Dancing isn't a crime either, Mr. Henderson."

Henderson pursed his lips and stared at a spot on the wall. "Your one better look where she steps, or someone's missus is going to be out for blood."

"We'll handle it, Mr. Henderson. Now. I bet you have a very busy morning, and you'll be wanting to be on your way." Traffic wardens had already issued two tickets on that caravan and sent out an inspector. The next thing she'd send would be a tow truck. Only she had to deal with the mastiffs. And from what she'd seen, they weren't the friendly sort of mutts. Henderson was right. Neely should have done more. The group was nothing but trouble. It wasn't as if she hadn't warned them. One of the lads swore they would be gone by the end of the day. That was two days ago. She didn't like being played for a fool. *Trouble.* She smelled trouble.

Neely turned and pushed the intercom button on her phone. "Ann?"

"Yes, Sergeant?" The front-desk clerk was perky as always. Neely wished that didn't annoy her. Maybe she and Garda Lennon would fall in love and breed uber-optimistic lads in short trousers.

"Do you have the calling card for that man from ISPCA? What was he called again?"

"Charlie Meade?" Ann said straightaway.

Neely hadn't met him, but from Ann's reaction, she took it he was handsome. Or at least handsome in Ann's eyes—the woman was generous to a fault. "That's it. Charlie Meade."

"I have his card right here."

"Can you make a copy for Mr. Henderson, and also give Meade a bell—let him know we may need him in the next day or so to pay another visit to our caravaners."

"There was something about the way the creeper was staring at the girl," Chris Henderson said. "Gave me the chills."

"Leave the caravaners to me," Neely said. She could not take one more second of this man. And Cormac never did get to have his say. She'd join him at the harbor to see what this vandalism was all about. She tried a softer approach with Henderson. "Why don't you go home and have a rest?"

"Not a chance," Mr. Henderson said. "I can rest when I'm dead."

CHAPTER 3

John Street in Dingle was a treat for the eyes with its colorful shops, pubs, and restaurants. Cormac couldn't help but think of all the history that was packed into this charming harbor town. He thought about how Dingle thrived in the fourteenth century by trading with France and Spain, exporting fish and hides, and importing wine. By the sixteenth century, Dingle had become one of Ireland's main trading points. But like everything and everyone else in life, Dingle also suffered. In the seventeenth century, the town was burned and plundered, and during the Great Famine in the 1840s, more than five thousand people died in the Dingle Poorhouse alone. Their burial sites in the pauper's burial ground overlooked the town. But then good luck struck again in 1984 when Paddy Ferriter, the Dingle Harbor lighthouse keeper, spotted a lone dolphin escorting fishing boats in and out of the harbor. Fungie would become the darling of Dingle for the next thirty-seven years, delighting locals and tourists alike. Sadly, he'd since disappeared without a trace.

Many of the buildings on John Street were historic—if only *those* walls could talk. But the writings they were looking at now, on at least ten shops, were scratched out in chalk. It would be easy enough to wash off, and three shops that were "hit" had already washed theirs away, but it was odd enough that at least one shopkeeper talked the rest into calling the guards. Cormac stood in front of the ice cream shop, reading the message over and over again, as if an explanation would suddenly appear.

WHO PUT BELLA IN THE WITCH ELM?

"Mean anything to you?" Cormac asked Neely. He knew she would follow. He was surprised it had taken this long. The guards had temporarily blocked access to the upper portion of John Street where the shops had been chalked. Tourists were starting to gather in clumps on the other side of the barrier, pulled in by the lure of the drama. Given that they were being treated to a rare dose of summer weather and the shopkeepers were eager to welcome in customers, they had to work quickly. The scent of sugary ice cream tickled his nose.

"Hold on," Neely said, bringing out her mobile phone. "Is the message exactly the same on every shop?"

Ten shops—three washed them off already. They're all the same except this one." He pointed to the lower corner of the wall in front of them. Neely bent down. She could make out four words, also in chalk:

THE HAND OF GLORY.

Was it akin to an artist's signature?

"I didn't bring me reading glasses," Neely said, straightening herself up. "Give it a read, will ya?"

" 'The Hand of Glory.' "

Neely repeated it to herself a few times. "Is it religious? Are we dealing with some kind of zealot here?"

Cormac shrugged. "The possibilities are endless." He crossed his arms. "Either way. He's definitely trying to send some kind of message."

Neely stood. "He?"

"Or she."

"Damn straight."

Cormac had mixed feelings about Neely joining him. He hadn't had a chance to confess his sins, and now that he was no longer in her stuffy office, he was having second thoughts about doing so. He was a grown man. He was allowed to have sex. Was she too young? Yes. Twenty-four. Jaysus. He should be ashamed of himself. And he was. He was also oddly proud of himself. It had been so long. He was impulsive; he went against his own grain. And he'd told the truth—he saw no evidence they were breaking any laws. He and a grown woman went out for lunch, had a few pints, and knocked boots in the great outdoors behind the pub. It was so out of character, but lately he'd been stressed and sad. His mam was going downhill. Motor neuron disease was cruel. Day after day, he watched her suffer and struggle.

He had sex. It happens. It *happened*. Maybe the caravaners would soon be on their merry way, and he would never have to think about it again. Maybe his mam was right, and he needed to find a good woman. Or a flawed one . . .

The only thing he knew for sure was that he did not want Dimpna Wilde to find out. Would she even care?

"Heya!" A male head popped out of the ice cream shop. "Take your photos, and let us get back to work." He gestured to the antsy crowd.

"We have our photos," Cormac said. "The sugar addicts will be coming your way soon, don't you worry."

The shopkeeper grinned. "Good man."

Cormac confirmed with the photographer that she had completed her task, then instructed the shopkeepers to wash off the messages, noting that, once that was done, the guards would remove the barriers. He also gave a warning that he did not want to see a single photo of the chalk messages on social media, but he had a nagging feeling it was going to happen anyway. Too many people had already seen them, and no doubt their camera phones had been flashing. It was exactly the kind of attention this scribbler wanted, and Cormac was loath to feed the beast.

Neely looked up from her mobile phone. "I knew it," she exclaimed. "I knew there was something familiar about Bella."

Cormac despised technology. But he had to concede that it had its place. Now that they were across the street, watching shopkeepers hose down their walls, the smell of ice cream was replaced with the scent of fish and chips wafting out from a nearby pub. Overhead, gulls cried and swooped. "Story horse?" he asked.

Neely had perked up, and her voice came out in an excited rush. "The original messages referred to a wych elm." She pointed out the misspelling on the wall:

WITCH.

"Original messages?"

She held up a finger. "However . . . in the 1970s, the incorrect spelling—witch, as in the broom-riding kind—appeared on a stone obelisk near Stourbridge." She waited to see if this resonated with Cormac. It did not. He waited. "In England," she added.

"I have absolutely no fecking idea what you're on about. The 1970s? England?"

"The entire case goes back to 1944."

"Case?"

She read off her phone. "The graffiti 'Who put Bella down the wych elm?' began appearing in England in 1944 after four young lads discovered the skeletal remains of a woman inside a wych elm in Hagley Woods."

"Jaysus."

"To this day, they've never identified her." Neely began to gesture. "Messages were written in a variety of renditions—

'Who put Bella in the wych elm?' 'Who put Bella down the witch elm?'—and there were all kinds of theories as to who she was, a German spy being the most popular. There's a lot more, but it's going to take ages to read through it all."

"I guess we're looking at a true-crime buff. Maybe this is all some kind of twisted advertising for her true-crime podcast."

"Or his," Neely said.

Cormac couldn't win. He gestured to the wall. "What about 'Hand of Glory'?"

Neely's tongue stuck out of her mouth as she googled again. "The pickled hand of a hanged man. The 'hand that did the deed.'"

Cormac took in the wall. "Someone is definitely trying to tell us something."

"Meteor showers," Neely said, shaking her head. "I knew it was going to bring trouble."

"Seems relatively harmless. Ready to head out?"

Neely nodded, and they began walking toward the car park at the harbor. There was a buzz in the air, a jovial atmosphere, and a hearty crowd. From a distance came the sound of tin whistles and guitars.

"What was it you came to see me about?" Neely asked. "You said you wanted a private chat?"

Cormac was hoping she'd never ask. He wrestled with the words he should say. *Remember when you sent me out to that caravan . . .* "When you sent me out to that caravan, there was only one of them at home"—Neely's mobile phone rang. She held up a finger, then put her phone on speaker. They had reached the dock, and they had to lean in to hear over the sound of boat horns, bustling fishermen, and amped-up tourists. The ocean rippled, and the sun shone down on them. It was picture-perfect. So why did it all feel so ominous? Maybe it was his shame, eating away at everything.

"Chris Henderson on the line for you," Cormac heard Garda Lennon say.

Neely groaned. "Tell him I'm in a meeting."

"He said it's urgent."

"Put him through." She gripped the phone, already regretting it.

His voice came across the line in fits and spurts. The connection was terrible. ". . . Never believe . . . pervert . . . wolf . . . sheep . . . clothing."

Neely glanced at Cormac to see if he could decipher it. He shook his head. "Mr. Henderson, this is a terrible connection."

". . . caught . . . station . . . Camp." She could hear the sounds of cars whipping past.

"If you're walking the roadways again, I'm begging you to stop." The connection severed. Neely sighed and stared at the phone. She hung up, then called Ann back.

"Can we send a squad car to Camp? I just want to make sure Chris Henderson isn't playing in traffic again."

"Absolutely."

Neely hung up and shook her head. "I'm over this meteor shower already."

They reached Neely's squad car. She inhaled. "Do you smell that?"

"The ocean?"

"Fish and chips."

"Did you want to stop for lunch?"

"I can't." She sighed. "If this diet lasts any longer, I'll be fighting the gulls for scraps of bread."

Cormac nodded sympathetically. His mam had already instilled in him the importance of staying far out of any conversations concerning women and their weight. "Here's the story," he said. "When you sent me out to that caravan"—Her phone rang again. This time, she left it off speaker, but he could tell from the look on her face that it was far from good news.

"There's been an incident in Camp," she said as she pocketed her phone.

Cormac felt his stomach drop. He'd had this sinking feeling of dread all morning. "What now?"

"A hit-and-run. We've got one dead. Driver screeched away."

"God," Cormac said, heading to the passenger side. "Tell me it's not Chris Henderson."

Neely threw open her door. They piled inside. "It *is* Chris Henderson."

"He was struck by a car?"

Neely nodded as she started the squad car. "Hit-and-run. Witnesses say it wasn't an accident."

"I don't understand. Either there was an accident or there wasn't." He held onto the dash as Neely pulled out. Throngs of people were crossing from the square to the harbor. She threw on the lights and sirens and waited for them to scatter. "Witnesses say the car seemed to be trailing Henderson. That it deliberately plowed into him and screeched off."

Like a bat out of hell . . . Cormac's heart was thudding in her chest. "Was anyone able to identify the driver?"

Neely shook her head. "All we know for sure is that Chris Henderson was struck and killed by a black Audi."

CHAPTER 4

"Wilde's Mixed Animal Practice," Niamh Dowd chirped into the phone. "Niamh speaking. Ah, Mrs. White, it's good to hear from ya. I wanted to remind you that Porky is due for his vaccinations. I know, I know! We're all going. I'm hoping to get off early to suss out a sweet spot. Do you think it will bring us luck?"

Standing in Exam Room 1 with her vet tech, Patrick Kelly, Dr. Dimpna Wilde could imagine the grin on her office manager's face as her booming voice pierced through the air vent.

Patrick winced as an orange tabby clawed up his chest. "It's like an amplifier," he said. "You can hear everything."

"Indeed." Dimpna had often wondered how her father knew so much about his patients when he didn't really engage them in chatter, but now that she'd taken over the clinic, she'd finally discovered Eamon Wilde's secret. You didn't even have to try to eavesdrop; the vents did the job for you.

Dimpna reached for the toenail clippers, while trying not to make eye contact with the feline. If Donovan locked eyes with you, it was as if he immediately knew everything you were about to do to him, and he'd freak out. Last time she cut his nails, he'd leapt onto the nearby cabinet, shaking medical contents loose and onto the floor. It took an hour to pick up everything, and she was still finding odd bits here and there. The cat gave Dimpna the side-eye and yowled some more. Dimpna peeled him off Patrick's chest, eliciting a few whines from both of them.

Patrick cleared his throat. "Mr. McCarthy wants his anal glands expressed too."

"I'm afraid he'll have to go to his own doctor for that," Dimpna said. "Unless you're willing. Some employees go above and beyond. In this case, I'm afraid you'd be going below and beyond."

Patrick stared at her for a moment, revulsion stamped on his handsome, young face. It thrilled Dimpna way more than it should have. Dimpna's lips finally betrayed her, and she smirked. Patrick's face flushed red once more, then he began to shake with laughter. "Donovan's anal glands," he said. "But now I'll never be able to look Mr. McCarthy in the eye again."

"Ah, you will, so. If this job doesn't toughen you up, nothing will." Humor was the one balm Dimpna couldn't do without, even if it was gallows humor at times.

Patrick chatted as he attended to Donovan's chart. "Do you think Niamh is right? Is the meteor shower good luck?"

"I do not believe in good versus bad luck," Dimpna said. "Just as I don't believe black cats are bad luck or that women are witches."

"I didn't say that last bit," Patrick said. "About black cats or witches." He handed Dimpna the chart. It brought a smile to her face.

"Maybe I do believe in luck." She rolled up on her toes before settling back down.

Patrick raised an eyebrow. "Why is that?"

"You're up next in the anal-gland rotation."

Patrick groaned. The phone rang again, and once more Niamh's chipper voice filled the room. "Wow," Patrick said.

"You can hear everything in here." He gave her a look as if she was a bona fide voyeur.

Dimpna shrugged. "Some conversations are more interesting than others." She hummed a soothing tone as she quickly trimmed Donovan's tough nails. She handed him back to Patrick and clapped him on the back. "Take your time with the anal glands. Really get in there."

Patrick mimicked a wretch, then reached for a pair of medical gloves. Dimpna tried not to laugh as he completed the task, taking notes on a clipboard from the corner of the room. "I'd say you're getting to be a pro," she said when he was finished. "Maybe you should be our go-to anal-glands expresser."

Patrick shook his head. "In that case, I would just go."

Dimpna laughed again. "There are far worse tasks. You'll see." She couldn't wait until he was elbow deep up a cow's arse at half-two in the morning. She gestured for him to leave the room with an even-crankier Donovan, who was digging his newly trimmed claws into Patrick's chest once more. In this profession, this was how their patients thanked them for their work. They strode to the waiting room, where Dimpna pried the cat from Patrick's chest and turned him over to Gordon. He was a retired chemist who lived downtown. He and his cat were a regular sight on a bench near the harbor. Donovan often perched on Gordon's shoulder as Gordon sketched boats.

"Hello, Donovan," Gordon said, setting him down on his sketch pad and scratching behind his ear. "How'd the appointment go?" The cat meowed and swished his tail.

"As well as can be expected," Patrick said.

"It was grand," Dimpna said. "He's all sorted."

Gordon held up a shaking hand. "I'm just not up to the task anymore. Me fingers won't hold the trimmers still."

"Don't ya worry about a thing," Dimpna said. "We can keep up a regular trim." She hoped he'd be able to continue with his sketches, but from the looks of his hand tremors, there would come a time when he would no longer be able to hold a pencil. Hopefully, he would enjoy every second while he could, or perhaps he would learn to sketch with a pencil in his mouth. Animals and people were resilient, a bright spot in a world that could be so dark. As Gordon and Donovan settled their bill and said their goodbyes, Dimpna checked out the patient-board. Niamh was an excellent manager, and Dimpna appreciated the color-coded board—red for those who needed immediate attention, then orange, and finally green. Their next patient, Toby, a hound with chronic bad breath and a penchant for eating inanimate objects, was a green.

"Is Toby here?" Dimpna asked Niamh, with a nod to the board.

"They just called to cancel," Niamh said. "Apparently, Toby swallowed a rubber shark, but he's already pooped it out."

Knowing the household consisted of four young lads, Dimpna didn't even need to ask. "Good for Toby," Dimpna said. She could only hope they threw the toy away.

"Soon it will be showtime!" Niamh said, pointing to a shining star she had pinned in her hair. "I'm getting in the mood!"

"I'm getting in a mood too," Dimpna said. "I just don't know what mood it is yet."

The phone rang, and Niamh snatched it up. She stared at Dimpna as she spoke. "Yes, we take emergency calls." She mouthed *Sorry.* Dimpna wanted to tell her there was no need to be sorry; after all, it was Dimpna's practice and policies, but there was no way Niamh could lip-read all that, so Dimpna simply gave her a thumbs-up. "What exactly is the nature of your emergency?" Niamh frowned as she listened to the reply. "If you could try and take a breath, I can't hear you that well, pet." Niamh bit her lip, then covered the mouth piece. "Some girl—she's sobbing—says she only wants to see you—she could be here in twenty minutes."

"What's the emergency?"

"She either refuses to say or she can't get it out without crying."

Dimpna felt a twist in her gut. If she had to put an animal down, it was going to make for a very sad day. "Tell her I'll be here," she said. "Tell her to hurry."

CHAPTER 5

Chris Henderson's body lay in the middle of N86, one of two roads into Dingle. Traffic was now backed up in an angry snarl, and guards were directing drivers to make U-turns. Once they were re-routed, Connor Pass, the other road to Dingle, would become a nightmare, despite its stunning cliff and ocean views. There was no good time for a man to die in a hit-and-run, but if there was a worse time, Cormac couldn't imagine it. Tourists clogged the area, trying to squeeze out the last of their summer holidays, and given that the town of Dingle had decided to make the meteor showers a celebratory night, folks had already started making the trek to secure a good spot. Thus the line of cars now snaking all the way through Camp.

A tent had been erected over the body, and as soon as the coroner arrived and communicated with the state pathologist, they would get the poor man on his way to the morgue at Kerry General Hospital. It couldn't come soon enough. Cormac had yet to make his way closer to the body; this would be Neely's jurisdiction, and he didn't want her to feel as if he was taking over.

"Multiple eyewitnesses confirm it was a black Audi that hit him and did a runner," Neely said. The look on her face was one of pure anguish. "Did you hear that now? A black Audi!"

"I heard," Cormac said. Just like Henderson had claimed.

Neely flicked Cormac a look that he couldn't quite decipher. "What was all that business about a wolf in sheep's clothing? He must have figured out who the pervert was." She wrung her hands. "I was sending a squad car. But it was too late."

She was getting emotional. He didn't blame her. It was hard not to in a town where you knew everyone. And anyone who *didn't* get emotional about an elderly man being purposefully run down was a poor excuse for a human being. But she would need a clear head. Guilt had helped exactly zero detectives solve cases. "This is not your fault. What else could you have done?"

"We could have *believed* him."

He noted her use of "we." She wasn't just blaming herself; she was also blaming him. "Mr. Henderson didn't give us a number plate or even a description of the man. If it even was a man. Could have been a woman."

"But I didn't really believe him," Neely said. "He was chewing on me last nerve."

"It doesn't matter what you believed; it mattered what you did. And you did everything you could."

Neely glanced at the body, the pain visible on her face. "He was probably wandering the street, looking for the car." She gulped. "Because he knew I wasn't going to take it seriously."

"Why would he be crossing this stretch of road?" Cormac asked. There was nothing but fields on either side. He turned around, looking at nature in all directions. No pub, no inn, no shop, no petrol station . . .

Neely chewed on her lip. "This area is a frequent crossing for red foxes. He patrolled this road most every day. Everyone who knew him knew that."

"Did witnesses see him chase after a fox?" Cormac asked.

"They did, so," Neely said. "A mother and her pup."

She was dancing around something, and Cormac could feel

his patience draining. "Did witnesses get a number plate?" Cormac asked.

"No," Neely said. "No one caught it."

"How is it possible that the man Henderson confronted earlier for peeping on a woman just happened to see him crossing the road after a fox?" It was too coincidental.

A determined look settled on Neely's face. "I don't know. But, by God, I won't let the bastard get away with this."

"I don't want to step on any toes here, but like I said, I'm available to help."

"I want this maniac caught yesterday," Neely said. "I'll take all the help I can get."

Cormac turned to a nearby guard. "Pull all CCTV in the area, and get all eyes on the footage. Station guards at all peninsula exits. We're looking for a black Audi. After that, see if we can get an update on the arrival of the coroner."

"We'll have to go back to those caravaners as soon as we finish here," Neely said. "Talk to the young woman Henderson was on about. Make sure she's alright."

"Brigid Sweeney." Cormac felt the back of his neck heat up. *Tell her. Get it over with and just blurt it out.* But just as he had talked his mouth into opening, Neely walked away and headed over to a clump of guards by the roadside. She filled him in when she returned. "We've set up checkpoints all around Dingle, and an FCI is also on the way."

A forensic collision investigator. Cormac was a bit surprised. "There are no vehicles to examine," he said. "What do you think the FCI will be able to accomplish?"

Neely gestured for Cormac to follow. She walked down the road until she came to a patch of grass with visible tire marks. The area was marked off by crime-scene tape. "I think the driver waited here."

Cormac studied the marks. There was no doubt that a car had pulled into this spot, and the driver would have a clear view down the road. It would be relatively easy for a tire expert to retrieve a few tire prints. Cormac knew where Neely was trying to steer this investigation, but he wasn't convinced. "If you're saying our driver was staked out, waiting for Mr. Henderson—"

"That's exactly what I'm saying—"

"But how did our driver know that a fox would be crossing this patch of road and Chris Henderson would be here to run after it?"

Neely shrugged. "I don't know how. I just know that he did."

"You're sure there were foxes?"

Neely nodded. "Brace yourself," she said. "This is where things get strange."

Neely crossed the road and gestured for Cormac to follow. Guards parted as they neared the tent and ducked under the white-and-blue crime-scene tape. Neely pointed to the body. Cormac moved in closer. There was something red and furry sticking out from underneath Mr. Henderson's hip. A paw. As he stared, it twitched. Cormac yelped and backed up abruptly, his heart pounding. "What the hell is that?"

"I believe it's her pup." Neely pointed down the road. Cormac had to squint, but then he saw it. A red fox was standing in the middle of the road, swaying. It seemed oblivious to the frantic human activity. As if sensing it was being watched, the fox slowly craned its head and stared at Cormac with dark, unblinking eyes. For a second, it was Cormac who couldn't move a muscle. It was an eerie feeling, and the hair on the back of his neck bristled.

"Jesus." Why hadn't Neely led with this? "What's it doing? I thought they didn't get that close to people?"

"My guess is that it's a *she*," Neely said. "That it's a mother."

"A mother," Cormac said, finally understanding what Neely

had been trying to say. His eyes flew back to the body. The protruding paw. "That's her kit?"

Neely nodded. "Just a wee thing." She grimaced. "As far as we can tell."

Cormac wanted to be anywhere but here. He could feel his throat closing up. "And it's . . . still alive?"

"It's been moving," Neely said. "Twitching."

"Are you going to move the body?" Technically, they were not supposed to. That was the role of the state pathologist, or, if granted permission, in mitigating circumstances, the coroner could move the body. Cormac would call this a fecking mitigating circumstance. He patted his blazer pocket for his inhaler, and when he found it, he breathed in heavily, causing Neely to tilt her head his way.

"The coroner is on his way." She glanced at the mama fox. "We can't be sure how she'll react if we move the body, and we have no idea whether or not the pup can be saved." Neely grimaced. "But it looks like the pup is somewhat protected underneath Mr. Henderson, and when we do make a move, we want to be guided by the experts."

Cormac couldn't take his eyes off the mama. "She's just . . . staring." He felt gripped by an intense dread and was actively fighting the urge to flee. He wanted to be an animal person. But even domesticated pets made him feel a bit—not scared, exactly, but he wouldn't be the first to run up and give one a pat, and they inflamed his allergies something awful. Medication helped calm down his sniffling. But this wild creature was a different story. This one was tapping directly into Cormac's fight-or-flight sensors. He prayed Neely wouldn't notice that his forehead had broken out in sweat. He was no expert, but this fox seemed . . . *unhinged.* Maybe Cormac wasn't far behind.

Neely dug in her pocket and handed him a crumpled tissue. "She may have been struck by the vehicle herself; she could be brain-damaged—that may explain the lack of fear," Neely said. "We're giving her as wide a berth as we can."

Cormac didn't want to seem ungrateful, but there was no way he was using that tissue. He liked his brand-new ones from the packet, thank you very much. He thanked her and stuffed it in his pocket, as if it was a treat he was saving for later. At times like these, Cormac wished he hadn't given up cigarettes. Cormac forced himself to look at the fox. "What are we going to do about that?"

"Her," Neely corrected. "Charlie Meade from ISPCA is on his way, but he's not going to be able to handle her on his own." She gave him the side-eye. "Shall I call a certain local veterinarian, or would you like to do the honors?"

CHAPTER 6

Dimpna maneuvered her green-and-white VW bus through traffic, stopping multiple times to explain to guards that she was called to the scene and wondering how close she would be able to get before she gave up, parked in a field, and hoofed it. The sobbing girl with the animal emergency had been a no-show, but if she did arrive, Dimpna trusted Patrick to handle it. Yet another guard ran toward her, waving his arms frantically. "This road is closed," he yelled. "What do you think you're doing?" He had a baby face underneath his navy-blue cap.

A sense of shame filled her, even though she'd done nothing wrong. At least she hadn't worn her platinum-blond hair in pigtails; if she had, he was liable to think she was a minor. It was embarrassing enough that, this close up, he no doubt could see she was sitting on phone books. When one was vertically challenged, one did what she could. "I was called out to the scene," she said, flashing her credentials. "Doctor Wilde. I'm a veterinarian."

"Right, right, I know you alright, Doc. Me wife is the one who brings our pup in."

"Who's the pup?"

"Emerald. He's a—"

"Jack Russell terrier." No wonder the man looked so tired; that dog was young and had boundless energy. "He's a spitfire, that one."

The guard grinned. "That's the one."

"A wee dote he is too."

"Aw, he is. But you must say that to all your clients."

"I don't. He's a special boy." She crossed her fingers, wondering if that did anything to balance out all the hot air she was blowing his way. Not that they needed any more hot air today. The sun was blaring, and she hadn't been able to locate a pair of sunglasses. "I was told there's an injured wee fox?"

"Right, right." He gestured for her to pull into the field alongside the road and pointed out the white tape in the distance. "Park just behind it, and head to the tent."

Bumping along, she pulled as close as she could get to the crime-scene tape. She parked, hauled out her medical bag, and proceeded to the tent. She was stopped by another guard, and she held up her credentials again. "Doctor Dimpna Wilde."

"It's alright," she heard a familiar voice say. "She's with me."

The guards parted, revealing Detective Inspector Cormac O'Brien. She was surprised to see him at an accident scene. He nodded to Dimpna and hurried over.

"How ya?" he said softly. "Thank you for getting here so quickly."

"Of course," Dimpna said. She gestured toward the tent. "It's still alive, is it?"

Cormac nodded and grimaced. "It's twitching." He pointed across the road. "We're all a little nervous about *her*."

Dimpna turned and took in an adult fox on the side of the road. "The mama, is it?"

"That's the theory," Cormac said.

"I'd say it's spot-on." She was standing very close to humans, seemingly unfazed by their presence. That was not natural. "Was she hit too?"

"I don't know," Cormac said. "DS Neely wondered the same thing."

"Possibly brain-damaged." That could pose a problem. For the most part, foxes were intelligent, nimble, and shy creatures. But if this one had a head injury and a kit to protect, things could get dicey. Dimpna edged closer to the body. She clocked a guard with a gun standing at the corner of the tent.

"He's standing by to shoot the mama fox?" she said, trying to keep her voice calm.

"Just a precaution," Cormac said. "If she charges."

"You're not in Spain, and she's not a bull. Tell him to put down the gun."

Cormac gave her a look. "If I came into your clinic and told you to put down your spatula, would you listen?"

"Yes," Dimpna said. "Because if I'm standing in a veterinarian clinic with a spatula, then I've got bigger problems than you bursting in to order me around."

Cormac was so freaked out by the fox that he was losing his words. "You know what I mean. Spatula. Speculum. Damn it. Scalpel. That's it. Scalpel." Sweat ran down his cheekbone. "Why is she just standing there?"

"Maybe she's frightened too." Dimpna gestured to the gun. "And who can blame her?"

"I have humans to protect."

"I'm sure he's quick on the draw. Either he puts that gun at rest, or I walk." She hadn't intended to bully Cormac, but she wouldn't be able to concentrate if some fool was holding a gun on a frightened mother. Even if that mother was the four-legged kind; mothers, not to mention women, had to stick together. Cormac's jaw twitched, but he strode over and spoke to the guard. The gun came down. Cormac turned to Dimpna.

"Happy?"

"As happy as a veterinarian with a spatula," Dimpna said. She couldn't help but grin as his face turned crimson. He was just too easy to mess with.

"The coroner is pulling up," Sergeant Barbara Neely said, coming up from behind. "He's asked you to wait for him."

Dimpna nodded. It might already be too late for the kit. But it was twitching. Twitching was good. Where there was life, there was hope.

"I have a mesh bag that can contain the kit," Dimpna said. "But I wasn't told about the mama. We need a cage and bait if we have any prayer of luring her away."

"I have a contact for a lad from ISPCA," Neely said. "He'll be here any minute."

"ISPCA?" Dimpna said. "For a wildlife call?" The agency normally only handled domesticated pets. Then again, so did she.

"He was already in the neighborhood, and he keeps cages in the back of his lorry."

That was a stroke of luck. "If he's nearby and has a cage, ask if he can get some crispy chicken and string or wire to set the trap. That would be our best bet," Dimpna said.

"Crispy chicken?" Cormac said. "For a fox?"

Dimpna shrugged. "Only if you want to catch her."

Cormac covered his face with both hands, then parted fingers to reveal his eyes. "Ask him to hurry."

Neely held up her phone, nodded, and walked a few steps away to place the call. "We're in luck," Neely said a few minutes later. "He's just down the road at the Village Pub—says they serve crispy chicken."

"Gary Flaherty is here," Cormac said. "The coroner," he added.

As if he'd been waiting for that introduction, Gary Flaherty came into view. He moved quickly for a stout man and was soon standing in front of them, heaving from the effort. "Jaysus, it's a warm one today, lads," he said. He removed a hand-kerchief and mopped his brow as he took in the body from where they stood. He wore a protective suit that was probably heating him up beyond his comfort zone. "I understand we have to let you get to the pup as soon as possible." His gaze fell to the mesh bag in her hand.

"We're waiting for a member of ISPCA to try and cage the mother fox before we approach her pup," she explained.

The coroner's gaze shifted to the mother fox. "Don't see that every day."

"No," Neely said. "You do not."

He tilted his head and shrugged. "Is it safe to start taking photos?"

Everyone looked to Dimpna. She wished it wasn't her call. If they shot the mother fox, it would be on her. "She's used to people moving around so far," Dimpna said. "Just no sudden or loud movements." Hopefully, if there were sudden or loud movements, the fox would take off in the opposite direction. There was something touching about a mother worried for her young, no matter what the species. It filled Dimpna with a sense of awe, but also a gut-twisting sorrow. As a mother of a grown son, Dimpna knew you never stopped fussing over them, and they never stopped being your babies. Her son, Ben, was a grown man, but that didn't stop Dimpna from being a mother bear when needed.

"I'll get the crime-scene photographer to get to work," Fla-herty said. He turned and gestured to a tall man in the distance with a large camera hanging around his neck. It was fascinat-ing, getting a glimpse of other people's professions. People often asked Dimpna how she could deal with sick and injured animals all day, and now she found herself wondering how these folks could deal with such human tragedy day in and day out. Dimpna stood to the side while they began to process the scene. Poor Chris Henderson. He was a regular at her veterinarian clinic and a crusader for their population of red foxes. From what she'd heard, someone had run him down and fled the scene. Horrific.

"Charlie Meade is here," Neely said minutes later, hurrying over to Dimpna. "He has the cage and chicken."

"Brilliant. I'm going to prepare a sedative." Dimpna knelt beside her bag and rummaged in it until she found the pills she wanted. An injection would be quicker, but she wouldn't be able to safely administer one in these circumstances. By the time she had it sorted, a muscular man in a red ISPCA shirt was headed her way, hauling a large wire cage. "Doctor Dimpna Wilde," she said as she came to her feet.

"Charlie Meade," he replied with a nod.

"You got here quick."

"I also nicked someone's lunch," Charlie said. "Figured you didn't want to wait around."

"You figured right," Dimpna said. "Score one for ISPCA. It's a great organization."

"I take it you don't work there," he said with a wink.

"Ah, now." She held up the pills. "I'm going to hide a few of these in the chicken." Luckily, with crispy skin, it was easy enough to wedge the pills into the chicken's flesh and cover them with the skin. "Hopefully that will do the trick." It wasn't perfect, but it was the best she could do on the spot.

Charlie Meade nodded, then as she worked the pills into the piece of crispy chicken, he turned to his side, as if blocking out the sight of the body. "Just one pup?"

"There might be others," Dimpna said. "Or they might have left the den already. It wouldn't hurt to sweep the area afterward."

"Got it." Charlie Meade and a few guards got to work. They set the cage and the chicken a few meters from the fox.

"Now, if you can, let's all move as far away from her as possible and ignore her," Dimpna said. *Please, go to the chicken . . .*

Dimpna donned her thick gloves and moved back with the rest of them. The fox lowered herself to the ground, crouching toward the cage. "Come on, Mama," Dimpna said. "I bet it smells good."

The fox took a few steps forward, the hair on her back lifting. Dimpna found herself holding her breath, and to their credit, everyone around seemed to be doing the same. Four more steps and she'd be right there. *Come on.*

"Go on ya boy ya," she heard a guard nearby say under his breath. The fox took a few steps back, and the guards groaned.

"Remain still," Dimpna said.

The mama fox edged forward again, and then, just as they thought hope was lost, the fox darted for the chicken, following it into the cage. The cage door shut with a snap. Cheers rose from the crowd. "Worked like a charm," Charlie said, giving Dimpna a thumbs-up.

"Brilliant. Now let's hurry and see if we can get the kit," Dimpna said.

"Is it kit or pup?" Cormac surprised her by asking.

"Either," Dimpna said. "Kit, pup, or cub."

"I'm ready to have the body moved," the coroner said. "Just waiting for your instructions."

"Now that the mama is caged, we don't have to worry how she'll react when we touch the pup," Dimpna said. "I'll be ready as soon as you lift the body." Dimpna had avoided looking too closely at Mr. Henderson until now. He was lying face up, his eyes open and staring at the sky. Blood pooled from underneath him and was smeared along the road as if the poor man had been dragged. "I'm sorry, Mr. Henderson," Dimpna whispered, her stomach clenching with sorrow.

"You knew him?" She could hear the surprise in Cormac's voice. He should know by now that everyone knew everyone around here.

Dimpna nodded. "He was a friend to many foxes."

Cormac nodded. "I heard."

"Should we get protective gear?" another guard asked. "Will it bite?"

Dimpna shook her head. "From the looks of the poor thing, it's still young. My thick gloves should be enough."

"Do we have photographs of the original position the body was in?" This came from Sergeant Neely.

The coroner nodded. "We have photos and sketches, and we've outlined the body for the FCI."

Dimpna crouched next to Mr. Henderson, and as soon as a pair of paramedics lifted his body, she used the mesh bag to scoop up the young fox. Male. She pegged him at about two months old. He was still alive, but barely. A short distance away, the mother fox thrashed in her cage and let out a blood-chilling screech. "Jaysus," she heard a guard say, and no doubt everyone's heart was pumping. The pup's heart, on the other hand, wasn't pumping enough, his chest barely rising.

"I've got ya, luv. Hang in there, you hear?" Dimpna pulled out the needle she'd prepared and administered the sedative, mostly to ease any of his pain, then slipped him into the mesh bag. Poor pup. Poor mama. Poor Mr. Henderson. Someone had caused all this pain. For what? But as horrific as it was, there was nothing she could do for poor Chris Henderson. She would focus and do what she could for the mama and baby fox. She could only pray it wasn't too late.

CHAPTER 7

Dimpna pulled her VW bus up to her clinic and was immediately greeted by Patrick. "Did the sobbing young woman with the animal emergency ever arrive?" she asked as she jumped out of the bus.

"Not a trace," Patrick said.

"Maybe the poor thing died."

Patrick glanced at the skies. "I'm starting to think meteor showers are bad luck," he said. They carried the cage with the mama fox between them, but just as they neared the front door, it flew open, and Moira Egan barreled out, struggling with a browned-off standard poodle named Danny Boy. He was sporting the "cone of shame" and not one bit happy about it. Before Dimpna and Patrick could react, the poodle lunged at the cage with a rallying cry, knocking its plastic cone into the bars. The fox snapped and hissed before backing up to the farthest corner of the cage. The sedatives had yet to take effect. Mrs. Egan let out a yelp of her own as she yanked on the leash. Danny Boy growled and bared his teeth.

"Patrick!" Dimpna said. "Treat?" Patrick looked startled. "For the dog," Dimpna clarified.

"Right." He nodded to his white lab coat. "It's in me pocket."

"Can you reach it, Mrs. Egan?" Dimpna said. The cage was growing heavy. "Whilst keeping the dog behind you?"

Mrs. Egan pursed her lips. "I can try." She squeezed her eyes shut, as if doing something naughty, then she reached into Patrick's pocket and pulled out the treat.

"Lure him away with it," Dimpna said.

Mrs. Egan finally coaxed Danny Boy a safe distance away. This morning, Danny Boy had unwillingly parted with a couple of bits down there; it was no wonder he was cranky.

"What in the world is that?" Mrs. Egan asked, tilting her head at the cage as the dog snapped up the treat.

"A poor red fox," Dimpna said. She left Mrs. Egan standing with her mouth open, as she and Patrick guided the cage inside. "Let's take her to the kennel. She can rest while we see what's going on with the pup. If the pills don't kick in soon, we'll see if we can inject her with a sedative, take X-rays, see what we're dealing with."

An older man seated in the far corner of the waiting room heaved his overweight beagle up. "You're going to try to save roadkill before you look at me baby?" His baby was here as a result of his misguided owner overfeeding him again.

"A red fox is not roadkill, Mr. O'Shea" Dimpna said.

"He looks evil," O'Shea said. "He's grinning!"

"Red foxes grin when they're scared," Patrick informed him.

"Fun fact," Dimpna added.

"It really is," Niamh, their clinic manager, said from behind the reception desk.

"Prioritizing a wild animal," O'Shea said with a shake of his head. "Who's going to pay for that now?"

"God and karma will settle it," Dimpna said. "Don't you worry." A wildlife grant would actually pay the bill, but Dimpna figured her human client wasn't really interested in the minutia. "As soon as we have our patients stabilized and in the kennel, I'll send Patrick out for Mr. Wiggles."

Dimpna turned to the reception desk. "Niamh?"

"Yes, Doctor Wilde?" Niamh had a big grin and bouncing curls. She was what some might call curvy, but Dimpna hated labeling other people's bodies. No doubt in part because she was a wee thing herself and had to put up with a lot of jokes. She'd been called an imp, a fairy, and her favorite—a miniature Viking.

She never let other people's opinions stop her, even defied conventions once in a while by wearing her hair in pigtails and sporting flower-laced dresses and colorful wellies. With her mint-green eyes and white-blond hair, she resonated most with the Viking comparison. She'd certainly been called worse. Animals came in all shapes, sizes, and shades, and so did people. Variety was the spice of life.

"There is a fox—a kit—in the bus. He's in a mesh bag. Do you think you could carefully glove up and bring him to Exam Room 2?"

"Of course," Niamh cooed, her big heart already turning to mush. She opened a drawer, grabbed a thick pair of gloves, and headed out. Minutes later, she met Dimpna in Exam Room 2, the kit cradled in her arms.

"Was this part of the hit-and-run in Camp?" Niamh asked, as Dimpna gently removed the kit from his bag. The sedative had done its job, and the poor thing was fast asleep. Dimpna began to set up for X-rays. "Is it true that Chris Henderson was killed and the car took off?"

"That news traveled fast," Dimpna said. "But let's not get our waiting room gossiping."

"Where do ya think I heard the news in the first place?" Niamh asked. Dimpna grimaced. She should have known. Clinic gossip was fierce. What better way to get one's mind off a sick animal than nattering on about other people's miseries? "Poor Mr. Henderson!" Niamh continued. "He was good old stock. It's so awful. And on the cusp of the meteor shower."

She took a deep breath that she seemed to hold for a count of three before expelling. "I was hoping it would bring us all good luck! What if I got it wrong?"

Dimpna didn't voice the worst part, the rumor she'd heard that Mr. Henderson was deliberately run down. "Luck is what you make it."

"I suppose," Niamh said. "But I'm still breaking into the chocolate drawer."

"Do what you have to do," Dimpna said. "Just leave a few for me."

"Are we still going to the meteor shower?" Niamh asked.

"Absolutely," Dimpna said. "We're all going." Once a year, the earth crossed into the path of Comet Swift-Tuttle, lighting up the skies with hundreds of meteors. Given that today had been a clear day, they were bound to be spectacular, and Dimpna had no intention of missing this. She needed it. Her staff needed it. But she'd be lying if she said the hit-and-run hadn't put a damper on it and raised a few anxieties.

Dimpna wasn't sure if meteor showers brought out the same insanity as full-moon evenings, but what if it was like that on steroids? During full moons, they were often clogged with visits. Animals displayed a variety of reactions to the gravitational pull. Dogs would howl, cats would hide, and birds often became disoriented. Owners swore their horses had worsening bouts of colic during a full moon, and more dairy cows were born during that time as well. Given all this, full moons resulted in a staggering 28 percent increase in visits to a veterinarian clinic. Dimpna had practiced most of her career in Dublin, where the skies didn't get dark enough to create this kind of sensation with the meteor showers, and so she had no way of knowing how this evening would measure up. She prayed it would stay calm long enough for her to enjoy a little of the sky-watching action.

Patrick came in to help with the baby fox. "I'll get his preop medications ready," Dimpna said to Patrick. "We'll get X-rays, and then he'll rest overnight. If he remains stable, we can see about setting any fractures in the morning. Same with the mama."

Radiology on the fox pup showed several limb fractures, and there was swelling on the brain of the mama. Fractures Dimpna could fix, but the brain swelling was extremely worrisome. The fox's eyes were fixed, and her pupils were nonresponsive to light. And now that she could see her up close, she'd also noticed some neck twisting—torticollis. Without medication, no doubt she'd soon be thrashing her head around in pain. At least they could give her a quiet place to rest, and sedatives. The mama fox must have crossed the street first, and the young pup had followed. No doubt the mother took the blow from the car. That must have been when Mr. Henderson darted out, along with the pup.

The odd bit was that no other pups had been in the vicinity. It was rare for a litter to have just one pup. The den must have been nearby. Or perhaps the rest had all grown up and left the den, and this wee thing was the lone straggler. *Failure to launch.*

If the hit was intentional, as Dimpna heard a few of the guards say, did that mean a car was lying in wait? It was true that Mr. Henderson regularly patrolled the streets, but it wasn't every day that a fox dashed across. That probably happened once every few months, if Dimpna had to guess, and usually in early morning or late evening, when humans were asleep. Perhaps the animals were already tuning in to atmospheric disturbances due to the approaching meteor shower and a killer got lucky. But what had Mr. Henderson ever done to anyone? Who among them would do such a thing? It was unfathomable.

CHAPTER 8

Dimpna switched off the last of the clinic's lights, plunging it into darkness. She heard a yowl and then felt her black cat, Spike, rub against her calf. "Heya, petal," she said as she bent down to scratch behind his ears. Spike purred. From the waiting room seats came the sound of three dogs snoring— her English bulldog, Guinness, her collie, Pickles, and the newest addition to her four-pack, an enthusiastic sheepdog, a border collie named E.T. She debated whether or not to take them to her flat upstairs, then decided to leave them be. She was anxious to get to the hill, where Niamh and Patrick had secured a good spot, according to their text. They had also picked up Dimpna's father, Eamon. Recently diagnosed with dementia, he had more bad days than good, but at least he was up for an outing. One just had to be prepared for his mood to shift like the Irish weather. When he wanted to go home, it was time to go home.

Her mam, on the other hand, had already declared that she would be spending the meteor shower in her caravan in the field giving tarot card readings. Supposedly, this was the perfect night to "bless" the cards. To each his own.

Cormac had texted that he was on his way, but his mam would not be joining. Dimpna felt a squeeze of empathy; it was such a powerless feeling knowing a parent was dying and not being able to stop it. It wasn't fair that some people suffered, and it also wasn't fair that others were struck and killed with no notice at all. That was why one had to enjoy every moment of life. She had just shut and locked the door behind her when a truck screeched up to the clinic, tossing up gravel. Dimpna groaned. She should have known she wasn't going to get out of here that easily. She stepped around Tiernan an old black Lab who never left the courtyard, and took a few steps forward, bracing herself for whatever chaos was headed her way.

The passenger door to the truck flew open, and a young woman jumped out. Seconds later, the truck screeched away. The woman stumbled forward, head down, left arm clutched to her chest. She was wearing a blue dress partially hidden beneath an oversized jacket. She lifted her head as if she sensed she was being watched. Her long black hair fell past her shoulders in waves, and her pale blue eyes seemed to be tracking her surroundings. The young woman before her was stunning, and Dimpna recognized her from a recent newspaper article about a colorful group of twenty-somethings in Camp. They had a pair of mastiffs that kept getting loose and a talking African grey parrot. In a town where any newcomer stuck out like a sore thumb, this ragtag group was infamous.

"Brigid Sweeney?" Dimpna blurted out.

Brigid, who had been moving toward Dimpna with her hand clutched to her jacket, came to an abrupt stop, and her eyes widened. "Have we met?"

"Sorry, no. I saw an article about you in the paper last week."

"And you recognized me in the dark?" Brigid looked down at herself. "Like this?"

"I can see well enough." Dimpna nodded to the courtyard light. "You also have a memorable face," she added. "What brings you here?"

Brigid stepped forward and opened the jacket, revealing a glimpse of brown fur covered in red splotches. It was only then that Dimpna noticed that Brigid's left hand was also smeared with red. There was more on her left cheek and all over the jacket. The jacket sported words, but they were marred by the red splotches. All Dimpna could work out was the last three letters of the first word—*den*—and three letters of the second word—*all*.

"Is that blood?" Dimpna asked.

"Rabbit's blood," Brigid said. "I saved him." Brigid moved closer to Dimpna, revealing more of the poor creature. "An evil man tried to cut its foot off!"

Dimpna instinctively took a step back. "While it was still alive?"

"Obviously." Brigid lifted her right hand. In it was a bloody knife. A butcher's knife from the length and heft of it. Who carried around a knife like that?

Dimpna took a step back. "What are you thinking, waving that thing around?" There were a lot of rumors swirling around the caravaners, some of which involved speculations of drugs. Anything was possible, and Dimpna was alone at the clinic. Tiernan, bless his heart, didn't have teeth for biting, even if he had the will. With her own dogs contained upstairs, she had to be alert.

Brigid lifted the weapon higher. "It's the knife he was using. *Psychopath.* He dropped it."

Even in the dim light, Dimpna could tell that its edges were razor-sharp. "Do you mind setting that thing down?"

"You should have the knife tested," Brigid said. "And the jacket."

"Tested?" Dimpna felt a sense of panic clawing at her. She felt as if the two of them were doing some kind of dance, only they were completely out of step with the music.

"Blood, fingerprints." Brigid's eyes flashed. "Maybe you will be able to identify him."

"Me?" Dimpna did not usually let fear run away with her, but her body was sending all sorts of alarm symbols. "I'm not a guard."

Brigid tilted the knife. "Are you going to ring the guards?"

"Did *you* ring the guards?" Dimpna could not believe they were standing here having this conversation. "You called my clinic hours ago, by the way."

Disappointment showed on Brigid's face as she shook her head. "I had to wait for a ride." She chewed her lips. "I need you to call the guards."

"That doesn't make any sense." Nothing the young woman said made any sense. She had to be experiencing a mental breakdown. Not to mention that Dimpna didn't normally treat wild animals, and after the foxes, this hare made three. She was starting to buy into Niamh's superstitions regarding the meteor shower.

"He was holding the rabbit down on a tree stub, and I saw him lifting this big knife." She lifted the knife once more.

"Put it down. I mean it. Put it down right now."

Brigid inched over to the stone wall and let the knife fall on top with a clink. "I know I must seem a fright." She stroked the hare, which had begun to frantically pedal his feet. "I just screamed. And screamed and screamed. And he ran. He left it all—the jacket, the rabbit, and the knife."

It was the strangest story Dimpna had heard in a long time, maybe ever, and Dimpna's poor head was filled with strange stories. "Where was this?"

"In Camp. Near the caravan. I was just having a stroll."

She was lying. Dimpna would have bet anything she was lying. But why? "Who dropped you off?"

"A friend. I told him he didn't have to stay. He's all jazzed up about the meteor shower." Brigid tilted her head to the sky. "I can feel them coming, can't you?"

"Them?"

"The meteors."

"I can't feel a thing." Except a twinge of fear, which was unusual for Dimpna. Premonitions were her mother's wheelhouse. But there was something seriously wrong here, and it had nothing to do with the injured hare. But Dimpna wasn't a psychologist, and she couldn't let paranoia run away with her. An animal was injured, and she needed to have a look at it. "Follow me." Dimpna held open the clinic door. "And, if you can, try not to drip too much blood on the floors." She was still hoping that she'd make it to the meteor shower on time. She turned and waited for Brigid to catch up. "My dogs are going to bark from upstairs when we come in."

"I don't mind," Brigid said.

"You might not, but it will startle the hare," Dimpna said. "He could scratch you."

"The jacket is thick," Brigid said. "I'll be grand."

"I'm going to get some gloves and protective sleeves, and then I'll take the hare."

"You'll get blood on you," Brigid said.

"Not a bother," Dimpna said. "I wash off easier than me floors." Dimpna grabbed a pair of pull-on sleeves and thick gloves, then returned and took the hare from Brigid. It thrashed in her arms, and Dimpna was grateful she'd waited until her arms and hands were protected. "Does your hare have a name?"

"I don't know," Brigid said quickly. "Do you really think the maniac names them before chopping off their feet?" She shrugged off the jacket and let it drop to the floor. "Maybe the guards can figure out who he is from his jacket." She kicked it away from her. "*Please.* He's a bad, bad man. He needs to be arrested."

"I'm a veterinarian," Dimpna said. "If you want the Gardaí, all you have to do is dial 999."

"They're out to get us," Brigid said. "They wouldn't believe a word I said."

Dimpna glanced at the jacket, unsure of how it would help, unless the woman was imagining some kind of Cinderella scenario where guards went door-to-door, forcing bad men to try it on. And why on earth had Brigid been wearing it? Did she know who this person was and was afraid to name him? Was it a boyfriend? A close friend? One of the lads in the caravan with her? What Dimpna really wanted to do was find out the true story, but accusing the lass of being a liar was probably not the best way to go. "Hunters who used to kill rabbits did so for the meat, and using the feet and skins were simply an attempt not to waste their kill. I've never heard of anyone targeting them for their feet alone, and certainly not while the animal was still alive."

"People don't really change," Brigid said. "No matter how hard they try. Not on the inside."

"Follow me." Dimpna headed down the hall to Exam Room 1. Brigid followed. Dimpna set the hare on the exam table and examined its back left paw. There was indeed a slice through it, as if someone was marking where a cut would be made. The cut was superficial, which threw Brigid's story into question and didn't explain the amount of blood on the jacket. "Are you sure you don't know who did this?"

"No one ever believes me," Brigid said. "Half the time, I don't even believe me." Her blue eyes were swimming in pain.

"Have you taken anything this evening? Alcohol? Drugs?"

Brigid let out what Dimpna could only describe as a growl. "See?" she said, clenching her fists. "Do you see?"

"There's way more blood on the jacket you tossed on me floors then there is from this hare."

Brigid looked shocked for a moment, then her face went still. "Perhaps it wasn't his first rabbit."

"Did you see other rabbits?"

"No. But does an absence of other rabbits prove whether or not there were other rabbits?"

She was strong-willed, this girl. Dimpna, possessing the same quality, normally admired it in others. But she couldn't stop her internal alarm bells from ringing. "How did you stop this person?" Perhaps a few practical questions would split Brigid's lie wide open.

"I ran at him and screamed louder than the rabbit."

"Hare," Dimpna said reflexively.

Brigid shrugged. "I don't know the difference."

"Hares are larger. Also longer ears and hind legs." Dimpna pointed his out. "This guy would have scratched and kicked up quite a fuss."

"You can see the cut for yourself," Brigid said.

"It's not a true cut. It's just a line across his foot."

Brigid shook her head. "I'm telling you—he had the knife raised over his head, as if he was about to hack the foot clean off."

Dimpna willed herself not to challenge the young woman. "But he took off when you screamed, leaving both his jacket and knife behind?"

"Correct."

"You're saying a dangerous psychopath with a knife ran away simply because you screamed and ran toward him?"

Brigid blinked slowly. "I'm not able to explain why it happened. I'm only explaining what happened."

"Animal cruelty is a very serious charge."

"I agree."

She had waited hours to come in, but the blood on the jacket was relatively fresh. What was Dimpna dealing with here? She usually felt so in control when she was at work. But everything about this visit was off. Serial killers often started by killing animals. But Dimpna wasn't going to mention that. She still wasn't convinced there even was a psychopath running around. Was this some kind of cry for attention? "If you know who this person is, you should be very careful around him."

"I don't want to be around him at all!" Brigid said. "He needs to be behind bars. Help me."

The hare twitched its nose. "I'm going to clean him up and bandage him. He'll be fine." Brigid watched as Dimpna set about cleaning and wrapping the foot.

"I can't believe someone is going around cutting off rabbits' feet," Brigid said. "Pardon me—hare. I suppose a hare's foot is considered just as lucky?" There it was again, the word of the day apparently. Luck.

"Not from the hare or rabbit's perspective," Dimpna said. Luck was only good or bad in the eye of the beholder.

"Don't you think someone like that needs to be put away for good?" Brigid sounded as if she were pleading. "The guards have to test that knife. Maybe he left fingerprints? And the blood on the jacket. They have to test that too!"

There she went again with the testing. She wanted someone to go down for something. "Once again, I am not a member of the guards."

"But you're friends with that detective inspector, aren't you?"

The comment caught Dimpna completely off guard. And yet it made perfect sense now. For some reason, Brigid Sweeney was using Dimpna to make contact with Cormac. Did she have a little crush on him? Dimpna wouldn't blame her. Cormac was undeniably charming when he wanted to be. And how did she even know about their friendship? Brigid ran her hands down her blue dress. "I left my handbag back at the caravan, and I don't want to miss the meteor shower. But I'm going to pay you, I swear. I'll be back tomorrow morning."

"Do you plan on keeping him?" Dimpna asked. The hare twitched his nose and tried out a hop with his new bandage. Dimpna patted his head.

"I'm not keeping him," Brigid said. "I just want to make sure you get paid."

"We work under grants when it comes to wildlife," Dimpna said. In this case, it would do no good. The hare was fat and happy. Comfortable around people. Dimpna was starting to suspect he was someone's pet. She'd go through her client roster and see what she could dig up. Dimpna let the hare down on the floor. He could hop around for a few minutes, and then she would find him a nice kennel for the evening. They returned to the waiting room. "Please report this incident to the guards."

Brigid's eyes bore into Dimpna's. "They hate us," Brigid said. "Please. I need you to call that detective inspector. He won't listen to me."

"And why do you think he would listen to me?"

"You're not the only one who reads articles. You two teamed up on a murder probe recently, didn't you?"

Dimpna hadn't teamed up with Cormac, but they had been thrown together when Johnny O'Reilly was murdered and her parents were accused of being murderers. There had been plenty of press about it. But what did she think Dimpna could do? "If someone is threatening you, I promise you the guards will take it seriously."

"But you won't?"

"If you want me to ask Inspector O'Brien to pay you a visit so you can report the incident, I'd be happy to do that."

"You're just like all the rest of them." A pained look came over her face.

"Let me say it again. Any person who abuses animals is a dangerous person," Dimpna said. "Whether or not I call them, the guards are going to need your help catching this man."

"It was the guards who told us to leave town," Brigid said. "First thing in the morning." She looked toward the exit as if she wanted to get a head start.

"Is someone picking you up?" Dimpna asked. "I can drive you to your caravan."

"You even know where I'm staying?" Brigid sounded horrified.

"You're the one who just mentioned your caravan, petal," Dimpna said. "In Camp."

"It's too easy to find someone these days. It's too easy!" Dimpna could say the same thing; after all, Brigid had tracked *her* down. Brigid brushed back her hair, causing the sleeve of her dress to slide up, flashing a large, angry bruise.

Dimpna could offer her a cup of tea, sit her down, get her to talk. But the meteor shower was starting soon, and people were waiting for her. Dimpna pointed to the bruise. "Are you alright?"

Brigid looked startled, then yanked her sleeve down. "I'm fine."

But she wasn't fine. Anyone could see that.

"This is a safe place. I can help you. But you have to tell me what's really going on."

"I hate this place," Brigid said. "Everyone knows your business."

"Do you need me to call the guards right now? You can wait for them in here."

"No!" Her eyes flashed with anger. She closed her eyes for a minute. "I'm sorry. I'm sorry. This was a huge mistake." Brigid turned and headed for the door. "I just need to make a call, and then I'm out of here."

"Make your call," Dimpna said. "I'll be here if you change your mind." Brigid lingered by the door as Dimpna headed back to Exam Room 1. She wasn't normally an eavesdropper, but when she reached the room, she lingered under the vents. Soon Brigid's voice filtered in.

"It's me," she said. "It didn't work. Please. We have to get out of here. *Tonight*." Seconds later, the front door slammed shut.

CHAPTER 9

Cormac O'Brien lowered himself on the hill next to Dimpna. "Best seats in the house." He wasn't wrong; from their vantage point, they had a clear view of the skies, far enough away from the downtown lights, but a front row seat to the ocean. The stars gleamed, and several meteors had already streaked across the dark skies. Dimpna felt a vibration in her solar plexus, the feeling that tonight was special. But it was overshadowed by the surprise drop-in from Brigid Sweeney. Dimpna hoped the lads she was with weren't abusing her. That was the only explanation Dimpna could come up with. It seemed she wanted to turn one of them in without getting blamed for it. She had to tell Cormac.

"I need this," he said suddenly. "I can't tell you how much I need this. A respite from the sadness and horror that was today."

Great. She was going to ruin it for him. Maybe she could give him a few more minutes of peace. "You can thank Niamh and Patrick for the primo spot," Dimpna said. "How's your mam?"

"She's resting." Cormac held up his phone. "But I'm going to take videos of the action to share with her." Meteors flashed down, and cheers rose from the people spread out across the grassy hill. Dimpna wished her son and brother and mam were here; she wanted to be near everyone she loved. "Amazing," Dimpna said. She was at a loss for words. It was raining meteors.

"We're so small," Cormac said. "So insignificant."

"Is that a good thing or a bad thing?" Dimpna said.

"Maybe a bit of both," Cormac answered.

"I can't get the image of poor Mr. Henderson out of me head," Dimpna said. "I told myself I wasn't going to ask, but here I am asking. Do they have any leads on the person who struck him?"

"I've offered my help, but Sergeant Neely has jurisdiction," Cormac said. "But no, they haven't found the car or the driver of the Audi yet." He sighed. "How are the foxes?"

"I'll operate on the little one in the morning as long as he's stable. But the mama has swelling to the brain, and I don't think she's going to see the morning."

Cormac reached out and covered her hand with his. "You're a good person, Doctor Dimpna Wilde."

"So are you, Inspector O'Brien." They shared some prolonged eye contact. There was a definite chemistry between them, but neither of them had acknowledged it. Dimpna had a full life and a long track record of falling for wounded men. And even though, on paper, Cormac seemed to have it all together, she sensed an intensity with him—the kind that was attractive in the initial stages of a romance but became an albatross as love wore on. And Dimpna didn't even know if she could handle whatever sadness lurked within him. Then again, maybe she should take a leap of faith.

"Good person," Cormac retracted his hand and looked away. "I don't know about that."

Just as she thought they were getting somewhere. He was moodier than usual. Dimpna took a deep breath. "Have you heard about the group of twenty-somethings who set up a caravan in Camp and have been selling their wares?" she asked.

"As a matter of fact, I paid them a visit yesterday," he said.

"Well, only one of them was home. Neely was hoping I could encourage them to move along."

"And did you?"

"Looking back on it, I could have done a better job."

"I see." Was Brigid right? Perhaps she had reason to think Cormac wouldn't believe her. He could be a little intimidating at times.

Astute as ever, Cormac picked up on her anxiety. "What's the story?"

"Brigid Sweeney came into my clinic just as I was headed out this evening."

Cormac focused on her. "Something wrong with one of the dogs? The parrot?"

Dimpna shook her head. "She had a wild hare and an even wilder story."

"And what story is that?" His voice was low.

"Said she rescued the hare from a man she caught trying to chop its foot off." She gave it a beat. "While it was still alive."

Cormac frowned. "What?" He swallowed hard. "Is that it?"

"Is that it?" Dimpna was gobsmacked. Had everyone gone off the rails this evening? "I've never heard of anyone doing such a bizarre thing. If you were going to take a rabbit's foot, you would kill the rabbit. I mean, otherwise, we're talking about a very sadistic person."

"Sadistic people do exist," Cormac said. "One of them ran down an old man in cold blood."

Could it be the same man? Dimpna shivered. "Serial killers often start with cruelty to animals." She paused. "But I still don't think she was telling the truth. She had a large knife and a jacket covered in blood—she said it belonged to the man trying to torture the hare—but there was a lot of blood on the jacket, and there was hardly a scratch on the poor thing, just a thin line across its foot."

"Did she have any idea who this person is?"

"She said she didn't, but she wanted me to call you."

"Me? Specifically?" He sat up straight, and Dimpna followed suit.

"Yes. She wanted the guards to test the jacket and knife."

"Test it for what?"

"Blood and fingerprints." Dimpna shrugged. "I guess she wanted you to figure out who the madman is."

"Strange."

Everything about this was strange, including Cormac's reaction. From a little ways over, Niamh let out a laugh, and Dimpna's father howled. Niamh laughed harder. "He's howling at the shooting stars," Niamh called out.

"Grand," Dimpna said.

Patrick threw her a desperate look. He was caught between her howling father and a very enthusiastic Niamh. "Meteor showers," Dimpna called to him.

"Meteor showers," he called back, sounding somewhat traumatized.

Dimpna turned back to Cormac. "There was hardly any blood on the hare at all. I don't know where the blood on the jacket—if it is indeed blood—came from."

Cormac fixed his gaze on the meteors. "That lot is definitely up to something. I just don't know what."

"I don't know either, but I really think she needs help." Dimpna told him about the angry bruise on Brigid's arm.

Cormac rubbed his chin. "Do you have her mobile number?"

Dimpna shook her head. "Normally, I'd have them fill out paperwork, but I thought this was a wild animal, not a pet, she brought in, and I suppose I was just trying to get out of the clinic." She wanted to be here on this hill. With him. Had she made a mistake?

"You thought it was a wild animal—it is a wild animal, isn't it?"

Dimpna shook her head. "The hare is very tame. I think it might be someone's pet."

"Maybe the owner is the one abusing it?" Cormac asked.

"Maybe."

"Was Brigid Sweeney alone?"

Dimpna nodded. "Someone dropped her off at the clinic and then peeled out. I offered her a ride to her caravan, but she refused. But I heard her on the phone. She was telling someone that they should leave now. She said it wasn't safe."

Cormac stood up. "Maybe I should pay a visit to the caravan now." He dug out his mobile phone. "I should call Neely." Dimpna suddenly remembered the butcher knife. She gasped and slapped her hand over her mouth. "What's wrong?"

Dimpna scrambled to her feet. "The knife. I told her to set it down on our stone wall in the courtyard. I wonder if she took it when she left or if it's still there."

"I want to go home." The voice in the darkness belonged to her father. He had snuck up on her. "I want to go home." Since his dementia had progressed, her father had very little patience.

"Sorry," Niamh said. "Do you want me to take him?"

"Not at all," Dimpna said. "You two enjoy the rest of the sky action." Although it was hard to see their faces, she imagined Niamh was grinning and Patrick was blushing. Niamh had a mad crush on Patrick. Dimpna hoped she wouldn't get her hopes up. Patrick didn't seem to feel the same way. He had many women in Dingle flitting about him.

"Did you enjoy it?" she asked her da. He was over six feet, and looking up at him strained the back of her neck. Had it not been for the same platinum hair and mint-green eyes, she might have been asking her mam a lot more questions about the postman.

"Enjoy what?" he frowned. "What are all these people doing out here in the dark? I want to go home."

"Okay, Da," she said. "Let's get you home."

Cormac's phone rang. He moved away to answer it, covering his free ear with his hand.

"I want to go home," Eamon said. "I want to go home."

"We're going home, Da," Dimpna said. "We're going to walk to the car."

"We're not going home," her father said. "You're still talking."

"Alright, let's go."

"Do you even know where I live?" His volume drew attention from those nearby, but everyone just as quickly looked away. Her father had been one of the most respected veterinarians in town. He'd taken care of all their lovely creatures during the past four decades. It just wasn't fair.

"I know where you live, Da."

"You do?" He sounded amazed. Dimpna began to walk downhill with her father, taking slow and deliberate steps. Her VW bus was parked just down the hill. It was a short drive to her father's house, but long enough that she wouldn't be returning. It would be bedtime soon, and her bones ached for a soft mattress. Patrick was taking emergency calls tonight, and unless she was needed too, she planned on getting at least four hours of sleep. Four hours was a good night. Five was a miracle. She couldn't remember the last time she saw six, let alone eight. Eight was for people who didn't take care of sick or injured animals.

"Dimpna." She turned around to find Cormac hurrying after them. "Speak of the devil," he held up his phone. "There's another complaint about that group. It's their dogs again. They're loose and chasing after cars. I'm headed there now."

"Do you want me to meet you there?" Dimpna asked. She glanced at her father.

"I can let you know when I get there," Cormac said. "It's possible we'll need some help with the dogs."

"I'll keep my phone handy," Dimpna said. "And treats."

"Treats?" Cormac had perked up.

"For the dogs."

"Right, so." He sighed, shaking his head as he walked away. "Always for the dogs."

After taking her father home and helping him get ready for bed, Dimpna returned to the clinic and searched the courtyard. The butcher knife was gone. Had Brigid taken it with her when she left? Tiernan whined and leaned against her. Dimpna gave him a pat, then checked to make sure his water bowl was filled and his bed was tidy. Sometimes good old Tiernan brought little gifts and deposited them in the bed; Dimpna was relieved tonight was not one of those nights. Dimpna's phone rang, and she glanced at the screen. *Cormac.* That was quick. She answered straightaway.

"The dogs are contained," he said. "Found stumbling down the road."

"Stumbling?"

"He said they seemed . . . *drunk.*"

"He?"

"An off-duty guard helped get them into his car. Can he bring them to you?"

She glanced across the street at their new boarding facility in what used to be a mechanic's garage. It was currently empty, and there was plenty of room for a pair of dogs. "Of course."

"Thanks. I warn you. They aren't the friendly sort."

"Even when they're drunk?" Dimpna couldn't help but say.

Cormac chuckled. "Touché."

"They're protective, and their adrenaline is pumping, but I'll have muzzles on the ready." She paused. "Did you find Brigid?"

"No. None of them seem to be at the car park, but the caravan hasn't moved. I bet we hear from them when they realize their dogs are gone."

"If there's any dog food around the caravan, tell the guard to bring it; an abrupt change in diet can be tricky with dogs," Dimpna said. "And obviously I'm not saying she's dangerous or anything, but it looks like Brigid took the butcher knife with her when she left."

"Good to know. Why don't you take the dogs to the caravan in the morning? I'm going to see if they'll leave in exchange for getting them back. And this time I'm going to personally watch them go."

"The earlier the better. I have a fox to operate on around ten."

Cormac chuckled, and Dimpna smiled in the dark. The meteors were fainter from this vantage point, but she could still make out sparks from above. It was like the universe was celebrating some grand occasion. She felt both awed and uninvited. She hoped that, wherever Brigid Sweeney was, she was okay. "Early it is then," he said. "Half-seven?"

"Half-seven," Dimpna said. "We'll be there with bells on. And give my best to your mam."

"She'll love that," he said with a laugh and then hung up before she could decipher what that was all about.

Dimpna had barely slept. The dogs, on the other hand—big mutts, the pair of them—had arrived sleepy and went into kennels without a fuss, only to break out and cause a ruckus in the middle of the night. She had awoken to the sounds of strange howling coming from the boarding facility. When she burst in, she found the entire place in disarray. Their dog beds had been shredded to pieces, their water and food bowls were knocked over, and giant muddy paw prints were all over the walls. These dogs could not have opened the latches to the kennels themselves. Had Dimpna been so distracted and tired she hadn't properly closed them in? Or had someone gotten into the kennels and set them free? The dogs barely even looked at her, their giant heads swiveled around causing the drool hanging from their massive jowls to spray in all directions.

When they tried to take a step forward, they faltered. Minutes later, they were both out cold again. There was only one explanation that made sense: emergence dysphoria. These dogs had been drugged—most likely with ketamine—and not by a veterinarian, who would have also given them Valium to prevent this kind of chaos as the ketamine wore off, but by an amateur.

Upon waking in their dysphoric state, and finding their kennels unlocked, they had kicked up such a fuss that they had exhausted themselves again. Someone had been in here. Someone had messed with the kennels. Dimpna couldn't be sure she locked the main door. She'd been exhausted. Had someone been watching her the entire time? At least the dogs were no longer playing in traffic. What if it was one of their owners who had drugged them? She wouldn't want to hand them over if they were being abused.

Dimpna took blood from both of them and put in a rush order with the lab. But given that it wouldn't be sent off until morning, it would be at least three business days before she had the results. Cormac seemed eager to see the caravaners go, and these dogs were his bargaining chips. But she could not in good conscience ignore the fact that someone was mistreating them.

She would take the dogs to Camp, as promised, but before giving them back to the caravaners, she would let Cormac know her suspicions that they had illegally been given ketamine. Had Brigid also been on ketamine? It might explain her bizarre story. She would urge Cormac to let her keep the dogs until the test results came back. As a precaution, Dimpna packed a pair of muzzles in her bag. Depending on the dose they were given, they could wake up disoriented again. Muzzles upset people, but if used correctly, they were safer not only for humans but for the dogs as well. She roused them from their slumber and coaxed them into her VW bus with a nice liver treat. They both fell asleep again once they were on the comfy blankets of the traveling kennels. Soon they were snoring. Dimpna was jealous. She longed for a good night's sleep. Last night, after the dogs had awoken her, the emergency-animal dam broke wide open, and Dimpna ended up teaming with Patrick until half-three in the morning.

They'd tended to a goat in need of stitches; apparently the meteors spooked him, and he tried to jump a fence. Then they had a beagle who wouldn't stop vomiting, followed by a cat who got in a fight with something that bit off part of its ear. And then, when she went to check on the mama fox and her pup, there was good news and bad. The pup was stable, but the mother had passed away. Patrick volunteered to bury her in the field, and Dimpna consoled herself that she had done everything she could, and given that the fox was on pain meds, her passing had been relatively peaceful. "We'll take care of your kit, mammy," she whispered. The surgery on the pup would proceed after ten this morning. They had to make sure they didn't handle him more than necessary, as the goal would be to release him into the wild. Dimpna was running on numerous cups of coffee, and there was no traffic at this hour, so she made it to Camp in good time.

She slowed down when she approached the section of the road where poor Mr. Henderson had been struck. Flowers and mass cards had piled up beside a bespoke wooden cross painted white. RIP CHRIS HENDERSON was written across it. Another handmade sign had been stuck in the ground near it: TO THE COWARD WHO STRUCK A DEFENSELESS OLD MAN: WE WILL OUTFOX YOU. CALL THE GARDAÍ IMMEDIATELY IF YOU SEE OR KNOW SOMEONE WITH A BLACK AUDI.

It seemed the details about the foxes had leaked. Perhaps there was no keeping an event like that under wraps. Vigilantes. Dimpna couldn't blame the outraged locals, and the callback to foxes was clever, but she had a feeling they were going to make the guards' job that much harder. On top of everything else, they did not need to deal with regular folk "hunting" each other down. Then again, having everyone on the lookout was necessary. Dimpna just prayed things weren't going to get too out of hand. She sent a prayer up to Chris Henderson. She told him that she hoped the mama fox had joined him on the other side and promised she'd keep his crusade to protect red foxes alive. "The pup is grand, Mr. Henderson," she said out loud, crossing herself before continuing on. "Thanks to you."

Camp was a quaint village with a gorgeous view of the mountains and Tralee Bay. Homes were well-maintained, and for the most part, the hikers and tourists who came through also treated it with respect. Dimpna found the caravan in the parking lot of the Airbnb, as described. She pulled over, somewhat surprised that Cormac's red Toyota was nowhere in sight. He was nothing if not prompt. The caravan was covered in stickers ranging from graffiti to politics to sports. The car park was littered with overturned rubbish bins, the remnants of a campfire, and a cooler with its lid flipped open. Compared to the pristine village, no wonder locals were complaining about this group. The guards would have to do something before people got a notion to take things into their own hands. A black pickup truck was hitched to the caravan, jacked up on enormous tires. There were no signs of the foursome, although it was possible they were all inside sleeping.

Dimpna decided not to park next to the caravan in case there was going to be trouble when the lads realized she had their dogs. She circled around until she found shaded parking a few streets away. The dogs were still sleeping. Poor things. It wasn't their fault they were troublemakers. The fault always lay with the human beings who took care of them and either trained them or failed to train them. She cracked the window, then hoofed it back. The sun was just coming up, and in the distance, the bay sparkled. It was a crisp morning, and Dimpna enjoyed the breeze. There was still no sign of Cormac. She glanced at her phone—no missed calls. She moved a safe distance away from the caravan and took a deep breath. The skies were bleeding a soft pink overhead. Two stakes were planted in the ground in back of the caravan. That must be where the dogs had been (unsuccessfully) chained up during the meteor shower.

Across the car park and to the right of the caravan stretched an open field edged by a patch of trees. Farther down was a crumbling stone bridge over a creek. Dimpna was staring in that direction when she caught a glimpse of a blue dress through the trees. It was a very specific shade of blue—royal blue—the same color dress Brigid Sweeney was wearing when she'd come into the clinic. Was that Brigid?

Dimpna headed toward the patch of blue. Soon, she was only a few feet away. Brigid was there alright, leaning against the tree, head flopped down and that gorgeous long dark hair covering her face like a curtain. Had she fallen asleep standing up? Dimpna could now see more of the dress and her body pressed against the tree, but something was wrong; she was abnormally still. Dimpna, on the other hand, felt every cell in her body firing a red alert. She edged closer.

"Hello?" Dimpna's voice was raspy and barely above a whisper. She didn't want to look, and at the same time, she looked. That's when she saw the rope. It was thick, and there was a lot of it. Brigid Sweeney was tied to the tree in two places: just above the chest, and at the knees. Was this some kind of prank? But even as Dimpna had the thought, she knew it was not. Blood pooled at the ground on Brigid's left side. It took Dimpna several moments of staring to realize what she was seeing. Or *not* seeing. She was not seeing Brigid Sweeney's left hand. The blood was flowing directly from Brigid's mangled wrist. The large butcher knife flashed through Dimpna's mind. It would have taken something like that to sever a hand. *Psychopath*. Brigid's strange tale came rushing at Dimpna, admonishing her for not doing more. She was dead. The beautiful girl was dead, left hand severed off, and left in the dark of the woods to bleed to death. Something furry and brown was tied to the wrist just above where Brigid's hand should have been. What was that? Dimpna forced herself to have a proper look at it. Tied to Brigid Sweeney's wrist, dangling from a piece of twine, was a rabbit's foot.

CHAPTER 10

Dimpna found herself scouring the ground for the hand, as if finding it was some kind of priority. She saw nothing but grass and stone and dirt and blood. "My God," she whispered to the trees. Dimpna's eyes welled with tears, as she fumbled in her pocket for her phone.

"Jesus." Dimpna pedaled backward, panic bubbling up in her, heart pounding. "Help," she called out as she turned. "Hello? Is anyone here?" Dimpna could have sworn she heard a barn owl screech in the distance, something they normally only did at night. After its eerie cry had faded, she heard nothing but the wind rustling the trees. *I'm sorry, Brigid. I'm so so sorry.* Her fingers trembled as she dialed 999. When the dispatcher answered, Dimpna stumbled through the call, the sound of her own terrified voice ratcheting up her blind panic.

"Please take a breath," the operator said. "Do you know the victim?"

"I'm not close with her, but I know who she is. Her name's Brigid Sweeney."

"Brigid Sweeney."

"She's with three other twenty-somethings—they have a caravan parked in Camp—they entertain the tourists . . ." Was it a tourist who killed her? *No, it was a psychopath, and last night she asked for your help . . .* Dimpna's insides pulsed with guilt.

"Are you in danger?" the operator asked. "Is anyone nearby?"

Was she in danger? My God. She hadn't even considered that. How could she be so stupid? "I don't know." This could not be happening.

"Do you see anyone around?"

"No. But that doesn't mean they aren't . . . watching."

"Help is on the way. Stay with me. What exactly are we dealing with here?"

"She's tied to a tree. There's so much blood. She . . . I didn't touch her. Should I touch her? She has to be dead."

"Did you check for a pulse?"

"She . . . her left hand is missing. *Severed.*" It tumbled out of her like a confession.

"Her hand is missing?" Dimpna could hear the shock in the operator's voice.

"It's gone. I think she bled out. I don't see her hand on the ground."

"Does she have her other hand?"

Dimpna couldn't believe they were having this conversation. "Yes."

"Please. Check for a pulse."

I'm a veterinarian. I know dead when I see it. Dimpna didn't want to go anywhere near her. But, of course, she should have checked for a pulse; she wasn't thinking clearly. Swallowing her revulsion, she forced herself over to Brigid, being careful where she stepped. She placed her hand on Brigid's intact wrist and pressed down. She tried to shut out her own beating heart and concentrated on trying to feel a pulse. "It's cold. There's nothing. No pulse."

"Okay, luv, you're doing great. No pulse. I assume there's no breath?"

Dimpna hated every moment, but she parted Brigid's hair. She had to lift Brigid's head, and it was dead weight. As it lifted, a horrific sight greeted her. Half-open bloodshot eyes, mouth open and rimmed in blue as if she died mid-scream. Dimpna squelched her revulsion as she gently let Brigid's head fall down again, her hair once more filling in the gaps. "There's no life left in her." No life, no light. Tears welled in Dimpna's eyes, and she bit the side of her mouth to stop from crying out. This wasn't fair. This wasn't right. Mr. Henderson's death had been an act of pure evil, but this young woman had had her entire life ahead of her. She'd stood in front of Dimpna just last night. *Begging for help . . .*

"Take some deep breaths for me," the operating was saying.

"It's so awful."

"I know, pet, I know. Can you go somewhere safe?"

"My vehicle."

"Get to your vehicle and lock the doors. We're sending emergency services."

"Thank you." *Murdered. Hand chopped off. A rabbit's foot.* Dimpna stayed on the call long enough to give her location, then hung up and hurried away from the scene. If she didn't calm down, she was going to be sick. Brigid's face was going to haunt her for the rest of her life. Why hadn't she done more for her last night? "I'm sorry," she kept saying out loud. "I'm sorry, I'm sorry, I'm sorry." Was this shock? She should call Cormac, and she would. As soon as she could catch her breath. From a distance, she could hear the pair of mastiffs howling. They knew. Somehow they knew. The air no longer felt fresh. It was downright chilling. Hands trembling, she dialed Cormac's number.

Cormac's mam had passed away in the night. His sweet, lovely, intelligent mam. He stood next to her bed—what *had* been his mother's bed the past few months—and wondered how her sheets and quilt and eyeglasses and book and teacup and crossword and the myriad of prescription bottles that had overtaken the last few years of her life could all still be here, yet she was just . . . gone. Life supposedly prepared you for death, so why did this feel so impossible? Why was his mind searching for ways to bring her back? He'd been with her in her last moments and held her hand. He'd come into her room after the meteor shower and his second trek to Camp to show her the videos he'd taken. They watched them together, but the quality was too poor, so he finally put his phone down and described it to her in detail. The darkness of the sky, the sound of the ocean lapping at the shore, the thrill he felt in his solar plexus as the first streaks of light came down, the soft blanket on the hill, the scent of the ocean in the air. He only left out one tiny detail; the feel of Dimpna Wilde's hand when it brushed against his and the jolt he felt when they locked eyes.

It wasn't lost on him that Cora O'Brien wanted more details about the people than she did the meteors, or should he say a particular person . . . the aforementioned Dimpna Wilde. The last few days, all she'd wanted to do was talk about Dimpna Wilde. *What a lovely woman. What an intelligent and empathic person, and musical too!* His mam was a little matchmaker. Even while dying from a horrible disease that he wouldn't wish on his worst enemy, she was worried about him. Even if he did fall in love, marry, have children—she would miss it all. She wouldn't see him walk down the aisle and kiss his bride, she'd never hold her grandchildren. He, her only child, had stolen that joy from her. Because there had been chances. Of course, there had been chances. But Cormac always fled, consumed by ethereal terror whenever he got close to committing. He pitied the women in his life. They deserved better. And his mam had deserved better.

"You only have one mother," she used to say to him. "You only have one mother." And what a brilliant mother she'd been. But she'd been much more than that. And definitely more than a woman stricken with a terrible disease. She'd been so many things. A sister. A wife. A retired school teacher. An avid hill walker. A lover of literature, poetry, and puzzles. Cormac knew it was fashionable to complain about one's mother, but his had been a friend and a great sounding board. She'd read three newspapers daily and could finish the crossword ten minutes faster than Cormac. This past year, she'd accepted her diagnosis of MND with dignity, suffering in the end, but quietly. No one would ever know him or love him like his mam. He felt a stab of self-pity as his eyes welled with angry tears.

He'd fallen asleep in the chair next to her bed, and he was there when he heard the death rattle. It startled him out of a light sleep and, for a moment, shocked him. He'd heard about the death rattle but didn't think of it as a real thing, a thing that would happen to his mam. He didn't know if she knew he was there, but he was there, and he held her hand. Those final moments, if any "silver lining" was to be found, were relatively quick. Her eyes widened, and she squeezed his hand as she focused on the ceiling. Her last gesture was pointing to the ceiling, her last words: "Oh, look!"

He looked, he really did. He *looked*. He saw an old ceiling with a water stain and a crack. She let out a shudder and a soft moan, and then her hand went limp in his. She was at peace. Or at least that's what he kept telling himself. She was at peace. *Oh, look! What did you see, Mam?* He hoped it was something beautiful. She had been something beautiful.

Today he was going to tell Sergeant Neely everything. He'd been too worked up about it. She'd probably shake her head, give him a little lecture, and never let him forget it, but he could live with that.

His phone rang, startling him out of his thoughts. *Dimpna.* He clocked the part of him that didn't want to answer, that was already hardening against the very idea of *them* . . . "Hello?"

"Hey." She was out of breath. "This is awful—"

"I know, I know. But she's no longer in pain."

"I'm sorry—what?" Dimpna sounded confused.

Now he was confused. "My mam," Cormac said. "She just passed away." It was then he realized that she couldn't have possibly known and they were like passing trains barreling down opposing tracks.

"I'm so sorry," she said. "I'm so sorry."

It was then that Cormac remembered. The dogs. The caravan. "We were supposed to meet."

"That's totally understandable, and if this wasn't an emergency, I wouldn't be calling."

"Are those horse-mutts giving you a hard time?"

"I called 999, and help is on the way, but it's horrible, it's so horrible—"

He could hear genuine panic in her voice. He was already reaching for his keys. "Talk to me."

She breathed as if she was gulping for air. "I just found Brigid Sweeney tied to a tree."

"Is she alright?" The words just tumbled out of his mouth as he fought the image. Had he really just asked her that? *Of course she isn't alright.*

"She's dead."

"No," he said. "No. No. No."

"Murdered. Someone . . . someone tied her to a tree, chopped off her hand, and left her to bleed to death."

CHAPTER 11

As Cormac entered the village of Camp, he felt its beauty
mocking him. His grief had turned to horror within seconds
of Dimpna's call, and now it was all balled into a fist in his
stomach. His confession, if he gave it to Neely, would already
be too late. He should be driving directly to her office now,
throwing himself at her mercy. In the distance, the curves of
the Slieve Mish Mountains were the backdrop for Tralee Bay,
and everywhere one looked, there were well-tended hedges
and a gang of wildflowers. Purple loosestrife, yellow honey-
suckle, vibrant fuchsia, and the orange flowers of montbretia
all ensured that summer would go out in a blaze of glory.
Nothing evil should ever come to such a spectacular peninsula.

It was supposed to be a feast for the eyes, a balm for one's
weary soul. From the mountains to the oceans to the ruined
forts and medieval outdoor architecture, this blessed land was
a haven for hikers, campers, fishermen, bird-watchers, boaters,
and tourists. Brutal murderers were nowhere on that list. And
yet here they were. Evil had snaked its way in, and here Cormac stood, hiding this cancerous secret. If he didn't confess
now, his lie would eventually come out. He knew this. But
could it wait until after he'd helped catch this madman? No

one could be more motivated to solve this than him. But if he went forward—even one more little action—it would be the end of his career. Maybe even his freedom. But his fellow guards needed him. Brigid Sweeney needed him. He could hardly bring himself to look at the silver caravan. It looked as if nothing had changed. It was hooked up to a black truck. If only they had left last night. *If wishes were horses, how Cormac would ride.*

What do I do, Mam? Guide me.

An ambulance and squad cars lined the street across from the caravan. As Cormac had requested, they were waiting for him and Neely. He parked his red Toyota slightly away from the hubbub and stepped out. This prompted the four guards who had arrived ahead of him to emerge from their vehicles. He gave them a nod and held up a finger. Right now, the fewer people they alerted to the murder scene, the better. It was bad enough that the town was riled up over the Henderson murder. Signs had been popping up all over Camp addressed to the killer:

WE WILL OUTFOX YOU.

He understood the rage, but the last thing the guards needed was a mob of angry vigilantes. He could only imagine the chaos once word of this second horrific death got out. But none of that mattered in the moment. The first few moments of any investigation were critical. The devil was in the details. As he lived through it, he had to pay attention to the details.

He approached the guards, who immediately pointed toward the line of trees. The guards reminded him of a Greek chorus, moving as one, warning the masses of the dangers to come. He instructed them to keep an eye on the crowd. He was already wearing protective gloves and booties; he'd donned them in the car to draw less attention to the scene.

Crime-scene tape had not yet been set up, but as requested, everyone was far away from the area. He quickly crossed into the patch of trees.

Even though Dimpna had described the scene, the shock of seeing Brigid Sweeney in such a state felt like a gut punch. Her long hair flowing down, the rope tight around her body, the stringy bits hanging from her severed wrist, and that rabbit's foot dangling down. Rage enveloped him. This was Cormac's second murder scene, and he'd felt nothing close to this emotional at the first one. He wanted to scream. He wanted to tear the ropes that secured her and part her hair and tell her how terribly, terribly sorry he was. When he'd arrived last night, was she already dead? There had been no light or life around that caravan. He'd knocked and knocked. No lights, no sound, no answer. He'd assumed they were out enjoying the meteor shower and had no idea someone had let their dogs loose. Or had they taken them with them and the dogs got loose from somewhere else? If the dogs had been at the caravan, then there was another possible explanation . . . the killer needed to cut them loose. Had Brigid Sweeney been at the caravan alone with the dogs?

Where was the rest of her group? Eve Murray. Billy Sheedy. Alan Flynn. Would they find more bodies? His little indiscretion had suddenly become a giant mistake. Cormac quickly stepped out of the trees. It was only a few steps from the road. She'd been so close to everything and everyone. Killed in plain sight. The killer could have gone farther into the patch of trees, and she might not have been seen for days or weeks. Or he could have put her in Tralee Bay or the Atlantic Ocean, and it may have been years or even decades before she washed up. The killer wanted her to be found.

Images of chalk scribbling on the shop walls in Dingle assaulted him:

WHO PUT BELLA IN THE WITCH ELM?
THE HAND OF GLORY

"My God," he said out loud. Not only had this murder been planned, the killer had foreshadowed it. The chalk messages weren't harmless acts of vandalism; they were a killer's calling card. Telegraphing his evil intentions on the walls of cheery shops that sold ice cream and souvenirs. Would they catch him on CCTV? Cormac had assigned a team of guards to it, but he'd yet to get an update. He fumbled with his mobile phone and left a message at the station, asking someone from the team to call him ASAP. He'd double the number of guards combing through the tapes. The street had been jammed with people, and many of the messages were written on obscure parts of the shop walls. Had he or she known exactly where to write the messages while staying hidden from the cameras?

The killer would not only enjoy Cormac's torment, he would feed off it. Some people liked to say they didn't believe in evil people. Only evil acts. Cormac believed in evil people. There weren't many out there; most murders were crimes of passion or a dreadful angry impulse left to fester too long. A deep well of hurt that led up to an unforgivable act. This was not any of those. This was the kind of evil that thrived in darkness. The kind that could not survive unless inflicting great pain. This was once-in-a-century evil. And it was here, in Camp, Ireland, in the Dingle Peninsula, in his backyard. And he was terrified.

He was also terribly conflicted. Should he confess his sins now? Should he recuse himself?

He could not let his emotions overwhelm him.

Cormac removed his gloves and booties, balled them up and stuck them in his pockets. If he kept acting like this was his case, anything he touched and anyone he talked to could be compromised. He wouldn't handle evidence, and he wouldn't officially interview the witnesses. He would recuse himself. *Of-*

ficially. Nothing he did would damage the case against the killer in court. He would make damn sure of that. But no matter what, nothing or no one was going to stop him from hunting down the killer. And if Sergeant Neely got the credit but he was the one to crack it, he was fine with that. More than fine. But right now, he was the only one here, and every moment was precious, and he was going to do whatever he had to do. A guard approached, and Cormac instructed him and the others to begin taping off the area. He gestured to the caravan. "We'll be including everything from this point all the way up to the caravan as part of our murder scene. But start back here. I'm going to approach the caravan."

He headed for the caravan, and before he even reached it, he had a partial answer. At least one of the remaining three was still alive. Billy Sheedy, the loose cannon of the group, was pacing in front of the caravan, cursing and shouting. The sun was beating down on his bald head. He really should be wearing a hat.

"He's just noticed his dogs are gone." Cormac turned toward the female voice and found Dimpna Wilde standing beside him. He felt gripped by an overwhelming sense of . . . something . . . whenever she was around. A release of sorts, when he hadn't even realized he'd needed one. The sun was directly overhead, making her platinum-blond hair shine. Her mint-green eyes looked even more ethereal in the morning light. He'd often seen her in colorful dresses, but this morning she was wearing faded denims and a flannel shirt. She probably loathed that people thought of her as tiny, but given that Cormac was short himself, he nearly felt tall next to her.

"I wouldn't be so sure," Cormac said.

"What?"

Cormac couldn't blame Dimpna for being confused. Hell, he was confused. He took a few steps back. He couldn't look at her like that. Not now. What kind of man was he? A woman had been brutally murdered just meters away, and he was lost in a schoolboy crush. He wanted to be rid of all these emotions swirling through him. Death all around him—his mam and Brigid Sweeney—yet here he was, blindsided by a maddening, flitting desire. It was the stress. He had better watch himself; he was very close to the edge. Cormac turned his focus to Billy Sheedy. "If he's the one who set those dogs loose, then he knows very well that they are gone."

"I see." He could feel Dimpna studying him. "Perhaps he expected them to return."

"That could be," Cormac said. "That tracks."

"The dogs are in my bus," she said. "I parked down the road." A look of concern fell over her face.

"Something on your mind?"

"I think the dogs were drugged. Ketamine is my guess. I took bloods, but it will be days before I get the results."

Cormac stared at Billy. Had he drugged his own dogs? Or was the killer a stranger, and he drugged the dogs in order to get close enough to release them?

"Can it be delivered orally?"

She nodded. "Yes."

"So, presumably, someone could have tossed them a piece of meat with ketamine in it?"

"Yes."

Cormac felt his jaw tighten. "You're sure our victim is the woman who came to your clinic last night?" He sounded so clinical. So cold. He had to ask the question, but he knew the answer. Even without seeing her face, he knew it was Brigid Sweeney. And she was dead because he hadn't done his job. Just twenty-four hours. Why couldn't he wind the clock back twenty-four hours? Who was he kidding? He needed that clock wound back forty-eight hours. *Forgive me, Father, for I have sinned* . . .

"I had to part her hair to check for breathing," Dimpna

said. "It's her. She's even wearing the same dress." She shuddered. "And a rabbit's foot where her hand should be."

He couldn't help but flinch as the image of the furry bit tied to her wrist rose up to mock him. What kind of sick bastard were they dealing with? Was he nearby? Watching? Cormac wasn't a profiler, but he'd bet his bottom dollar the sadistic killer was nearby. The thought made his pulse race. "It matches the story she gave you last night." A mysterious man about to hack off the foot of a live rabbit. It had sounded so outlandish. Yet here they were. And there she was.

"I didn't believe her," Dimpna said. "I should have done something. I should have insisted she stay while I called the guards."

"You did tell a guard. Me." If anyone was going to beat himself up over this girl, it was going to be him. "You are *not* to blame."

People were starting to gather around the caravan. The guards were busy securing the patch of woods, but no one had thought to barricade the road from the other direction. Hikers, who were used to stopping at the caravan in the morning for photos and trinkets and a glimpse of Brigid Sweeney, were multiplying along the roadside, drawn to the drama. First the hit-and-run, now this. Every single person that now stood along the road across from the caravan was a potential witness. Or a killer, watching the drama unfold. And Cormac still didn't know if Eve Murray or Alan Flynn were still alive, or on the run, or obliviously sleeping away while Brigid's dead body was tied to a tree only meters away. Dimpna stepped back as Cormac waved over a few guards. "I want all these people to step across the road and stay there. No one leaves until they talk to me."

The guards nodded and headed for the group. Cormac counted fifteen people around the caravan, mostly hikers. Was one of them their suspect? "Thank you for calling me," Cor-

mac said to Dimpna. "I'm sure you have to get back to work."
He wanted her gone, away from all this. He couldn't afford to
be distracted. He needed his anger.

"I don't know how I'm going to concentrate," she said. "But
I do have patients that deserve my full attention." She nodded
to Billy Sheedy, now leaning against the caravan and smoking a
cigarette. "Should I tell him I have his dogs?"

"I'll take care of that. Do you mind keeping the dogs safe
until further notice?"

"I don't mind at all. Especially if one of them is the psychopath." She started to walk away, then stopped and ran
back, and before he knew it was happening she had wrapped
her arms around him. She smelled like lilacs and rain. She
pulled back but kept her hands on his arms, holding him in a
gentle squeeze. "I'm so, so sorry about your mam. She was a
good soul."

He felt his throat constrict. He couldn't think about her
now. "She was indeed."

Dimpna dropped her hands and stepped back. "Please let
me know if there's anything I can do. I mean it. Anything."
She started to walk away, then stopped. "I don't know if it
matters . . ."

"Talk to me."

"Brigid left a jacket at the clinic. There's a lot of blood on
it . . ."

"That's right." He felt his spirits tick up slightly. Evidence.
He'd take it. He'd take every little scrap. "Use gloves, and put
the jacket in a plastic bag. I'll have a guard pick it up."

"I may be in surgery, but I'll leave it with Niamh."

"Don't let her know what it is. Make sure the jacket isn't
visible."

"Of course."

"Thank you. And I hope I don't offend you by saying this,
but please don't—"

Dimpna held up her hand. "I won't say a word. To anyone."
He nodded. "What you saw was very traumatic. I know
you're used to seeing animals in pain, but—"

Dimpna bit her lip and nodded. "Nothing like this. And I
hope I never do again. I can't get it out of my mind."

"You probably never will. I don't think I'll ever get it out of
mine. If you need someone to talk to, I can refer you to a psychiatrist that the station uses."

"I promise to ask for that name if I need it."

Relief settled over him. "Thank you." She smiled, and he
watched her walk away. What a morning. He wanted a cup of
coffee, and even the thought of wanting something so frivolous
when Brigid had died such a violent death made him feel
guilty. Brigid would never have a cup of coffee or tea or a pint
or a toast at her wedding with a glass of champagne. But he
needed a cup. He needed a cup because he wasn't going to
sleep. Maybe not for days. Cormac should be at the funeral
home right now, going over the arrangements his mam had already set up. Family and friends had been called, and they
were on their way in. He could only imagine their reaction
when they found out he was going to work a murder inquiry.

His mam would have understood. She would have insisted
he take the case. *I'm dead*, he could imagine her saying. *I can
wait. You need to find this killer before anyone else gets hurt.*
First Henderson, and now Brigid Sweeney. Were the deaths related? One killer or two? Had the killer been watching his prey
(Brigid) through his binoculars when Chris Henderson ran up
to him, outing him as a pervert? The poor man. He'd done the
right thing by going to the guards, and he was punished for it.
Did this killer think Henderson could identify him? Did he
know Henderson had gone to the guards? In the distance,
Dimpna held two enormous dogs on leashes.

"And just when we thought things couldn't get any worse,"
Garda Lennon said, sneaking up on him from behind.

Cormac jumped. "Jaysus," he said. "You put the heart in me sideways."

"I'd say it's those mutts making your heart race," Lennon said.

"They're beasts," Cormac said.

Lennon laughed. "Just imagine them in cute little pajamas."

"What?"

Lennon shrugged. "They do that on social media. Dress aggressive dogs in cute little outfits to make us go all soft on them. I'm imagining them in sky-blue jammies with yellow duckies."

Cormac cocked his head and stared at the dogs. "Still wouldn't give them a cuddle," he said. "Even if they were wearing pink onesies with winged babies strumming the harp."

"Shit!" Billy Sheedy disappeared into the caravan, and the door slammed shut behind him.

"Four people sleep in there," Cormac said, shaking his head. *Now three . . .*

"Plus two dogs and a talkative parrot," Lennon added.

"Jaysus." Cormac snuck in a few head taps, which were supposed to be a calming technique. It didn't work.

"Did you go inside when you paid them a visit the other day?" Lennon asked.

Was he onto Cormac or just trying to be part of the team? He'd never heard the lad so talkative. Cormac shook his head. "No."

"I thought Sergeant Neely said you had a long talk with them."

"With Eve Murray," Cormac said. "We stood outside. But then she said she was going to faint if she didn't eat, so I accompanied her to the Village Pub." *Accompanied her.* Is that what the kids were calling it? *We smashed. Knocked boots. Drank too much. Had sex against the back wall of the pub. I completely lost my mind.*

Just then a small window in the caravan cranked open, and Eve Murray stuck her head out, as if Cormac's thoughts were all being broadcast on a bullhorn. Billy Sheedy flew out of the caravan and began pacing. "What's the story?" Eve called to him. Cormac had to watch carefully. Was he about to see a performance? Had they turned on Brigid together?

"Hell and Fire are gone," he yelled back. "Someone's taken them."

Eve leaned farther out the window and stared at the stakes in the ground. "Their chains are gone too. Maybe they're with Brigid?"

Their chains are gone too . . . Cormac stilled himself to listen. What did that mean? What had someone done with the chains?

Billy spat on the ground and shook his head. "She's with the poetry arsehole. They left last night."

Poetry arsehole. Once more Cormac didn't know if he could trust what he was hearing. His craving for a cup of coffee morphed into a pulsing need as he took out his mobile phone. He pulled up his notes app. He needed to type in everything they were saying. *Poetry arsehole. Last night.*

"Has anyone seen our dogs?" Billy Sheedy called into the crowd.

"Your dogs are safe," Cormac called out.

Billy came to a stop and turned to Cormac. "Who are you?" he said, not hiding his disgust.

"Detective Inspector Cormac O'Brien." He flashed his badge, which accomplished exactly nothing.

"We have every right to be here," Billy said. His eyes flicked to the numerous squad cars lining the road. "Don't tell me you brought the entire garda station to intimidate us?"

The caravan door opened, and Eve tromped down the steps with the parrot on her shoulder. "You," the bird said. "You, you, you."

"Why is he saying that?" Cormac asked. He had to remind

himself that he had never been inside the caravan, that he had never met that parrot.

Eve gave Cormac the once-over, then a naughty grin lit up her face. "She knows everybody's secrets." Eve winked. The look on her face told him everything he needed to know. She was going to use their moment of insanity as leverage. She could even be a killer. It was over. Cormac's career was over. The parrot suddenly screeched, making even Eve jump.

"Help me!" it cried. Its voice was in a higher pitch than the previous utterance, and her tone sounded panicked. "Help me, help me, help me."

CHAPTER 12

"She's never said *that* before," Eve said, tilting her head to look at the parrot. "Was someone watching a horror movie last night?"

Cormac froze, his mental gears locking as he fought the instinct to shake the feathers off the parrot until he told him who did it. "You've never heard him say that before?"

"Her," Eve said.

Cormac had to silently count to three. "You've never heard *her* say that?"

Eve shook her head. "Never." She turned to Billy, who looked just as confused. "What were you watching last night?"

"The skies," Billy said. "Like everyone else."

"Who else is inside your caravan right now?" Cormac asked.

Eve frowned. "Just Alan."

"Wake him up and tell him to come out here," Cormac said. Eve looked to Billy. Was she asking his permission? Was Billy controlling the group? "Now," he added.

"We're not leaving until we get our dogs," Billy said.

Cormac took a step forward. "You're not leaving at all."

Billy's face scrunched. "What?" He took in the squad cars. "Is this about the Audi? Are you here for Robert Brannigan?"

"He left," Eve said. "He and Vera both."

Cormac felt a zap up his spine. "Who's Robert Brannigan?"

Eve and Billy exchanged a look. "He's Vera Brannigan's brother-in-law." Billy pointed to the cottage/Airbnb on the other side of the car park. "He parked his car here Friday for the weekend."

"His car," Cormac said. "A black Audi?"

Eve and Billy nodded. "And you've been sitting on this information since that poor old man was run down?" Cormac could feel the blood pumping through his veins. *Your anger will not serve you, your anger will not serve you . . .*

"Like you would believe a word we say," Billy said. "You've been harassing us since day one."

"We mind our own business," Eve said. "You should be happy about that."

Cormac's stomach turned. A mistake he'd made that lasted only a matter of seconds was going to reverberate for his entire life. "I'm not the least bit happy."

"Help! Help! Help!" the parrot screeched.

"Where is Alan Flynn?" Cormac asked. "I want him out here now."

Eve whirled around and went inside.

Billy spat on the ground. "Do you happen to know Robert Brannigan's number plate?" Cormac asked.

Billy shook his head. "It was parked here Friday morning. Before the old man was killed. That's all I know." Billy crossed his arms.

Cormac caught a glimpse of Garda Lennon across the street and waved him over.

"Inspector?"

"I need you to notify me the minute Sergeant Neely arrives."

"Absolutely."

"And I want every available guard looking for Robert Brannigan and his sister-in-law, Vera Brannigan." He pointed to the cottage. "She runs this Airbnb, and I've just learned that her brother-in-law, Robert, drives a black Audi that was supposedly parked here Friday morning, hours before the hit-and-run."

Garda Lennon straightened up. "That's huge." Garda Lennon indicated the group of hikers across the street. "They're all clamoring for information. Demanding to know why we closed down the entrance to their hike."

Cormac held up his finger to Billy. "Don't you move." He crossed the street. The hikers were indeed getting restless, their voices growing in frustration.

"What's going on?" a woman asked, pushing her way forward. "Was a hiker injured on the trail?"

"We're dealing with a police emergency," Cormac said. "The trail is shut down until further notice." The guards were combing it now, looking for any signs that a killer had used it as his escape. Drops of blood . . . anything. Or the killer could be one of these hikers, hiding in plain sight. "Who has paper and a biro?" he asked.

For a moment, everyone just stared at him. Finally, a man dug an envelope out of the pocket of his trousers. "Will this do?"

"It will." Cormac took the envelope.

"I have a biro." Cormac turned to find Charlie Meade standing behind him. He was wearing another ISPCA T-shirt, this one in blue. Cormac moved closer.

"What are you doing here?" He didn't realize he was advancing on Charlie until the man took a step back.

"Sergeant Neely sent me here to collect the dogs," he said, holding up his hands. "Just in case the lads refused to leave." He glanced around. "Has something else happened?"

Cormac forced himself to relax. He couldn't afford to incite panic. "One thing at a time," he said. "The dogs are no longer in their custody." So much had happened so quickly that Cormac had forgotten to keep Neely in the loop.

Charlie glanced at the caravan. "Are the dogs alright?"

"Relatively," Cormac said.

Charlie arched an eyebrow. "Relatively?"

Cormac wasn't ready to inform anyone outside the Gardaí that the dogs might have been drugged. He nodded. "They're in a safe place. I'm sorry you had to make the trip." But maybe it wasn't an entire waste. "Listen." Cormac lowered his voice. "Can you hang tight? I'm going to need you to take their parrot and drop him off at the Wilde's veterinarian clinic in Dingle. Can you do that for me, or do you need additional paperwork?" He had no idea how Eve Murray was going to react to that. But those three were going into the station for questioning, and it had to be done.

Charlie glanced at his phone. "If I'm just dropping him off, it doesn't need to be official."

"Her," Cormac found himself saying. "It's a she."

Charlie took this in stride. "I can drop her off."

"Thank you." Cormac paused. "One more thing. If the parrot says anything while you have her, I want to know."

"Are you joking me?" Charlie laughed.

"I am not."

Charlie's grin faded. "Will do."

Cormac clapped him on the back. "Hang tight."

"Not a bother." Charlie leaned in, his eyes inquisitive. His gaze traveled to the line of squad cars and waiting ambulance. He wanted intel.

"I appreciate you," Cormac said.

"Of course." Charlie Meade stepped back. Cormac took the envelope and the pen and held it up to the group of hikers. "I want everyone to write down their name and their digits. Everyone. After you do that, I want you to patiently wait here until a guard can ask you a few questions before he or she dismisses you."

"I'm not going to stay here all day like I'm some kind of criminal," an older man called out. "I'm going for a hike."

"Not today you aren't," Cormac said. "Let me repeat what I

just said. The entrance to the hiking trail is closed until further notice."

"Closed?" another the hiker said. "You can't close a hiking trail." All the folks with backpacks, Kerry-Camino maps, water bottles, and walking sticks were getting rattled.

"Watch me," Cormac said. How many hikers took that trail every day? How many of them either started the trail in Camp or stopped in Camp? Their suspect pool was deep and wide. Then again, hiking was supposed to soothe the soul. But their killer could easily be pretending to be a hiker, hiding in among them.

"Just waiting to get a picture of me with the talking bird," another would-be hiker said. "I promised me niece."

"Well now, you're going to write down your name and digits on this envelope, and wait here until a guard can confirm you've given us the correct information and we've had a word with you, and then *maybe* you can be on your merry way."

"When are you going to tell us what's happening?" someone cried out. Murmurs of agreement rang out. Cormac crossed back to the caravan, ignoring the crowd's thirst for information. He could only imagine how their tongues would wag once they knew all the gory details. It was human nature, but there was nothing "natural" about it. It turned his stomach.

Billy approached the minute Cormac returned. "My dogs," he said. "Where are they?" He was a lid ready to blow.

"Don't you worry," Cormac said. "We'll definitely be having a word with you as well." Cormac was anxious to get back to his murder scene. Neely had to be here by now, but he had to deal with this crowd first and gather their statements as quickly as possible. He didn't want to give any of them time to concoct a story.

Four more squad cars, followed by a lorry with GARDA TECH-NICAL BUREAU stamped across it, pulled up. Heads turned as voices rose.

"What's the story?" a man called out.

"Is that for us?" Billy Sheedy asked, running a hand over his bald head. "We'll leave, okay? This is madness." He looked around to see if anyone else agreed with him.

"Lads," Charlie Meade could be heard saying from across the street. "All this can't be about the dogs."

"Then what?" Billy shouted back, opening his arms. "Because we didn't report the Audi?"

"Audi?" Charlie said. "As in the one that ran down the old man?" He took a step closer. "I didn't realize that was the one. I helped the woman who lives in the cottage the other day—"

"Garda Technical Bureau," Billy said, panic leaking from his voice. "Why is the Garda Technical Bureau here?"

"What is taking Eve and Alan so long?" Cormac demanded. As if they were standing on the inside with their ears pressed to the door, it opened, and Alan Flynn stepped out. He wore his hair long and wild, and his shirt sported a peace sign.

"Step out," Cormac said. "Hands where I can see them." Alan frowned but raised his hands and stepped out, followed by Eve Murray and the parrot. "Anyone else?"

The three of them shook their heads. A series of doors slammed as additional guards emerged from their cars. Finally, Cormac spotted Neely among them, and it appeared as if she was getting briefed.

"What's the story?" Alan Flynn asked as his eyes darted around.

If one more person uttered that phrase, Cormac was going to lose it. Not that he could blame them. He studied his three caravaners. "Where is the fourth member of your group?" Cormac's stomach curled at the question, but he needed to judge their reaction and answer. Every moment he was living through right now could become important evidence.

"She went off with a local," Billy said.

"What's the name of this local, and where does he live?" Cormac asked.

"Peter something," Billy said. "And we have no fecking idea where he lives." He turned to Eve and Alan. They shook their heads.

Peter something... Useless titles went through his head, *Peter Pan, Peter Peter Pumpkin Eater*... *Tell me, does Peter need a hand?* Cormac hated his inner mind. "Where did she meet this local?"

"He came around here all the time," Eve said. "Is Brigid in some kind of trouble?"

"When were you expecting Brigid back?" He nearly cursed himself for using the past tense, but the three in front of him were so rattled they didn't seem to notice it. *Or they already knew*...

Eve frowned again. "We all agreed to leave before noon." She shook her head. "Should I give her a bell?"

Cormac held up his hand. "None of you know this Peter's surname?" The three shook their heads. "What about his phone number?"

More shakes of the head. "He writes her poetry," Eve said. "That's all I know."

"It's shite," Billy said.

"It's shite," the bird perched on Eve's shoulder said. "Help me, help me, help me!"

"What is with her?" Eve said. "Calm down, Bette Davis. Calm down."

"Bette Davis?" Cormac couldn't help but ask.

"Look at her eyes!" Eve said. "She has Bette Davis eyes."

"I'm Bette Davis," the bird said. "Pretty bird."

Cormac personally saw nothing but parrot eyes, and he resisted the line going through his head: *Fasten your seat belts; it's going to be a bumpy night*... It wasn't lost on him that the woman in front of him was named Eve—perhaps another reason she named her bird Bette Davis. None of that mattered now. "Are there any other animals inside that caravan?" Cormac asked.

"No," Eve said.

"We don't abuse our animals," Billy said.

"You also don't keep a good eye on them, now do you?" Cormac hadn't meant to say it, but the lad was working his nerves.

"If you're referring to our dogs, they didn't break loose; someone must have taken them." Billy completed his sentence by spitting on the ground.

Cormac came to attention. "What makes you say that?"

Billy pointed at the stakes in the ground. "The times they broke loose, the chain was still there. Both chains are gone. Someone had to have unhooked them."

The dogs were massive. Who but a fellow member of that caravan would have felt comfortable approaching them? "How do I know one of you didn't unhook them?" Cormac held their gazes. Alan raised his hand, which was off-putting; it reminded Cormac of a schoolchild. Was he being too hard on this group? Not if one of them was a killer. "Yes?"

"Why would we unhook our own dogs and leave their chains hanging after them?"

"If you have our dogs in custody, as you say," Billy chimed in, "why are you asking us about them?"

Detective Sergeant Neely was finally here and making her way over. She and Cormac nodded to each other. They stood close together.

"Have you seen the body yet?" she whispered.

"Briefly. You?"

"Not yet."

"Brace yourself."

Neely groaned. "Right." Cormac pointed to Vera Brannigan's cottage. "Do you know her brother-in-law?"

"Robert?" she said. "I do."

"Did you know he drives a black Audi?"

Her eyes widened. "I do not."

"According to the lads, he parked it there Friday morning. A few hours before the hit-and-run. They also claim that the pair of them were going out of town."

"Together?"

"That's unclear."

"He's a businessman—insurance? Investments? He travels frequently. Mostly Dublin." Neely's gaze shifted toward the patch of trees. "I can't believe this is happening."

"There's one more little thing," Cormac said.

Neely straightened up and narrowed her eyes. "What little thing?"

Get it over with. "I had sex with Eve Murray, so I'm going to need you to take the lead on all of this."

CHAPTER 13

Neely stood open-mouthed and staring. "You did *what*?"

"It's not what you think. It was well before all of this. Before Henderson. And Brigid. I came out here—they weren't breaking any laws—we went to a pub—"

Neely held up her hand. "I don't need every detail."

"I'm going to tell Superintendent McGraw. And my name won't be attached to any official interviews or evidence collection. Just—bear with me until then, okay?"

She shook her head. "I don't know."

Cormac barreled on. "We need a guard to take these three into the station." Cormac thought he was speaking softly enough, but he misjudged it.

"Station?" Eve Murray said. "Why do we need to go to the station?"

What else had she heard? His confession? "I understand that you're going to have a lot of questions," Cormac said. "We have that in common. But for now you're going to surrender Bette Davis to . . ." He looked across the street and whistled until Charlie Meade's head popped up. He waved him over. Charlie came immediately.

"You remember Charlie Meade with the Irish Society for Prevention of Cruelty to Animals?" Charlie lifted his hand in a wave. No one waved back. "I'm going to have him take your bird—"

"African grey parrot," Eve corrected. "And no. No fucking way."

"I'm going to have him take Bette Davis to the same safe place where your dogs are being held," Cormac said, doing his best to put on a soothing voice. "We have an emergency situation, and I'm afraid you'll be speaking with us all day today."

"What emergency?" Billy demanded. "We have a right to know."

"You'll know when I decide the time is right," Cormac said. Billy pressed his lips together and glared.

"Why are you doing this?" Eve cried. "The safest place for Bette Davis is with me." Her lips quivered. "She's my emotional support bird."

"There's no legal provision in Ireland for that," Neely said.

"There should be," Eve said. "Bette Davis keeps me calm."

"Help me, help me, help me!" Bette Davis said.

Eve grimaced. "What is wrong with ya?"

"You're going to be very busy the rest of the day," Cormac said. "I promise you Bette will be in good hands. If there's any food or medicine you want to go with her, we'll have a guard escort you into the caravan to retrieve them."

Billy Sheedy crossed his arms. "Is this about that man Brigid was worried about? The one who tried to cut up the rabbit?"

"What do you know about him?" Cormac asked.

Billy's eyes narrowed into slits. "Just what I said."

Cormac wanted them in an official interrogation room when he delivered the news about Brigid. He wanted to slide a photo of her tied to the tree across the table, and he wanted to watch every single tic, widening of the eyes, and exclamation. He wanted to record exactly what came out of their gobs next. None of it would be anything they could use in court, but it would definitely help tilt his compass in the right direction. "Did you see this man with your own eyes?"

Billy shook his head. "Nope. But I saw the knife and the blood and the rabbit."

Cormac looked to Alan and Eve.

"Nobody saw him but Brigid," Eve said. "And she isn't exactly a truth-teller."

Cormac stepped closer. "What does that mean?"

"It means she could have been messing with us," Billy said. "She likes messing with people."

Alan turned on Billy, the Celtic knot tattoos on his pecs tightening. "She *wasn't* messing."

"You don't know that," Billy said.

"She was genuinely freaked out." Alan seemed to give up on Billy and directed the comment to Cormac and Neely. "Is she in some kind of trouble?"

"Do you know where exactly Brigid saw this man?" Neely asked.

Billy relaxed his arms. "She said something about a tree stump." He pointed to the tree line where Cormac knew Brigid's body was tied. There was no tree stump in those woods, not that he'd seen. The location was so close to the caravan. Why hadn't one of them heard her scream? Or were all three in on it together? Or perhaps the two lads did it, and the remaining female was terrified. The problem is, she didn't look terrified. None of them did. And if there really was an insane man trying to torture a live rabbit, had anyone else come forward about it? They were going to have to comb through any reports received in the last week. Wouldn't an animal who was being cut while alive make hideous noises? He was back to thinking there was something very off about this story.

Cormac turned back to Neely. "We're also trying to identify

a local poet by the name of Peter." He paused as Neely took this in. "I'm guessing around their age."

Neely frowned. "Maybe the Nosh family?"

"That's it," Billy said. "Nosh. Peter Nosh."

Cormac felt a sliver of hope. That was one good thing about a small town, a leg up over a murder in a city like Dublin. Everyone here knew everyone else. Peter Nosh. They now had four persons of interest, and if they thought they were under pressure now, wait until he turned up the heat.

Neely jotted down a note, then turned back to the other guards with another nod. "Let's send a squad car to bring Peter Nosh into the station." It wasn't normal that things were happening this fast, before he even got a look at the body, but he already knew this case was going to be anything but normal. And if this Peter Nosh was their killer, there was no time to waste.

"This isn't just about our animals," Alan Flynn said. "What is this?" His eyes landed on the Technical Bureau's lorry. "Isn't that a forensics truck?"

Guards stepped up as Charlie Meade took the African grey from Eve. "Help me," the bird said. "Help me, help me, help me."

Charlie threw a stricken glance to the group. Eve threw up her hands. "Why do you keep saying that?"

Charlie gave her a pointed look. "I'll help you," he said to the parrot in a calming voice.

"Get what you need for the bird, and let's go," Cormac said. He nodded to Neely. It was time she saw the extent of what they were dealing with. It was time she saw the body.

Sergeant Neely stumbled away from the trees and onto the road. She had just laid eyes on poor Brigid. Cormac had waited in the clear; he'd seen enough. "Alright?" he asked for the second time. "It's alright if you're not." He shook his head. "No one should be alright with that."

"Fine." She turned her back to him. He watched her cross herself, muttering something. When she turned back, she was all business. "Peter Nosh did not do *this*," she said. She thrust her finger toward the crime scene. "Not that."

"Let's keep our minds open." This was also the trouble with small towns. Everyone *thought* they knew each other. But they were often wrong.

"I've known that lad since he was in short trousers. He wouldn't even know how to do this. He's a poet, a nerd."

"What would Brigid Sweeney be doing with a nerd?" Cormac blurted out.

Neely squinted and studied him. "Why? She was too beautiful and should instead choose a lad based on superficial attraction?"

He would not let Neely shame him. He didn't make the rules. Was it his fault if most men were superficial? *Visual creatures.* He did see how that one was agitating. As if only men were visual creatures and women lived with blindfolds on, sensing everyone's soul. Hogwash. *Humans* were visual creatures. He had no excuse for his fellow man. They could be pigs. But he wasn't going to solve it here and now with Neely. "Isn't that the way of the world?"

"And yet you chose the other one." Neely looked stricken that the words had come out of her mouth. "I'm sorry. I'm just extremely disappointed in you."

"It just happened. I didn't plan it."

"I need you on this. What was done to her? I've never seen anything like that."

"I swear to you. I will be on this. I don't need any recognition. I just need to make sure that everyone knows you're in charge. When we catch this bastard—and we will—I cannot let my indiscretion jeopardize the case."

"McGraw will want to remove you entirely."

"He will. But he can't follow me around twenty-four-seven."

"You're asking me to pretend you're not investigating this?"

"I'm not asking you to do anything. Technically, Eve Murray was not any kind of suspect in anything when she and I . . . you know."

Neely took a deep breath. "This does *not* happen here. What was that yoke around her wrist?"

"A rabbit's foot."

"I didn't see her hand. Did you . . . find it?" Cormac shook his head. Neely shuddered. "Why? Why would someone do that?" Cormac filled her in on Brigid's visit to Dimpna the night before and the tale she'd told about a madman trying to hack off the foot of a live rabbit. "My God," Neely said. "And Doctor Wilde didn't call the guards?"

Cormac found his defenses rising. "Dimpna tried to convince Brigid to call the guards, but Brigid said . . ." He stopped short. Neely already seemed wound tight.

"She said what?"

"She said we—specifically, me—that I wouldn't believe her."

"I see." Neely nibbled her lip, no doubt remembering their visit to the caravan.

"But I saw Dimpna that evening."

"I *see*."

Cormac felt his frustration growing. She saw nothing. "We met up for the meteor shower. Not long after, I got a call that the mastiffs were running loose again. They were picked up by a guard and brought to Doctor Wilde's clinic." From now on, he was calling her Doctor Wilde. And keeping his distance. "I came back out to the caravan personally."

"Last night?" Neely asked. "You swung by here last night?" He nodded. "And it never occurred to you to call me?"

She was taking her anger out on him. He couldn't react to it. He wanted to—he was only human. But one of them had to stay calm. "There was no one here. I planned on phoning you this morning." He began to pace. "The guards we assigned to this caravan left their post to chase the dogs."

Neely seemed to be considering his statement. "Did someone release the dogs because he or she was afraid of the dogs or because they wanted to get rid of the guards?"

"That's one thread we have to pull on," Cormac said. "Although it could have been both."

"And when the guards returned?" She let the rest of her question hang in the air.

"When the business with the dogs was all over, I told the guards to go home."

"Why?"

"Because I figured they would eventually figure out *we* had the dogs, and I thought it would keep them under our control." He'd messed up. And they both knew it.

"What time was this?"

"Around half-ten." He checked his notes. "Billy Sheedy mentioned that their chains were gone. But when the guards picked the dogs up, there were no chains." He paused. "The dogs were acting funny when the guard picked them up."

"Funny how?"

"Wobbling, stumbling. Like they were drunk. Dimpna thinks they were drugged with ketamine."

"She thinks or she knows?"

"She took bloods, but it's going to be several days before she can confirm her professional opinion."

"If they were drugged, does that rule out our caravaners?"

"Not necessarily. Either they were recreationally using ketamine and the dogs got into it, or they wanted us to think someone else did this."

"Do you think they're that clever?"

"I think whoever murdered that young woman is that clever."

Neely crossed her arms and gazed around. "You think the killer has the chains?"

"Brigid is tied with rope, but I am wondering if the killer used the chains somehow. Or perhaps it was the easiest way to unhook the dogs without getting too close? But if the dogs both ran off with their chains dragging after them, how and where did they come off?"

"It certainly leads to numerous questions," Neely said. "We're going to have our hands full."

"There is something else I need to tell you, but it has no bearing on this case."

"Don't tell me you knocked boots with another one of our suspects." Neely had her hackles up. He couldn't blame her.

He shook his head and swallowed past the lump in his throat. "My mam died this morning."

Neely placed her hand on her heart. "No, Cormac, no."

"It was peaceful. She's no longer suffering."

"I am so sorry to hear that." She stepped forward and gave his arm a squeeze. "That's what we tell McGraw. You can't officially investigate this case because you're mourning."

"No. I'm telling him everything. I won't have this blow back on you or anyone else."

"I'm so sorry, Cormac. What a terrible, terrible morning."

Her pity was genuine. But it was the last thing he wanted. "Thank you. But she was suffering. And now she's not."

"May she rest in peace." Neely crossed herself.

Cormac hated the phrase *rest in peace*, but he understood people had to say it anyway. His mam was a go-getter. She wasn't lounging on some fluffy cloud gossiping with the rest of the departed. She'd spent the last year of her life watching her body fall apart. His mam was on the *move*, having an adventure worthy of her spirit. "The point is, I had planned on meeting Dimpna—Doctor Wilde—at the caravan this morning."

"Why Dimpna?" Her annoyance was back. Perhaps he'd take the pity after all.

"Because she had the dogs. I was going to tell them they could have the dogs back if they left immediately."

"Right, right. Go on."

"Because of Mam, I lost all track of time. Dimpna arrived first, and she saw Brigid's blue dress through the trees."

"Dimpna Wilde found the body?" Neely said. "Your Dimpna?"

"I don't know what you're implying by 'my Dimpna,' but yes. She was meeting me here with the dogs."

"And she found her." Neely sounded as if she was finding this difficult to swallow.

"Yes."

"Poor thing. She'll never forget a sight like this."

"Neither will we."

"The only way we'll ever have a bit of peace now is if we find her killer."

"Agreed."

Neely sighed and rubbed her left wrist. "What is all this business about rabbits' feet? It's meant to be good luck, isn't it?"

They sat with the irony for a moment. "The symbolism either means something to this brutal killer or . . . he's sending a message."

"Or she," Neely said. "Although my money is on a male." She slid him a look. "No offense."

"None taken. But we do have to keep an open mind." He couldn't help but think about her severed hand. Had she bled out quickly? Damn it, he hoped so. He couldn't even imagine her terror. He was glad he wouldn't have to go home to his mam and relay this wretched tale. Her absence was already creating a gaping hole inside him. He knew he'd have much more grieving to do on the other side of this case. In a strange way, they were twisted together. His mother's death and then

Brigid's death at the hand of a sadistic killer. Sealed in fate. He could not grieve one until he found justice for the other. Or maybe he was just coming up with excuses to kick his grief down the road.

Neely said, "I need to walk." Cormac followed. The weather was in transition. The sun had faded behind a layer of thick clouds, and the wind was picking up.

"We should get a tent over Brigid before it rains," Cormac called after Neely as he jogged to catch up.

Neely nodded, then spoke into her radio. "They're on it." Cormac filled her in on the missing knife from the clinic, the jacket with blood on it that guards were on their way to pick up, and the utterances of Eve's parrot. Neely groaned. "A bird? Our prime witness is a bird?"

"An African grey parrot," Cormac said. "So we have the caravaners—Billy, Eve, and Alan. We have Peter Nosh, and we have Robert and Vera Brannigan."

"Henderson must have interrupted the killer staking out his prey. When he came to our office, he had no idea who was driving the Audi. But it didn't take him long to find out." Neely gazed at the caravan.

Cormac gave a solemn nod. It had been a traumatic couple of days. "Somehow, right after Henderson leaves your office, he figured out the identity of the creeper. Let's say it was Robert Brannigan. Maybe they had another run-in. And that's why Henderson was killed." It was never about Henderson. It was about Brigid.

Neely shook her head. "I can't believe any of this is happening."

"Start believing it. Because we need to be all-in."

"You have a funeral to plan. You should be with family."

"My mam would have wanted me on this case, and that's enough for me," Cormac said. "She already made all her own funeral arrangements. I will, of course, attend her funeral and spend some time with family. I promise you. I will be a shadow. But I will not drop this case." A news helicopter was circling above them. It would not be long before the media showed up. They needed to control the message carefully. "It's going to be a shit show," Cormac said. "We'd better brace ourselves."

"You mean *I'd* better," Neely said. "Because, apparently, I'm now the head shit."

CHAPTER 14

DO NOT CROSS THIS FIELD UNLESS YOU CAN DO IT IN 9 SECONDS BECAUSE THE BULL CAN DO IT IN 10.

Unlike some warning signs—BEWARE OF DOG, when the dog was a mushy labradoodle who would lick an intruder to death before biting—this sign was a truth-teller. The bull it referenced was old, mean, and quite capable of killing a man. Dimpna stood by the edge of the fence with Donie Bailey, the farmer who owned Cujo. In the distance, Cujo snorted and pawed the ground, as if waiting for his next victim. Cujo was old, and he had been showing signs of aggression. But his fate was sealed when a neighboring lad had wandered into the field with a red cap and the naïve idea to see if he could make the bull charge. The bull not only charged, it nearly killed him. Thankfully, there was an old underground burial chamber on the property—a small, cave-like structure—marked in the distance by a rusty tractor that was now part of the landscape. The lad had been able to reach the chamber, crawl into it, and cry for help. The parents stopped making threats when Donie finally agreed it was time to put Cujo down. But even though Donie had a gun and knew how to use it, when it came down to it, he couldn't pull the trigger. Dimpna had given him the name of a humane group that would take care of it for him. But when they arrived to pick him up, Donie had changed his mind. Niamh had given her a bell when Dimpna was leaving Camp. A concerned citizen had spotted the bull in the field pawing the ground and butting the fence as if it was a mortal enemy. Given that Donie's farm was on the way back to the clinic, she'd decided to stop and see if she could persuade him to do the right thing before someone else got hurt or killed.

"I have the sign," he said to Dimpna pointing to it. "The lad was trespassing."

"You may not get so lucky next time," Dimpna said. "You don't want the death of a child on your hands."

"I'm not ready," Donie said. "When I'm ready, I'll shoot him meself."

"You should keep him in the barn until you're ready," Dimpna said. "It's not safe for anyone to let him roam this field."

"The sirens got him all riled up," he said. "Something is going on in Camp."

"I'm not here to talk about that, Donie. My professional advice is that Cujo is now a danger not only to himself and to any living creature who wanders into the field; he's a danger to you."

"How is he a danger to me?"

"If one more lad wanders in and is hurt—or killed—you cannot claim ignorance. You will be liable."

"The blood will be on my hands, is that what you're telling me?"

Dimpna felt a chill at the words and couldn't help the images from this morning that flashed into her mind. "Yes. It is your responsibility. Cujo has had a long life. Shall I call our friends to come back out?"

Donie waved her comment away. "They won't be coming back out. I'll shoot him meself. I'm going to let him have the day. Look how happy he looks."

Dimpna looked. He was pawing the ground. As if sensing her gaze, he looked up, nostrils flaring.

"I won't be coming out to see him anymore, Donie. And until he's been put down, I won't be able to come out for the others either." Donie had a herd of dairy cows. Dimpna placed her hand on his shoulder before climbing into her bus. "The sooner it's done, the sooner you can heal," she said.

Donie stared at her, then waved her on down the road.

"Someone has an admirer," Niamh sang out to Dimpna as she returned to the clinic. Dimpna stood by the call board, willing herself to focus on the day ahead, when her mind was firmly on Brigid Sweeney. She couldn't stop seeing the horror. At least a guard had promptly arrived to pick up the jacket that Brigid had kicked across the floor, begging Dimpna to tell the guards to have it tested. She felt the itch to tell someone (everyone), the horrific drama of her morning. But until there was a media briefing or someone else got wind of the details, she had to keep the ordeal to herself. Her father had often lectured her on patience: *Where's the fire, Dew? Slow down. Mistakes made in haste lead to waste.* There were times Dimpna was gripped with a sense of grief over losing her father despite the fact that, physically he was still here.

She missed Ben too. She made a mental note to pay her son a visit as soon as she was out from under all these burdens.

"Did you not hear me say that someone has an admirer?" Niamh said. The cheer in her voice was usually welcomed, but today Dimpna found it painful. Keeping a secret this big felt toxic.

"Oh?" Dimpna forced a smile and turned to face her office manager.

Niamh held up a folded note. "I didn't mean to read it, found it under the seats." She indicated the seats in the waiting room. Dimpna felt her heart rate tick up. Had Brigid dropped it?

"I think I know to whom it belongs," Dimpna said. She held out her hand.

Niamh grinned and clasped the note to her chest. "It's *poetry*." She leaned in and whispered. There were three folks in the waiting room, and they all seemed eager to hear more.

"Is it good poetry?" Dimpna couldn't help but ask.

Niamh shrugged. "It rhymes, and it's obvious *someone's* in love." She reluctantly handed the paper to Dimpna. Heart tripping in her chest, Dimpna opened it:

> *I could sit upon a thousand hills*
> *And dream of you all night long*
> *You're a goddess from another world*
> *And I'm your lifelong pawn*

It had to be for Brigid. What was it like to be so beautiful that men dropped everything to bare their souls? Then she thought of how things had turned out for the young woman and felt a deep shame spread through her. She tucked the poem into the pocket of her lab coat and turned to the board.

"Is it yours?" Niamh asked.

"No," Dimpna said. "It's definitely not mine."

"But you're going to keep it?"

"I believe I know to whom it belongs," Dimpna said. *For Whom the Bell Tolls . . .* She refocused on the call board, hoping that would be the end of the conversation.

"Are you alright, Doctor Wilde?"

Niamh usually called her Doc or Dimpna. She'd already picked up on Dimpna's shift in mood. This was the one downside of having a tight-knit staff in a tight-knit town. "Grand, I'm grand," Dimpna said. "Out a bit late, I suppose." Although Niamh had arrived bright and early, Dimpna and Patrick had spent the rest of the morning operating on the wee fox, so this was their first moment to speak. Dimpna had managed the operation quite well. She'd been forced to wall off her emotions during the surgery. No matter what else was going on, in the moment of need, her patients were the world. But now her emotions were threatening to overflow.

"How did it go with Mr. Bailey?" Niamh asked.

Dimpna sighed. "He's being as bullheaded as Cujo."

Niamh nodded sympathetically. "I'll pray to Saint Francis to give him the strength to do the right thing." The patron saint of animals. Was there a patron saint for bullheaded men? If so, Dimpna would be praying round the clock. "Patrick said you were jammers last night," Niamh continued. "That's why I brought you this." She lifted her arm to reveal a small bag hanging from it, then reached in and pulled out a large coffee and a lemon tart. "Sugar and caffeine. You deserve it."

"Thanks a million," Dimpna said. She meant it. If there was ever a day to load up on sugar and caffeine, today was that day. Dimpna treated herself while continuing to think through her workload. The next few patients were calls out to farms, which would keep Dimpna away from the office and thus the office gossip. And even though rain was moving in, the fresh air would do her good. The wee fox had had several fractures that they had set, on his front and back leg on his left side, and he would be sleeping it off for quite some time. His recovery would take time. They would not be able to release him back into the wild immediately, and Niamh had been tasked with calling wildlife rescue centers to see if anyone could take him. Dimpna needed to go outside and breathe, and tried not to look too eager to escape, but there was only so long she could stare at four walls before she was ready to be outdoors. Especially in the last month of summer. At least the jobs today were pretty basic. There was a colt and a few sheep that needed their hooves tended. Patrick could handle the clinic while she was gone.

Niamh plopped down in her seat and twirled. "That love poetry was definitely for you," she said. "Otherwise, you'd be spilling the details."

Dimpna pretended not to hear Niamh as she headed upstairs to fetch her four-pack, then with Guinness, Spike, Pickles, and E.T. tripping behind her, she grabbed her gear, told Niamh she would be back at the end of the day, and headed outside. A man was coming up the walk with an African grey parrot perched on his shoulder. The caravaners had a parrot. Dimpna stopped and eyed him. He looked familiar, but she couldn't place him. "Did Inspector O'Brien send you?"

For a second, the man looked startled. "Bette Davis is a good girl," the bird said. "Help me, help me, help me!"

Dimpna felt the hairs on the back of her neck raise. "What's the matter with ya, luv?" Dimpna cooed.

"This is Bette Davis," the man said with a nod to the parrot. "And yeah—that inspector sent me. Something is going down with those caravaners. Guards are swarming all over the place." He held out his hand. "We met briefly the other day."

"You look familiar, but I'm having a hard time placing you."

"I trapped the fox with ya?"

"God, right, right. You came through with the cage and the crispy chicken! How could I forget?"

He grinned. "Charlie Meade with ISPCA. Lucky I happened to be in the pub when the call came in that you needed my lunch for a fox." He glanced at the clinic. "How are they?"

"The pup is going to be fine, but I'm afraid the mother didn't make it."

"That's a shame." She held her arm out to Bette Davis, and she jumped off Charlie Meade's shoulder to Dimpna's fist, then wasted no time climbing up to her shoulder. "She likes you better than me," Charlie said.

Dimpna shrugged. "Comes with the territory."

"Bette Davis, Bette Davis, Bette Davis," the bird said. "Get a record."

"Thank you for dropping off the parrot. Do you need any forms signed?"

He shook his head. "Not for the bird. But I do have other clients here."

"Oh?"

"Hell and Fire," he said. "The mastiffs."

"Right." She had to be coming off as a clueless eejit. What a morning it had been.

"Would you mind if I see them? I can mark them as healthy and secure for my paperwork, and a signature would be appreciated for that."

"Absolutely. You can see Niamh, our office manager inside. She'll be able to take you to the kennel and sign your forms."

"Thank you, Doctor Wilde."

"Please. We've rescued a fox together. Call me Dimpna."

"Call me Charlie," he said with a wink. He headed for the clinic.

"Do the caravaners know I have their animals?" Dimpna asked. From what she'd seen of the bald lad, he wouldn't hesitate to turn up and demand she release them.

"Not by name," Charlie said, stopping and turning around. "The detective just told them they'd be safe and taken care of while they're wanted for questioning." He took a step toward her. "I'm dying to find out what happened, but the detective is keeping it mum." He looked at her as if she might have something to add.

She shrugged. "I'm sure there will be an announcement at some point." This was a tight-knit community, a Gaeltacht region, and gossip spread quickly, so she was definitely keeping her gob shut. In some ways, it would be a relief to share the horror with others. But it was also going to rile up the entire area. Fear and rumors would swirl. The gorgeous lass tied to a tree with her hand severed.

"Are you alright?" Charlie asked. Dimpna was starting to realize she did not have a poker face.

"Help me! Help me! Help me!" the parrot squawked. Dimpna flinched, she'd nearly forgotten the bird was right by her ear.

"I'm grand," Dimpna said, already irritated at the prospect that folks might be asking her that all day. She was already putting on the best front she could, considering the circumstances.

The door to the clinic opened, and Patrick Kelly stepped out. "Niamh said you were out here with a parrot on your shoulder," he said. "Do you need a hand?"

Dimpna flinched at the phrase, and Charlie Meade picked up on it. He cocked his head and stared at her. "Her," Dimpna said to Patrick, forcing a smile before he could ask her what was wrong. "Say hello to Bette Davis."

"Help me, help me, help me," Bette Davis said. Dimpna flinched again.

Patrick tilted his head. "Are you torturing Bette Davis?" he asked with a glint in his eye. He held his arm out, and Bette Davis immediately hopped onto it, then climbed all the way up to his broad shoulder and nuzzled his ear.

"All the birds in town like our Patrick," Dimpna said.

Charlie Meade laughed. "I can see that." Patrick's face turned ruby-red.

Dimpna resisted the urge to joke that Niamh would be jealous. Patrick seemed oblivious to Niamh's crush on him, and it was better for the clinic that it stayed that way.

"Wait," Charlie said. "Do you think the parrot saw or heard something happen last night?"

"Last night?" Patrick said. "What happened last night?"

"Nothing," Dimpna said quickly. "We were just chatting about the meteor shower." Had Bette Davis witnessed Brigid's abduction? *Were they hearing Brigid's last words?* She turned to Patrick. "There's a giant birdcage in the back kennel, but if she seems distressed in it, you can take her upstairs to my flat, and maybe see if you can set up a perch and food and water. My four-pack won't bother her. Will you, lads?" She looked to them now—Spike, Pickles, Guinness, and E.T. They looked back expectantly.

"Well trained," Charlie Meade said. "Even the pussycat. I'm impressed."

"Don't let them fool you," Dimpna joked. "They're little terrorists."

"Are you ready for a little holiday?" Patrick said to the parrot. "Your guest cage is huge, and it has a swing and toys. I think you'll like it."

"Brilliant," Charlie said. "Sounds like something I might like."

"I'm headed to John Noble's farm," Dimpna said.

"Can I come with you?" Patrick said. "We've had a cancellation, and there's nothing on the board for another two hours."

"Come on, then," Dimpna said. "I'll wait in the bus while you sort out Bette Davis."

"Two shakes," Patrick said. He turned and headed into the clinic, talking to the parrot the entire time.

Charlie dug in his pocket, then held out a calling card. "Here's my private number. If you need me or get any updates, I'd appreciate a call."

Dimpna tucked the card in her pocket. "We do sometimes come across abused animals," she said. "I'm grateful ISPCA is always on the lookout." She paused. "And if you know any wildlife rescue centers, we'll be trying to find one to take in our wee fox."

He nodded. "I can definitely ask around."

Dimpna sighed. "It's been a crazy few days around here."

"I'll say." He shook his head. "I'm wondering if they've got a suspect in custody."

"Oh?" Dimpna said.

"As I said, the guards swarmed that caravan this morning. Taped it off like it was a crime scene. Do you think they tied one of them to the hit-and-run?"

Tied. She tried to stop the image of Brigid and the rope and the tree, but it came anyway. She was shocked the public still hadn't gotten wind of it. "Sounds like it," Dimpna said. Lying was getting easier with practice.

"If so, I'm thrilled they caught the bastard." He took a deep breath. "What kind of sicko runs over an old man and takes off?" He clenched his fist. "It's unforgivable."

"They'll catch him," Dimpna said, in a tone that any psychologist would peg as someone trying to convince herself. "They'll catch him."

Patrick exited with a file. "Dimpna?" he said. "Can I have a moment with you in the boarding facilities?" Dimpna knew from his tone there was something afoot.

She turned to Charlie. "Do you mind seeing Niamh first? She can take you to see the dogs in a bit."

"Not a bother," said Charlie. He headed into the clinic, and Dimpna followed Patrick to the boarding facility across the street. Patrick moved with purpose, and his earlier jovial self was nowhere to be seen. What now? She wondered as dread thudded through her. What now?

CHAPTER 15

Cormac and Neely ducked under the crime-scene tape and moved away from the murder scene as the forensics team moved in. "I'm sending guards over to Peter Nosh's house to keep an eye on it and see if he's home," Neely said.

"We need to get our three caravaners to the station, put eyes on Peter Nosh, and get a bead on Robert and Vera Brannigan," Cormac reiterated. "I'd say that's a good start." He thought of something. "Does Robert have a wife?"

Neely nodded. "Lorraine. I'm sure the guards are already at her house."

"Let's confirm that," Cormac said.

Neely nodded. "I'll send Garda Lennon a text. He's going to be point on this."

"Let's put the request in for a warrant to search the caravan. Although if our three caravaners are willing to let us search it, that will speed things up."

"I keep thinking of George O'Malley," Neely said. "But he couldn't possibly have anything to do with this."

Cormac stopped. "Who is George O'Malley?"

Neely walked ahead a few steps before realizing Cormac wasn't following. She stopped and faced him. "He's a local eccentric. He's mute. He can hear, but he doesn't speak. He walks around with his donkey. Sells little trinkets."

"And?"

Neely sighed. "I believe I've heard something about him selling rabbits' feet alright."

"We've got quite a list of suspects started already," Cormac said.

"Persons of interest," Neely corrected.

"Dimpna Wilde said she got the distinct feeling Brigid was lying—or at least not telling the whole story. She said she's never heard of anyone severing the foot of a live rabbit. But if it's this George O'Malley, is it possible he's mentally ill?"

"I don't want to assume he's mentally ill just because he doesn't speak."

"Of course not. I'm simply trying to see if there are any dots we can connect."

"Well, here's one that doesn't connect. O'Malley doesn't drive a car, so he's not our man for the hit-and-run."

That would blow Cormac's entire one-killer theory. "Maybe he sold this rabbit's foot to our killer. But if he doesn't talk, how will we know?" First the parrot who spoke but couldn't comprehend; now a person who comprehended but couldn't speak.

"I think he draws," Neely said. "That's how he communicates."

"Let's hope he draws us something good," Cormac said. *Like a confession . . .* "I had one of those yokes when I was a lad," Cormac said. "Now I wish I didn't."

"A rabbit's foot?" Neely sounded surprised.

"Aye. I got it at a carnival," he said. "Carried it around for about a year until I realized it wasn't bringing me any luck."

"It never brings the rabbit any luck either," Neely said.

A guard approached, and they stopped and looked at him. "We've got the entire field past the caravan cordoned off."

"Good man," Neely said. The guard nodded and moved away. "She had to have screamed," Neely said, looking around. "No one heard her?"

"I had the same thought," Cormac said. "There was a large crowd last night for the meteor shower, so there would have been competing noise. Horns, cars playing their music, cheers," Cormac said. "It was quiet when I arrived, but later in the night, I think the volume picked up."

"Do you think he arranged her hair to fall over her face like that?" Neely asked. "Is he hiding her face?"

"Maybe he's ashamed," Cormac said. "Or maybe he's playing a game." This was someone overconfident. Determined. Was this something that had been in the planning for ages?

"Someone had to have seen something," Neely said. "We'll figure this out right quick." She did not sound convinced.

"Right," Cormac said. "Unless everyone was too busy looking at the skies." This killer had seized an opportunity. There had been a large crowd gathered, but everyone was looking up.

"I can get started on a warrant to search the caravan," Neely said.

"I want to speak with her three roommates. Come to think of it, I think it's best to chat with them here in a relaxed setting before bringing them into the station."

Neely looked around. "Here? You want to chat with them here?"

Cormac nodded. "If we take them to the station, it's going to eat up loads of time."

"It also makes it official," Neely observed.

Cormac hoped she wasn't going to stop him. "This will just be me, having a chat. I won't read anyone their rights. But you know as well as I do, we need to know what they know as soon as possible."

"I think I'm the one who should have that chat," Neely said. "Including reading them their rights. You're the shadow, remember?"

"As long as I can listen—and maybe text you additional questions?"

Neely crossed her arms. "Where exactly were you thinking of having this chat?"

He gestured to the cottage. "There's a plastic table and chairs at the side of the Airbnb." He cleared his throat. "I also need the crime-scene photographer to get some shots of Brigid. I want to see their reactions."

"It's a bit unconventional," Neely said. "But the sooner we interview them, the sooner we can speak with the rest of our lineup."

"That's the spirit," Cormac said.

"Let's hope they know how to contact Brigid Sweeney's family," Neely said. "It wouldn't be right for them to hear about it on the news first."

Gawkers stood near the roadside, staring open-mouthed as guards placed crime-scene tape around the entire area. A white tent had been placed around Brigid, leaving a somewhat eerie-looking encampment around her remains. Once the body was removed, the tree would become a resting place for Mass cards and flowers and candles. Cormac also guessed the killer had taken her hand. Some kind of trophy? There hadn't been anything else visible on the ground around her. No phone. No handbag. And given that it had been dry lately, there weren't any obvious footprints. Cormac was itching to get into the caravan to see what was in there. Guards had closed the nearby entrances to the Dingle Way trail and were questioning hikers. Cormac headed for the three caravaners, who had been relocated to the far side of the Airbnb near a plastic table-and-chair set. Neely was already there and gave him a nod as he approached.

Billy Sheedy and Alan Flynn were smoking, while Eve Murray paced. Were her restless feet the sign of a guilty conscience? She stopped as he approached, and soon Cormac had three pairs of eyes on him.

"What's the story?" Billy said. He dropped his cigarette and crushed it with his shoe. "Why are you taping up the car park?"

"Is it Vera Brannigan?" Eve asked. "Has something happened to her?"

"Sergeant Neely is going to have a little chat with each of you individually," Cormac said. "When we're finished here, you'll be off to the Tralee Garda Station where you can give an official statement."

"Statement?" Eve said. "What kind of statement?"

"If someone was hurt, why is the ambulance still here?" Alan asked.

"Is someone dead?" Billy asked. Eve and Alan's heads snapped toward Cormac as they awaited his answer.

"One at a time," Cormac said.

"He didn't say no," Billy said, jabbing his index finger at Cormac. "Is someone dead?"

Cormac ignored the question. Although the skies had darkened, the weather was still mild enough to hold an interview outside.

"We'll talk to you first," Neely said with a nod to Eve. Eve gave Cormac the side-eye. Did she think she had leverage? Cormac felt a twinge of relief that he'd come clean to Neely. He would still have to face Superintendent McGraw.

"What are we supposed to do?" Billy said. "Can we go back to the caravan?"

"No," Cormac said.

"Our truck?" Alan asked.

"No."

"We're just supposed to stand here, twiddling our thumbs?" Billy took out his mobile phone. "I'm calling Brigid."

"I'm going to ask you not to call anyone," Cormac said. He'd soon find out if they would voluntarily submit their phones to a search. He had an impulse to snatch them now, but then nothing he gleaned from them would be legal.

"Why are there so many guard cars?" Billy said. "Just because our dogs broke loose and nipped at a few tires?"

"Oh, Jesus," Eve said. "Did they cause an accident?" She glared at Billy. "I *told* you they were going to cause an accident."

"Do you *see* any smashed-up cars?" Billy said, rolling his eyes.

"The earlier accident," Eve said. "The hit-and-run."

Cormac's phone dinged. The photographer had texted him the photo of Brigid. As instructed, he had taken the photo at such an angle that neither her severed hand nor the pool of blood was visible. Cormac wanted this information kept secret as long as possible. He hoped that withholding that gruesome detail would incite the killer. He forwarded it to Neely. She took one look and grimaced.

"I have to go to the jax," Eve said, crossing one standing leg over the other. "Like really, really bad."

Neely sighed. "I'll have a garda escort you to the Village Pub." Neely pointed to Billy. "I'll have a chat with you first."

"I've never needed an escort to the jax in my life," Eve said.

"There's a first time for everything," Neely said, as a female garda approached.

Alan, sensing he was in for the long haul, lowered himself to the ground and crossed his legs in a yoga pose.

Cormac felt a prick of jealousy. He wasn't even that old, and he'd have a hard time making his legs do that.

Neely asked the garda to take Eve to the restroom at the pub. The garda glanced at her watch. "Do they open this early?"

"Someone will be there. Tell them we'd consider it a favor."

The garda nodded and gestured to Eve. "I'm not a criminal," Eve said.

"It's for your own safety," Cormac said. "Please. Trust us."

Eve stared at him for a moment, then strode off, the garda following.

"I'll need you to give us some privacy," Cormac said to Alan as Neely led Billy to the picnic table. Cormac signaled for another guard to escort Alan across the street. Alan reluctantly stood, but then he whirled on Cormac.

"We can't leave. We can't go back to the caravan. We can't call Brigid. We can't go anywhere alone. I can't get in my truck. And you say it's for our safety? When the fuck are you going to tell us what's going on?" If yoga was supposed to center him, it wasn't working.

"As soon as it's your turn," Cormac said. Alan scoffed, then trailed after the guard. Several times, he turned back to glare at Cormac. Cormac hurried to where Neely was questioning Billy. He got there just in time.

"When is the last time you saw Brigid Sweeney?" Neely asked.

Billy frowned. "This again? Last night." He crossed his arms. "What did she do?"

The comment was an interesting one. What was he thinking she'd done? "What time?" Cormac asked without thinking. Neely shut him down with a look.

"What time?" she repeated to Billy.

"Dunno."

"Your best guess."

Billy squirmed in his chair. "She tried to save some fecking rabbit. Alan dropped her off at a vet's, and that's the last I saw her. Told you she spent the night with the freak who calls himself a poet."

Cormac sidled over and whispered in Neely's ear.

"If the last time you saw her, she was headed off to a vet, then how do you know who she spent the night with?" Neely repeated.

Billy frowned. "Because she mentioned it before she left. We were making plans to see the meteor shower." He crossed his arms. It was obvious from his expression that he hadn't been happy with Brigid's decision.

"Where did you watch the shower?"

"Outside the pub up the road." The Village Pub. Cormac felt his interest tick up. It should be easy enough to pull CCTV footage from the publican. "Did you have any contact with her after she left? Phone call? Text?" Billy shook his head. "We'll get the records, so I suggest you tell the truth."

"I resent the implication that I'm not telling the truth," Billy said. He spat on the ground. "Whatever trouble Brigid's got herself into this time has nothing to do with me."

Cormac had an urge to fling the plastic table away and grab Billy by the neck. Just the thought was satisfying. "What other trouble has Brigid gotten herself into?" This time he ignored the look from Neely.

"I'm not answering that. If you have any more questions about Brigid, you can ask her yourself."

Neely took back the reins. "Have you ever had a romantic relationship with Brigid?" she asked.

"On and off." Billy uncrossed his arms. "Lately, it's been off."

"Quarreling?" Cormac asked. Billy shrugged. *Interesting.* "Do your arguments get physical?"

Billy jumped to his feet. "No!" he shouted. Guards nearby turned their heads. Billy looked at them, then Cormac. "Fuck no. Is that what she said? Is she spreading her lies?"

Another disparaging comment about the lass in a matter of minutes. "Sit down."

Billy shook his head but took the seat again. Cormac waited.

Billy scratched himself behind the ear. Cormac eyed his arms and hands, trying to work out if they had any scratches or cuts, or blood. He was somewhat dirty, bare-chested, and there were indeed three angry scratches on his arm. Cormac nudged Neely, and she snapped a photo.

"Hey," Billy said, leaning forward and hunching his shoulders. "What the fuck is your problem?"

"What happened there?" Neely pointed to the scratches.

"What do you mean?"

"Your arms. The scratches," she persisted.

Billy shrugged. "We were exploring."

Neely didn't look up from her notepad. *Good move*, Cormac thought. *Keep it casual. Just having a friendly chat here.* He had to remind himself to unclench his fists. "Who is we, and when and what were you exploring?" Neely continued.

Billy glanced at Cormac and frowned before turning back to Neely. "You name it. The woods, the hiking trail, the old train tracks, the beach." He spread his arms out. "We love it here."

Neely looked up, looked out at the bay, nodded. "Where is it you're from?"

"Monahan."

Up north. Cormac already knew that; his accent was distinctive. "She's going to need your full name and address," Cormac said as he slid a notebook and biro across the table. Being a shadow was harder than he anticipated.

Billy leaned in. "I'm not answering a goddamn thing until you tell me what you think you're hunting here."

"Do you hunt?" Neely asked.

Billy closed his eyes and bumped his fist on his forehead several times. "I need a smoke." He sighed, opened his eyes, and then, as if just waking up, he swiveled his head to look at the crime-scene tape that was being erected as they spoke, all around the line of trees down the road, guards walking it back as they dragged it toward the caravan. Then he took in the ambulance, then the Garda Technical Bureau lorry. Suddenly, he stood, knocking the chair out from under him. Before Cormac could even stand, Billy Sheedy was off like a flash toward the crime scene.

"Brigid!" he screamed. "Brigid!"

CHAPTER 16

"Damn it," Cormac started after him. "Stop." Billy kept running. "I said stop," Cormac repeated, as he and Neely sprinted after him. Cormac reached him first, grabbed his shoulder and swung him around.

"Tell me she's not over there," Billy said, pointing to the tree line. The sarcasm was gone; his voice was filled with panic. "For the love of God, tell me it's not Brigid." Alan had heard the commotion and was running toward them in one direction, while Eve and the garda escorting her were approaching from the other.

Alan reached them first, his hands clasped near his lips in a prayer position. "What's wrong?"

"It's Brigid," Billy said. "They're asking me about Brigid." Eve caught up, and the three of them stood in a fortified clump facing Cormac and Neely.

"Where is she?" Eve asked.

There was no avoiding this now. "We cannot let you cross into our murder scene," Cormac said.

"Murder scene," Billy said. "Murder scene." He put his hand over his mouth. "What are you fucking on about?"

"We have a deceased female victim," Neely said, delivering the news with a calm that Cormac knew she did not feel. "We'll need to get a positive identification. But we believe it's Brigid Sweeney, and she's met with foul play." She pulled out her mobile phone and held up the partial crime-scene photo of Brigid. Cormac tried and failed to get the image of her severed hand out of his poor head. The three leaned in to have a look.

"No," Billy was the first to reel back. "No!" he screamed. He put his head in his hands. "No, no, no."

"Jesus," Alan said. "Is this some kind of sick prank?"

"That's her, lads," Eve said. "That's her." Eve's hands flew over her mouth. Alan closed his eyes and put his hands in prayer position.

"Brigid. Oh my God, Brigid." Billy lunged forward, only to be stopped by several guards. "Who did this?" He continued to struggle against the guards. "Brigid!"

"Calm down," Cormac said. "Or we're going to sedate you." He had no idea whether or not he could do that, but it did the trick. Billy stopped.

"Where's that poet? Peter? Where is he?" Billy was practically foaming at the mouth. "I'm going to fucking kill him."

"Can I see that photo a little closer?" Alan asked.

Somewhat reluctantly, Cormac held the photo closer.

"Maybe it's someone who looks like her," Alan said. He threw panicked looks to the others. "How do we really know? We need to see her face."

Cormac held up his hand. "We're waiting for the coroner or state pathologist to arrive. Until then she cannot be touched."

"It's her," Billy said throwing Alan a death glare. "You know it's her. She went to that poet. She spent the night with him," Billy repeated.

"She didn't," Eve said. All heads turned to her, and she seemed to wait until she had a captive audience. "I saw Peter last night at the pub."

"Which pub?" Cormac asked.

"The Village Pub," Eve said. "Where I was just escorted to

the jax. Among other things . . ." She stared openly at Cormac, a smile playing at the corner of her lips.

Him. She was talking about him. Cormac got the feeling she had not told the lads about their tryst, and she was thoroughly enjoying what she thought was their dirty little secret. How long would that last?

Alan nodded. "I saw Peter there too. With an older woman."

"His mam, I think," Eve said.

"Then he killed her before he went to the pub," Billy said. "Or after."

They didn't have a time of death yet. But Cormac was taking notes nonetheless. It was too late to separate them. They would do that later. "When was the last time you saw Brigid?" Cormac asked Eve. She glanced at Billy and Alan. "Look at me," he said. "Not them."

"Yesterday."

"What time yesterday?"

Eve shook her head. "I can't remember."

"You dropped her off at that vet with the bloody rabbit, remember?" Billy jabbed his finger at Alan. "She never came back."

Alan stepped into Billy's personal space. "What are you saying?"

Before Cormac could separate them, Billy gave Alan a shove. Alan stumbled back, then prepared to charge. This time, Cormac caught him and held him back. "She didn't want me to wait for her," Alan said. "She insisted. Peter was going to pick her up."

According to Dimpna, Brigid had called someone from the clinic, saying something about it not being safe and that they needed to get out of here. It had to be one of these three. Cormac whispered this to Neely.

"I want each of you to check your mobile phones and tell me the last time Brigid called you," Neely said.

"You sealed off our caravan," Billy said. "Our phones are in there."

"All of yours?" Cormac asked. Alan flipped the pockets of his shorts inside out and spread open his arms. Cormac ignored him.

Eve nibbled on her bottom lip. "My phone is in there too."

It was possible Brigid had left a message with one of them and they hadn't heard it. "I will get warrants for your phones. But it will speed up my investigation if you give me passwords and permission to search them."

"No," Billy said, making eye contact with the other two. "We need representation."

"If you had nothing to do with this, why are you jumping to that conclusion so early?" Cormac stared Billy down.

"Gee, let me think. You were *just* here the other day doing everything in your power to get us to leave town. And now what? You have our best interest in mind?"

"How did she die?" Eve asked, her voice barely a whisper.

Neely jumped in right away. "We won't be disclosing that until there's been a full examination by the state pathologist."

"We're supposed to tell you everything, but you won't even tell us how she died?" Billy snarled.

"That's how a murder inquiry works," Cormac said. He needed to get them back on track before they stopped talking altogether. "Are you sure none of you saw the man who hurt the rabbit?" Cormac asked. One by one, they shook their heads.

"She came running to the caravan with it clutched to her chest, bleeding like," Alan said. "She was wearing some man's jacket. I dropped her off at some clinic. I don't remember the name of it." He bit his lip. "It's in Dingle."

"I've got the name," Cormac said. He didn't supply it. If Alan was telling the truth and he didn't remember, then at least he couldn't harass Dimpna. They'd station a guard near the clinic in case his memory came back. For all he knew, they'd try and break out the dogs so they could skip town. "I'm going to need each of you to write down your movements last night, but why don't you talk Sergeant Neely through them right now? I want to know where you went, what you did, and what you heard."

"Heard?" Alan said. He tucked a long strand of hair behind his ears. When he pulled his hand back, it was shaking. "We didn't hear anything that sounded violent, if that's what you mean." He glanced at the others.

"Oh my God," Eve said. "Was that why Bette Davis was screaming for help?"

Cormac needed to keep his wits about him. They sounded panicked, but this could have been rehearsed. "Was it possible Brigid returned to the caravan last night?"

"It's possible," Eve said. "The three of us were out all night."

"Not all night," Billy chided.

"From about ten to two in the morning," Alan said.

If that was true, then Cormac had at least a partial time line.

"I want to see her," Billy said.

"You can't." Cormac said. "End of story." If just one person found out about the severed hand and a reporter got wind of it, their biggest advantage would vanish. This killer wanted that detail out. And Cormac wanted to thwart every single desire this killer possessed. Cormac's phone beeped. He glanced at the text. Dingle Daily News on the scene.

Shit. It was as if the reporter had been summoned by Cormac's thoughts. No one says a word. Tell him to wait for a press conference.

Cormac turned back to the threesome. "Were the three of you together the entire night?"

"Absolutely," Billy said.

Eve and Alan exchanged a look. "What?" Billy said.

"I won't lie for you," Eve said. "That's what."

Billy's face morphed into one of rage as he squared off with Eve. "I was with you all night."

Eve was shaking her head even before he finished. "We were together *most* of the night," she said, winding a streak of pink hair around her finger. "But we were all on our own after Brigid went to the vet."

Billy's mouth dropped open. "If Brigid was at the vet, then you can't be accusing me of hurting her."

"I wasn't accusing you of hurting her. I was just saying we weren't always together." Eve and Billy engaged in a staring contest.

Eve bit her lip. "Are you sure her death wasn't an accident?" She swallowed. "Is it possible she killed herself?"

"She would *never*," Billy said. "Don't say that!"

"She's tied to a tree," Alan said. "She couldn't have done that to herself."

Cormac came to attention. "How do you know whether or not she's tied to a tree?"

Alan crossed his arms, his tattoos flexing. "You showed us a photo. She's standing up against a tree. I can't see how a dead person would stay upright unless it involved rope of some kind."

Three heads swiveled to Cormac. "I cannot confirm or deny anything about my murder scene—"

Neely cleared her throat. "*My* murder scene, and we expect the three of you to keep your mouths shut as well. Unless you prefer we *don't* catch her killer."

"We won't say a word," Alan said.

"Tied to a tree?" Billy said. "Tied to a tree?"

"Do you keep rope inside that caravan?" Neely asked.

"There's rope in the back of my truck," Alan said. "Or there was."

"Your truck is part of the murder scene," Cormac said. "The guards will be searching it."

Alan shrugged. "Be my guest. But anyone could have reached in and taken the rope."

"Oh my God," Eve said. "Oh my God." She launched herself into Alan's arms. He was stiff for a moment and then hugged her.

"Poor Brigid," Alan said as he rubbed Eve's back. "Our poor, poor Brigid."

Billy groaned, then once again pounded his forehead with both fists. Cormac wanted to tell him to cut it out, but it was only himself he was hurting.

Eve pulled away from Alan and swallowed. "It was late when I saw the poet. Around half-ten. What time was she murdered?"

"We're going to wait for the state pathologist to tell us that," Cormac said.

"How did he do it?" Billy said, clenching his fists. "I'm going to kill him."

"Shut up, you eejit," Alan said. "You can't talk like that in front of a detective."

"He's an inspector," Neely said.

Billy glanced at Cormac. "I'm going to kill him, *Inspector*," he repeated, jabbing his index finger at Cormac. "You'd better get him first because I'm going to tear him apart with my bare hands."

CHAPTER 17

Billy Sheedy bounced around like he was preparing for the boxing ring.

"I'd listen to your friend here," Cormac said, gesturing to Alan Flynn. "If you're making a genuine threat, you can be locked up."

A gull screeched and circled above, causing everyone to look up.

Billy stopped bouncing, then began to pace. "I swear to God, you'd better get to him before I do."

"That's it." Cormac turned and motioned to Neely, who was conferring with a nearby guard. "Sergeant Neely?" Neely gave a nod, then headed over.

"What's the story?"

Cormac pointed to Billy. "This lad has threatened to kill Peter Nosh three times. I think he needs some alone time to think."

"You can't do that," Billy said.

"You've made three threats in a matter of minutes in front of multiple witnesses," Cormac said.

"It's a figure of speech!" Tears streamed down Billy's face. "Just let me see her. Just let me see her."

Neely took him by the arm and led him toward a squad car.

"I knew we shouldn't have questioned them here," Neely said. "From now on, I *am* calling the shots."

"Your movements last night," Cormac said to Alan while Neely was distracted. "Take me through them."

Alan seemed eager to comply. "After I dropped Brigid off at the veterinarian clinic, I went straight back to the caravan. The others were gone."

He glanced at Eve. She refused to make eye contact with him. "Once Alan and Brigid left, I was alone. Billy was out," Eve said. "I figured he was at the pub sucking down jars. I didn't know if Alan was coming straight back or not. I went down to the bay." She stared at him. "I was thinking of a certain someone, but I didn't have his phone number."

And she wasn't going to get it.

Cormac jotted down a note, raging that she was trying to be cute with him on the sly. Flirting when her friend was just murdered. Was she a psychopath? Could she have murdered Brigid alone? Did she have the strength to take off a hand? Would it have required strength? Or just the right knife? "Why were you seeking calm?"

"Because Brigid had just found a rabbit whose foot was almost hacked off." She glared at Cormac. "Any animal lover would be upset."

"But you went without your parrot?" Cormac asked.

Eve glared. "So?"

"I thought she was your emotional support animal." Cormac kept his tone neutral. It took two to argue, something he'd learned way too late in life.

"Water calms me," Eve said. "I didn't need Bette Davis for that."

Cormac turned back to Alan. "Continue."

Alan shook his head. "I don't remember where I left off."

"You dropped Brigid at the clinic."

"Right. I came back to the caravan."

"Back up a second," Cormac said. "Why didn't you stay with Brigid at the clinic—wait with her so you could drive her home?" Cormac liked asking the same question multiple times. It often produced new answers, especially if someone was lying.

"Because she said she was meeting Peter in Dingle."

"I see. Go on."

Alan sighed. "I came back to the caravan. No one else was here. I took a nap. Heard Billy and Eve arguing outside the caravan at half-nine," Alan said.

"Talking," Eve said. "We were just talking."

"Fine," Alan said. "At half-nine, I heard Billy and Eve talking very animatedly with raised voices and emphatic gestures." He gave her a look. Eve frowned and looked away.

"How can you be so sure what time it was?" Cormac asked.

Alan scoffed as if the answer was obvious. "Because I was surprised I fell asleep, so I checked the time on me phone."

"And then?"

"Searched the Internet for the highest elevation to watch the meteor showers. Smoked a joint. Then we went to the pub."

"Oh my God," Eve said. "He doesn't need every stinking detail."

"Actually I do," Cormac said. "And you better believe I'm going to find out every gory little detail, and if I find out any of you are lying to me, including lies of omission, you'll be joining your pal Billy."

"Brigid's parents," Eve said. "Do they know?"

"We're going to need you to give us their names and info," Cormac said. Although the Gardaí had family-liaison officers, Cormac wanted to notify the parents himself. Rather, he would accompany Neely if she agreed with the decision. It was the worst part of the job. The absolute worst. But he needed to learn more about Brigid, and home was often the place to do that. Had she issued any complaints about her three traveling companions?

"They live in Kerry, forty or so minutes away, Brigid said. Her mam's name is Emma. I think her da is Daniel. We don't have their number, like."

Emma and Daniel Sweeney, somewhere in Kerry. That would be enough to track them down. Cormac took a note. "I'd like to ask the three of you to give my guards permission to search your caravan." Their heads snapped to attention, and then they looked at each other. "Otherwise, the guards *are* going to get a warrant. If you give Neely permission to enter, that would speed things up."

"If you're not allowed to enter without our permission," Alan said, eyeing the caravan, "how can you keep us from entering?"

"We have twenty-four hours before a judge could even rule on the caravan," he said. "In the meantime, I've got a dead girl a few feet away who lived in that caravan and may have been abducted from that caravan or even killed in that caravan. That's how I can keep you from entering."

"Just let him search it," Eve said. "Unless you have something to hide."

"Me have something to hide?" Alan said. "That's rich, coming from you." Eve was needling Alan, and it was working. The veins in his slim neck bulged. Cormac couldn't imagine the four of them living on top of one another in that caravan. Had one of them snapped?

Cormac turned to her. "So what were you and Billy so animated about last night at half-nine."

Eve pursed her lips. "He was upset about Brigid. But not like 'I'm going to kill her' upset. If he was going to kill anyone, it would have been Peter."

"Very helpful," Alan said.

Eve was wearing long sleeves. Alan's arms were bare, but free of scratches. Then again, the killer could have worn a long-sleeved shirt and gloves. There must have been a struggle. "How did your friend Billy get those scratches on his arms?"

Alan shook his head. "I have no idea what you're on about."

"Yes, you do," Eve said. "I heard you ask him about them."

Alan swiveled on Eve. "Jesus," he said, "would you shut your ever-loving piehole?"

"I'm not covering for either of you," Eve said. "Do you hear me?"

"I don't need you covering for me," Alan said. "You're the one who hated Brigid."

"That's a lie." Eve felt Cormac's gaze on her. "Brigid was full of herself. Did she annoy me sometimes? Of course. She always had drama swirling around her, and she loved it."

"And by drama, she means admirers," Alan said.

Eve scrunched up her face. "Lunatics." She shook her head. "Brigid attracted men, yes. But most of them were rubbish."

"Last year, we had to leave a camping ground because of one fella," Alan said.

This got Cormac's attention. "Where was this?"

"Dublin," Eve and Alan said in unison.

Cormac removed his notebook. "Is there anything about that I should know?"

"Some fat, married yoke who was creeping on her," Alan said. "Brigid reported him to the guards."

"She also humiliated him in front of his wife," Eve said. "Caused a huge row between them."

Cormac took notes. "Was he arrested?"

"By the time the guards showed up, he was gone," Eve said.

"Did she ever see him again?" Cormac asked. Eve and Alan exchanged another look. Cormac took a step forward. "You need to tell me everything. Believe me. We want this animal behind bars yesterday."

"She was really losing it the past week or so," Eve said. "She was convinced someone was watching her. She thought maybe it was him."

"Do you have a name for this fella?"

"No," Eve said. "We never knew his name."

"We just called him fatso," Alan said.

"Or pervert," Eve added.

There was something about this story that sounded rehearsed. Were they making it up? "How long ago was her first run-in with him?"

"Nearly a year ago to the day," Alan said.

"And where was this?"

"A caravan park outside of Dublin," Alan said. "Hidden Valley."

Depending on how well it was run, they may have a record of the incident. "What exactly did she experience with him?"

"Caught him peeping in the windows numerous times. He'd follow her to the jax, to the lake, a little store they had at the park; he was right behind us every time we went for a hike, that kind of thing," Eve said. "Your typical stalker shite."

"Only he was really out of shape, so he never continued on the hikes," Alan said.

Cormac nodded. "Did he ever get physical with her?"

"Once," Eve said. "Brigid had screamed at him in front of everyone. As she turned to walk away, he grabbed her arm really hard. Left ugly bruises."

She had ugly bruises now too. Coincidence?

"Were there witnesses to the attack?" Cormac asked.

"Loads," Alan said. "But we couldn't tell you who they were because we didn't stick around."

"That's when we stopped parking at caravan parks," Eve said. "And yet even though detectives like you try to chuck us out, that car park is the safest place we could have been."

"Sadly, that's not true," Cormac said, his gaze shifting to the patch of trees where the body of poor Brigid remained.

"Oh," Eve said, staring at the ground. "Right."

"How old was this somewhat-stalker?"

"Old," Eve said. "Maybe forty-something."

Old. Cormac hoped his face didn't give him away. *Old.*

"I'd say late thirties," Alan corrected.

"You have no idea what his name was? His wife's name? Anything?"

"It's not like we were trying to get to know him," Alan said. "And anyway, that was a year ago."

"I hope she didn't suffer," Eve said.

"She's tied to a tree," Alan said. "She suffered."

"Was she stabbed?" Eve asked.

Cormac felt his spine tingle. "Why would you ask that?"

"Because of the psychopath who cut off the rabbit's foot," Eve said. "She said he had a knife," Eve said, holding her hands apart a foot. "The sharpest knife she'd ever seen."

"But neither of you actually saw this man?"

They shook their heads in unison. "I saw the rabbit, though," Alan said. "And the knife." He mentioned the rabbit and the knife, but not the jacket. Cormac made a mental note.

"There is something I just remembered," Eve said. "I just don't know if it's helpful to Brigid's case." She gestured to a guard in the distance. "I heard your one say something about binoculars. Are those important to the case?"

Cormac tried to keep his reaction calm, despite the adrenaline pumping through him. Which one of his guards was openly discussing the Henderson case? "They might be," he said, as if they probably weren't. "What about them?"

Eve smacked her lips. "Nothing sinister. But. When we met Vera Brannigan and were working out the particulars of using her car park, she let us into her mudroom, and hanging from the coat rack was a giant pair of binoculars."

CHAPTER 18

Patrick and Dimpna stood in front of the mastiffs snoring in their crates. "The bloods came back," Patrick said.

"Already?"

He nodded. "We called and put in a rush specifically for ketamine. The results are positive. They were definitely tranquilized, and in high doses."

"Tranquilized and then set loose," Dimpna said. Given the size of these dogs, and depending on the dose, the effects could have taken fifteen to twenty minutes to set in, enough time for them to terrorize a few car tires before the guards got to them. Had this been the work of the killer? Sedating the dogs so that he could sneak into the caravan? She had to call Cormac right away. "It's a miracle these pooches weren't struck by a car." She hadn't even known their names until Charlie Meade mentioned them (poor things, with such wretched names), and given that they'd been snoozing the entire time with her so far, she hadn't been able to gauge their personalities either.

"They'll sleep it off, but we'll need to inform the guards in case it's one of the three caravaners who drugged them."

"Three?" Patrick asked. "Aren't there four of them?" She kept forgetting he knew nothing of this morning's drama.

"Right," Dimpna said. "I'll handle speaking with the guards. I'm off to the farm call, but can you keep an eye on Bette Davis—"

"I'm coming with you, remember?"

"Right."

"Are you alright, Doctor Wilde?"

"It's been a morning," she admitted.

They headed outside. "Niamh asked if Bette Davis could stay with her in the reception area," Patrick said as they crossed back to the clinic.

"Perfect. Tell her it's a brilliant idea, and let her know to text me if the parrot gets unusually sleepy."

"Will do," Patrick said. Dimpna held up her mobile to indicate she was going to step out to make the calls. "Do you want me to take the farm call?" Patrick asked. "You must be exhausted."

"You've been up just as long," Dimpna said.

Patrick flashed a grin. "I'm a bit younger."

"I should dock your pay for that cheeky comment," Dimpna said. "Thank you, but I need a change of scenery as well. And the work will go faster with the two of us. But I am going to work on hiring another vet tech or vet for the near future."

"I've heard that before," Patrick said with a wink. He headed off to speak with Niamh as Dimpna stepped outside. She gazed on her mother's caravan in the field. She would speak with her after the murder had been announced and let her know she didn't think it was safe for her to sleep out there all alone in her caravan until the killer was caught. Even an enormous pair of guard dogs hadn't stopped the brute. Where did he or she get ketamine? Dimpna supposed it wasn't all that difficult these days, and it didn't even have to be stolen from a veterinarian or a medical facility. It was considered a street drug now, "special K." What a world. She rang Cormac and filled him in on the test results. She also relayed her fear that the killer might have followed Brigid to the clinic and that the missing butcher knife was possibly the murder weapon. Cormac said he was going to send a guard to watch the clinic, at least for today through this evening. "Thank you," Dimpna said. She knew the guards in every nearby station would be busy, but she was relieved he was sending someone to watch her clinic. She had her staff and the lovely creatures under her care to think about.

She hung up and hurried into the clinic. Niamh and Charlie were engrossed in a conversation.

"Sorry to interrupt," Dimpna said, noting the flirtatious look on Niamh's face. And if she wasn't mistaken, Charlie was looking equally interested. "Charlie, you're welcome to see the dogs, but I have to let you know that they're rather sleepy. I can't fill you in on all the details, but the detective inspector would be happy to."

"As long as they're not going back to those owners until everything is cleared up," Charlie said.

"They are staying here for now."

"Got it. I'll be off then." He treated Niamh to a smile. "I'll see you around."

"Not if I see you first," Niamh said loudly, with a laugh. She watched him walk out the door. Dimpna normally would have teased her, but she had more pressing issues on her mind. She gathered Niamh and Patrick in the back room. Given the brutal nature of the crime and her fears that the killer had been to the clinic to retrieve the knife, she had to give them some kind of warning. "I don't know what you've heard, but there's a situation unfolding in Camp."

"Does it have anything to do with the caravaners?" Niamh asked. "And a guard picked up that jacket—it looked like it had blood on it."

So much for keeping secrets. Dingle was a small town, and the gossip grapevine was swift. Dimpna nodded. "I don't want to keep things from you, but I'm under strict gag orders not to reveal any details. You'll hear about it soon enough."

"That doesn't sound good," Patrick said, his forehead creasing with concern.

"It's not," Dimpna said. "It's awful."

"I knew you weren't yourself this morning," Niamh said.

"Until I am able to fully explain what's going on, I would feel better if you kept the clinic doors locked."

"You mean during the day?" Patrick said.

Dimpna nodded. "Not only that, I've decided to leave my four-pack with you. E.T. and Pickles are pretty good guard dogs."

"You're both going on a farm call, right?" Niamh said.

"We are," Dimpna said. "Which is why I want you to keep the doors locked to everyone but our scheduled clients."

"Do you want me to stay?" Patrick asked.

Niamh shook her head. "I'm fine. Especially with E.T. and Pickles."

Patrick lowered his voice. "You can't tell us anything?"

Dimpna shook head. "There's going to be a media briefing this afternoon."

"That sounds serious," Niamh said.

Dimpna nodded. "You should only admit our regular clients into the clinic and, of course, our feathered and furry patients. If anyone you personally do not know tries to make an appointment, take down their name and number, but do not make any appointments with any persons you have not met, and do not accept anyone at the door who hasn't made an appointment."

"Wow," Niamh said slowly. "Okay."

"There is going to be a guard watching the clinic for today and this evening. If anything makes you feel funny, call 999 immediately."

Niamh's eyes were wide, and Dimpna could see a million questions swimming in them.

"Got it," Patrick said. "Should we be worried?"

Dimpna thought of the hand, the ropes, the knife, the rabbit's foot. "Better safe than sorry." Dimpna swallowed hard. Soon, everyone in the Dingle Peninsula was going to be a whole lot worried, and they'd be fools not to be.

CHAPTER 19

The media briefing was scheduled for noon in Camp. The state pathologist was due to arrive, but time was of the essence. They needed to be able to part Brigid's hair, photograph her face, and get a positive identification, preferably from her caravan-mates as opposed to her poor parents. Most likely the parents would eventually see the photos, and once they did, they'd never be able to erase the macabre image from their minds. Cormac would do everything he could to convince them not to look at the photos. Unless, of course, he thought they were guilty. The state pathologist granted their local coroner permission to part Brigid's hair and photograph her face, so at least that would happen today, and the pathologist herself was due to arrive by late afternoon. A family liaison officer had been assigned to Mr. and Mrs. Sweeney, and the officer was willing to notify them of Brigid's murder, but Cormac informed Neely that he wanted them to personally give them the news. Neely agreed. After, they'd make sure to connect the liaison officer with the family so they could be kept abreast of any developments. Superintendent McGraw was on his way to Tralee from Dublin headquarters, and an incident room was being set up at the station.

Cormac had heard from Dimpna that the dogs tested positive for ketamine. He had a pretty good hunch they'd find it in Brigid's system too. It's possible someone accompanied her into the patch of woods and they recreationally took ketamine near the tree where she was found. In this case, even someone as slight as Eve could have done the deed. Had Cormac had sex with a monster? He'd been trying to wipe every trace of their encounter out of his mind, but it only resulted in him replaying it. How he'd come out of the jax at the pub to find her waiting by the door. How she'd taken his hand and led him outside. How she'd backed him up against the exterior wall and reached for the snap in his denims. He'd allowed it, but he wouldn't say he'd encouraged it. The entire thing had taken him by surprise; up until then, they hadn't even been flirting. Had they? He'd asked her questions about their travels, and she'd talked at length about how they'd suddenly become popular with tourists, not in small part due to her talking African grey parrot. Cormac had been just about to leave when it all went down. When he replayed the memory, he skipped the jax and went straight to his car. It never happened.

But it had. Why had he let it? That was the question he had to face. Did it have anything to do with the fact that his mam had been pressuring him about Dimpna Wilde? Was he so afraid of commitment that he self-sabotaged, or had he simply gotten stuck at the intersection of biology and Guinness? And when had he reached the age where spontaneous sex was a bad thing? Maybe he'd always been that age.

He was dreading Superintendent McGraw's reaction. Absolutely dreading it. Would he be demoted? Shoved into some pencil-pushing job that he could not tolerate? Eve Murray hadn't been involved in any crime when it happened. Would that matter?

Armed with a few photos that did not reveal her missing hand, Cormac and Neely went straight to the Tralee Garda Station, where Brigid's three traveling companions had been taken and were waiting to give official statements. Neely conducted the interviews with Garda Lennon, while Cormac watched behind one-way glass. So far, Neely seemed to want Cormac involved. He prayed that, once McGraw arrived, they could keep it that way. The caravaners' reactions upon seeing Brigid's death photo varied.

Billy Sheedy had burst into tears—big, heaving sobs that overtook his body. Alan Flynn developed a twitch in his right eye and covered his mouth with his hands as he rocked back and forth, a motion that was soon joined by a crooning moan. Eve Murray seemed the most at ease. She displayed no outward signs of stress, apart from eagerly accepting any offer of food or drink. The three of them would give their official statements today in writing, and if the search of the caravan did not bring up any direct evidence of their involvement and they agreed not to leave town, they would be free to go. But if anything triggered the officials' suspicions further, they had twenty-four hours in which they could hold them.

Cormac thought it would be more useful to set them free. In that case, he would put plainclothes guards on them. He wanted to see where they went, what they did, and, if possible, who said what to whom. And if they did attempt to leave town, Cormac would be notified straightaway, and he assured them he would personally pursue them as if he or she were the killer. But for now, they were here in the hot seats, and extremely uncomfortable—just the way he wanted them.

Cormac had one more question for each of them—and he'd already stressed it to Neely: Did Brigid Sweeney wear any jewelry, especially bracelets or rings? He refrained some saying left or right hand. If she wore a big diamond on her left hand, perhaps this had been some kind of botched robbery. Eve was not wearing any jewelry, but Alan wore both a silver ring and a necklace. Billy wore a gold cross. All three said that during this trip they had not seen Brigid wearing any rings or bracelets.

"Did she have any tattoos?" What if her hand was severed because of a tattoo?

"No," Billy said. "I teased her about it—she hated needles."

If they were telling the truth, then her hand wasn't severed for her jewelry or over a tattoo. He'd partly guessed that. Besides, he'd never heard of a tattoo so troubling that someone else felt the need to literally cut it off. So why did the killer do that to her hand? Was it a trophy? One question everyone answered straightaway—yes, Brigid was left-handed. Did the killer know this? Why not both hands? Did he simply think it was an efficient way to kill her? And why the call-back to Bella and the wych elm? Was it a distraction or someone obsessed with the cold case? A copycat?

The rabbit's foot . . . he'd nearly forgotten about that bit. The rabbit's foot had something to do with why he severed her hand—a hand for a rabbit's foot? Was there some kind of rabbit vigilante out there? Then again, hadn't Brigid tried to *save* the rabbit? Was there really a madman out there mutilating live rabbits? And if so, was he so enraged at Brigid catching him in the act that his revenge was to cut off her hand and leave her to bleed to death? Chris Henderson had interfered, and he was struck down in broad daylight. They were looking for a madman. But were they looking for a serial killer?

Cormac was dying to ask the caravaners to tell him everything they knew about Brigid's story and rabbits' feet, but he had to be careful. Along with her severed hand, the rabbit's foot tied to her wrist was a detail only the killer knew, and for now, he had to keep it under wraps. If she was wearing a rabbit's foot around her wrist before she died, one of them would have mentioned it. When Neely sat them down for a second interview, she'd be able to ask them about the man Brigid had supposedly seen cutting off a rabbit's foot, without giving it away yet that one was now tied to her wrist, but first Cormac wanted to see what information they would reveal unprompted.

Sometimes what a suspect left out was just as revealing as what they "remembered."

Once Neely held the press conference, no doubt the revelation of Brigid's murder was going to cause widespread panic. Not that they planned on giving the public all the gory details, but they did need to give folks enough information to keep them vigilant. Everyone needed to know this killer was extremely violent. Cold-blooded. They needed to lock their doors and not let anyone go out alone and—he hated to say it—especially women. This killer might have a type. Then again, if he was Henderson's killer, anyone who got in the way of this killer stalking his next victim—male, female, old, young—anyone and everyone was in danger. They needed tips, they needed eyes and ears everywhere, and they needed everyone to lock their doors at night and not go out alone. Not let their children go out alone, not until this brazen and evil soul was caught. But before they could hold a press conference, they had to break the hearts of Emma and Daniel Sweeney.

They were in Cormac's red Toyota now on the way to see them. It was a forty-minute drive. As Dingle fell away, the roads took on more curves, and the hills rose sharply. The Sweeneys were out in a very rural area, as close to being off the grid as you could get without actually being off the grid. And although the scenery was second to none—curved roads outlined by limestone walls, rising hills patched in shades of green and brown, glimpses of water when the car reached a high enough peak—if you were a young person this far away from creature comforts, Cormac could see how the desire to travel could take hold. How Brigid would have yearned to hang out with people her own age, see a bit of the country. Travel and dance and live and breathe. She should have been able to do that. He didn't realize he was gripping the steering wheel until he felt Neely's intense gaze on him.

"I don't mind driving, if you're not up for it."

"Sorry," he said. "I'm fine."

Neely sighed. "I don't think either of us are fine."

"Nor should we be."

"Maybe we don't have to tell McGraw *why* you're taking a back seat in the investigation. He'll assume it's because of your mam."

"I can't ask you to do that."

"Do what? If you get caught, I can play dumb. I'm good at that."

"Let's just take it one step at a time."

Neely had a file on Brigid Sweeney in front of her. "She was a competitive Irish dancer when she was a young one. Cute as a button. Won first place in numerous competitions."

A multitude of losses. Murderers didn't just take a person, they took all their hopes and dreams and shining possibilities. Getting him or her off the streets so that they could never hurt another human being again was the worthiest of goals. But there was never true justice. The form of true justice that Cormac desired was the impossible kind. The kind that found a way to reverse the evil that had been done. The kind of justice that would allow Brigid Sweeney to live out the rest of her life as she should have done. *Wishful thinking.* Illogical, but he couldn't stop replaying variations of a rescue fantasy.

His mam would have understood. His throat closed at the thought of her, and he'd taken six calls from family members—rushing through all of them, hearing the confusion and disgust in their voices that he was working a case. He had to keep reminding himself that they might not approve, but his mam would have insisted he take this case. He was going to go to the funeral home early this evening; then he would have supper with some of his relatives and do a bit of begging for forgiveness. He wanted to hold the funeral service as soon as possible, and given that many had driven hours to get here, he assumed so did they. He'd call a local caterer and figure out a place everyone could gather afterward. He was also going to have to break it to them that his mam was adamant in her wishes. She wanted to be cremated and her ashes spread on the cliffs near the ocean, where all the beautiful wildflowers thrived. *I was never much of a gardener in me life, Mac. I'll be one in me death. You can wave to me whenever they bloom.* Had she not requested that, he'd most likely be going to Killarney for a burial, and with this case, there simply was no time. But the next day or so, he'd be forced to take at least four hours for her service and gathering with relatives, so the more he accomplished today, the better.

"Let's hope those three young souls are sweating it out in the station right now, and that we find hard evidence of something in the caravan," he said.

Neely's phone rang. "Sergeant Neely," she said. "Yes . . . Is that right? . . . Right . . ." Neely let out a sigh. "Have a guard keep an eye on him, but don't approach. We'll see if we can figure out a way to communicate with him."

She hung up. "We've tracked down the man I was telling you about. George O'Malley."

"Your one with the donkey who sells rabbits' feet?"

"That's the one. Apparently several witnesses saw him interact with our caravaners on multiple occasions."

Cormac nodded. "We'll pay him a visit right after the briefing."

"I thought you were going to the funeral home after the briefing."

"I'm due there this evening," he said. "We should have time after the briefing if we limit the questions."

"I know you're anxious to cover a lot of ground quickly, but you have to spend time with your family."

She was right. This was the worst possible time. Couldn't everyone just understand that? "We should have time," he repeated. "Any word on Robert and Vera Brannigan?"

"Still in the wind."

"They could be our killers."

"Maybe there's more going on in that cottage than an Airbnb," Neely said. "But if Vera's involved in this, something had to trigger it. She's never been in trouble in her life."

"What about Robert?"

Neely gazed out the window. "According to his wife, he's in Dublin, and Vera is not with him."

"Sometimes wives are the last to know," Cormac said.

"And sometimes wives lie," Neely replied. Cormac had this panicked feeling that they were losing valuable time; he wanted to be out there right now, knocking on doors, shaking down trees. "Don't worry," Neely said. "We're off and running."

She was right. That didn't stop Cormac from wanting to sprint.

CHAPTER 20

The Sweeneys lived in a small stone cottage fronted by a relatively flat and neglected garden and backed up by a large hill. Sheep bleated from the top of the hill as they approached, and Neely accidentally kicked an old tin can, sending it rattling over stones in the yard. It took twenty minutes of knocking to bring Emma Sweeney to the door, and when she finally answered, she only opened it a crack, peering out at them with one leery blue eye.

"Mrs. Sweeney?" Neely said, taking the lead. "I'm Detective Sergeant Neely, and this is Detective Inspector O'Brien." They flashed their badges.

"What brings you here, Detectives?" she asked. The door remained cracked.

"May we speak with you inside?" Neely asked. "And your husband. Is he home?"

"He's not awake," Emma said. "He works nights."

"Mrs. Sweeney, I'm afraid we're here on a very somber and urgent matter, and if at all possible, you're going to want to wake him," Neely said.

The door shut, and they heard the sound of the chain being disengaged before it swung open again. Emma Sweeney stood before them wrapped in a blanket. She was an older version of

Brigid, with long dark hair and pale blue eyes. Cormac found himself staring at her face and then her two good hands. He hated knowing the pain the news would soon inflict. "I'm not waking him," she said, then stepped back to let them in. "Cup of tea?"

Cormac wanted a cup of tea—hell, he wanted a shot of whiskey, then a cup of tea, then another shot of whiskey. "No, thank you," he said, and Neely shook her head. Emma gestured to a sagging couch. Above the wood stove were shelves. Pictures of Brigid took up every inch, most of them from Irish dancing competitions throughout the years. There were fewer and fewer pictures of Brigid as she got older. Had they had a falling out? On one end of the couch, some kind of creature was curled into an orange ball. "That's Baby," she said. "I wouldn't wake him either." Emma sat in a rocking chair and once more gestured to the sofa. Cormac made a beeline to the end opposite of the cat, his nose already twitching. Neely perched close to him.

"I'm afraid we're here about your daughter, Brigid," Cormac said. Their home was lived in, but he wouldn't go so far as to say cluttered. Balls of colored yarn lay in a basket by Emma's chair, a china cabinet showed off a collection of Waterford crystal, and a shelf in the back housed a collection of books and records. The television in the corner was turned on, but the sound was turned off. Because the husband was sleeping? Above the telly hung a plain wooden cross. Cormac found himself staring at it.

Emma thrust herself up from the chair. "What has she done now? Arrested, is she?"

Interesting. Cormac was going to have to follow up on that, but not until the news had been delivered and she'd had time to process it.

"No, no," Neely said. "Please. You're going to want to sit down."

Emma eyed the pair of them, then settled back into her chair. Cormac cleared his throat and started them off. "Were you aware that your daughter was in the town of Camp, traveling with three friends in a caravan?"

Emma shrugged. "I didn't know where they were at the moment."

"When is the last time she . . ." Cormac stopped. "I'm sorry. We'll get to that. Mrs. Sweeney, it is with the deepest sorrow that I tell you this. This morning we found a young woman deceased, and her three traveling companions have positively identified her as Brigid Sweeney."

Emma, who had been sitting still, began to rock. "What do you mean?" she said.

Neely and Cormac exchanged a look. Neely nodded that she would try. "We found your daughter's body this morning in the village of Camp. There are details we cannot share yet, but I'm so sorry to tell you that it appears she was murdered, and we have opened an official inquiry." Emma continued to rock. "You will be assigned a family liaison officer who will keep you informed of our investigation and help answer any questions, but in the meantime, both myself and Detective Inspector O'Brien wanted to personally deliver the news."

"We will not stop until we find the person responsible for your daughter's death," Cormac added.

"It's not her." Emma's rocking increased. Cormac had an urge to tell her to stop. He wanted her to take off the blanket. Was she hiding something? Had she driven out to Camp in the middle of the night and murdered her daughter? He was having a hard time picturing it, but everything and anything was possible. And what of this husband?

"We did bring photographs of your daughter," Neely said. "But you're under no obligation to look at them. They're quite disturbing, and we do have her identification confirmed by the three mates she was traveling with."

Emma lifted her eyes to them briefly, then slowly shook her head. "What if?" She rocked. "What if I wanted to see her in person?"

Neely looked to Cormac, and he nodded. "Once the OSP completes their examination, they'll let us know the body can be collected."

"OSP?"

"I'm sorry. Office of State Pathology."

"Oh." She sounded small, as if that blanket had swallowed most of her.

"We can have her transported to a funeral parlor in Dingle, or Tralee, or if you're bringing her home to bury, I'm sure your local funeral parlor can make arrangements to pick her up."

Emma closed her eyes briefly. "I'll talk to me husband."

"Do you think you should wake him?" Neely asked. Emma simply shook her head no.

"We're waiting on the state pathologist to arrive on scene," Cormac continued. "He or she will conduct a thorough examination to determine the exact cause of her death, and then the postmortem will be done, so I'm afraid it's going to be a while before we can share details and release her body for a burial."

Emma stood, throwing off the blanket, then clasped her hands below her chin. She wore a plain housedress, and Cormac wondered if she had been embarrassed to be seen in it. She squeezed her eyes shut tight and began shaking her head. "No, no, no, no."

"We wanted you to hear it from us before a noon media briefing," Cormac said. He glanced at the telly, now showing an ad for tooth whitener. Brigid's blue lips flashed before his eyes. "Once the news is out, I'm afraid there's a chance it's going to take over headlines all over Ireland." A gorgeous young woman on her summer holiday, tied to a tree the night of a meteor shower. They wouldn't even need the severed hand to cause a stir. But once they did get wind of it, and Cormac knew that was only a matter of time, the meteor storm would be replaced by a media storm. The village of Camp—and Dingle, for that matter—had no idea what they were in for.

"We don't really watch telly," Emma said. Cormac glanced at the telly, and despite the fact that it was on, he simply nodded as she pointed to a dusty record player in a dark corner of the room. "Sometimes we play our music." She began humming to herself, as she rocked back and forth.

"We can give you and your husband a ride to Camp and put you up in an inn at our expense," Cormac said.

"We don't leave home anymore," Emma said.

"Do you use mobile phones or a landline?" Cormac said. "When is the last time you heard from your daughter?"

"Me husband has the phone. She calls us every Wednesday morning. So that's the last time we heard from her."

"Can you tell me about that conversation?" Cormac asked. He was having a challenge getting a bead on Mrs. Sweeney, but he did know that shock was a powerful balm, and right now, it was wrapped around her tighter than any blanket. She had yet to ask what they did know about how her daughter was killed, and often that was a red flag for Cormac, but in this case, he believed it was shock rendering her mute. If they could prove they were home, they lived too far from the crime scene to be persons of interest. Then again, without close neighbors, it would be difficult to prove they were home.

"She said they were leaving soon," Emma said. "Maybe it's not her. Maybe they left."

"The other members of the caravan are still there," Neely said. "They positively identified our victim as your daughter. And they have confirmed that Brigid never returned to the caravan the night after the meteor shower." At least while they were there. Cormac hadn't dismissed the possibility that she was abducted from the caravan. That parrot had heard something troubling.

"How could one girl have such bad luck?" Emma said. "I told her. I told her not to push it." She sunk back into the sofa. She glanced toward a hallway that led to the back of the cottage. "I can't tell him. It's going to kill him."

"Let us tell him," Neely said. "Do you want to see if you can wake him?" Emma shook her head.

Cormac edged forward. "What did you mean when you said, 'How can one girl have such bad luck'?"

Emma wrung her hands together. "Last year when they traveled in their little caravan, Brigid ran into trouble."

"What kind of trouble?" Cormac asked, taking out his notebook. Was this about her somewhat-stalker?

"Some man was bothering her," Emma said. "We were so proud to have such a beautiful child. Until we realized that beauty like hers was a curse."

"You asked if we had arrested Brigid," Cormac said gently. "Has she been arrested before?" Emma stilled. "I'm not trying to speak ill of her, but this may be important."

Emma sighed. "That group is trouble. Those lads and that one with the colored streaks in her hair."

Cormac could feel Neely's gaze on him—the mistake that kept on taking . . . "Billy, Alan, and Eve?" he asked.

Emma nodded. "They get in a bit of trouble everywhere they go. Mostly I blame the lads. If they nick things, it's their fault."

Neely and Cormac exchanged a look. This was news. "They've been arrested for petty theft?" Cormac asked.

"They've been accused of it, run off because of it, but no, they've never been arrested. Yet. We told her if she kept hanging out with them and she got arrested, not to call us. We'd already warned her."

"And the trouble she got in with some man?" Cormac asked.

"What about it?" Emma sounded defensive. "Blame the woman, is that it?"

"That's not it at all," Neely said. "We're trying to figure out who might have hurt your daughter, and more often than not, a person is harmed by someone they know."

"Then look no further than the three she was with," Emma said. "I told you, they're trouble."

"We are definitely questioning them, and we will turn over every stone in their background," Cormac said. "But I still would like to hear more about this man who was bothering her last year." He flipped through his notes. "A caravan park outside of Dublin—Hidden Valley."

Emma flicked a glance at his notebook. "He was a married man camping with his wife and children. He started following Brigid around, trying to get her to engage with him. The wife didn't like it."

"Did she happen to give you a name?" Cormac asked.

Another shake of the head. "Brigid could be very secretive. But she seemed almost gleeful that she got your one in trouble with his missus." She suddenly stopped rocking and looked up at Cormac with familiar blue eyes. "What happened to my baby?"

"I think you need a cup of tea," Neely said to Emma. "Would it be alright if I fixed you a cup? You can keep chatting with the inspector."

Emma nodded and pointed to the kitchen. "Kettle is next to the cooker, and you'll find cups and biscuits in the cupboards above the sink."

"Thank you," Neely said.

Cormac gave it a beat while Neely headed for the kitchen. "This man," he said. "Did you get any kind of description?"

Emma rubbed her forehead as if trying to conjure up an image of the man. "She said he was fat and old."

Cormac jotted that down, wondering how old "old" was to Brigid Sweeney. "And when you say he attacked her, can you tell me exactly what happened?"

"He came up from behind and put a knife at her throat."

Cormac fumbled with his notes and nearly dropped them. "A knife?" Her travel companions had not mentioned a knife.

Emma's hand flew to her own throat for a moment. "He told her she was nothing but a tease. Only the dogs—they must have smelled him, for, thank God, they came running. Brigid said from then on, she was going to love those dogs like they were her babies. Even though they really belong to Billy." Emma craned her head back and let out a wail. Cormac, who hadn't been expecting it, jumped. Soon after, a thump was heard from the back of the cottage, followed by a man cursing. Emma continued to wail. Cormac's heart filled with the sound of it, the raw grief of a mother. In the kitchen, teacups rattled. Neely hurried out without a single cup and stood awkwardly, her hands covering her mouth. Heavy boots clomped down the hall, and a large figure emerged. It was only as he reached the sitting room, muttering angrily, that he saw Cormac and Neely. He stopped and rocked back on his heels, nearly toppling backward.

"Daniel," Emma wailed. "It's Brigid. It's our Brigid."

"What's our Brigid?" His tone was that of a frightened man.

"I'm Detective Inspector O'Brien, and this is Detective Sergeant Neely," Cormac said, coming to his feet. "I'm afraid we've come with distressing news."

"What have they done to her?" Daniel said, hurrying toward his wife. "What have those lads done to our Brigid?"

CHAPTER 21

Sergeant Neely faced the media from an outdoor podium set up in the parking lot of the Village Pub, down a ways from the murder scene. The rain had stopped for now, but clouds had gathered above, and the bay was obscured by a thick mist. Appropriate weather for the grim news they were here to deliver. In addition to reporters and their flashing cameras, there was quite a large crowd gathered, and the street was lined with cars that had pulled over to see what the drama was all about. Was the killer in the crowd right now? Gloating? Anticipating? Pale Irish faces stared back at Cormac as he scanned the group. One in the crowd caught his attention. He'd been one of the hikers gathered across from the caravan the morning they'd found the body. And as Cormac remembered, he'd been the most vocal in trying to get information from the guards. He was short but athletic-looking, with brown hair and a short brown beard. Cormac held up his phone, as if trying to suss out whether or not he had a signal, and snapped the man's photo. His head pivoted to Cormac just as he brought the phone down, and Cormac was faced with several seconds of awkward eye contact. He was relieved when Neely stepped up to the microphone.

"It is with great shock and sadness that I stand before you

today," Neely said. "This morning at half-seven, the body of a woman was discovered in the patch of woods down the road. Although we cannot release the details of the crime scene to the public at this time, and we will need to wait for the official findings of the state pathologist, we are treating her death as a homicide." Voices rippled through the crowd. "Her family has been notified and assigned a family liaison officer, and we have opened a murder inquiry."

Hands thrust in the air as reporters shouted questions:

"What can you tell us about how she died?"

"Do you have any suspects?"

"Do you have an identification on the victim?"

Neely held up her hands as if to stop the onslaught of questions. "We do have a positive identification; the victim's name is Brigid Sweeney. She is not a local of Camp or Dingle, although she is from County Kerry. She was traveling with three others in a caravan, and it is the remaining three that have positively identified her remains." She cleared her throat. "We have set up a tip line, and we are asking the public for their help. If you saw or heard anything suspicious last night during the meteor showers, or if you believe you saw or spoke with Brigid Sweeney—and there is a photo of her on our website—please call either Tralee or Dingle garda station. We'll give the numbers at the end of the briefing."

"How was she killed?"

Neely was prepared for these questions, but Cormac could see that she was struggling. "We are very early in this investigation, and as I stated, we will not be giving out any information until after the state pathologist has conducted his or her examination. The main points we are emphasizing in this briefing are twofold: One, the section of the Dingle Way hiking trail from Camp to Annascaul will be closed for a few days. However, if you were in the area of Camp last night and noticed or saw anything unusual, or heard or witnessed any kind of struggle, we ask that you call either the Tralee Garda Station or the Dingle Garda Station. We also urge the public not to roam outdoors alone. What we can tell you about this murder is that it was the act of a very violent and deranged individual." Cormac took a moment to scan the crowd, once again wondering if the killer was among them. "We urge the public to be aware of their surroundings, and we encourage you to go out in pairs. If you have any suspicions, please be careful who you share them with. It's best to take them directly to the guards."

She paused as voices in the crowd began to speak at once. "Is the killer one of the other caravaners?" a male shouted. "The dogs are gone, and there's crime-scene tape around the caravan."

"We do not have anything to share on that front," Neely said. "Suffice it to say we are taking every measure possible to find this killer and bring him or her to justice."

"What time did the murder occur?" a female reporter asked.

"We are waiting for an official finding to narrow down our time line, but what we can say at this juncture is that the incident took place between eight p.m. and seven a.m."

"During the meteor shower?" the first reporter called out.

"Correct," Neely said.

"Do you have any suspects at all?" the female asked.

"All I can tell you at this point is that we will leave no stone unturned," Neely said. "Our tip lines are open, and once again, we urge everyone to remain vigilant. If you see or hear anything, no matter how inconsequential you think it is, we want to hear from you. In the meantime, we once again urge you to go out in pairs and keep a special eye on young ones; do not let them wander around alone. I know this is a safe and close community. Having a young life taken in an act of violence is not something any of us ever expected when we woke up this morning. We will return to the peaceful place we all know and love. But until then, watch your backs, and most importantly, watch each others." Neely waited for the murmurs and comments to die down.

A reporter raised his hand and stared at Cormac until he nodded. "What about the hit-and-run that killed Chris Henderson?"

"That is still an open investigation," Cormac said. "We also encourage anyone with any information related to Mr. Henderson and the hit-and-run to call the guards. If you or anyone you know owns a black Audi, please have them contact the guards so we can eliminate them as a suspect."

"Is it true you're looking for Robert Brannigan, the co-owner of the Airbnb where the caravan is parked?" This came from the hiker Cormac had just photographed. He wasn't a reporter. Who the hell did this man think he was? Cormac's radar pinged. There was also new information in that question. Co-owner? "We are interested in speaking with both Vera Brannigan and her brother-in-law, Robert," Cormac said. "In fact, we want to hear from anyone who was in this vicinity in the last few days. Sergeant Neely will make sure you all have the number for the tip line."

"Is it true that Robert Brannigan drives a black Audi and you still haven't located the one involved in the hit-and-run?" That man again.

"What is your name, sir?" Cormac asked. "Are you with the media?"

"Me?" He shook his head. "I'm a hiker." He had an Irish accent, so he wasn't a tourist.

"Your name, sir?" Cormac asked again.

"Brendan," he said, sticking his chin up. "Brendan Keyes."

Given that he could hardly whip out his notebook and write it down, Cormac committed the name to memory.

"Do you have the number plate for the Audi involved in the hit-and-run?" a reporter interjected.

"I'm afraid we do not."

"Is there any reason to believe that the murders are linked?" the reporter continued. A sharp reporter. Cormac's worst nightmare. "There is currently no evidence to suggest they are linked," Cormac said.

"Have you ruled out the possibility?" the reporter pressed.

"We have not ruled anything out, but the murder scenes are very different." There was an obvious connection—Henderson reporting a creeper staring at Brigid through binoculars—but Cormac wanted to keep that under wraps.

"Was Brigid Sweeney violated sexually?" another reporter called out.

"We will all have to wait for the state pathologist for the answers we seek," Cormac said. He understood the reporters were just doing their jobs, but this was excruciating.

Neely stepped in. "That concludes the media briefing. We will schedule a new one as soon as we have any new information to relay. Garda Collins here will read out the digits for the tip line. You can also find it on our website. And until we hold a second briefing, we will not be taking questions." Regardless, questions were shouted as Neely left the podium. She and Cormac crossed the street to the caravan, now blocked off with crime-scene tape. Garda Lennon soon joined them. Cormac was itching to go inside, but as promised, he hung back as Neely and Lennon suited up. Cormac held his breath as they entered the caravan, and the door slammed shut behind them.

There were two sets of twin-sized bunk beds in the rear of the caravan, so tiny Neely knew Cormac would have felt claustrophobic just looking at them. Only one of the four bunks was neatly made, the top left, and Neely made a note of it. Given that the lads claim that Brigid had not slept here last night, perhaps that was her bed, or perhaps one of the four was the type who routinely made his or her bed. Beyond the bed was a cramped restroom, and in the main "cabin" was a built-in dining table with bench seating and a built-in sofa. Every surface was littered with something—books, papers, plates and cups, dog toys. How in the world did two large dogs, a parrot, and four people reside in here? Neely had often complained to her husband that they needed to expand their house to accommodate his Lionel train collection—more often than not, he was setting up a new track on their dining room table—but standing here, she realized they had a mansion, and she vowed never to complain about his train sets again. He could run them through the whole house if he wanted, although she'd let him figure that out on his own.

"I can easily see one of them snapping," Garda Lennon said, as if reading her mind. "What exactly should we be looking for?" he added.

"Anything to do with Brigid—her handbag or her mobile phone would be a big score, or any signs of violence—any mention of Peter Nosh, or Robert or Vera Brannigan, or the Hidden Valley Caravan Park, or George O'Malley—anything to do with rabbits' feet—diary, poetry, love notes, stalkers—we can start there."

Garda Lennon's face reflected the gravity of their task. "How about I take the front and you take the back?"

"You sure?" Neely asked. "You don't want to root around the jax and the sweaty bedsheets?"

"No, God, no. That's not why I—Let's switch." Lennon turned himself sideways as if to squeeze past Neely.

"I'm only messing," Neely said as she headed for the back of the caravan. "It doesn't look as if any tussles took place in here."

"Could the three of them have killed her together and cleaned up?" Lennon asked.

"Anything is possible," Neely said. "And if that is the case, we'll make sure at least one of them cracks."

They quickly found and bagged three mobile phones. All of

them were password-protected, and getting into them would take time. Neely assumed the killer had taken Brigid's, but they would have to wait and see. Lennon stood by the front door, examining the lock. "There's no sign of forced entry."

Neely nodded. "Either Brigid knew her attacker and let him in, or they were careless about locking the door."

"Or he was already inside," Lennon pointed out. "Waiting."

The thought gave Neely the shivers. It was one of her worst nightmares, the thought of waking up in the middle of the night and finding a stranger hovering over her in the darkness. Neely headed for the jax, figuring she might as well get the most unpleasant task over with first, when she noticed something on the top left bunk, the only one that was made. Not only had the bed been made, it was tight and neat, the plain gray cover smooth, the pillows propped up. But that's not what had caught her attention. A piece of paper was sticking out from underneath the pillow. Gloves on, Neely pulled on it. She found herself staring at a message scrawled in red ink. The letters were blunt and disproportional, as if the scribbler had used his or her nondominant hand:

YOU MADE YOUR BED

What in the world? "Lennon," she said, wishing Cormac were here.

Lennon made his way over. Neely held up the note.

He frowned, then edged in closer. His lips moved as he silently read. "Where was that?"

"Under the pillow," she said. "As if waiting for the tooth fairy."

" 'You made your bed.' " She glanced at the bed. "It's technically correct. One of these beds is not like the other." She snapped a photo of the beds and the note and sent it to Cormac. Had she done something to someone? Had her death been some kind of warped revenge?

Interesting . . . Cormac texted back immediately. **What else?
Still looking** . . .

Neely returned to the front of the caravan, where she'd stashed evidence bags, then dropped the note into one. She then returned to the beds and stared at them. "We need to ask the three about this bed."

"What are you thinking?" Lennon asked as he scribbled down a note.

A thought struck Neely. "What if the killer made the bed?" she said.

Lennon cocked his head. "Just so he could leave that note?"

"Yes," Neely said. "Just so he or *she* could leave the note."

"She?" Lennon said. "Do you really think the killer could be a woman?"

"We have to leave room for that possibility," Neely said. "It's very dangerous to make assumptions when you're conducting a murder inquiry."

"That is sage advice," Lennon said. "Thank you."

Neely nodded. "Should be easy to find out whether or not Brigid routinely made the bed."

Lennon took the evidence bag with the note from Neely and held it up to the window to catch the light. "You think we can get fingerprints off it?"

"We should be so lucky," she said. "Right, so. Let's keep looking."

Neely caught sight of a book underneath the built-in dining table. She saw no other books in the caravan. Wishing her knees weren't so creaky, she knelt to have a closer look. It was a large hardback, like a coffee-table book. It was open to a page. Staring back at her was a photograph of a stone obelisk. Over the face of the obelisk was a familiar message written in white chalk:

WHO PUT BELLA IN THE WITCH ELM?

"Oh my God." She immediately called Cormac via video. Lennon hustled over.

"Talk to me," Cormac said, hunching over the screen.

"Look what I found underneath this dining table and open to this exact page." It took several tries of aiming the camera until he could see what she was on about. Outside, the wind had picked up, rattling the windows and making the caravan rock.

"My God," he said. "The killer was there. He was in there."

"Could be all three of them," Neely said.

"Why would they just leave it out in the open then?" Lennon asked.

Cormac arched an eyebrow. "Maybe that's what they want us to think," he said. "That they couldn't be that stupid."

"Talk to ya in a bit," Neely said and disconnected the call.

Lennon knelt with ease next to the book and placed an evidence marker near it. "I've been reading up on this murder ever since the chalk drawings," he said.

"Give me the story," Neely encouraged. "Tell it to me like I know nothing about it all."

Lennon swallowed and nodded. "Hagley Woods. Near Birmingham, England. In 1944, four young lads were illegally poaching for bird eggs on the land when they went peeking into a hollow in a wych elm to see if there was a nest inside. Instead, they found a skull peering back at them. Scared the bejesus out of them, and they swore a pact not to tell a soul. Thought they'd be in trouble for trespassing and poaching. But one lad broke down and told his parents. The police arrived and recovered not only the skull, but a female skeleton. Given that she was stuffed in the hollow of the wych elm, they surmised she'd been placed there just after death, or even while still alive. Otherwise, she'd have been too stiff to fit inside. The murder probe soon became a sensation. They never did figure out who she was, or who killed her. Rumors ran wild. Given that there was a war on, some say she was a German spy, killed for being a traitor. Others thought she was a prostitute, and some say, no, she was an innocent—a local. To this day, she has not been identified, and her case is still unsolved." Lennon pointed to the obelisk with the message written on it. "Soon after she was found, graffiti like this began popping up all over town. Chalk writing on stone, mostly, with some version of 'Who Put Bella in the Witch Elm?' Sometimes it was spelled correctly, *W-y-c-h*, sometimes it was like you see here—*Witch.*"

"Murdered woman, tree," Cormac said. "Are those the only similarities?

"Hmm," Neely said. "Four lads? Four caravaners?"

"Interesting," Neely said. "But probably coincidental."

Lennon gasped. "There *is* another similarity." His baby face shone with anticipation.

"Well?" Neely urged when he didn't spit it out.

"Her hand," Lennon said. "Bella, as they called the skeleton, was missing her left hand."

CHAPTER 22

"Sheep," Patrick Kelly said, crinkling his nose, as they headed up the drive to the barn. "Whenever I work with sheep, I end up on me knees." He grimaced. "It's a long way down."

Dimpna laughed. "Don't be telling me about your too-tall problems, lad," she said. Patrick joined his laughter with hers, a sound that helped lift her dark mood. "Besides, you've got me here today."

They were halfway to the barn, weighed down by their medical bags, when the skies opened up. Their wellies squelched as the ground beneath them turned to muck. John Noble was waiting for them at the opening of his barn and gave a friendly wave as they approached. "Thanks be to God the vits are here," he said with a grin.

"Vits," Patrick said softly, and Dimpna gave him a little shove until he laughed.

"At your service," Dimpna said with a salute.

"I've got all sorts of problems with me sheep, Doc," John said. "Have a look for yourself." He pointed just inside the barn, where several sheep were lying about like lads after a drinking binge. Dimpna set her veterinarian case down, popped it open, and removed two sets of boiler suits and gloves. "Bucket of hot water and soap and a clear bucket of water are over in the corner, just as you requested," John said.

"Appreciate it," Dimpna said.

"I gave you a head start," John said, gesturing to the inert pile of wool before hiking up his overalls and scratching his head.

Dimpna raised an eyebrow. "Oh?"

He nodded. "I did everything I could for their hooves, used some herbs, some flowers, some olive oil, some Vaseline, some Windex." He pointed to the rail of a stall, where items were lined up like evidence in a trial. Herbs, flowers, olive oil, Vaseline, and Windex. Patrick faked a cough to cover his laugh.

Dimpna held up her hand. "Got it." She and Patrick exchanged a look. People were always trying every homemade cure they could think of to avoid calling a vet. Often by the time they arrived, it was too late. It was even worse with all the "advice" floating around online. Luckily, Dimpna didn't have to worry about John researching anything online; he was a throwback—had never owned a computer and would stay that way until his dying day. There was something Dimpna deeply admired about that.

"Do you need me to stay?" John said. "I'm behind in me morning chores."

"I don't think this should take long, if you have a minute to spare, so," Dimpna said. The last time Noble had pulled that trick, it had taken five months to get paid.

Noble fidgeted but remained in the barn, watching them as they examined the sheep. "And while you're here, Doc, I've got a cow with pink eye."

That request wasn't on the list, but this was typical with house calls. The old "while you're here, Doc" happened nearly every single time.

"Even more the reason for you to stick around," Dimpna said.

Most of the sheep had chronic foot rot. The misshapen feet had to be cleaned; then they needed antibiotics. Dimpna suspected another one had meningitis. She gave him some anti-inflammatories to see if the swelling would go down, as well as a long course of antibiotics.

"When might we see a turnaround?" the farmer asked. "That one there is Clancy." He pointed to a rather stout one in the corner. "He's me favorite."

"Why is that?" Patrick asked.

"Because he keeps to himself," John said. "It's a quality I admire."

"With this course of antibiotics, you'll want to see it through the full five days," Dimpna said. She found a third sheep with ringworm. They ended up being there longer than Dimpna had expected. By the time they finished with the sheep and treated the cow for pink eye, two hours had flown by. For billing and medication, she'd brought a handheld system that allowed her to order and administer the prescription, and even print out a receipt and instructions on the spot. John shifted back and forth several times as he watched her work the handheld device. Finally, she sorted out the medications and labeled each bottle with the prescription number. She began to print the invoice and receipt.

"I miss the old-fashioned ways," John said, staring as the device spit out what she needed. What John really missed was putting off paying his bills until someone came knocking on his door.

"We're able to treat a lot more animals this way," Dimpna said. "And keep the lights on in the clinic."

"I heard something was going on in Camp this morning," John Noble said as he stared at the invoice Dimpna had just handed him. "Did you hear anything?"

"Our phones have been ringing off the hook," Dimpna lied. "I'm afraid I haven't heard a word."

"But it's all over the news, like," John said. He may not own a computer, but he certainly watched telly. He glanced at Patrick. "What about you?"

"What about me?" Patrick asked.

"Have you heard about that colleen they found murdered in Camp?"

Patrick shook his head. "I don't have any more details than you."

"First a hit-and-run, and now this poor lass!" John said. "It's not safe these days," John continued. "Too many tourists."

"Mr. Noble," Dimpna said, "when you find yourself getting too interested in local gossip, just ask yourself, 'What would Clancy do?'"

They all turned to look at Clancy, who immediately turned and faced the wall, showing off his wooly arse. Noble frowned, then nodded.

This was another part of the job—chin-wagging. Farmers mostly kept to themselves, but they still managed to hear things through the grapevine, and they often wanted Dimpna to bring news from the outside world. She could only imagine his reaction if he knew what she'd seen this morning . . . Patrick picked up both of their medical bags and headed for the bus, leaving them to chat. Dimpna was really hoping he was ready to pay today; her father had been way too lenient with him. "I'm about to head back to my bus," Dimpna said. "Shall I wait for you to retrieve payment?"

He blinked. "What?"

"You can give me a check, cash, credit card?"

He stared at his fingernails. "You want it now, do you?"

"It would be the easiest for both of us," Dimpna said, plastering on a smile. "I have bills to pay myself."

"Follow me to the house then," John said, as if she were

putting him out. The rain was coming down hard now, and Dimpna hoped this wasn't an excuse to invite her in for a cup of tea.

"I'm still washing up. Why don't you run and get the payment while I do that?" Dimpna said. "I really have to be on me way." She had already washed up, but she really couldn't get pulled into the house. John was a lonely man; it was probably a long time between visitors.

"Mary's lad next door has been running wild with the colleen that was murdered," John said, lingering in the door to the barn.

Dimpna stopped pretending to wash up and ran over to him as he headed out the door.

"You said Mary's son was seeing Brigid Sweeney?" she cried over the wind and rain.

"Too bad you don't have time for a cuppa," he called back.

Patrick looked like a giant squeezed into one of the small wooden chairs in John's cramped kitchen. It wasn't until they were on their second cup of tea that John began to talk. "That's right, Peter Nosh was courting that caravan girl."

Patrick threw a look to Dimpna and mouthed, "Courting." She was more stuck on "caravan girl."

"He was writing her poetry and everything. Poor lad. Imagine your first love gets murdered? Poor, poor lad." Dimpna set her teacup down, and John popped up to fetch the kettle.

"I'm grand," Dimpna said, covering the teacup with her hand. "We really must collect payment and be on our way." Dimpna stood.

"I must say, I wonder if that explains his odd behavior this morning," John said.

"Odd behavior?" Patrick asked.

"Never mind me," John said, gesturing to Dimpna. "This one needs to be on her way."

Dimpna clenched her fist as Patrick tugged on her coat, and she reluctantly sat. "I suppose it wouldn't hurt to wet me tea, given that it's lashing out."

John poured more hot water into her cup, then Patrick's. "I saw him standing in his field this morning, holding something. Looked like women's clothing."

"That's odd," Patrick said. He glanced at Dimpna.

"He was just standing there?" Dimpna asked.

"Like one of my sheep when crossing the road and a car starts honking the horn. *Frozen.* He stood there until his mammy came out onto the porch and started screaming at him. I suppose the lad is heartbroken." John quickly switched gears and began talking about his farm, and the weather, and Clancy, his favorite of the sheep, and how the cow probably got pink eye from Peter Nosh because the other day Peter Nosh was leaning over the fence talking to Tootsie (named so because the cow is a female, but she looks masculine to him, like she's a he dressed up as a she), and Peter was sniffing and bawling, and his eyes were all red. Perhaps he and the dead girl had been having problems for a while, and then he switched to the latest hurling match, and how his local publican was having trouble with one of his taps, and John would have offered to help him out, only he's playing the music too loud, and given that John is nearly deaf, you can only image how loud that is, now, and who did they think was out there, running over elderly people?

By God! John for one wasn't going to go near nor next to Camp until they caught the filthy bastard. And had they been to Mass lately? If there was ever a time to turn out and pray, it was now, or maybe they needed one of those neighborhood watch meetings again like they did back in the day, when the heads of dead seals began appearing all over the harbor in Dingle. Forty minutes later, Dimpna knew they had to make a run for it, and she stood once more. This time, Patrick joined her, the pained looked of a tortured captive stamped across his face.

"If we can collect the payment, we'll get out of your hair," Dimpna said. "You must have a very busy day."

"A farmer never rests," Patrick added. "We've taken up too much of your time already."

Dimpna smiled. Patrick was learning.

John mumbled to himself as he headed out of the kitchen. "I have to find me credit card."

Dimpna stood. "We'll wait outside your door." She was dying to get out of the stifling kitchen. Relief settled over Patrick's handsome face, and they escaped together. Outside, the rain was coming down sideways, and the wind sent a bucket stuttering across the yard.

"Do you think Mr. Noble is going to make a run for it?" Patrick joked as they waited.

"If he does, you'll be the one running after him," Dimpna replied.

"Do you think Peter Nosh had anything to do with Brigid's murder?" Patrick whispered.

"I wouldn't have the faintest idea," Dimpna said.

Patrick arched an eyebrow. "Just felt like having tea with Mr. Noble, did ya?"

"It's coming down in buckets," Dimpna said.

"Literally," Patrick said, pointing to the one that had danced across the yard until being stopped by a fence post.

"I'd rather drive home when I can see beyond me windshield."

"Uh huh." Patrick gave her the side-eye.

"The guards need our help," Dimpna said. "If Peter was seeing Brigid, he needs to speak with the guards. He may know something." Patrick still had no idea that Dimpna had been the one to find Brigid's body. She'd been grateful her name hadn't been leaked at the press conference. And even though it wasn't logical, Dimpna felt tied to the case. Responsible somehow. She wished she could do things over, keep Brigid at the clinic, call the guards.

Was it Peter's poem that Brigid had dropped in the clinic? It was still in Dimpna's lab coat at the clinic. She'd put it in a plastic bag and sent Cormac a photograph. Given that she hadn't mentioned to Niamh that it was possible evidence in a crime scene, Cormac said he'd meet up with Dimpna personally to get it. The rain began to taper off. "I'll take our bags to the bus," Patrick said, heaving them up.

"Might as well start her up," Dimpna said. "I'll be right there." As Dimpna waited for John, she focused her gaze on Mary's farm next door. It was twice the size of John's. Mary Nosh and Dimpna's father had had a falling out some years ago over billing, and she'd been using Dr. Connolly, the other vet in Dingle, ever since. It suited Dimpna fine; her father had been a fair man, and she didn't like anyone who wanted to take advantage of him. If Peter Nosh was dating Brigid and writing her poetry, Dimpna had no choice but to tell Cormac. Minutes into her thoughts, John reappeared with a credit card. It was shiny and looked as if it had never been used. She tapped it against her reader and, once it was approved, printed out a receipt that she handed to John.

He stared at it sadly. "Your father used to send me a bill in the mail."

Patrick was waiting for her in the passenger seat of the VW bus. "Did he pay?"

Dimpna grinned. "He paid."

Patrick held up his fist, and they bumped. Dimpna buckled up and backed out of the driveway. She was nearly to the road;

the rain was lashing down once more, and the sound of the wipers filled the bus.

"Watch out!" Patrick yelled. A figure had dashed in front of the bus. Dimpna braked hard, sending the tail end of her bus sideways.

"What the hell?" The windshield wipers scraped, while the rain pounded, along with Dimpna's heart.

"Someone darted in front of you," Patrick said. "Not your fault, but I think one death is enough for today." Dimpna squinted and looked to the right. In the distance, she saw the back of a man, sprinting down the road. His arms were occupied; he was carrying something. Dimpna felt anger surging through her, her adrenaline pumping. She unbuckled and opened the door.

"Hey!" she yelled. The man took off. She was shocked at his speed. He ran straight ahead, disappearing in the rain. She took a few steps forward. He'd dropped something red. It stood out in the gray rain. She moved in closer. It was a lacy red bra, splayed out on the road. Normally, she'd never think to go back to the bus, put on a pair of gloves, and pick it up. She should just leave it. But it was odd, wasn't it? Why was there a man racing down the street in a rainstorm with a handful of women's clothing? *Peter Nosh. Just like John Noble said.* Should she pick it up or leave it? It was probably nothing. Maybe she shouldn't pick it up. Maybe she should leave it and call Cormac.

"What is it?" Patrick shouted.

"Maybe nothing," Dimpna said. "But maybe something." She got back in the bus and placed the call.

Cormac and Neely arrived thirty minutes later, which was good timing considering the slick roads. Neely bagged the bra in an evidence bag. "Fill me in on this morning," Cormac said.

Dimpna went over the incident. It wasn't until she mentioned that the Nosh farm was next door that Cormac's alarm raised to the next level.

"Peter Nosh?" he said. "This is where he lives?"

"Do you know him?" Dimpna asked.

"I've been meaning to speak with him," Neely said.

"I wish I had the poem on me," Dimpna said. "It's at the clinic."

"Do you remember any lines from it?" Cormac asked.

"I took a photo." Dimpna hunched over her mobile phone, trying to avoid getting wet, as she brought it up on the screen:

> *I could sit upon a thousand hills*
> *And dream of you all night long*
> *You're a goddess from another world*
> *And I'm your lifelong pawn*

Cormac studied it. If he had any opinions on it, he kept them to himself. "To recap—Peter Nosh was running away from his farm with women's clothing in his arms?"

"I can't be sure it was Peter," Dimpna said. "Patrick saw a lad dash in front of the bus, but I didn't see him until after. Then I saw him drop something red; it stood out in all this gray. I saw it was a bra. It might be nothing, but given the morning everyone's had and the fact that John Noble also saw Peter standing in his field, holding what appeared to be women's clothing, and everything else that's going on . . . it seemed right to phone you."

"You did the right thing," Cormac said.

She didn't know much about the lad or his mam, Mary, other than she was a few years younger than Dimpna. They were a family that kept to themselves, and if Dimpna knew anything about Mary Nosh, she knew the guards at her door asking about her son would not be well received. Could Brigid's murder soon be solved? Could Peter Nosh be a killer?

In the distance, John Noble stood by his barn door next to a clump of sheep, watching them through the rain.

CHAPTER 23

Cormac could feel DS Neely's eyes on him as he watched the taillights of Dimpna Wilde's bus disappear in the rain. "I suppose we just walk this way," Cormac said, pointing in the direction where Dimpna and Patrick said the lad had traveled. "Hopefully, we'll be able to see him through this shite."

"If that lad wants to hide, he knows this area better than we do," Neely said. "We should start at his house with his mam."

"Lead the way," Cormac said, wishing he'd brought a raincoat.

Neely headed toward a white farmhouse in the distance. "Dimpna Wilde," she said. "Don't you find it odd?"

"I find a lot of things odd," Cormac said. "Dimpna Wilde isn't one of them."

"I see." Neely did nothing to disguise her concern.

"What are you on about?"

"Never mind."

"You can't do that. You have to say it now."

Neely picked up her pace and raised her voice. "First, Dimpna Wilde discovers the body, and now suddenly she has what might be another piece of evidence?"

"It could just be a lad tossing out a bra so his mammy doesn't know he's riding someone," Cormac said. "But what exactly are you suggesting?"

Neely stopped in the road. Her visibility jacket flapped in the wind. "Is there a chance you might be a little too close to our suspects?"

He wasn't expecting this. "You consider Dimpna Wilde a suspect?"

Neely began counting on her fingers. "She was the last person to see the victim—"

"That we know of—"

"She had a knife, a poem, and a bloody jacket at her clinic—"

"Left by Brigid Sweeney—"

"She 'loses' the knife—"

"Didn't lose it; it was taken from the courtyard—"

"Which very well may be our murder weapon—"

"Probably taken by the killer, which means he knows Brigid went to Dimpna. He knows she has his jacket—"

"She found the body, took the dogs, and the bird, and now she finds evidence against another suspect?"

"She's a target now," Cormac said. "Tell me you'll protect her."

Neely sighed. "Why is it that every woman you're involved with is complicating my life?"

Cormac pressed the bridge of his nose. "I'm not involved with her."

"Just because you haven't made your move doesn't mean you're not involved."

"I asked her to take the parrot and the dogs, and it's not her fault the victim brought a rabbit into her clinic before she was murdered." Neely looked ready to say something else, and Cormac held up a finger. "And the rabbit, the bloody jacket and knife, and Brigid's visit to the Wilde's Clinic—all of that was verified by Billy, Alan, and Eve."

"I still don't like it," Neely said. "And since you seem to want to know what I think—"

"I do—"

"Between sleeping with one of the suspects—"

"*Before* she was a suspect—"

"But you were on duty. You were supposed to go to that caravan and ask them to move along."

"I did that. I did."

"You slept with her."

"She said they were leaving after the meteor shower. She said she was hungry. We went to a pub."

"Don't take this the wrong way, but between your personal relationship with one of our suspects, your whatever it is with Dimpna Wilde, and the very recent passing of your mother, I don't think you should be investigating this case." Cormac came to a dead stop, and Neely nearly slammed into the back of him.

"Is there a right way to take that?" Cormac could not believe his ears. Her words landed like a slap. Was Barbara Neely really going to turn on him? Even if she wanted to handle two murder probes at once, headquarters wouldn't hear of it. But the pair of them answered to a super. And Superintendent Mc-Graw wasn't the friendliest, even when things were going well. If Neely didn't have his back in this, he'd be in a world of trouble. He shouldn't have told her. Damn his compulsive need to do the right thing. Neely began walking toward the Nosh farm, forcing Cormac to run to keep up. He also had to hold his hat so it wouldn't blow off and shout against the wind to Neely's back.

"If you want to blame someone, blame me," Cormac said. "Leave Dimpna Wilde out of this."

"Leave her out of this, but protect her, is that what you're telling me?"

"Yes."

"It's not a matter of blame, Inspector, it's a matter of judgment."

"One mistake, Sergeant. Was it a colossal fuckup? Yes, it

was. Okay? I'd do anything to take it back." He stopped to catch his breath. "But you need me. Catching this killer has to be more important than punishing me."

"I'm not out to punish you, Inspector. I just don't like the mess you've dumped on me." She shook her head. "Your actions are very much like the current weather."

Stormy. Clouded. Mercurial. Unpredictable. She had him there. In the distance, sheep bleated, a mournful sound. He felt a sudden kinship with them. "Dimpna told me all about Brigid Sweeney's visit *well before* she found her body. I would have immediately gone to the caravan to see if the lass was alright, only Brigid said she was meeting a friend—aka *Peter Nosh*—in Dingle for the meteor shower. It was soon after that I received a call about the dogs running loose. A guard picked them up, and I not only asked Dimpna to meet me at the caravan in the morning, I asked her to take the dogs that evening and take them back to the caravan in the morning. All of this is on me. I was hoping to use the dogs to get the group to move on out. If my mam hadn't passed away, I wouldn't have been late, and perhaps I would have found the body. Would you have been suspicious of *me* then?"

Neely stopped and turned to him. "I don't think you should be mixing business with pleasure."

"Pleasure?" Cormac said. "Believe me, there's no pleasure."

"Let's just table this. We need to focus, and we're almost at the house." Cormac was surprised to see she was right. They were at the drive. A horse stood at the edge of the fenced pasture, staring at them.

"I assure you, my judgment is clear, Sergeant, and even if it's not official, I have no intention of walking away from this case."

"You need to grieve your mother."

You need to mind your own business. "People grieve in their own way and on their own time."

"I've had my say. Now, let's go see what we can get out of Peter's mam." She stopped as a few sheep hurried down the road. "Sheep," she said. "Clothing."

"What?"

"Remember my last phone call from Chris Henderson? Something about sheep and clothing. I thought wolf's clothing, but maybe it was just sheep and clothing. Do you think he was talking about Peter Nosh?"

"It's possible, but . . ." Cormac looked out over the pasture and hills. "We're nowhere near Camp."

"Maybe he saw Peter taking clothing from Brigid's caravan."

"And . . . what? Peter had sheep with him?"

"Maybe he was just referencing that Peter lives next door to a sheep farm."

"It's Kerry. Everyone lives next door to a sheep farm."

"He said something like, 'You're not going to believe this.'" Neely tapped the quote in her notebook, hovering over it to keep the rain off.

"I believe you. We have a legitimate suspect in Peter Nosh."

"This is it," Neely said. "I can feel it in me bones."

Cormac looked up to see a modest stone home. In the distance loomed a large barn. He nodded.

"Let me do the talking," Neely said. "Mary Nosh does not like strangers."

CHAPTER 24

Mary Nosh stepped out onto her porch and slammed the front door behind her. She was a thin woman with hard eyes. She wore a shawl that she wrapped even tighter around herself at the sight of them. "Hello, Mary," Neely said.

"Barb," Mary said, despite the fact that Neely was in uniform. "I wasn't expecting to see you here, now."

"We won't take much of your time." Neely gestured to Cormac. "This is Detective Inspector O'Brien."

"I saw you on the news." They could hear the telly blasting from within.

"We're here to speak with Peter," Neely said.

Mary adjusted her shawl and shifted her gaze toward the road. "He's not here."

Neely nodded, giving it a beat. "Do you know where we might find him?"

"He's taken to his bed; he's got a bug."

"You just said he wasn't here," Cormac couldn't help but interject. "Now, which is it?"

"Do you see him standing here?" Mary said.

"We can go up to his room and speak to him, if that's the way it has to be," Neely said. "But we will be speaking with him."

"Come back later."

"I'm afraid we need to see him right now," Cormac said.

"I don't know when he'll be back," Mary said. "He went out."

"In the span of a few seconds, you've told us he's in and he's out," Cormac said. "Which is it?"

Mary Nosh glared at him and pressed her lips together tightly.

Neely took a step forward. "We'll wait in the kitchen," she said. "And we'd love a cup of tea."

Although he was chuffed at the way Neely had bulldozed her way into Mary Nosh's kitchen, it was the worst mug of tea Cormac had ever had in his life, and dollars to donuts she had done it on purpose. There was a chalk-like consistency to it, and for a moment, he wondered if it had been poisoned. Mary Nosh sat at the front of the table, her eyes constantly flicking to the large ticking clock on the far wall, next to a painting of Jesus on the cross. Cormac wasn't sure which one she was staring at, probably both.

"How is Peter these days?" Neely asked. Cormac was eager to hear the answer. He was quite surprised that Mary Nosh had yet to ask why they wanted to see her son. She also hadn't brought up the reason she'd seen them on television this morning, and Cormac found that extremely troubling.

"It's going to be lashing rain all day," Mary said. "Did you happen to see that female vit was next door this morning?" Mary made a clucking sound. "I told John he should switch to Doctor Connolly, like we did. Your one never did use the sense God gave him."

"Now, Mary," Neely said. "Don't tell me you don't approve of a female veterinarian?"

"Have you seen her?" Mary said. "Itty bitty thing. We stopped using the Wildes when Doctor Wilde ran it."

"Doctor Wilde still runs it," Cormac said.

"No," Mary said. "He has memory holes now. Big ones."

"Doctor Dimpna Wilde," Cormac said. "His daughter, a renowned veterinarian in her own right."

Mary pursed her lips, but if she was going to make a reply, she thought better of it. The rain pummeled the windows, making them rattle. Cormac prayed the technical team had gathered all the evidence they needed before the skies opened up. They'd been left with so little to go on. At least the coroner had arrived, and he'd been granted permission to cut the poor woman down from the tree; her body was on the way to the morgue at Kerry General Hospital. The state pathologist was aware of the violent nature of the crime, and they'd been assured the case would get top priority. Neely's gaze suddenly shifted to the window. Cormac glanced over just in time to see a hooded figure headed for the door. Mary stood from her chair so fast she nearly knocked it over. They had purposefully parked the squad car in the drive next door. They didn't want the lad to see them and do a runner.

"Sit down, please," Cormac said to Mary Nosh. She was poised to warn Peter.

"He's a good lad," Mary said, as Cormac headed for the door. "We don't want any trouble. Barb, please. Tell him we don't want any trouble."

The door opened, and a young man stepped in, dripping water. His hair was slicked back. He wasn't conventionally handsome, but he was tall with a strong face. "I got rid of them, Mam. No one will ever know."

"Got rid of what, Peter?" Cormac asked.

Peter's head whipped around, and his mouth dropped open at the sight of the detectives. "Nothing," he said. "I'm on about nothing, as usual. Right, Mam?" He could not hide his air of desperation.

"Don't take him into the station," Mary Nosh begged.

"Station?" Peter said. "Me?"

Mary threw off her shawl, letting it land on the back of a chair. "This is all my fault. I told him to get rid of the clothes. I didn't want ye to think he had anything to do with that business with that lot."

"And which lot are you referring to?" Neely asked.

"You know which one, Barb. In Camp. The dead girl."

"I'm on duty now, as you can see, Mary, and you'll need to address me as Sergeant Neely."

Mary nibbled on her lip, then shrugged her consent. Cormac turned to Peter. "Whose clothes were you getting rid of, lad?"

"No one's," Peter said. "Donated some old clothes of me mam's. Isn't that right, Mam?"

"You dropped one of the items as you ran," Cormac said. "It was a lacy red bra."

Peter swallowed hard, then shut his eyes. "Listen to me, Peter," Neely said. "I know Detective Inspector O'Brien." She pointed to Cormac. "He's a truth seeker. And you better believe he finds it. You'd best tell him everything, no matter how embarrassing for you or your mother, because if you don't, you're going to find yourself in a whole world of trouble."

"Trouble?" Mary said. "For sneaking around with a girl?"

"What's the name of this girl?" Cormac asked.

"I was donating some of my mam's clothes," Peter said.

"You were sprinting down the road in the rain with a handful of women's garments," Neely said. "And you've now just lied straight to our faces twice."

"You can answer the questions right here and now, or we can bring you into the station and you can answer them under the spotlights," Cormac added.

"I need to change me clothes," Peter said. "I'm soaked through."

"Your mother can pick out a fresh set for you, and you can

change at the station," Cormac said. The lad was squirrelly and eager to get as far away as he could.

"Are you joking me?" he said. "What do you think, I'm going to jump out me window?"

"Are you?"

"This has nothing to do with Brigid Sweeney," Mary said. "He had nothing to do with that awful business."

"And yet, from what we hear, they were supposed to meet up the night of the meteor shower. We found a poem he wrote her that was in her possession. He's lying to our faces and was seen running down the road with women's clothing clutched in his hands, just after our press conference about the lass," Cormac said. He wished he had a search warrant. "Mind if I take a look around?"

"Around where?" Mary asked, as she straightened her spine.

"I could start with Peter's room," Cormac said.

"You wouldn't find anything," Mary said. She shot a look to Peter. "I told you. I told you she was bad news."

"I can't stand being in these wet clothes," Peter said. He headed for the stairs. "I'm going to change."

Cormac held up his hand. "There's no need to change. You're going to show us where you ditched that armful of clothing."

Peter swallowed again. "It's too late," he said. "They're gone."

"Gone?" Neely stepped forward. "Gone where?"

Peter shook his head as he backed up. "It was raining hard. I don't even know meself."

Cormac moved in on him and lowered his voice. "You'd better remember right quick, because you're taking us there now, and if you lead us astray one more time, you're headed for a tiny little cell and you can keep those wet clothes on as they turn your skin—not to mention your manly parts—into moldy little bits." He could feel Neely's scrutinizing gaze on him, and yes, he was angry, but this cheeky lad had it coming, and so did the mother, for that matter.

"All this fuss for getting rid of some unwanted clothes?" Mary said.

"Enough of the ridiculous banter," Neely said. "No one rushes out of the house to dump clothing outside in a storm, and I will not stand here and listen to the two of you claim that's anywhere near normal."

"How did you find out? It's that Dimpna woman, is it?" Mary held up a clenched fist.

"She almost ran me over," Peter said, sounding outraged.

"That's what happens when you dash out in front of someone's vehicle," Cormac said. He couldn't help it. "And we all know the clothing belongs to Brigid Sweeney, isn't that right?" Cormac did his best to sound sure of himself.

"What does it matter now?" Peter said, his shoulders rounding in defeat. "Dead girls don't care about their clothes."

CHAPTER 25

"Peter!" Mary Nosh cried. Neely turned to her and shushed her, then turned back to Peter. "Go on, so."

Peter removed his wet jacket and started on his boots as he talked. "Mam didn't want the clothes around in case someone got the wrong idea. Brigid is the one who gave me a bag of her clothes. She was going to leave those lads."

"We have a lot to unpack here," Cormac said.

"There's nothing to unpack," Peter said. "I threw the clothes out."

"He was speaking metaphorically," Neely said.

Peter stared at them, his eyes wide, his mouth open in a pant.

"You should know something about metaphors," Cormac said. "I heard you're a bit of a poet."

Peter took a sudden interest in his fingernails. "Where did ye hear that?"

"I don't like any of this talk," Mary said. "Does he need a solicitor?"

"You decide," Cormac said. "But first he's taking us to where he dumped that clothing, or you better believe he's going to need a solicitor."

Peter straightened up, a look of pure horror on his face. "But I just took off me wet boots."

"Well, then," Cormac said, "you'd best pull them on again."

"We could have called in the team for this," Neely said as they trudged through the muck. They had grabbed gloves and evidence bags from the squad car and were following Peter as he tried to retrace his steps. Cormac was determined they would search the surrounding area until they found every scrap of clothing that belonged to Brigid. Every once in a while, he could imagine her presence, see her walking next to them in her bare feet and her royal blue dress. *I'll find him*, Cormac said to her via his thoughts. *Did Peter do this?* He tried to imagine her answer, but even her ghost remained silent. Cormac had yet to figure out if Peter Nosh was way too simple to have murdered Brigid in such a gruesome way, or if he was a genius for making them think he was too simple to have murdered Brigid in such a gruesome way.

"Do you own knives?" Cormac asked as Peter muttered to himself in the rain.

"Everyone owns knives," Peter said.

"Big ones?" Cormac asked. "Sharp ones?"

"My mam has cooking knives," Peter said. "Why?"

"Just making conversation," Cormac said. Regular cooking knives would not be enough to sever a hand at the wrist. He'd have to wait for the state pathologist's findings, but his best guess was a butcher's cleaver. They needed to find the knife that Brigid left at the clinic. Had she taken it with her? Did she *provide* the weapon of her death to the killer, or was he the madman chopping off rabbits' feet and he simply took back his knife?

"Do you hunt rabbits?" Cormac asked.

"What?" Peter sounded truly confused.

"Are you a rabbit hunter?"

"I'm not any kind of hunter."

"Peter's more of a bookish lad," Neely said. "I bet you have a grand library."

Peter frowned. "No," he said. "But I do go to the library."

"What are your last few reads?" Cormac said. "Are you into any true crime?"

"True crime?" Peter said. "Not a chance. I'm a *poet*." He sounded truly appalled. "There." Peter stopped by a small hill. Just beyond it was the bay. "I don't know if they'll be washed away or not."

"Take us to the exact spot you threw them in," Cormac said. "And you better hope they're not washed away."

The rain lightened up as they reached the water's edge, and just a few feet in, clothes were bobbing on top. "Those belong to Brigid Sweeney?"

Peter nodded, his teeth chattering. "She was supposed to spend the night last night. I met her in Camp, and she gave me the clothes. That was the last I saw of her."

Neely stared out into the water. "I guess it's going to have to be me."

"I would do it, you know I would," Cormac said. "But it's evidence. And if I touch it—"

"It could be thrown out of court," Neely finished. She sighed, donned her gloves, and opened the plastic evidence bag. "Tell us about that meeting," Cormac said as Neely waded into the water. From the squeal she let out, it was freezing. "Your last meeting with Brigid?" Cormac prompted Peter.

"We met at the Village Pub in Camp about half-six. The clothes were in a SuperValu bag."

"Where's that bag now?" Neely asked.

"It's in my room."

"We'll be taking that as well," Neely said. Peter shook his head, then shrugged. "Go on," Cormac urged.

"She said she was in a hurry. Said she'd text me later to find out where we were watching the meteor shower. She had to take a rabbit to a vet in Dingle." He shook his head. "I told her we don't use the vet's daughter, we use Doctor Connolly. But she wouldn't listen." Peter stopped, then scratched his head. "Why were you asking me about rabbits?"

"Were you supposed to meet after in Dingle?"

"She was going to meet me in Camp. At the Village Pub."

Cormac watched Neely place a pair of denims in the bag. Red panties floated a ways out, and she waded farther in. Cormac thought over Brigid's story about the rabbit. According to what she'd told Dimpna, Brigid had grabbed the rabbit, the knife, and the jacket right after screaming and scaring away a man who was attempting to hack its foot off. That was the reason she gave for wearing the jacket—wrapping the rabbit in it, getting blood on herself in the process—but if Peter was telling the truth and hours earlier she was talking about the rabbit, yet not wearing a man's jacket and no signs of blood on her . . . well, what did that mean for her story? *It was made up.* "What was she wearing?" Cormac asked.

"A blue dress," Peter said. He rubbed his eyes. "She was so fucking gorgeous."

The blue dress tracked. "Did she have a man's jacket over the dress, or any blood on her?"

"What?" Peter asked. From the sound of his voice the question shocked him. "No."

"And then what?" Cormac pressed as Neely grabbed the panties, waded back to shore, and added them to the bag.

"I gave her a poem."

"Does it end with the line 'I'll be your lifelong pawn'?" Cormac asked.

"You read it?" Peter asked. "That was private." He stared at Cormac. "What did you think of it?"

Brigid must have dropped the poem in the clinic . . . or had she purposefully left it, perhaps wanting it to lead to Peter in case anything happened to her? "Nothing is private when there's a murder probe," Cormac said. "You'd better think long and hard about that, and if there's anything you're not telling us, now would be the time." The last items were a pair of red shoes and a top. Neely reached the shoes first and placed them in the bag. She had to wade out farther for the shirt. She scooped it out of the water and held it up for Cormac to see. It was white, with a peace symbol. But there was something else. Smears of red paint across the chest, spelling out a word. Cormac moved closer to see if he could read it: BITCH.

She placed it in the bag and waded back to shore. They both looked at Peter, who was suddenly fascinated with his shoes.

"I'm going to have to change out of these wet clothes before I catch sick," Neely said. "We can't have us both out of commission."

Cormac nodded and addressed Peter. "We're going to need you to come with us to the station so you can give an official statement."

"I need to tell my mam."

"We'll call her," Cormac said. "Let's go."

"What if I say no?" Peter said.

"Then I'm going to read you your rights and arrest you," Neely answered. "Would you like that?"

"No."

"We're parked up at Noble's. Let's pick up the pace." Neely led the way. Peter slouched with his hands in his pockets, trailing his feet.

"Better pick it up, lad, before she gets browned off," Cormac said. He sighed but picked up his pace.

"Did you see or speak with Brigid after she gave you the clothing?" Cormac asked.

Peter shook his head. "I texted her like twelve times that night. I never heard back."

"Did she say where she was going next?" Cormac asked.

"Back to the caravan to leave them a note."

A note.

You Made Your Bed.

That note?

"Was she anticipating trouble?"

"No. She said they'd all be out, that this was the best time to sneak out." Peter ran a hand through his wet hair, flattening it even more to his head. "I'm sorry." His voice squeaked.

"Sorry about what, Peter?" Cormac asked. "Are you sorry about what's written on her shirt?"

"Is it blood, Peter?" Neely chimed.

Peter's lips quivered. "Brigid said they'd be gone." He swallowed. "But one of them must have been home. One of them must have killed her. I think it has to be Billy."

"Why Billy?" Cormac asked. He hadn't even acknowledged their question about the shirt. Maybe he was gruesome enough. Smart enough.

"Billy Sheedy was in love with her. She'd rejected him over and over. She told him she was with me now."

"And she was coming to spend the night with you?" Cormac pressed.

Peter hesitated. "That's right."

"Are you telling me your mam was fine with you having relations with Brigid Sweeney under her roof?" Neely asked.

"We're both adults," Peter said. "But of course not. She was allowing Brigid to sleep in the guest room."

"Keep those thoughts fresh in your mind," Cormac said as they reached the squad car. "We're all going to go to the Tralee Garda Station and have ourselves a proper chat."

"Look, I'm really sorry, okay?" Peter said. "When I heard what happened to her, I panicked. That's the reason I threw her clothes in the bay."

"Did you also write BITCH on her shirt in blood?" Neely asked.

"It's not blood. It's spray paint."

"That sounds like a yes," Cormac said.

"I thought she was standing me up! I didn't know she'd been murdered!"

"Save your breath," Cormac said. "We need all of this to be official."

"I didn't kill her. I loved her."

"The inspector is right," Neely said, opening the back passenger door of the squad car and gesturing for Peter to get in. "Save your tears for later."

"I want to go home and shower and put on dry clothes," Peter said.

"We'll give you some dry clothes at the station. A nice little jumpsuit."

"You're arresting me?"

"We are taking you in for questioning," Cormac said. "I'd cooperate if I were you."

"You can wear the jumpsuit until your mam brings you some dry clothes," Neely said. "That's the best we can do."

"My Mam was right," Peter said. "I should have stayed away. That lot she was with, they're nothing but trouble. It's one of them that killed her. It's one of those caravan lads."

An hour and a half later, Peter Nosh sat in front of them in an interview room at the Tralee Garda Station, looking rumpled but dry in his white T-shirt and gray tracksuit bottoms. He had been read his rights but had declined a solicitor. Gone were the earlier denials; now he was like a puppy, wiggly and eager to yap. Once again, Cormac watched from behind one-way glass as Neely and Lennon interrogated him.

Neely slid the poem Dimpna had found at the clinic in front of him.

I could sit upon a thousand hills
And dream of you all night long
You're a goddess from another world
And I'm your lifelong pawn

Peter nodded. "Where did you find that? Did she . . . ?" He swallowed. "Did she have it on her?"

"I'd like to see any other poems you wrote to Brigid," Neely said.

"Do you think it's any good?" Peter asked.

"A woman has been murdered," Neely said. "And you want to know if we like your love poems?"

"That's not fair. I just . . . hope she liked them. She was my muse." His smile soon faded. "Or she *was.*"

"What about Chris Henderson?" Neely asked.

Peter frowned. "The old man who was hit by a car?"

"Did you know him?" Neely asked.

Peter shook his head. "Are you trying to pin that on me too? I don't even drive."

"Mr. Henderson mentioned you," Neely said. "Why would he do that if he didn't know you?"

Cormac squirmed in the next room. Although technically they could lie to suspects, he, for one, didn't like it. Lies got you in trouble, no matter how good the intention. Then again, it was because of this philosophy that he was sitting in the dark, unable to badger Peter Nosh. Maybe if he was more comfortable with lying, he'd have a seat at the table.

"Me?" Peter said. "What did Mr. Henderson say about me?" Sweat dripped down the side of his face, and he looked as if he was about to burst into tears. It was easy to forget how traumatizing an interrogation could be. If Peter was innocent, they were probably inflicting some psychological damage here. How would he eventually act out? Drinking? Drugs? Poetry?

"What happened last night?" Lennon said. "Take us through it."

"I've told you everything."

"You told us about meeting up with Brigid," Neely said. "I want to know about *after.* I want to hear about your evening."

Peter swallowed. "You want everything?"

"Everything," Neely confirmed. "The whole devil."

"What?" Peter looked stricken.

"The details," Lennon said. "She wants all the dirty little details."

"The night of the meteor shower was supposed to be the best night of my life." Peter leaned back in his chair. "But it ended up being the worst."

CHAPTER 26

The Village Pub, two and a half hours before the meteor shower

Peter Nosh changed his outfit three times before deciding on a green shirt and denims. He was early to the Village Pub; he needed to be early, needed to be in control. He ordered a pint and took it outside to the picnic table. There were three hikers standing nearby, two women and a man consulting a map, chatting about flora and fauna they expected to see on the route. *Losers.* He hoped they'd go away; the man especially was annoying. Peter could tell he'd just met up with these women, and he was really flirting with the younger one. He was like a cartoon character with his tongue hanging out. And she wasn't anywhere near as pretty as Brigid. Peter wanted him gone before Brigid arrived. He could tell the older woman didn't like yer man either. She kept trying to break away, but the younger one was laughing and enjoying the attention. If they didn't leave, Peter was going to have to think of another meeting spot.

"We'd best get our legs out from under us," the older woman said.

"Maybe she wants to stay," the man said, tugging on the arm of the younger woman. "One for the road. My treat."

"No," the older woman said. "We want to be fresh for the hike."

"What time are you setting off?" the man said. "I'll meet you."

"Early, I think," the young woman said. "What time are you setting off?"

"Early," he said with a shit-eating grin. "Why don't we meet here?"

"Let's go," the older woman said. She took the arm of the younger one and dragged her away. The man watched them until they were out of sight. Peter's fists clenched as he waited to see if he was going to leave. Finally, he went back inside the pub. *Loser.*

Brigid was going to meet him and his mam outside the pub, and then they would find a spot to watch the meteor showers. Brigid had already met him at this exact pub earlier to give him the clothes, so she'd be able to find them quickly. Peter worried about everything, so it was one less worry. Brigid wouldn't be able to claim that she couldn't find the pub. He wasn't calling her a liar, exactly, but this way she couldn't pretend to get lost. She did that once. Stood him up and then said she went to the wrong pub. He then had asked a lot of questions regarding the incident that she just couldn't answer. Or wouldn't. *What pub? Why didn't you text me? Who else was there? Why did you stay when you knew I was waiting for you? How did you get confused?*

It was new for him, getting this worked up over a girl. Every minute he wasn't with her, he was writing about her. She was his muse. She was perfect. Well, almost. The thing is, she didn't seem like the kind of girl who got confused. A little voice whispered to him, one he tried to ignore. *She's a liar. She's a fucking liar.* And maybe she was. But he forgave her. Because love meant forgiveness, didn't it? And let's be honest. He couldn't believe she was into him in the first place. The lads living with her couldn't believe she was into him either; he could see it in their eyes. Billy Sheedy thought he was a joke. Billy also hated him. Peter had been expecting Billy to jump out at him whenever he stopped by the caravan. Last time, he'd given him the two-finger gesture when Brigid wasn't looking. He was getting really worked up about that too. That was probably why he wasn't sleeping. He'd never dated at all, let alone a beauty like her. And even though part of him knew there had to be a reason, one that had nothing at all to do with liking him, he didn't want it to end. She could use him all she wanted. As long as it lasted. That was the bit that bothered him the most. The little voice that kept whispering it was never going to last. It kept him up at night that voice.

It was half-eight. He perched on the picnic table outside and texted her. His mam was here now; she was in the pub chatting away with someone. He'd wanted Brigid to get there first, which is why he told Brigid to meet him at eight and his mam at half-eight. He imagined his mam walking in, seeing him with Brigid, seeing how happy Brigid looked with her only son. He wasn't a loser. He wasn't an outcast. If a girl like that could love him . . .

But she was making him wait. Again. Peter hated waiting. And this time she was making his mam wait too. She couldn't say she went to the wrong pub this time. There weren't any other pubs in Camp. He grabbed his notebook. Tonight was the perfect night to tell her he loved her. She'd given him her change of clothes, which meant they weren't just dating; they were a couple. He'd tell her how he felt; he'd do it with another poem. He was pretty sure she liked the other six he had given her, even though she'd been very quiet about them. That's when he realized that she probably wanted to hear him say it. In a poem. That he loved her. Which he did. He'd never loved a woman before, but this was it; he loved Brigid

Sweeney. He wanted to shout it from the rooftops, but he wasn't a shouting it from the rooftops kind of lad. But he could shout it in a poem, and then anyone could read it however they liked; they could shout it from the top of the nearest cliff, if they so wished. He wanted to see Brigid's face light up; he wanted to hear her say it back. He had a plan too. A plan that she could stay in Dingle and let the rest of those eejits go on their merry way in their cramped little caravan.

How could she stand sleeping next to those dirty lads? They creeped him out. And those massive, smelly dogs. And that stupid talking parrot. And the other woman, Eve; she was a rude one, she was. Brigid needed to get away from them. Out of respect for his mam, she could sleep in their guest room until Peter saved up enough money to get them an apartment. He'd sneak in at night, of course, but at least he'd appease his mam in the meantime. They didn't need something real big, and it would still be bigger than that caravan, and you'd always know where to find it because it didn't move all the time.

She was late. She was always late. If he said something to her, would she break up with him? Her mam said lateness was a sign of disrespect. Thirty minutes late. She wouldn't want to be late for the meteor shower. He texted her: **Where are you?**

No answer. He called her. It went to voice mail. He left the same message. "Where are you?" He hung up. His mam exited the pub and he could see it in her eyes when she looked at him. She'd been telling him that Brigid was trouble, that a "girl like that" was only using him. And then his mam really went off the rails.

"I think that girl is a thief."

"What are you on about?" Peter hated when his mother got worked up.

"My heart-shaped locket is missing," his mother said. "It disappeared the day you brought her into our house."

"Mam," he whined. "It has to be there. Brigid wouldn't take your locket."

"I looked everywhere. She had to have taken it."

"She didn't."

"I'm telling you that girl is a thief. And she's standing you up."

"She's coming," he said firmly. A man had to be firm, or a woman would take over. It was always the way.

His mam set her lips and flashed him a look. In that moment, he hated her. Forget the guest room; Brigid was sleeping in his room tonight. "Give her a minute."

"It's getting dark."

"Give her a minute."

"We've given her thirty minutes. She's being very disrespectful." His mam's eyes flashed with anger. "Women who look like that think they can walk all over everyone."

There it was. The angry side of his mam. He was the only one who ever saw it. She was like the weather. You could be chatting away with her one minute, everyone in a good mood, and the next a dark cloud would take her over and she'd turn into a banshee. Sometimes he hated her. Brigid was nothing like his mam. His mam was a storm; Brigid was the rainbow after. He stared at his notebook. He wanted to say something about her eyes, compare them to the meteors. Flashing? Streaking? No. *Filled with otherworldly light.* God, that was it. That was good. And that was her. *Filled with otherworldly light.*

He played around with a new poem, drowned out his mam.

> *Brigid, my love*
> *Filled with otherworldly light*
> *You're a shooting star in the dark*
> *An eagle that will take flight*

He scratched out that last line. He didn't want her to take flight. Where was she? He texted her again. **Mam is impatient. Where are you??**

Should he ask her about his mam's locket? Why would she take it? Was she a troubled girl? If so, she needed him. He wasn't like the other lads she went out with. He was a sensitive soul. Maybe if she went to Mass more, she would be punctual. Father O'Toole was always talking about showing up. Showing up for church. Showing up for your neighbors. Showing up for God. Brigid needed a Father O'Toole sermon; that would sort her out. Peter would be good for Brigid. He'd cleanse her of her bad habits. *Cleanse her of her sins . . .* He stared at his notepad again.

She's late . . . Maybe she was changing her clothes too. She did that a lot. Ever since, he started changing his clothes too, never sure of what to wear. She made him nervous. He wanted to look just right. What would she be wearing? He hoped she was still wearing the blue dress. She was gorgeous. His mam thought she was too good for him. That's what she was trying to say every time she said, "A lass like that."

But she wasn't too good for him. She was just right. He called her again. It went directly to voice mail. What the fuck? Was she still at the caravan? It was just down the road. He'd walk over. Maybe she was staring in the mirror, trying to look all perfect and gorgeous for him. She didn't need to do that! She was already perfect. *Gorgeous.* He didn't even mind if she sinned a little. His mam and her friend came out of the pub, and they asked if she and Peter wanted to join them.

"You go ahead, Mam," he said, eager to get to the caravan. "Brigid and I will meet up with you later."

His mam tried to resist; she hated not being able to control him, but luckily, she hated making a scene in front of other people even more, and her friend was waiting. Peter waved goodbye to them and headed down the road toward the caravan. And by the time the silver caravan came into view, those massive dogs straining on their chains, he knew what he had to do. Even if it meant there was going to be some serious trouble.

CHAPTER 27

Tralee Garda Station—present day

"That's how I heard Brigid and one of the lads arguing," Peter said, as he finished his account of the evening. "I'm pretty sure it was Billy." He shook his head, and his expression was that of disgust. "She called him an animal." He jabbed his finger at Neely. "I *told* you it was him."

"You'd better put that finger down before I put it down for you," Garda Lennon said.

"What?" Peter dropped his finger. "Sorry," he mumbled.

Cormac felt a flush of pride for the young garda, even though he had nothing to do with it.

"Did you actually see her and Billy?" Neely asked.

"No. I was approaching the caravan when I heard them yelling at each other."

Cormac felt himself growing tense. Peter was a slippery one. He'd previously told them that the last time he'd seen Brigid was at half-six when she'd given him the clothing. Now he'd supposedly heard her at half-nine at the caravan, arguing with one of the other lads. Both lads had insisted they hadn't seen Brigid after she was dropped off at the vet. If Peter was telling the truth, this was huge. The difficulty Cormac was having was that he made it a rule never to trust a liar. He texted Garda Lennon. Lennon glanced at the text and thankfully didn't glance at the one-way glass. "So even though Brigid was supposed to meet you at the Village Pub and she wasn't answering your many calls or texts, you decided to go find her," he said.

Peter shifted in his chair and crossed his arms. "I told you, I wanted to see if she was alright. She was thirty minutes late."

"Go on, so," Neely said. "What happened next?"

"I left."

"You left a woman in distress?" Lennon said.

Peter traced the tabletop with his finger. "If I'd known what was going to happen, I would have called you lot, now wouldn't I? But those dogs were chained out front, and she sounded like she was holding her own. She didn't yell for help or nothing. She was just yelling at him." He swallowed. "I thought she was telling him that she was leaving, that she was going to live with me, and they were just working it out is all."

"Live with you?" Neely asked. "Live with you and your mam?"

"Right. Well, I was going to ask Mam if she could stay in our guest room. Just until I could afford to find us a flat."

"How do you know it was Brigid?" Neely asked. "Couldn't it have been Eve?" *Or a parrot . . .*

"I know the voice of the woman I love," Peter said.

"And yet you just left her when she was screaming at someone," Neely said.

Peter opened his mouth in horror. "Nobody can get past those dogs! They would have torn me to shreds."

"Why didn't you call the guards?" Neely asked.

"And say what? That Brigid was humiliating one of her mates?" He shook his head. "I tell ye, I wouldn't have wanted to be him. She was eviscerating him."

"You just said she sounded terrified," Lennon pointed out.

Keep it up, lads, Cormac thought. *He's getting flustered . . .*

"She was all over the place. First she sounded frightened; then she started calling him a loser."

"I'm going to need you to write down everything you heard either of them say," Neely said, sliding a blank sheet of paper and a biro over to him.

"I already told you what I remember." He pointed to the recording device. "Just play it back."

Neely gave him a minute to stew. "Did you see any other vehicles parked in the lot?"

Peter chewed on his lip. "It was jammed. People were parking for the meteor shower."

Cormac knew that's why the killer had chosen that night. Everyone felt safe in large numbers, and no one in that crowd was expecting trouble. The killer knew no one would be looking.

Peter smacked his lips together. "There is one more thing I remember. I found it strange. Very strange indeed."

"Go on, so," Neely said.

Peter crossed his arms and stuck his chin in the air. "What's in it for me?"

Cormac couldn't believe the cheek of this lad; he wanted to come through the glass and throttle him. Instead, he texted Lennon again. "Excuse me?" Neely said.

Peter twisted in his chair. "I'm willing to work with you, but don't I get something for it?"

"How about this." Lennon stood and slammed his hands on the table. "Maybe. And it's just a maybe. Maybe Sergeant Neely will overlook the fact that you just lied straight to her face."

"How did I do that?" Peter was back to sounding like a scared little boy.

"Your mammy was your alibi. But now you've just told us you left your mam and went to the caravan. What really happened when you went to see Brigid?"

Peter's face was beet red. Cormac was starting to come around to Neely's opinion. This could be their killer. An immature killer, no doubt. But he was turning out to be more complex than Cormac had thought possible. A knock sounded on the door to the interrogation room. It opened, and a guard popped her head in. "There's a solicitor here for Peter Nosh."

"Damn right there is." The solicitor, a large man carrying two bags of takeout—Chinese, if Cormac had to guess; he could smell it from his little hidey-hole. The solicitor squeezed past the guard and entered the room. "My client is done talking." He dropped one of the bags in front of Peter, then pulled out a chair next to him, heaved into it, and opened the bag. "But while we have a table and a room, we're going to eat our lunch. I'm starving."

"What did you remember, Peter?" Lennon said. "It could help us find her killer."

"You know it's not me, right?" Peter asked. "Right?"

"What strange thing did you remember?" Lennon asked again.

"Not a word," the solicitor said.

Cormac pounded his fist on his thigh.

"When did you paint BITCH on Brigid's shirt?" Neely said. "The one that looks as if it has blood on it."

Yes. Cormac pumped his fist.

"Spray-paint," Peter said. "But I didn't do it. I swear."

"You know it was spray paint, but you didn't do it?" Lennon asked.

"Correct."

"Do you ever write your little poems on buildings in chalk?" Neely asked.

"What?" Peter said.

The solicitor sat up and frowned. "You're done here, Detective."

"I swear," Peter said. "I didn't kill her. I didn't."

"Shut your gob," the solicitor said, sliding a bag of food his way.

Peter swatted the bag out of his way and leaned across the table. Neely and Lennon had risen and were at the door. "I'll tell you something, just to prove that I'm innocent." The solicitor started to interrupt, but Peter held up a finger and glared at him.

"I'm listening," Neely said.

"She was upset about a drawing," Peter said.

"What drawing?" Neely asked.

Peter shrugged. "I heard her say, 'this drawing' . . ." He shook his head. "She sounded really freaked out."

The solicitor slurped his drink. Neely stared at him; it was obvious he didn't know what to make of the comment. Neither did Cormac. *This drawing . . .*

"I can't be sure, but I feel like she was showing him whatever drawing she was talking about." He slumped further. "That's when I left."

"I believe you," Neely said. "But I don't believe you about the shirt."

"Bitch," Lennon said. "Not a very nice thing to call the girl you love."

The solicitor stopped mid-bite and waited.

"It wasn't me!"

"Then who was it?"

"Mam! Okay?" He set his fists on the table and rested his forehead on them. "It was my mam."

"Your mother?" Neely said. "Why would she do a thing like that?"

"Because Brigid stood us both up, like. She was *rude*. And if there's one thing my mam hates, it's rudeness."

CHAPTER 28

Cormac was late by the time he greeted Aunt Grace and Aunt Jane at the harbor; as predicted, they were none too happy that Cormac was not only still working, he was (in their interpretation) heading up a murder probe. The chances of him explaining why he wasn't officially heading up the probe were exactly zero. A large boat was pulling out of the harbor, its red and white sails fluttering in the summer wind. "We worry about you," Grace said. "I thought you had a nice promotion in Killarney and you wouldn't have to do this messy business anymore." Grace and Jane, both in their late seventies, looked so much alike. Plumper than his mam (who had lost all her weight due to her disease), their hair gone white; they were each dressed in black, from their shoes to their dresses, even their hats. His mam would not have liked that either. The sadness of it all. Hugging them felt good, though, and he realized he was glad they were here.

"I'm just not built to sit behind a desk," Cormac said. "I'm where I belong." He would go absolutely mad back in Killarney, pushing paper around. He'd tried it. It was not the life for him. "Let's have supper, shall we?" If their mouths were full, they couldn't lecture him. They went to a nearby seafood restaurant—fish and chips for Cormac, bacon and cabbage for

Aunt Grace, and curry chicken for Jane. His aunts chattered away while they ate, and Cormac was content to stuff his gob and listen. When they were finished, his aunts refused desserts; then they said they might as well have a look at the dessert list, then they said, no, they didn't have room, then they said perhaps just a little sorbet, then they ordered toffee pudding with vanilla ice cream. Cormac settled on a coffee.

"How is that doctor friend of yours?" Grace asked. "Your mam loved her to bits."

"She did," Jane said. "She thought the two of you were well suited."

"Doctor Wilde is a good friend," Cormac said. "There's nothing more to it, Aunties. We play a few trad sessions now and again." Their gazes remained steady on him.

"What does she play?" Grace asked.

"She's a brilliant fiddler," Cormac said.

"There you have it," Grace said. "The squeeze-box and a fiddle. You wouldn't need much more than that, now would you?" Her warm brown eyes steadied on him.

"Now. That is a nice match," Jane said. "And she isn't too tall."

Cormac nearly choked on his coffee. For all he knew, these two had promised his mam they would see to it that he found a good woman and settled down. And they weren't wrong. If he was ever to be in a relationship again, he would choose a woman like Dimpna. He could only imagine his aunts' expressions if they'd known he'd already dragged Dimpna into this murder probe. *Shame on him.* They'd be mortified. His mam would be mortified. Hell. He was mortified. Dimpna was tough, but she was sensitive. You had to be to work with vulnerable animals. But now she was probably feeling out of sorts, and it was in part Cormac's fault. He never should have left those dogs at her clinic, and he made a mental note to have that lad from ISPCA pick them up. Otherwise, he'd put a bull's-eye on her back. What if one of the caravan lads came looking for them?

With only two veterinarians in Dingle, it wouldn't take much to find which clinic had the dogs. And what if one of those same lads was a killer? Namely, Billy Sheedy. He had enough anger to kill, of that Cormac had no doubt. Then again, so did Peter Nosh, not to mention the mother. Peter's anger came out as their interrogation dragged on. And Dimpna had nearly hit him with her VW bus; was he the type that would start harassing her? He was if he was the killer. Cormac couldn't stand the thought that Dimpna was involved in this. He would not rest until this evildoer was brought to justice.

"Earth to Cormac," Aunt Jane said. "Where did you go?"

"Away with the fairies," Aunt Grace said, clicking her tongue.

"Sorry, sorry," he said. "You have my full attention."

"Why don't we take your mam's remains back to Killarney?" Aunt Grace said. "We can have a proper burial at the cemetery."

"Those weren't her wishes," Cormac said. "She wrote them down. I showed you." His mam had known this was going to happen; she'd warned him. *They're going to be persistent. Stay strong.* They'd had a good laugh. Here he was a detective inspector, shaking in his boots at the prospect of going head-to-head with Grace and Jane Kehoe. Neither had ever married, which made their attempts to couple him up even more humorous. Maybe he should scour the harbor for a pair of lonely, eligible fishermen.

Grace and Jane were the younger sisters, and he knew their grief was deep and wide. "But Mam said you're free to take some of the ashes to the cemetery and put up a headstone, if you'd like," Cormac added. "In fact, it was Mam's idea."

"She always did go her own way," Jane said. "What did the parish priest have to say about that?"

"I couldn't tell you," Cormac said. "But somehow she worked it all out."

Jane looked startled. Her teacup rattled as she set it down on the saucer. "What do you mean you can't tell us? You do know the local priest, don't you?"

"I believe he's called Father O'Toole," Grace said.

"Mam worked it all out," Cormac said. She'd been a power-house. What was life going to be like without her? He didn't want to think about it.

"Cormac James O'Brien," Jane said. "Are you telling us that you haven't been going to Mass?"

The pair stared at him.

"Let's not get into that now," he said.

Grace sighed. "I suppose some of her ashes and a nice head-stone in Killarney is better than nothing."

"I suppose it is," Jane said. "But it would have been nice to have all of her."

"I'll see to it then," Cormac said. The funeral was set for 1:00 tomorrow. Cormac had agreed to take the rest of today and tomorrow off, but he had no intention of sticking to it. He would spend the rest of the day today with his family, and to-morrow as well, but he planned on going into the station late tonight to start laying out his bulletin board. This case was be-coming complicated quickly, and visuals always helped him think. And given that he couldn't accompany Neely on her visit to George O'Malley, not to mention Robert and Vera Brannigan and Mary Nosh, he would need to catch up with her shortly.

"The others will be arriving soon," Grace said. "We're meeting at the pub in an hour. I'd like to go back to my room and freshen up."

"As would I," Jane said.

"I'll walk you ladies back to the inn and then meet you at the pub." Cormac hoped they didn't hear the relief in his voice. An hour was long enough to go to the station and start setting up his bulletin board. He'd ride his bike to the station, squeeze in a bit of exercise.

Although the Dingle Garda Station no longer operated twenty-four hours a day, Cormac was given leeway to work out of the incident room. He commandeered the large whiteboard. In the center, he placed the photo of Brigid tied to the tree, her long hair covering her face. Above it, he'd printed out the chalk drawings from John Street and put them side by side with the photo of the obelisk from the book in the caravan:

WHO PUT BELLA IN THE WITCH ELM?

Garda Lennon had done a good job of researching the story, but Cormac learned a few new tidbits. In addition to finding her entire skeleton, they also found a shoe, a gold wedding ring, and tattered bits of clothing. Although it was true that her left hand was not with the skeleton, they did eventually find it some distance from the tree. The most likely scenario was that an animal had absconded with it, for there was no determination from the coroner that it had been purposefully severed. Given all of this, Cormac was starting to think that this book and the chalk drawings foreshadowing the murder were more of a distraction than anything else. *Smoke and mirrors.*

This psychopath was inviting them to go down a rabbit hole.

Was *that* the reason for the rabbit's foot? Who was this person? Or maybe he was losing his mind. The rabbit's foot could mean something to the killer. A good-luck symbol. A talisman. He or she was definitely playing games with the guards by leaving the book open in the caravan.

Brigid had obviously known she was in some kind of danger. So much so that she concocted a bizarre story—unless, of course, everything she said was true. But it just didn't fit. Brigid didn't feel like she could directly tell the truth. Why not? She didn't feel as if she would be believed?

And what if Eve knew who the killer was? Cormac had decided to avoid her, but maybe that was a mistake. He could not let her suffer the same fate. He would not let this killer take one more life.

But what if Eve herself was the killer? He'd considered this scenario before. That Eve and Brigid had walked into the woods together to do "special K." Eve could have pretended to do it with her. Or Eve did a little but made sure Brigid had the lion's share of the dose, then subdued Brigid as soon as the drug took effect. Therefore, Eve could have managed it all by herself. It would have meant it had been carefully planned in advance. The knife and rope could have been stashed beforehand near the tree.

There were still too many questions, too many possibilities. He had to focus on one thing at a time. And right now, there were more pressing questions to answer: Were the guards getting anywhere with CCTV footage of the chalk scribbler? And to whom did the book belong?

Dimpna was so hungry she could eat a small horse. She entered the clinic, wondering what she had up in her flat for dinner. The rain had calmed into a drizzle. Dimpna was surprised to see Niamh standing behind the reception desk, rifling through drawers. She should have gone home ages ago.

"Are we out of chocolate?" Dimpna asked hopefully. That was something she could easily fix.

"No," Niamh said. "I've got good news and bad news, I think I'd better get the bad news out of the way first, like."

"Help! Help! Help!" Bette Davis screamed.

"Jaysus." Dimpna had all but forgotten about Bette Davis. She was perched on top of a filing cabinet, bobbing up and down.

"Pretty girl. Want a biscuit?" the bird said.

Niamh gave Dimpna a look. "I've never, ever wanted to hurt an animal in me life. You know that."

"Of course, I know that," Dimpna said.

"But this one." Niamh pointed at the bird. "This one is tempting me. She never shuts up! And given that I listen to folks yammer on all day long, that's saying something."

"How often has she been screaming for help?"

"It's nearly all she says," Niamh said. "Do you think the bird witnessed Brigid's murder?"

"I think they had their telly on all day long, and it's repeating something it heard on a show," Dimpna lied. "But maybe we should put her up in my room; I can play music for her. I'm just worried her screaming is going to upset our clients."

Niamh nodded. "It would be a relief, to be honest. It's so creepy. I can't believe it. Two murders in Camp in a few days? It's horrific."

"Is that why you look so upset?" Dimpna asked. "It's very understandable, and if you need to take some time off, we can figure that out too."

"I'm grand," Niamh said. "And no, the reason for this look on me face, besides a murderer running around, it's about the mother fox."

"Don't tell me she's come back to life," Dimpna quipped.

"It's possible," Niamh said. "She's gone."

"I know, luv, she passed."

Niamh shook her head. "No, I meant . . . her body is gone."

Dimpna wasn't sure where Niamh was going with this. "I asked the volunteers to bury her in the field."

"That's what I'm trying to tell you," Niamh said. "When they went to bury her, she was gone."

Dimpna frowned, then headed out to the kennel. Niamh followed her. She stood in front of the now-empty cage where the mama fox had rested and then passed. Indeed, it was empty.

"Strange, isn't it?" Niamh said.

"You're sure they didn't bury her?"

"I'm sure."

"You asked all the volunteers?" They had four regular volunteers at the clinic who rotated shifts.

"I spoke to every single one of them," Niamh said. "And Patrick, of course."

"Do you think any of them are messing with you?"

"I never considered that, but if they are, I hope I have your permission to give them the boot."

Why would anyone steal a dead fox? This made no sense whatsoever. "I don't know what to say."

"I didn't hear anyone back here, but it's possible. You know. With that bird yap, yap, yapping, I did finally turn the music up. Loud." She rubbed her ear. "Me ears are still ringing." Niamh dropped her hand and continued to stare at Dimpna.

"Right," Dimpna said, as she headed back to reception and Niamh followed. "Give me the good news." They stood in front of the reception desk, and Niamh's cheeks flushed red, which was when Dimpna knew it involved a man. *Please don't let it be Patrick.*

"You know that Charlie fella from ISPCA?"

"I do."

"I think he's single," Niamh said. "Because he mentioned he has kids, but they live with their mam. That's his way of telling me he's single, isn't it?"

Dimpna smiled. Niamh was on a mission to find love. "We've never discussed our personal lives. I can find out, if you'd like."

"I mean, he's an animal lover, and that's the most important thing."

Dimpna nodded, thinking about Cormac. She was convinced his "allergies" were a cover. He was nervous around animals, that was obvious. Was it something she could work with him on? "I believe Charlie will have to come back for the cage we used to transport the mama fox," Dimpna said. "Maybe you can have a chat with him then."

Niamh grinned. "I'll do that."

"Now. We've all had a long day. Go home and get some rest." Dimpna followed Niamh out to the courtyard and took the time to give old Tiernan treats and a cuddle. Her gaze shifted to her mother's caravan. Was she heeding the warning to lock her doors? Was she still living out there? Dimpna returned to her flat and released her fur-babies, then headed across the field to her mother's caravan, her four-pack following. She'd take them for an official walk after she checked in on her mam, and then it would finally be time to sink into bed. She had a busy day tomorrow, including the funeral for Cormac's mam.

It was hard not to think about Brigid Sweeney, and now Peter Nosh. She was not a guard, but she just didn't see him as any kind of killer, let alone the kind who would do what had been done to that poor young woman. Dimpna couldn't help but replay Brigid's visit to her clinic over and over again. In every reenactment, Dimpna convinced Brigid to stay and wait for the guards. Dimpna had checked on the hare early this morning and confirmed that the cut across its foot did not seem like a sincere attempt to cut it off. And the hare was way too domesticated; it had not been raised in the wild. If Brigid had been telling a partial truth—perhaps she took the hare from an owner she deemed was abusive—would finding the owner lead to the killer? Were they one and the same?

CHAPTER 29

As soon as Dimpna was a few meters away from the caravan, she knew her parents were not there. Her mam's car was gone. She stepped up to the door anyway and opened it easily. Dimpna tensed. It was more than likely, given Bette Davis's constant screams for help, that Brigid had been abducted from her caravan. Dimpna was going to have to convince her stubborn mam to lock her doors at all times. Better yet, she wanted to talk her into giving up the caravan altogether while this maniac was on the loose. If she wouldn't agree, then perhaps Dimpna should see if her mam would at least agree to keep E.T. with her. The newest member of her pack was not only smart as a whip; the sheepdog was an excellent guarder.

Dimpna stepped into the caravan. Purple velvet curtains hung from the windows. The small built-in table was cleared off, the sofa neat and plumped with pillows, and the back bed was made up. It was for this reason that a single cupboard above the sofa caught Dimpna's attention. It wasn't closed all the way, whereas the rest of them were properly shut.

If Dimpna wanted to open it, she would have to stand on the cushions of the built-in dining benches. Perhaps she should let it go. She slipped off her work shoes, then climbed onto the bench and opened the cupboard. White envelopes poured out of the space, raining down on her head. She caught one, then two, then three. They were all addressed to Ben O'Reilly in care of Dr. Dimpna Wilde. She didn't have to look at the return address, but she saw his name anyway, recognized his handwriting. *Sean O'Reilly*. Her son's biological father. Ben did not go by Ben O'Reilly; he went by Ben Flor. It was Niall Flor who'd raised him, and despite the tragic end to Niall's life, he had been a decent father to Ben.

Why was Sean O'Reilly sending letters to Ben in care of Dimpna? But she knew the answer; of course she did. Sean O'Reilly was up to his usual game-playing tricks. He wanted to torture her. Little surprise, given that the son they shared had been conceived during an act of violence. Rape. How she hated that word. It triggered her. But given that she'd spent decades hiding the truth, she was now determined to face it. Sean was incapable of change. This was yet another pathetic attempt to dominate her. Would she give the letters to Ben? How long would Sean wait until he made sure that Ben knew his mother was holding on to the letters? Sean wanted to drive a wedge between them. Little did he know that time and distance were doing that all on their own. Not to mention that Dimpna wasn't the one Ben was choosing to spend his free time with. That honor went to her brother, Donnecha, and Ben's half sister, Aisling O'Reilly.

Ben had recently cultivated a relationship with Aisling, Sean's daughter with his wife, Helen. She was going on ten years of age, and an adorable girl, but Dimpna cringed at the thought of Ben being sucked into the O'Reilly orbit. A once rich and powerful family—well, the matriarch, Róisín O'Reilly was still rich, and arguably powerful. So much drama they were practically a Greek tragedy. And apparently, Sean had not learned any lessons. He could have sent the letters to Helen instead.

Dimpna wasn't even speaking to Sean. "What have you

done, Mam?" Dimpna said out loud. She was torn between fury at her mam for hiding these from her and fury at Sean. Fury at Sean won out. She gathered all the letters, twenty-five of them, and exited the caravan. As she strode across the field, fuming, her phone rang. *Niamh.* She rarely called her after hours.

"Are you okay?" Dimpna asked, her heart thumping.

"I had the office calls forwarded to me phone," Niamh said. "Detective Sergeant Neely asked you to give her a call. She needs your help."

Another bright and early morning, another favor for a detective. But this time, when Dimpna pulled into George O'Malley's property, Sergeant Neely was already there, waiting next to her squad car.

"Thank you for doing this," Neely said.

"Not a bother." It was a bit of a bother; poor Patrick would be on his own for a spell. But Dimpna wanted to be helpful. Like it or not, she was in this now, and given that she didn't have the power to bring back the dead, the least she could do was help find this brutal killer.

They found George O'Malley by the side of his cottage, brushing his donkey. His chubby face lit up when he saw Dimpna Wilde, but it changed to a scowl when he noticed DS Neely, then lit up again when he saw Dimpna was carrying a cage with a hare in it.

"Hello, George," Dimpna said. "I brought you a friend." George clapped his hands and gestured to the hare and then himself. "Yes. He's yours, is he?"

George nodded and continued to point to himself.

"I thought as much," Dimpna said. "He's rather tame. In fact, I was wondering if he had wandered away from your property?"

"Hopped away, you mean," Neely said. She then leaned into Dimpna. "You're leading the witness."

"Sorry. I won't do it again."

But she already had her answer to the question. George was nodding so hard Dimpna was afraid his head was going to sail off his neck. "Could someone have stolen the rabbit?" Neely asked, glancing at Dimpna as if she were a translator. George seemed to be thinking about it.

Dimpna could feel Neely's energy shift into a higher gear. If the hare belonged to George, that connected him to Brigid. Dimpna was glad she was here; she had informed Neely that George O'Malley was one of the gentlest men she knew. He was an animal lover through and through; he treated his donkeys and hares like treasured friends. He had a decent farm, inherited through generations, and he'd been managing to survive all on his own. Despite the extra money his side business brought in, Dimpna surmised it was the socialization that George enjoyed. The donkeys were a buffer; George would stand quietly in the background, grinning as people loved up his companions, Frick and Frack. The pair stood close to the drive, their big noses sticking through the wood fence, hoping the visitors had brought treats. They were in luck. Dimpna snuck them each a couple of carrots and apples she'd brought along. Their wet, gritty tongues lapped up the treats, and then they lifted their gums and flashed their teeth. She laughed and loved them up for a minute.

George whipped out a pad and a pencil. He sketched something and turned to show them a perfect caricature of the hare; written above it in all caps was his name: FERGUS. George was partial to names beginning with F, it seemed.

"Lovely name," Dimpna said. "And may I introduce you to my friend? This is Detective Sergeant Neely." He held up a finger, then sketched something else and turned it around. A mug of tea with steam coming off it.

"We'd love a cup," Dimpna said before Neely could protest. She knew George O'Malley, and that's why Neely wanted her alongside; therefore, Neely would have to follow her lead. George took the cage with the hare, quickly removed a squirming Fergus, and handed Dimpna back her cage. Dimpna set it down. The hare was docile in George's arms as he examined the bandage. He looked questioningly at Dimpna. "Someone made a superficial cut across his foot."

George's mouth dropped open. He lifted both palms up. *Who?*

"That's what Detective Neely wants to find out."

George's glance slid to Neely. He pointed to the cut, then himself, and shook his head. George stroked the rabbit as he led the way to his house. It was a modest cottage; the real value was in the land. He stood by his front door and held up a finger.

"Shall we give you a minute?" Dimpna asked.

George nodded then disappeared inside the house.

"He can understand us," Neely said.

"He's very bright, Detective," Dimpna said. "A brilliant artist; caricatures are his specialty. He's wonderful with animals—a very gentle soul."

"I hate caricatures," Neely said. "I suppose no one likes to see their flaws."

"George is also known to make people appear a little heftier than they are in real life." Dimpna laughed. "But he has good intentions."

"Has he ever spoken?" Neely asked.

"I don't know," Dimpna said. "Not since I've known him, and according to Niamh, she's never heard him speak either."

"Even gentle souls have dark sides," Neely said.

Dimpna wanted to protest further but recognized it might do more harm than good. And when it came right down to it, Neely had a point. Everyone had a darkness within them. Even the nicest of humans had moments when their inner monster reared its ugly head. Dimpna had seen that in her husband, Niall, although by the time she did, it was far too late to save him from himself. Nothing was more terrifying than the enemy in the mirror. She'd seen it over and over again in Sean O'Reilly, and at times, she even felt a hideous rage churning within herself. *Inner demons.* Most people learned how to wrestle with them, keep them at undetectable levels. But anyone, at any time, could spring a leak.

George was back and holding the front door open for them, flashing a mouthful of crooked teeth. Dimpna had no idea how old he was, but if she had to guess, she would put him in his late sixties. Besides entertaining the tourists, he mostly kept to himself. But they had a mutual friend in common—Paul Byrne. Paul was Dimpna's first love, although their romance had been sidelined before it could be consummated, sidelined by her best friend, Sheila Maguire, jumping into his bed first. But all of that was in the past. They were tentatively rebuilding a friendship. Paul was a retired detective; technically, he'd been kicked off the force for beating a man who had been abusing his family. Now he was a bird-watcher and a volunteer at a local children's home where Frick and Frack were regular guests. It never failed to amaze Dimpna that everyone and everything in the Dingle Peninsula were connected. Like trees sharing a root system, the folks of Dingle were entwined. As soon as Dimpna and Neely entered the cottage, George held up the hare with a nod, then turned and exited.

"He built a rabbit hutch behind his house," Dimpna explained. "He's putting Fergus back."

"Wouldn't that be a hare hutch then?" Neely said.

Dimpna laughed. She was starting to see that Sergeant Neely had a healthy sense of humor. "Touché."

Neely gave it a smile and a beat. "You didn't recognize Fergus when Brigid brought him in?"

"I've not met Fergus before this," Dimpna said. "But according to Niamh, George often takes in injured hares and rabbits. He's been doing it for ages."

"I don't suppose you can ask your father," Neely said.

"Unfortunately, not anymore," Dimpna said.

"I need to know everything about George O'Malley's connection to Brigid Sweeney and rabbits' feet," Neely said. "And I must stress that you cannot let it slip that Brigid had a rabbit's foot tied around wrist or that her hand was severed."

Dimpna let her wave of resentment wash over her before letting it go. Neely had to do her job, and lashing out at her that she would never be so stupid would not get her anywhere. "Of course."

Dimpna watched Neely take in George's cottage. All of the walls were covered in caricatures of children and some adults, sitting or posing with one or both of the donkeys. Dimpna was surprised to come across her brother, Donnecha, in one, flashing a pair of rabbit ears behind the donkey. Her stomach flipped when she saw one of Aisling O'Reilly; standing in the background was Sean. Instantly, an image of letters raining out of her mam's cupboard assaulted her, and Dimpna had to shove it away. She'd deal with that later.

George returned and beamed when he saw them taking in his drawings. Neely gave him a thumbs-up, a gesture he enthusiastically returned. "If you ever sketch me, you have to make me skinnier," Neely said as George O'Malley pulled out chairs from the dining room table, then put the kettle on and began to prepare the tea. Minutes later, he set steaming mugs in front of them, along with a tin of biscuits. He opened a sketch pad, and before Neely asked a single question, he'd sketched a picture of Brigid Sweeney wearing angel wings and wrote RIP above it.

"That's lovely," Dimpna said. This man did not kill her. Neely could see that, couldn't she? Instead, she was staring at the drawing as if it were a confession written in blood.

"Were you friends with Brigid Sweeney?" Neely asked.

George tapped his lip with the pencil as he thought about it, then sketched another picture. It showed two people exchanging money. "Business partners?" Neely guessed. George nodded enthusiastically and touched his nose with one hand while pointing at her with his other.

"Did you sell rabbits' feet to Brigid?"

George nodded.

"Where did you acquire the rabbits' feet?"

George gave Dimpna the side-eye. "Maybe I should wait outside," Dimpna said. George shook his head, then patted Dimpna's arm. He then thrust his finger in the air, pushed back from the table, and left the room. He came back carrying a cardboard box that he dropped on the table with a thud.

"It's not a live animal, is it?" Neely asked as she scooted her chair back.

George laughed, then shook his head and wagged his finger at Neely. He opened the cardboard box, and before either could tell him it wasn't necessary, he turned it upside down, and rabbits' feet rained down on the table.

"Shit," Neely said, screeching back from the table and standing up. "Stop."

George looked startled. "It's alright," Dimpna said. George reached for one.

"Stop," Neely said again. "Don't touch them."

George pounded his chest. *Mine.*

"How many of those did you sell to Brigid and the lads?" Neely asked.

George looked up to the ceiling as he counted on his fingers. He flashed both hands twice. *Twenty.*

Neely was donning gloves. "Did the ones you gave—*sold*—

to Brigid and friends . . . did any of them have dried blood on them?"

George pulled a face, then frowned, then shook his head. Neely began examining the rabbits' feet while George rubbed his chin. "Listen. I think I need to take these into the station. You'll get them back. But we need them for comparison."

Dimpna understood why, but George did not. He looked to Dimpna for an explanation. "You'll get them back," is all Dimpna could say. "She promises."

"I don't make promises," Neely said. "But if you do not wish to voluntarily hand these over, then I will get a warrant, and that means a lot of people coming through your house." George gestured that she could have them. "Thank you," Neely said. She began putting them back into the cardboard box.

Dimpna dug in her handbag and was relieved she had at least seventy euros in her wallet. George probably depended on the money from the rabbits' feet to feed himself and his animals. "I'd love the drawing of Aisling, and my brother," she said.

George's eyes lit up when he saw the euros. He snatched them, nodding up and down. He hurried over to the wall and began removing the drawings.

"You had to do that now?" Neely asked.

"He depends on selling his trinkets," Dimpna said. "I don't want him stressing that you've just taken a month's worth of income."

Neely pursed her lips. "I have a killer to catch."

"I'm aware. This won't take a minute."

George hurried back with the sketches and handed them to her. Then he sat, and for a moment, they all fussed with their tea. The biscuits he'd set on the table were dry and crumbling. Dimpna had an urge to go through his cupboards and fridge to see if he was eating alright, but Neely would definitely frown on that.

"When is the last time you saw Brigid Sweeney?" Neely asked, removing a notebook. "I usually record interviews, but I suppose this one would need to be videotaped. I'll just take notes for now, but please be aware you may be called into the station to give an official statement."

George rose from his chair and fetched a calendar from his refrigerator. He returned to the table and tapped a date. *Friday.*

"Morning, afternoon, or evening?" Neely asked.

George jotted down his answer and turned it toward her. "Morning."

"Was there anyone else there?"

George nodded and started sketching. He turned the sketch pad around to show a crowd of people gathered around the caravan. Brigid was holding court, her dress lifting as she twirled. The dogs were tied up and staring lovingly at her. Billy was in the background, arms crossed, scowling. Eve and her parrot were sitting on top of the caravan. Dimpna nearly missed Alan, but he was there, standing by his truck. Staring at Dimpna, tongues literally hanging out, were at least four men. Behind them stood a woman, hands on her hips, a scowl on her face. "Wow," Neely said. "You're a very good artist. I'm going to need to keep this; it may help us identify who else was there." George nodded. "Do you know the names of any of these people?"

George pointed to Eve, Billy, Alan, and Brigid.

"No one else?"

He shook his head. He pointed to a man with a beard, a walking stick, and a backpack. Then he quickly sketched a man on a sign with a walking stick. "The Yellow Man," Dimpna said.

Neely nodded her understanding. The Yellow Man was a familiar signpost guiding hikers along the Dingle Way. "You're saying they're mostly hikers?"

George nodded. He then pointed to a large man behind an angry woman and then tapped the cottage by the bay.

"Vera and Robert Brannigan, I'm assuming," Neely said. She pointed to another man with a baseball cap. "He's actually quite muscular in person, but I'm guessing that's Charlie Meade." George pointed from Charlie's sketch to the two mastiffs that were tied in front of the caravan.

"Yes," Dimpna said. "He was there to check on the dogs."

Neely tapped the drawing of the angry woman and tilted her head. "It looks as if Vera went on a three-month eating binge."

George grinned, shrugged, and patted his own belly.

Neely sat up straighter, and unless it was Dimpna's imagination, she sucked her stomach in. "Why does Vera look so angry?"

George hesitated, then tapped the man in the drawing who stood closest to Vera. "Was she angry with Robert?" Neely asked. George went back to the drawing of Robert, then added his eyes popping out and his tongue hanging loose. "She didn't like her brother-in-law lusting after Brigid." George nodded and gave a thumbs-up. "I need you to be very clear. This was Friday morning? The morning of the meteor shower? You saw both Vera and Robert at the caravan?"

George nodded. He tapped his calendar, then the drawing, and nodded. Dimpna could tell this was having a big impact on Neely. She wasn't sure why, but of course, she wouldn't get anywhere by asking. Vera did look angry. Like an aggrieved wife. Robert was her brother-in-law. But she had been widowed for a year. Was she having an affair with Robert? What a mess that would be. He was married, and Vera had been married to his recently deceased brother. But it was definitely possible. Sordid things happened all the time. Neely suddenly cried out, as she zeroed in on something else in the photo. Something was hanging down past Vera Brannigan's hip. At first Dimpna assumed it was a handbag. Now she saw it for what it was. A pair of binoculars. Neely circled them. "You're sure? You're sure you saw her with these?"

George nodded, then mimicked using a pair of binoculars. He tapped a window in the cottage. Neely frowned.

"Was Vera looking out her window with the binoculars?" Dimpna asked. George drew a clock, then pointed to it over and over. "She does this all the time," Dimpna said. Another thumbs-up from George.

"Did you sell Brigid more rabbits' feet yesterday?" Neely asked.

George shook his head. He took to his sketch pad again. When he turned it around, the photo showed him walking down the road with one of the donkeys.

"Frick or Frack?" Dimpna asked.

George wrote FRICK above him. Sitting on Frick's back was a large hare. Dimpna didn't mean to interfere again, but before she could stop herself, she leaned in and pointed to the rabbit. "Is that Fergus?" George nodded and tapped the rabbit. "Sorry," Dimpna said.

"That's the same rabbit Brigid brought to your clinic that evening?" Neely asked.

"Yes," Dimpna said.

"Did your rabbit have a cut across its foot?" Neely asked, pointing to Fergus in the photo. "Like he does now?" George shook his head. "Are you certain?" George nodded.

"Did you lose the rabbit after this?"

George nodded and tapped the sketch of the dogs. Then he quickly drew a picture of Frick rearing up and the rabbit jumping off his back.

"The dogs scared Fergus," Dimpna said. "He jumped off Frick's back and ran off." Dimpna gave it a beat. "Hopped off," she corrected.

George nodded, approving Dimpna's interpretation.

Neely turned to Dimpna. "Could the rabbit have scraped his foot jumping off the donkey?"

"No. There was a deliberate cut across the foot, but not deep enough to do any damage."

"I could have retired this year," Neely said out of nowhere. "George, this is very helpful. Very helpful. I have one more question for now, and we'll leave you in peace."

George shrugged, then nodded.

"Have you ever seen anyone besides Vera or Robert with those binoculars before?"

He nodded.

"Who?" Neely asked.

He took to his sketch pad. He turned it around, shrugged both shoulders, and held his hands palms out, as if to say *I don't know*. The sketch once again depicted the caravan. Brigid danced in front of it. Parked across the street was a car. And poking out of the driver's-seat window was a pair of binoculars.

CHAPTER 30

Cormac dashed into the church and found Father O'Toole stepping down from the ambo. Guests were already starting to filter in, and organ music played softly in the background. Cormac approached the priest and explained his situation. The priest reluctantly agreed to delay the spreading of his mam's ashes, but Cormac would miss her Mass. He could still feel Grace and Jane's disapproval clinging to him like too much cologne as he dashed out the doors and to his vehicle. He had no choice. Despite the fact that he was in his suit and ready for Mass, a call had come in that possible evidence had been found at the crime scene. Now here he was, joined by Neely.

It was easier to be at the crime scene now that Brigid was no longer tied to the tree. Cormac and Neely had both received the call. Cormac had dashed from the church, and underneath his protective suit, he was wearing his best black suit. He wasn't sure if his family would ever talk to him again. It was hard enough to stand behind the crime-scene tape and not touch anything. On the ground in front of the tree, marked with an evidence-marker, was a long white feather.

"Swan," Neely said, bending down to examine it.

"Swan song?" Cormac guessed as he stared at it.

Neely cocked her head and considered it. "You don't think that's reaching a little?"

"I'd expect to find swan feathers near the bay, but in the woods?"

"Another bird could have snatched it to make its nest," Neely said.

Cormac nodded. "Or the killer is communicating."

"If the rabbit's foot around her wrist matches the ones from George O'Malley's collection, what will you think then?" Neely asked.

Cormac frowned. "How would we even match them?" This he had to hear.

Neely threw open her arms. "I don't know. I'm sure some nerd with no social life and a microscope could find a way."

Cormac gave her a minute to calm down. "George sold rabbits' feet to Brigid. She resold them. Even if they did come from George originally, the killer could have purchased it from Brigid or she had one of George's on her when she was abducted."

"Or George O'Malley is our killer." She studied the feather. "He does like to draw. And you've mentioned that this killer is communicating. Since he doesn't speak, perhaps it's his way of revealing himself?"

"Does he have a motive?" Cormac asked. Neely wasn't necessarily on the wrong track; at this stage, everyone was an equal suspect. But O'Malley was well known in the area. In Cormac's opinion, people didn't just wake up one day and turn sadistic. There would have been other signs, rumors, complaints, stories. They were still checking into O'Malley's background, but so far no one had reported anything sinister about the man.

"He didn't like that they were taking over his sales territory," Neely said.

"But his reaction was to sell his product to them instead, and it seems that was working out for him."

"It appears Brigid ended up with his rabbit," Neely said. "Fergus."

"More proof that large portions of her story were fiction," Cormac said.

Neely nodded. "Maybe she was setting him up to be the evil man who was hacking off their feet. He had an entire box full of the things." She shivered.

"We will see if the jacket fits him or the blood on it matches George's," Cormac said. He turned his attention to the item situated near the next evidence marker. It was a torn map. He asked Neely to hold it up.

"Glanteenassig Forest Park," she said turning it toward him.

"Maybe it's unrelated to our crime scene," he said. "Or maybe the killer was considering hiding her body here instead?"

Neely nodded and jotted down a note. "Although the park gets a lot of visitors, if he tied her to a tree all the way out there, it could have been ages before we found her."

"Make a note that we need to ask the other three if they've been to the park," Cormac said. "It's possible that Brigid had both the feather and the map on her."

"All of these items, including this map, may be incidental to our crime scene. The wind could have blown them here." Neely gestured around with her notebook, as if she expected a wind to sweep in a few more trinkets.

"And yet we'll have to follow them as leads."

"Chasing swan feathers and ripped maps?"

Neely was cranky this afternoon. He wondered if there was something else going on with her. Perhaps it was the chief superintendent's impending arrival that had her on edge. "If that's what it takes," Cormac said. "Can you hold that map closer?" She did. A portion of the bottom half was torn off. On purpose?

"Have you been?" Neely asked.

Cormac shook his head. "No."

"You're missing out. It's stunning. Mountains, two lakes, hiking trails with giant Sitka spruces."

"We could go now, camp overnight, skip the morning meeting." Cormac wasn't looking forward to the debriefing tomorrow morning. He was going to have to look at a room full of practical and intelligent guards and try to convince them that this killer very much believed, or wanted them to think he believed, in omens. And when he showed them the connection to the long-ago murder mystery in England, and explained that he thought this killer was very much aware of that case, he could only hope he wouldn't be singing his own swan song. And then there was the matter of Cormac's indiscretion. Neither he nor Neely knew exactly how Superintendent McGraw was going to react when he confessed his sins.

Neely's expression turned to one of concern. "Let's go," she said. "You don't want to be late for your mam's funeral, and I have to make sure me dress suit still fits me."

Cormac's family and friends had gathered in a pub while waiting for him (and after, to the pub they would return), so by the time they were gathered on the cliff by the ocean, everyone was relaxed and somewhat happy—exactly the mood his mother had envisioned. This was to be a "celebration of life." Father O'Toole had been decent enough to indulge their spreading of the ashes ceremony, though no doubt he would have preferred them to be at a cemetery. His mam had spoken to the priest at length to get them to this point, and Cormac was grateful for that.

Dimpna was in the crowd, and Cormac was surprised to see

her entire family was with her—Ben, Donnecha, her father and mother, and even Aisling O'Reilly. Aisling stayed by Ben's side. Each of them carried a red rose; everyone present had a red rose, another detail his mam wanted. After they tossed the ashes off the cliff—*Let the wind take them wherever they want to go*—they would then toss the roses into the ocean. *When the last rose disappears, go home. I'm free.*

"Eternal rest grant unto them, O Lord, and let perpetual light shine upon them . . ."

As the priest continued the prayer, Cormac made eye contact with Dimpna. She nodded and gave him a smile. A lump formed in this throat as he nodded back. The priest had finished. He stepped back and nodded to Cormac. He nodded back, then stepped up. "My mam always said I could be a poet. I don't know about that, but given that she wanted nothing more than a remembrance that fitted who she was—which is why we're all standing out here, with an amazing backdrop of the Atlantic Ocean, the mountains in the distance, the heather and gorse by our feet—this was where my mam felt closest to God." He cleared his throat. "In that vein, I've written a little something for you, Mam. I hope you like it." His encounter with Peter Nosh and his juvenile poetry had nearly stopped him from doing this, but he'd pushed that all aside; he wasn't entering any literary contests—this was for his mam. And when he typed out the poem, the spacing resembled a Celtic cross. His mam would have liked that too. In the distance, a figure stood in a black raincoat, hood pulled over his or her head. The skies were currently blue, but in Ireland, that could change at any moment. He supposed the figure was a local wondering why a crowd was gathered on the hilltop. Or was it the killer, taunting Cormac? For a split second, he had an urge to tear across the field and confront the hooded figure. But his mam deserved better.

Father O'Toole gave him a nod. "Whenever you're ready."

Cormac swallowed past the lump in his throat, held up the red rose, and directed his words toward the heavens:

> *She was smart, she was fearless*
> *She was like no other*
> *And she reminded me often*
> *You've only got one mother*
> *She was witty and warm and frighteningly clever*
> *If the sign told her not to, she was sure to push the lever*
> *She loved the outdoors, from the hills to the sea*
> *She never once took it for granted, take it from me*
> *I'll love her forever, as will all of you*
> *But we'll meet her again*
> *In a field kissed with dew*
> *In Eire she was born*
> *And in Eire she did die*
> *But her presence lives on*
> *In the earth and the sky.*
> *She was wild, she was free*
> *She was like no other*
> *And even though I've only got one . . .*
> *God bless, what a mother*

The next morning, the incident room in the Tralee Garda Station was standing room only. Cormac had spent the better part of the morning going over what they had with Neely and Lennon. And given that many had been in the pub with Cormac after his mam's funeral, this was a hungover lot to boot. Cormac had set the stage by using the whiteboard to lay out everything he felt they needed to investigate. He had the photo of Brigid tied to the tree, this one showing her severed hand, and another close-up of the rabbit's foot dangling from her wrist. He had an enlarged photocopy of the note tucked under the pillow of the single made bed in the caravan, which had already been confirmed to be Brigid's bed.

You Made Your Bed

Next, the chalk drawings from the shop in Dingle and the page from the book found lying open underneath the dining table:

WHO PUT BELLA IN THE WITCH ELM?

Peter Nosh's poem and a photo of the clothing he had tried to discard were also on the board. Front and center was the T-shirt with BITCH emblazoned across the front.

A few of George O'Malley's caricatures were included, along with the one of the rabbit being startled off the mule. Next to it, Cormac had added a sticky note: WHY DID SHE LIE? According to George O'Malley, Brigid knew it was his rabbit. (*Hare*, he could hear Dimpna Wilde correct him.) Yet Brigid pretended it was a wild hare and never mentioned a word about George. Had she been hinting that George was the madman chopping off their feet? Had something gone wrong with their little sales deal?

Another category had been added to the board: STILL MISSING. Underneath he wrote: HAND. KNIFE STOLEN FROM WILDE'S CLINIC.

A copy of the cover of the book found open in the caravan, *Murderous Tales and Talismans*, was taped to the board along with Cormac's note: WHOSE BOOK?

The man's jacket with blood that Brigid had brought into the Wilde clinic was out for testing, but he had added a photo along with: WHOSE JACKET?

Next, and most likely to cause a controversy, Cormac had included the hit-and-run death of Chris Henderson, detailing his morning visit to the Tralee Garda Station, the report of the creeper in the black Audi, a photograph of the binoculars, another copy of one of George's caricatures with the binoculars in Vera's hand circled, and single question above it: SAME KILLER? VERA BRANNIGAN AND ROBERT BRANNIGAN—AFFAIR?

Neely cleared her throat and faced the sea of guards in front of them. "We think this killer used the meteor shower and Chris Henderson as distractions to take out his intended target, Brigid Sweeney."

Superintendent McGraw stood in the back of the room, arms folded across his chest. In his sixties, he was a somber man who was pretty much "average" in every way. Average height for an Irishman, although taller than Cormac, average receding hairline, and average disdain for anyone who ranked below him. The only time he broke out a smile was when someone he deemed important was in the room. Today there was no trace of a smile. He seemed to be staring at Cormac's other notation on the whiteboard: THE HAND OF GLORY. Cormac would need indulgence and patience to get through this meeting. He had also jotted down their persons of interest: Peter Nosh, Eve Murray, Alan Flynn, Billy Sheedy, "hikers," George O'Malley, Vera and Robert Brannigan, Emma and Daniel Sweeney. He was going to have to delegate everything related to this case, and he could only hope the guards would take this seriously.

The super had suddenly noticed that Cormac was uncharacteristically quiet. Cormac had meant to fill him in on the situation before the meeting, but McGraw had arrived too late. "Your take?" McGraw said.

Neely cleared her throat. "I do have jurisdiction, and as you know, Cormac recently lost his mother. I've advised him to take bereavement leave."

Cormac was startled. Had she changed her mind about

spilling the beans to their super? McGraw's mouth dropped open.

"We can have a chat about it after the meeting," Cormac said.

"Your take?" McGraw asked again.

Cormac had no choice unless he wanted the entire incident room to hear about his sordid encounter with one of their suspects. "I think we're either looking at a serial killer, or if these are his first two murders, we're looking at a budding serial killer." Cormac said. He paused for the inevitable murmurs his statement caused. He let this settle with the group and added a note to the whiteboard: UNSOLVED CASES IN IRELAND. A groan went around the room. Cormac held up a hand. "If you're thinking this case is going to be overwhelming and all-encompassing, you would not be wrong. This is going to take all of us. It is going to test us. We have not just one but two murders to solve. It stretches credulity to say that these murders are not linked. And given that Chris Henderson came into the station to report a mysterious man creeping on our second victim with binoculars, there is a very straight line we can connect between his report and his death just an hour later. The first thing we must do is identify the driver of a black Audi seen in Camp that morning." He cleared his throat, dreading this next bit. "We do have a confirmation that Vera Brannigan, who owns the Airbnb and the car park where the caravaners are renting a space, has a brother-in-law with a black Audi."

"Is he in the station?" McGraw asked, dropping his arms and looking around.

"We've not yet been able to locate either him, Robert Brannigan, or his sister-in-law, Vera," Cormac said. "They're in the wind."

Neely stepped up. "Actually, we did just get word that they were located in Dublin." She caught Cormac's eye and mouthed:

Sorry. "They're on their way to the station as we speak and are expected by this afternoon."

"Where were they?" Cormac asked.

"Robert insists he was at a two-day training with his phone turned off, and Vera decided to go along for a bit of shopping." Neely hesitated. "Apparently, this decision was made without the knowledge of Lorraine, who is Robert's wife." Murmurs went around the room. Neely held up her hand. "They did take separate cars. Robert rode with a fellow employee in his vehicle, a white Volvo, and Vera took her Nissan. They say the Audi was left in the car park near the Airbnb. I've no proof of an affair."

"We'll be digging into their cell-phone records," Lennon said. "Make sure they were where they said they were."

"They'd better have receipts," McGraw said.

Garda Lennon popped up. "We also just received a statement from Billy Sheedy." He tapped Billy's picture on the whiteboard. "He recalled that a man by the name of Charlie Meade moved the black Audi on Friday morning at the request of Vera Brannigan."

"What?" Cormac nearly shouted it. Neely shook her head at him as if to warn him not to lose the plot altogether. How had they made so much progress without him?

"It's been a busy morning, Inspector," Neely said. "Or we would have already filled you in."

"Why couldn't Vera Brannigan move the car herself?" McGraw asked. Cormac had been wondering the same thing.

"It's a newer model and uses a key fob," Lennon said. "Vera is an older woman and didn't know how to start the car." McGraw's arms folded again. "Mr. Meade said she told him to just leave the key fob in the car. So, according to him, that's what he did."

Cormac was stuck on the fact that Billy Sheedy hadn't mentioned this until just now. Let alone Charlie Meade. "Did Charlie say why he never mentioned this to us?"

"Yes," Lennon said. "He said—I'm quoting—'I tried to tell that detective inspector when he asked me to take the parrot, but uderstandably he was very distracted.'"

Cormac glanced at McGraw. "Possible," Cormac admitted.

"The important bit is that Charlie says Vera told him just to leave the key fob in the car," Lennon said. "She insisted no one would bother it."

"Meaning any yoke could have stolen it?" McGraw sounded outraged.

"Correct," Neely said. "If Robert proves that he was in Dublin, and Vera attests to Billy and Charlie's claim about moving the car, it means anyone could have been driving the Audi."

"I don't understand why you didn't lead with this," McGraw said. "We've got the car that matches both the scene of Henderson's murder and the young woman." He gestured to the board. "Can't see the forest for the trees."

"We can see them, Superintendent. But these 'trees' have a lot of twisted branches. And speaking of trees, we are also going to be canvassing Glanteenassig Forest Park." Cormac tapped the photo of the ripped map he'd included on the board. "And given that our resources are limited, we will work with the park system to inform any campers or hikers to be on the lookout for anything unusual."

"You want them to give us a hand, do ye?" someone in the back chimed in.

Cormac waited until the laughter died down. "I guess that's a good segue, even if it is slightly disrespectful." It was incredibly disrespectful, but this was his team. Humor was often used to tolerate the intolerable. "I believe the killer has Brigid's hand. That he's keeping it as some kind of trophy."

Garda Lennon edged in. "Thank you for the segue." Cormac frowned as Lennon pulled down the screen and began a slideshow. Across the top, his title drew attention: THE HAND OF GLORY.

"I hope you're not planning on going too far astray here, Garda," McGraw said.

Cormac was hoping the same thing. He personally didn't want to focus on the symbolism. He was convinced the killer was using it all as a distraction. But he also didn't want to humiliate Garda Lennon.

"So far, the other residents of the caravan have claimed that Brigid was not known for wearing rings, bracelets, or anything that suggests the killer severed her hand in order to confiscate, say, a diamond ring." Lennon's voice was excited but wobbly. He wasn't used to speaking in front of large crowds. "It was her left hand that was severed, her dominant hand. I'm a lefty myself—"

"Focus," McGraw barked. He then slid Cormac and Neely a look. He knew there had to be a reason Lennon was getting so much airtime, and he already didn't like it.

Lennon swallowed hard and nodded. "As you know, tied to her wrist, almost like it was a replacement, was a rabbit's foot."

"And this George O'Malley is the one who sold Brigid rabbits' feet?" McGraw asked. "The one whose rabbit she brought into the veterinarian clinic?"

"Hare," Cormac said before he could stop himself.

"Excuse me?" McGraw's jaw tightened.

"Sorry, doesn't matter. Apparently it was a hare, not a rabbit."

McGraw looked as if he'd been slapped. "Fucking hell, Inspector," McGraw said, "I don't care if it's fucking Thumper from *Bambi*. What does that distinction have to do with the case?"

Cormac closed his eyes briefly. "Apologies. It has no bearing on anything other than—well, I got it wrong myself, so I just thought—"

"You just thought we all had the same stick up our arse as you, did ya?" This garnered a laugh from the room, which delighted McGraw. God, this was not the morning Cormac had expected. He hadn't even told McGraw the worst bit, and he was being publicly dicked down. Why was this arsehole still alive and his sweet mam was dead? McGraw, he decided then and there, was a small and bitter man.

"The book in the caravan, the one we found open to the page about Bella, had another interesting section: 'The Hand of Glory.' " Lennon flicked the slide until the picture flashed on the screen. It was a black-and-white photo of a bandaged hand. Even though most of the hand was wrapped, the bits you could see made it clear the hand had shriveled long ago. The room went silent. He had their attention. "The Hand of Glory, often being the left, or 'sinister' hand, historically was the dried and pickled hand of a hanged man." He hesitated and took in the confused faces he knew would greet him. "Although Brigid was not hanged, she was tied to the tree with rope. And given that this book was found open in the caravan, I do believe the killer was aware of the Hand of Glory." Lennon flicked to the next slide, a closeup photo of the lucky rabbit's foot. "Some speculate that what eventually replaced this practice, the practice of pickling and drying a human hand as a good-luck talisman, was the lucky rabbit's foot."

Murmurs rippled through the room, and he hadn't even reached the good part yet. "The Hand of Glory was also postulated to be related to another murder case." He had reached the third slide, this one of the obelisk with the chalk message:

WHO PUT BELLA IN THE WITCH ELM?

"It's 1944 in England. True-crime aficionados may be familiar with this case. Four young boys discovered a woman's skeleton in the hollow of a wych elm in Hagley Woods. Her murder was never solved, but soon after her remains were discovered, graffiti began appearing all over town, sometimes using the correct spelling w-y-c-h, sometimes using the incorrect spelling: witch."

The super moved in, clearly interested. "You're saying the book in the caravan was open to that specific page?"

Lennon nodded eagerly. "In 1944, in England, near Hagley Woods—"

"Jaysus, we don't need the entire bedtime story all over again, now do we?" the super chimed in.

Cormac's anger flared. "When they found the skeleton, her left hand was missing," he said, mostly to save Lennon from being the punching bag.

This brought a gasp from the room, and several voices began speaking at once. Neely stood. "Bella's hand was recovered when they searched the crime scene. It was most likely taken off by an animal."

"Our crime scene has not yielded a hand," Cormac said. "But Brigid's was still severed by an animal. This one just happens to be human."

"And it's the same message in chalk that someone wrote on the shop walls in Dingle," Neely added.

"Where are we with the CCTV footage?" Cormac asked.

"There's big news," Lennon said, looking slightly disappointed as if Cormac had jumped to the good part before he could. Lennon inserted a thumb drive into the laptop, and soon CCTV footage of a figure dressed in black, including a black sweatshirt and hoodie, was seen standing in front of a shop, hand raised. Partial writing could be seen on the wall:

WHO PUT

McGraw was the first to state the obvious. "He's short. Or she. Is it a woman?"

"Keep watching," Neely said. Lennon flicked through more photos of the same hooded figure moving down John Street. The last photo showed the figure hurrying toward the harbor. The wind had blown the hood partially back. The image was unmistakable. Cormac found himself open-mouthed and staring at Eve Murray.

CHAPTER 31

McGraw turned to Neely, confusion stamped on his face. Cormac could hardly move or breathe; it felt as if the room were tilting.

She'd seduced him on purpose . . .

She'd seduced him to make damn sure he wasn't on this case. He'd fallen for the oldest trick in the book. He'd been well and truly played. He was the worst kind of fool, the kind that knew better. And now look. One night of drinking in the pubs to honor his mam, and a flood of new evidence had poured in. He felt as if he'd been swept downstream and had no idea where he was or how to get to shore. Rage beat against his chest. What a fool he'd been. What a fucking fool. And here he'd been feeling shame and remorse that he'd allowed himself to be seduced. Wondered if she was having regrets. *Idiot.*

"Who is she?" McGraw said, his voice booming through the room.

"Eve Murray," Sergeant Neely answered. "One of Brigid's caravan mates." She pointed to Eve's photo. "The one with the talking parrot."

"She's a little thing," McGraw said. "She wouldn't have been able to do it alone."

"We're looking at the possibility that all three of them were in on it," Neely said. "Eve Murray, Alan Flynn, and Billy Sheedy."

"None of them have any violent incidents in the past, but there have been accusations of petty theft," Lennon added.

"So it's the three of them or nothing?" McGraw said.

Cormac groaned. "There is a scenario in which Eve Murray could have acted alone," he said. He was forced to tell them his theory. Two friends wander into the woods, to do drugs. Special K. Brigid's dose knocks her out. Eve ties her to the tree with rope that was stashed nearby and cuts off her hand with the cleaver, most likely also stashed nearby.

"A woman could have cut off Brigid's hand?" McGraw asked.

Cormac nodded. "It would have been difficult. Some anatomy knowledge needed. Severing the arteries and breaking the wrist, for example. But possible? Yes. I can only pray that Brigid Sweeney was unconscious for all of it."

Cormac could feel Neely's intense gaze on him. Did she think he'd cover for Eve?

"Have you confronted her with this?" McGraw asked. He was excited now. Like a child abandoning an old toy for a new one, he'd lost complete interest in Brannigan and his Audi.

"We are treating them as persons of interest. We recently obtained their written statements, and then they were released with the knowledge that they cannot leave town," Neely said. "But, no. We have not yet presented Eve Murray with the CCTV evidence."

"Why the hell not?" McGraw asked.

"Because we literally just received this," Neely said. "And as soon as we bring her back in and we present her with the footage, I have no doubt she'll clam up and ask for a solicitor."

"It might be worth putting a man on them," Cormac said. "See where they go, what they do."

"What about their alibis?" McGraw asked.

"They claim to have been out watching the meteor shower and say when they returned, at around half-two in the morning, there was no sign of Brigid, nor were there any signs that a struggle had taken place," Neely answered.

"What else would they say?" McGraw said. "They obviously killed her, and now they're hoping you run around chasing after these symbols and myths."

Cormac felt as if a tablecloth had been yanked from under him. "There are also more threads to pull at, sir. Last year, Brigid was having trouble with some man at the Hidden Valley Caravan Park outside of Dublin—"

The super held up his hand, not for permission to speak, but as a cue to Cormac to shut his gob. "I say we focus on our top suspects first. I don't have to tell you that the sooner we have a confession, the better."

McGraw started to walk out of the room.

"There's one more man we need you to take a look at," Neely said.

McGraw stopped, crossed his arms, waited.

"We received a tip that a man by the name of Brendan Keyes had been seen in various photographs on Brigid Sweeney's Instagram account." She stepped up to the laptop and started a new slideshow. First up was a photo of hikers gathered at the Village Pub, featuring one man in particular. He was a thirty-something with brown hair, smiling, the all-around outdoors type. "This is Brendan Keyes. He was hiking the Dingle Way when he stopped in Camp. Peter Nosh, when interviewed, mentioned a man fitting his description flirting with a woman half his age at the pub. George O'Malley's drawing also portrays a man who I believe is Brendan." She flashed a slide of O'Malley's drawing on the screen, with a red arrow pointing to the sketch; it did, in fact, resemble Brendan Keyes. "A background check came up with a hit; five years ago, he served a sentence for assault." Now it was Neely who had everyone's attention. "Mr. Keyes was supposed to be staying at the Dingle Inn. We had asked him not to leave town until we officially interviewed him. But when we arrived at the inn, he was gone. Nothing left in his room. He did not check out in person, and based on the last time he was seen, he snuck out after dark."

Cormac had been taking notes. He didn't want to step on Barbara Neely's toes, and yes, they needed to find this man to rule him out, but the profile wasn't matching the case. "Did he assault a woman?" Cormac asked.

Neely shook her head. "I believe it was a bar fight." *Not who they were looking for.* "He broke a man's nose."

"The man we're looking for probably chops off noses," Cormac said before he could stop himself.

"Let's find out if Brendan Keyes is still around," the super said. "If he's done a runner, I say let's go after him."

"This isn't a killer who would flee," Cormac said. "This is a killer who *wants* to stick around. He wants to cause panic, and believe me, he's made sure he has a front-row seat."

"He's checked out of the Dingle Inn," Neely said to McGraw. "But I can't be sure he's left town."

"As far as this business about her missing hand," the super said, "for all we know, a wild animal took it."

"I'm sure our state pathologist will inform us that it was a deliberate cut," Cormac said. "And it's too much of a coincidence that they're pointing us to a case where the Hand of Glory was a murder theory, not to mention the rabbit's foot."

The super looked poised to argue when a clerk stuck her head in the room. "Sorry to interrupt," she said. "Detectives? Superintendent McGraw?"

"Yes?" they all answered as one.

"We've found something you're going to want to see."

CHAPTER 32

Dimpna was standing in the courtyard when her mother pulled up and parked next to the new boarding facilities. She exited her vehicle and headed across the field toward her caravan without so much as a backward glance. Dimpna wasn't going to let her get away that easy. "Hey." Her mam kept walking. Dimpna had to run to catch up. "Where have you been?"

Maeve Wilde stopped and slowly turned. She looked stellar in a black pantsuit and turquoise coat. "I had to take your father on an errand."

Dimpna's father was nowhere to be seen. "Where is he?"

"I dropped him off at home; the aide is there, and he needs a nap." Her father was napping a lot these days, and sadly, those were the times everyone around him got the most relief. His moods were becoming more erratic, and he was having more bad days than good lately. Wandering around late at night was the latest development.

"What kind of errand?" Her mother was being cagey, which was nothing new.

Maeve waved her hand as if it didn't matter. "Just taking his mind off his worries." Her mother headed off.

"I don't think you should be sleeping in the caravan."

Dimpna could feel her mother's frustration as she turned

around. She was avoiding her. Was it because of Sean's letters? "Is this about that awful business in Camp?" her mother asked. She flicked something off her black pants—a speck of . . . something. Anyone who didn't know Maeve Wilde might wonder why she was so dressed up this early, but her mam always dressed sharp. In another life, she could have been an actress. She was in her seventies, but well-preserved.

"It *is* about the murders in Camp," Dimpna said. "I'm glad you've been paying attention to the news."

"How do you know I didn't get the information from a client?" Her mother arched an eyebrow. "Perhaps a little birdie whispered in my ear."

Dimpna took a step forward. "Did a little birdie whisper in your ear?"

"I'll never tell. You know I'm like a priest."

"You are nothing like a priest."

"My tarot vows are sacred, and whatever happens in a reading stays in a reading."

"I understand that completely," Dimpna said. "However . . ."

"However?"

"This is an extreme case. This was no ordinary murder, Mam. If you know anything that could help the guards . . . I'm sure they'd appreciate a heads-up."

"My cards said we were entering dark days," Maeve said. "It started with the meteor shower." Dimpna had yet to decide whether or not she believed in tarot cards or psychics. What she did know was that her mam had a way with people, and whether or not Maeve Wilde's predictions came true, people always came back for more.

"Have you seen anyone lurking around? Have you had any new male clients?"

"Have you?" Her mother placed a hand on her hip and tilted her head.

"Mam." Deflecting. Dimpna knew better than to push her

mother too far. She was here to address the letters. "I do not appreciate you hiding my mail."

Her mother dropped her hand, causing her handbag to bounce on her thigh. "How dare you go through my cupboards?"

"Are you joking me? You were hiding my letters."

"Ben's letters."

Dimpna silently counted to three. "Addressed in care of me."

"And why do you think he did that?"

"It's a crime to tamper with someone else's mail."

Her mother sighed as if Dimpna were keeping her from more pressing matters. "You're not someone else; you're my flesh and blood."

"Do not hide my mail from me."

"Don't open them." Maeve wagged her finger at Dimpna. "I can feel them. They're trouble." Dimpna didn't need her mam to tell her that. "Ben is spending a lot of time with his sister," Maeve added. "He's planning her birthday party."

"Half sister." Dimpna felt both pride and a little jealousy that Ben was taking an interest in Aisling O'Reilly. *Planning her birthday party.* She wondered how that was playing with Róisín O'Reilly. Probably not well. Most likely Aisling's mother, Helen O'Reilly, was the one allowing it. "I feel like he's avoiding me," Dimpna said. "He barely spoke to me at Cora O'Brien's memorial. Donnecha too."

"Lads will be lads," Maeve said.

"My son and my brother," Dimpna responded.

"The pair of them get on like a house on fire," Maeve said as she continued across the field. "No doubt sharing war stories about you."

"I mean it. Stay out of my mailbox."

"Tell it to your father. He's your thief."

Dimpna groaned as her mother receded into the distance. She could see it. Her father snatching the mail and bringing it to her mother like a cat dropping mice at her doorstep. Aisling's birthday party . . . was Ben going to invite her? Dimpna's mobile phone pinged. A text. It was from Cormac. **Need to visit an old friend of yours. Want to help smooth the path?**

When Dimpna and Cormac pulled up to Paul Byrne's cottage on the hill, there was no sign of him or his loyal German shepherd, King. She had tried calling him on the ride over, but he wasn't answering the phone.

"He's an avid bird-watcher," Dimpna said, stepping out of Cormac's Toyota. "He could be scouting." Overhead, as if listening in on their conversation, a red-tailed hawk soared. "Or he could be at the group home."

"That's right, he's a do-gooder."

"He is." Dimpna stared at him. "Did you mean it to sound snarky?"

"Binoculars," Cormac said. "I bet he owns a few pair." Something had definitely crawled under his collar. Most likely a combination of grief and two cold-blooded murders. He'd thrown himself into Brigid's case, pushing his mam's death aside. She would have to give him a wide berth; he hadn't even told her why he wanted to speak with Paul.

Sheep wandered along the roadside, flashing blue dye that linked them to their farmer. The layer of fog that had blanketed the peninsula this morning had dissipated, but gray clouds had moved in.

"He's bird-watching?" Cormac said. "How can he see in this?"

"I don't know where he is or what he's doing," Dimpna said.

Cormac lingered near Paul's old red truck. "Does he drive anything else?"

Was he trying to peer into the windows? "He barely drives that," Dimpna said. "He mostly walks."

"Did he ever mention Brigid Sweeney to you?"

"Never," Dimpna said. She did not add that she hadn't spoken to Paul in quite some time. It was becoming apparent that Cormac was considering him as a suspect. Paul didn't have an evil bone in his body. It was maddening to have so much information on this murder she couldn't share, yet be left out of new developments. If she pressed Cormac, he would start to lose trust in her. He was carrying a bag, and she had a feeling that whatever was in there was the reason they were here.

Dimpna headed to the front door and knocked. Then they waited. "Paul," she called out when she grew tired of the silence. "It's Dimpna Wilde."

She didn't expect an answer, but she received one in the form of a bark. She turned to see a blur of tan and black fur racing toward her. It was King, and he was old, but he was still a fierce protector, and they were on his turf.

"Watch out," Cormac yelled, hightailing it toward the street.

"It's okay," Dimpna said, willing herself to stay calm. "King, settle." At the mention of his name, the dog stood still and cocked its head. "Hey, lad, you're alright." He emitted a low growl, his ears flattening. Shit. "Settle," she said.

"King?" It was Paul, calling him from a distance.

The shepherd advanced, then lunged, pinning her against the front door, with one giant paw on either side of her head, and his rancid breath in her face. She was going to have to talk to Paul about his dental care. King was not going to allow her to move, not until his owner had a look at her. Dimpna slowed her breathing and kept her eye contact at a minimum. He was a very old dog, and his instinct to protect his threshold would win out over any other vibes she tried to give out.

"What can I do?" Cormac called. King didn't even turn his big head in Cormac's direction.

"Stay calm," she said. "We're just having a moment."

"I do carry," Cormac said. "A gun," he added, in case she hadn't worked it out.

"Not on your life," Dimpna replied. "We're on his property."

"All bets are off if he sinks his teeth into you," Cormac said.

"Sit," Dimpna said in a low voice. "Good lad." The good lad did not sit.

Paul's voice drew closer, and King's head swiveled toward it. Dimpna was surprised to hear another voice join him—female. She knew that voice. Sheila Maguire. Her once best friend. Dimpna's stomach curled in a familiar jealousy. The old Paul–Dimpna–Sheila love triangle. Were they together? Just good buddies?

"Paul," Dimpna called. "Sheila?"

"Dimp?" Paul answered.

"A little help here," she said.

Soon Paul jogged around the corner. "King," he called. "Heel." The dog immediately obeyed and joined Paul at the hip.

"Thank Christ," Cormac called. Paul's head whipped toward Cormac.

"I see," Paul said, turning back to Dimpna with that intense gaze of his. "I take it this isn't a social call?"

Sheila rounded the corner, coming to an abrupt stop when she saw Dimpna. Her face was flushed as if they'd just had a nurturing hike, which was also evident in her wind-tossed red hair. Sheila Maguire was a force of nature. Jealousy bubbled up in Dimpna, a gut reaction that proved the passage of time had done little to scrub clean their past. The crazy thing was that Dimpna didn't know who she missed more, her once best friend or her unrequited love. *Both.* Time marched on, but it also had a funny way of boomeranging one right back to the beginning. "It doesn't look as if you have time for a social call," Dimpna said.

"This is quite the surprise," Sheila said, narrowing her eyes.

"Sorry to ambush you," Dimpna said, making eye contact with the two of them. "I tried calling."

"No apology necessary," Paul said. "Why don't you come in?" He didn't look at Cormac as he delivered the invitation, but it wasn't necessary.

"Do you mind putting the dog away first?" Cormac asked. "I'm allergic."

A look of amusement flickered on Paul's face, and he tried to share it with Dimpna. She felt wedged in the middle and was sorry she'd come. Paul turned to Sheila. "Would you mind taking King for a walk?"

"Are you joking me?" Sheila said. "We just hiked for ages." No man would ever have to wonder how Sheila Maguire was feeling. It was in her tone, her stance, her gaze. Her red hair, so untamed, so beautifully wild. She still had that stubborn streak in her. Dimpna felt a twinge of longing, wishing she could have their youth back, just for a moment, ideally a single afternoon. They could once more wander the beaches and shriek as they dipped their bodies into the cold ocean, whisper secrets to each other in the dark. If they were still friends, there were so many things Dimpna wanted to know. What did Sheila think about Cormac? Had she ever met Brigid Sweeney? And what in the hell was she doing here at Paul's? Did they hike every day? Was "hike" a euphemism? And why on earth did Dimpna even care?

Paul eyed Cormac. "Are you wanting to speak with me alone, Detective Inspector?"

"Doctor Wilde can stay."

Sheila crossed her arms. "Typical. Come on, King." She turned and headed for her car. King trotted after her. "Need anything from the shops?"

Paul shook his head. "I'm sorted."

She wasn't going home; she was just going to kill time. They were dating. For all Dimpna knew, Sheila was living there. And now Cormac was studying her as if he was trying to suss out how she was feeling. Sheila nearly knocked into her on her way past. She got in her car, slammed the door, and peeled out.

"You'd best come in," Paul said, shifting his gaze to the darkening skies. "The heavens are about to open up."

Paul had the fire going, and he poured himself a whiskey after serving Dimpna and Cormac tea. He did not sit near her on the sofa; instead, he stoked a fire and barely made eye contact with her. She instinctually felt the same teenage angst she'd always felt around Paul. Those awkward edges, the signals from her heart and pulse and nerve endings that all fired at the nearness of him. That gaping wound he seemed to always carry, the one she could never heal but could never ignore. Was he ashamed that Dimpna had found out about him and Sheila this way? *Again.* Perhaps they were one of those couples who thrived under the perfume of secrecy.

"I'll get right to it," Cormac said. He lifted a book out of his satchel and set it on the coffee table. It appeared to be a large book. Dimpna was having difficulty reading the title. It was encased in a plastic evidence bag. Paul set his whiskey on the mantle and approached.

"Is that mine?"

"*Murderous Tales and Talismans,*" Cormac said. "Your name is on the inside flap."

Paul frowned, then turned and headed for a bookshelf near the door. He stood by it for a moment. "Well, I'll be."

"You're not denying it's yours then?"

"Why would I deny it?" Paul rubbed his chin. "Where did you come across it?"

"You didn't know it was missing?"

"I certainly did not."

"When is the last time you saw it?"

"The last time?" He flicked a look Dimpna's way. She remained still.

Cormac leaned forward. "When is the last time you noticed this book?"

"I couldn't say. I like keeping a collection of books, but the only ones I regularly thumb through are books on birds."

"A bird-watcher," Cormac said. "You must own a pair of high-powered binoculars."

"Several."

"Tell me. Are any of those missing as well?"

"Not that I'm aware of."

"Why don't you check? I can wait."

Dimpna was starting to regret that she had come. She'd never seen Cormac behave so rudely with anyone else. He couldn't possibly think Paul had anything to do with Brigid's murder. She wondered what that business about the book was all about.

Paul returned. "My binoculars are all accounted for."

"Tell me about this book," Cormac said.

Paul grabbed his whiskey, and this time he lowered himself next to Dimpna. "I bought it years ago at the bookstore in Dingle. It's a mishmash of old legends, lores, talismans. The title pretty much sums it up."

"Is there any one particular story in this book that you re-member?"

Paul arched an eyebrow. "I've heard of flash mobs for danc-ing, but I've never heard of a flash mob book group." He grinned. It was a grin that used to melt Dimpna on the spot. He was charming, and she couldn't help but like him. Cormac, on the other hand, was not showing his best side, but she sup-posed that was the job of a detective in search of a murderer.

"I'm deadly serious."

Paul sighed and set down his whiskey. "I only skimmed the book, and I only bought it because I think it's rude to browse a bookstore for hours without making a purchase. If you have something to ask me, come out and ask me. I'd tell ya you can borrow the book if you're so interested, but it looks like you beat me to it."

"Did you loan this book to anyone recently?"

"No."

"Have you ever visited the caravan in Camp? The one that entertains hikers and passersby with a talking parrot?"

"Of course he hasn't," Dimpna said.

"Actually, I have," Paul said. "At least three times."

Cormac instantly came to attention. "And what would bring a man of your age over to a caravan of twenty-somethings three times in a row?"

"Cormac," Dimpna said.

"It's Detective Inspector, Doctor Wilde." Cormac fixed her with a look, and a sense of shame mixed with panic washed over her.

"I didn't realize what this was all about," Dimpna said to Paul. "I wouldn't have come."

"I have nothing to hide," Paul said. "I volunteer at a group home, Detective Inspector. There's nothing children love more than a talking parrot and lively twenty-somethings that dote on them. All three outings were sanctioned by the group home, and we have photos of the children with the parrot and the car-avaners."

"With Brigid Sweeney?" Cormac was glued to Paul.

Paul nodded slowly. "And Eve Murray. I believe she owns Bette Davis."

"She does," Dimpna said. "That parrot is driving Niamh mental."

Cormac turned and stared at Dimpna until she shut her gob. It took him another few seconds to turn back to Paul. "On any of these visits, did you bring this book?"

"Absolutely not."

"You sound very emphatic."

"If you've looked through the book, you'll see the content is not appropriate for children." Paul crossed his arms. He was getting defensive. Dimpna had an urge to tell him to drop his arms. *Look casual. Who cares if he thinks you're a psychopath. Offer him a biscuit . . .*

"Sacrifices, cults, murders?" Cormac pressed.

"Detective, I don't know why I seem to have put you on your back foot. What is it you're implying?"

"Can you explain how this book was found inside the caravan of that group you visited three times?"

Dimpna nearly cried out. Was Cormac lying? Was he allowed to lie? Why hadn't he warned her of any of this before he brought her along? Had she just been used?

Paul picked up his whiskey. He rubbed his chin, then shook his head. "No," he said, "I cannot." He finished the drink in one go and slammed it down.

"Have you had any visitors lately? Other than your girlfriend?"

Was it Dimpna's imagination, or did Cormac just stress the word *girlfriend*? She could feel Paul stiffen beside her. "You think someone came in here and stole one book?"

"Do you have any other explanation?"

"Until just now, I didn't realize it wasn't on my shelf." Paul gazed at his bookshelf, then stood up abruptly. "King," he said.

"King?" Cormac asked.

"My dog."

"I've heard of dogs eating homework, but nicking books?"

"Hilarious," Paul said. He turned to Dimpna. "A few days ago, he was sniffing around the bookshelf like a lunatic. I didn't know what to make of it. I thought maybe I'd dropped a tasty morsel on the floor."

"Do you think he was tracking someone's scent?" Dimpna asked.

Paul nodded. "Given that I didn't touch that book, I can't think of any other explanation."

Cormac guffawed. "Now I've heard everything."

Grieving or not, Dimpna was losing her patience for Cormac. "German shepherds have two-hundred and twenty-five *million* scent receptors. It makes them one of the top breeds for detection. They can detect scents over a mile away on land, up to twelve meters below ground, and in twenty-five meters of water."

Cormac held up his hands in surrender. "Noted." His jaw clenched. He turned back to Paul. "On any of these multiple visits to the caravaners, did you ever step inside their caravan?"

"Absolutely not." Paul threw a desperate look to Dimpna. "I won't pretend that I haven't heard what happened to that young woman. But if my book was found in her caravan, I have no idea how it got there."

"Maybe you were sleeping with her," Cormac said casually.

Paul stood. "Get out."

Dimpna wanted the floor to open up and swallow her. If she wasn't Cormac's ride back to town, she would walk out right now.

"Is there any particular reason that question makes you defensive?"

"You don't know me. I don't sleep with women half my age."

"Brigid was an adult. No one is suggesting she wasn't free to sleep with whomever she liked."

"It wasn't me." Paul remained standing.

Cormac took his time getting to his feet. He headed for the door. Dimpna threw Paul an apologetic look as she got to her feet and followed Cormac. How had his book ended up in the caravan? Had Sheila put it there? Sheila wasn't above nicking a book, but why would she plant it in the caravan? Cormac opened the door and turned back. "Would you mind stopping into the Tralee Garda Station sometime today and giving us a sample of your fingerprints and DNA?"

Paul shook his head. "I'm afraid I have somewhere else to be."

"The group home?" Cormac asked.

"I don't believe my schedule is any of your business."

"Dimpna?" Cormac said. "Do you mind waiting in your vehicle?"

Dimpna looked at Paul. "I'm sorry," she said. "I think I've been used." She glared at Cormac, then strode past him, and if it wasn't for the fact that it was Paul's door, she would have slammed it in his face. She stood outside and gazed into the curtain of rain falling sideways in front of her. She was caught between two powerful emotions. Fury at Cormac for using her, and absolute terror over Paul's reactions. Maybe she was wrong. Maybe she didn't know anyone in this town after all. Because the old Dimpna thought she knew Paul. And the old Dimpna would bet her life that just now, Paul Byrne had lied. About what? She didn't know. But she knew him. And he had lied.

CHAPTER 33

The Dingle harbor should have calmed her. Water. Boats. Activity. The colorful wash of shops and pubs and restaurants. The cry of the gulls just before they swooped down. In the distance, she could hear the gentle beat of drums and the lilt of a tin whistle playing through the rain. This was supposed to be a happy place. Look out at the ocean and just forget about your troubles for a moment kind of place. Was this it for her? No more joy? Was she about to lose everything because of Brigid Sweeney? But the most terrifying bit was that the lads had gone quiet. Rage she could handle. But this silence was excruciating.

They made their way across the street and huddled underneath the awning of a pub to stay dry. Billy was smoking cigarette after cigarette, and Alan had bummed a few. Meditating, yoga-pose, try-this-disgusting-smoothie Alan. One of them had to hold it together. "What are we going to do?" Eve missed Bette Davis so much she felt as if she might die. She'd kept her little secret with that inspector, and he'd still taken her beloved parrot away. She should have never listened to Brigid. And it didn't even seem to work. He was definitely still nosing around. They were going to have to do something. Maybe something drastic. But not until she had Bette Davis back.

Which meant she was going to have to talk to that female vet. Stop by in the morning and politely explain that she needed Bette Davis. She *needed* her. The condescending face of that garda rose in front of her. Sergeant Neely. She'd tried to tell her the parrot was her therapy animal. *Ireland doesn't recognize that as law* or whatever shite had come out of her mouth. Who did these people think they were? Brigid was their mate. *Theirs.* Everything they'd done, they'd done together. When shit went sideways, it was called an accident. How many times had Eve warned her—warned all of them—that they had to stop. *Countless.* Yet no one would care about that now. No one was going to look out for her, not Billy, not Alan, *no one.* If she didn't get her parrot back tomorrow, she was going to break into that clinic and take her back. And while she was at it, she'd mess with that stupid animal-control man. Charlie Meade. Hanging around the caravan acting like it was his duty to save Ireland from Hell and Fire. Then taking a defenseless parrot just because some short detective inspector ordered him to? The man had no balls. She'd tell him that to his face. Forget the ocean; the kind of therapy she needed right now was revenge.

See what you've done, Brigid? Do you see?

Eve was tired of people thinking they could run right over her. Everyone underestimated her. Including Brigid. Billy and Alan wouldn't even look at her. What if they turned on her? What if they were plotting against her?

"I say we get the hell out of town," Alan said. "Tonight."

"Not without the dogs," Billy said. "But there are only two vets in Dingle, so they won't be hard to find." He tossed a cigarette butt into the sheet of rain.

"I told you," Alan said. "They're with the female vet. The itty-bitty one."

"What about Bette Davis?" Eve demanded.

"She's all yours," Billy said.

"You're rotten." Eve shoved him. Billy stumbled away from the awning, and when he straightened up, she could see rage swimming in his eyes. *Good.*

He advanced on her.

"Billy," Alan said, "calm down."

Billy poked Eve in the chest. "That bird never shuts up."

"That's funny," Eve said. "Neither do you."

Alan made an attempt at a laugh that got swallowed up by a departing boat horn.

"And listening to her scream—'Help me! Help me! Help me!'" Billy stepped aside as Eve dodged under his armpit. "*Come on,*" he said, grabbing her arm and swinging her back to him. They were all getting wet now. "You know that was Brigid." His voice tightened and went all high-pitched. Was he going to cry?

Eve pulled out of his grip and slapped her hands over her ears. "Stop it."

"Both of you, stop it," Alan said in a low but menacing voice. He gestured to the crowd. Despite the weather, people were going on about their business. There were people walking along the harbor. Fishermen disembarking and tying their boats to the dock. Tourists huddled under brellies and gathered around the busker in the square. Rain be damned; it was still summer, and people wanted to be around people. They were probably hyped up on the murder, feeding off the horror. Eve wanted to get out of there before Brigid's parents showed up. She did not want to see their faces.

"Have you been taking your meds?" This came from Billy, who was back in her face.

"Fuck you."

"No, Eve. I'm serious. You need to keep taking them. Especially now."

She should have never told them about her medical history. Fuck them. "Brigid's dead. She's *dead.* How am I supposed to act?"

"Seriously," Alan said, "if you guys don't lower your voices, I guarantee that one of these busybodies will be calling the guards."

"And say what?" Eve said. "We're talking in loud voices in the rain? It's the harbor, not a fecking library."

Billy found this hysterical and began to laugh. He stopped just as suddenly. "We find the dogs, we find the bird. And we ought to give the vet a reckoning while we're at it."

"No," Eve said. "We get in and out. Like always."

"It isn't like always," Alan scoffed. "It's a business. With animals."

"A vet's clinic is a different horse altogether," Billy agreed.

"A horse of a different color," Eve corrected. *Eejit.*

"No," Billy said. "A horse that colors differently. You know. Like, he's *independent.* Like us."

Alan laughed to himself and rolled his eyes as Billy aimed another cigarette butt like a dart into the wind. Seriously. What had she ever seen in these lads? She couldn't let them ruin her life. Brigid had done enough damage. Why hadn't she just listened for once in her life? Why did Eve have to scream to get anyone to listen?

Billy spat on the ground.

"We should get them tonight," Eve said. "The guards have searched the caravan."

"They're watching us," Alan said. "And we can't ride these bikes around forever." They'd nicked them from a pub. He was right. They couldn't keep drawing attention to themselves.

"We could spray-paint the bikes," Billy said. "Buy some time."

Alan frowned, then shook his head before turning back to Eve. "Who cares if they searched the caravan?"

"Think about it," Eve said. "Our little collection?"

"They won't even know what they're looking at," Billy said. He exhaled smoke through his nose. Eve was always fascinated when he did that. "That's what made Brigid a genius." Billy's eyes welled, and he turned away. Crying made him angry, and he was angry all the time now. Maybe she should cast off on her own, get the hell away from this place. Spain. Italy. America. But then they'd pin it all on her, wouldn't they? Eve, the original sinner. Eve, the one who ruined it for absolutely everyone on the face of the earth. She was convinced that's why her mother had named her that. As if her very existence had ruined her mam's life. You heard something enough, maybe you eventually just became that thing. Slid into it like a second skin. *Sinner, sinner, sinner.* She hated her parents for burdening her with such a name. And Billy was right—Eve was going to have to get Bette Davis to stop screaming for help. It was creepy AF.

"If we're going to be in the rain, we might as well walk," Alan said. They headed up John Street.

"We need to talk about the jacket," Eve said. "Do you think that's going to work?"

"It was a dumb idea in the first place, and I told her so," Alan said. "If she wasn't so stubborn, maybe we wouldn't be in this mess."

"No," Billy said. "If we'd only listened to her earlier, we wouldn't be in this mess."

"Are you back to that?" Alan squared off with him. "She wasn't right in the head. You know that."

"And yet, as Eve so delicately pointed out, she's dead. Who's the crazy one now?"

"We have bigger problems at the moment," Alan said. He was twitchy. The dread in Eve's stomach expanded. "Someone saw us."

Billy whipped around, his eyes red. "What do you mean?"

"That book. The old guy in the cottage that always goes bird-watching at half-six with his dog?" They nodded. Alan gulped. "His dog saw us."

"Are you fucking joking me?" Eve said. "You put the heart in me sideways over a dog?"

"I'm serious," Alan said. "What if he comes around us again, and the dog, like, recognizes our smell?"

"We get the dogs—and the bird—and we get the hell out of here the minute we get our vehicles back," Billy said.

Eve chewed on her lip. "As long as we're spilling the beans . . ." Both lads stared at her. "Did either of you notice that the mute with the donkey really upset Brigid the other day? I mean, like really upset her."

"No," they said in stereo.

"Well, he did. He gave her one of those drawings, and she completely freaked out."

"He drew her as a fat girl," Billy said. "She hated that."

Eve shook her head. "It was more than that. The way she looked at the drawing, then looked at him. It was like he was some kind of creature. She went in the caravan and didn't come out the rest of the morning."

"You sure she wasn't just surfing the crimson wave?" Billy said.

"Don't be gross. I'm telling you—I haven't seen her that upset since Hidden Valley." No one wanted to revisit that nightmare. Brigid had unraveled. And then, strangely, she rallied. Came up with her little plan. She only had herself to blame.

"Brigid's going to haunt us," Billy said. "She's never going to forgive us."

"She did this to herself," Eve said. "I tried to talk some sense into her."

"What's that you're saying about the woman I loved?" Billy was in her face, his fury overwhelming, his breath reeking of cigarette smoke. She'd been wrong. They weren't in this together. It was every man for himself. And she was not going to be anyone's victim.

"Back away from her," Alan said. Billy didn't move. Eve wanted to move. She wanted to kick him in the balls or shove him. At least she wasn't going to back down.

"Maybe we need to do a little stakeout," Alan said. "Find out what the mute is up to."

"No," Eve said. "We can't. They're watching us."

"Maybe they'll stop watching us if we give them someone else to chew on," Alan said. "Where's that drawing now?"

"I suppose it's in the caravan," Eve said. "Unless Brigid threw it out."

Billy clutched his head with both hands, as if afraid it was going to pop off and roll down the harbor, plop into the ocean, and bob away. For a moment, she imagined Billy's severed head floating away. Billy let out a guttural cry. "Damn it, Brigid. Can you see the shit storm you got us into this time?"

CHAPTER 34

Dimpna scratched the four-year-old beagle behind the ears as Vera Brannigan wrung her hands in worry, making her silver charm bracelet jingle. In her fifties, she was a fit woman with cropped hair colored a deep red that bordered on purple. "I don't know what to tell you," Dimpna said. "Molly is perfectly healthy."

"I see," Vera said, sounding none too happy about it. "But she just hasn't been herself since that poor girl was murdered."

"Maybe you haven't been yourself since," Dimpna said.

Vera seemed taken aback. "Excuse me?"

"It's natural," Dimpna said. "Animals pick up on your energy. Given that the caravaners live in your car park, I can't imagine how upsetting this has been for you." It was upsetting for everyone, but Dimpna was trying to be kind.

"Spot-on," Vera said. "It has been quite traumatic." Vera was usually a client of the other vet in town. Why was she really here? Even though Patrick had been available for the visit, and most women preferred handsome, young Patrick, Vera Brannigan had insisted on waiting for Dimpna. "If you have further concerns, I would need to take a look at her medical history."

Vera moved in closer. "Do you think she *saw* something?" She spoke in a hushed whisper.

"I don't know what you mean."

"My brother-in-law had been visiting that caravan," she said. "Sometimes he'd take Molly."

"Okay . . ." Dimpna had no idea where Vera Brannigan was trying to steer this ship.

"What if poor Molly witnessed something untoward and that's why she hasn't been herself?"

Was this plain gossip, or was she trying to throw her brother-in-law under the bus? The mystery of why Vera Brannigan showed up at Dimpna's clinic with a perfectly healthy dog had been solved. Everyone in town seemed to know that Dimpna and the new detective inspector had a friendship. Or had. She hadn't spoken to Cormac since that awful business at Paul's cottage. She was starting to see why her father withdrew from people. They could be maddening. "All I can tell you is that Molly's vitals are great, and she seems very lively and content."

Dimpna set Molly down on the floor and headed for the door. Vera remained by the examination table. "I've read quite a bit about you, Ms. Wilde."

"Doctor Wilde, if you please," Dimpna said.

"My apologies. Men are strange creatures, are they not?"

The comment struck out of nowhere, like a bird thumping into a glass window. "Some certainly challenge us," Dimpna said honestly. "But I could say the same thing about women." *Including the one standing before me.*

"I married Robert's brother, Noel. When he passed away, I thought that was the start of my very lonely race to the end."

"The end?"

"Of my life."

"Losing a spouse is profound," Dimpna said.

"Exactly," Vera said. "Of all people, I knew you'd understand." She stared at Dimpna. "Did you know he was going to do it?"

"What are you on about?" Dimpna felt her heartbeat tick up. This woman had some nerve. To think it was appropriate to walk into her place of business—her *sanctuary*—and prod her about her husband's suicide. The answer was no. Dimpna had been absolutely blindsided by Niall's death. And all the secrets that came with it.

"I'm very sorry for your loss," Dimpna said. "But my personal life is off-limits."

"I'm not *blaming* you," Vera said. "I'm on your side."

"I didn't realize we needed sides."

"Of course, we need sides," Vera said. "Venus or Mars." Molly whined. Dimpna knew how she felt. "Robert has taken me completely by surprise," Vera continued. "So now . . . now I'm torn. I'm due to talk to the guards. I don't want him to think I'm not loyal. And to be honest—I know this sounds crazy—but somehow he knows everywhere I go and who I speak with, and what I do. I don't know if he has spies or has hacked into me mobile phone and traces my movements. And it's not a crime to be perverted, or shall we say 'taken in,' by a siren."

"Brigid Sweeney wasn't a siren. She was a young woman with her entire life ahead of her." Dimpna was sick of this. It wasn't a crime to be beautiful. Nor should it be a currency.

Vera crossed her arms. "I saw her every day. I know what she was like."

"You're lucky to have a sweet and healthy dog like Molly." Dimpna glanced at the clock on the wall. "I am afraid that's all the time we have for today." She sounded like a psychiatrist trying to kick out a patient at the end of a session.

"That detective inspector—the handsome one I've seen you with—will be speaking with my brother-in-law."

"I don't know anything about that," Dimpna said. "I keep very busy here."

"It's Robert's black Audi, not mine. And I had no idea someone would steal that car. I hate those key fobs, so I asked that man from ISPCA to leave it in the car."

"The man from ISPCA?" Dimpna asked. "You mean Charlie Meade?" Dimpna hoped that Vera hadn't gotten Charlie in over his head.

Vera nodded. "I do hope I didn't get him in trouble," she said as if reading Dimpna's mind. "He was very kind to help me out." She shook her head. "Honestly, anyone could have stolen it."

Dimpna wanted to lecture her that it was ludicrous to leave the key in her vehicle, but she'd done it herself many times. Dimpna stood near the open door. "You can trust Inspector O'Brien. Just tell him the truth."

"I see," Vera said. "I'm bothering you." And yet she still made no move for the door. "But I really am in a difficult spot. You see, if Robert is innocent, I can't be the one to bring suspicion on him. I don't have anyone else in my life. But if he's guilty . . . I couldn't in good conscience keep quiet."

Molly, who was more than ready to go, lifted her head and howled.

"What exactly would you like me to do?"

"There's no harm in looking at a pretty girl, or even harmless flirting, I suppose, but when one starts to *deny* it, then I worry there may be a larger problem." Vera removed a manila envelope and set it on the exam table. "Now," she said, "I should be going." She swooped up Molly and exited.

Dimpna shook her head, nearly wanting to yell down the hall at Niamh, instruct her to charge Vera Brannigan double. She reached for the envelope; then, due to the growing sense of dread in her belly, she put on a fresh pair of medical gloves and opened the envelope. She was surprised to see photos slide out. They were all of Brigid Sweeney, taken at a distance. Brigid caught mid-twirl, her dress flying up and flashing toned legs. A close-up of Brigid's cleavage. A close-up of her face, lingering on her mouth, open in laughter. The last two were the least intrusive but the most damning: Robert Brannigan holding a giant pair of binoculars and standing next to his black Audi.

Cormac and Neely emerged from the Dingle Garda Station just as Dimpna was heading for the entrance. The sun was ablaze, and Dimpna wished she'd remembered to fetch her sunglasses. Cormac was carrying a cardboard box, and the pair wore grim expressions. "Hey," Cormac said.

"Are you moving offices?" Dimpna asked.

"Something like that," Cormac said. He nodded toward his Toyota. "Let me drop this in me car."

"Can I help you with something?" Sergeant Neely said. She eyed the envelope in Dimpna's hand.

"I came to see both of you." Dimpna said.

Cormac returned, his hands shoved in his pockets. Something had gone down. Dimpna had obviously interrupted something.

"Listen," Cormac said, "I owe you an apology. I got a little carried away with Paul Byrne." He cleared his throat. "It definitely won't happen again. I'm—"

"Taking some bereavement time," Neely said.

Dimpna knew immediately there was more to the story. Cormac O'Brien wasn't the type to take some time off. Not with a murder probe like this.

Dimpna held out a manila envelope. "I guess this is just for you then."

"I'm sure she'd let me have a peek," Cormac said. He took the envelope and handed it to Neely. Neely looked to Dimpna.

"Vera Brannigan came into my clinic today," Dimpna said. "I didn't realize it was meant for you until I looked inside."

"Why would she come to you?" Neely asked.

Dimpna swallowed. "She thinks Robert is somehow able to see where she goes and who she talks to. She brought her dog, Molly, in to see me, but the dog was perfectly healthy. She started talking about Brigid and how she was a siren, and what strange creatures men could be. Anyway, she finally said she didn't want Robert to think she turned him in, but that if he was guilty, she couldn't not do something."

Neely had already opened the envelope and was looking at the photos. Cormac looked over her shoulder. "Looks like we caught our pervert," he said. "And possibly her killer."

Dimpna headed for the harbor. She had wanted to talk to Cormac alone, find out exactly what was going on, but after handing over the envelope, Neely seemed eager to keep him there. It's not like he owed her any explanation. But she had been rather involved—she'd helped both of them with this case—but, of course, the street only went one way. She needed to have a walkabout, clear her head. Ben had texted her that they were having a stroll, and although he didn't quite invite her, she was going to invite herself. Gulls circled and cried overhead, and in the distance, a boat horn sounded. Shoppers were out on John Street, and a one-man band was set up near the Fungie the dolphin statue, playing drums, the squeeze-box, and a tin whistle simultaneously as a crowd gathered around to cheer him on. She headed for the boats, and it didn't take long to spot Ben, Donnecha, and Aisling O'Reilly strolling along the harbor path. They were easily identifiable, Ben's sand-colored hair blowing in the wind, Donnecha's skinny legs.

Aisling carried a big ice cream cone in her hand, and the

wee dote was sporting an equally large grin. Sean O'Reilly's daughter was cute as a button, and now partly because of Dimpna, she was without her father. An unwelcome image of Sean's letters to Ben floated in front of her. Although she didn't open them, she also hadn't handed them over. She was no better than her mam, keeping secrets from Ben. It was a hard pill to swallow, but she still couldn't bring herself to do it. Sean O'Reilly was a master at playing games. Her heart tugged for Aisling. It made her heart swell with pride that Ben was stepping up. But he was also leaving her out, and she was going to have to work harder to keep him in her orbit.

Ben spotted her first, but his expression was unreadable. "You're out in the wild," he joked as they drew closer. "Have you run away from your veterinarian practice?" She threw her arms around him, then reached up to ruffle his hair and kissed him on both cheeks as he groaned. Aisling let out a giggle.

"Hello, petal," Dimpna said to Aisling. "Are my lads treating you well?" She was going to make every effort to love the girl Ben so obviously adored. Maybe she would be the first O'Reilly who would break the evil mold.

Aisling looked up with a shy smile. "Your lads?" she asked, casting a glance at Ben and then Donnecha.

"My son," Dimpna said looping an arm around Ben. "And me brother," she said, roping Donnecha in with the other arm.

Her brother audibly groaned. "Don't let her fool you," he said. "I've always been the thorn in the family rose."

"You have?" Aisling stopped licking her ice cream and considered Donnecha. The lads shrugged out of Dimpna's embrace. "But roses have many thorns."

"Amen," Ben said.

Dimpna patted Aisling on the head; her face was too sticky with ice cream to kiss.

"You're very affectionate today," Donnecha said.

"I'm always affectionate," Dimpna said. "You should visit more often."

"How are Eamon and Maeve?" Ben asked. At their request, he called his grandparents by their names.

"Busier than me, it seems," Dimpna said. "I've barely seen them."

"You don't know about Eamon's new friend then?" Ben said. His voice had a teasing note to it, and there was a glint in her son's eye.

"Who is his new friend?" Dimpna asked. Why was everyone in her family so secretive? Was there something in their DNA? A shady link?

"I think I'll let him introduce her himself," Ben said.

"Definitely," Donnecha chimed in. "She's a gas."

"She?" Dimpna sputtered. Did her father have a girlfriend? In what world did that make sense? "Does Mam know?" Her father was suffering from a disease and aging rapidly, and he had time to fall in love? Her parents had stayed married but had been estranged for a decade. It wouldn't be wrong for him to want to find a companion—but now? And was her mother really as progressive as she purported herself to be? After all, if she was seeing other men, she was certainly keeping a low profile, and that was difficult to do in Dingle.

"Oh, she knows," Ben said. "I think she encouraged it."

"Is it me?" Aisling asked. "Am I his new friend?" Ben picked his half sister up and swung her around.

"You're part of our family now, lass," he said. Aisling squealed with joy. Dimpna was dying, just dying to ask how Róisín O'Reilly was dealing with everything. Was she being horrid to Ben?

"She's going to toss her ice cream if you keep that up," Donnecha said. For once, Dimpna agreed with her brother.

"We'd better hurry," Donnecha said. "We're going to be late."

Once again, Dimpna was in the dark. Jealousy gave her a horse kick to the stomach. "Late for what?"

"Aisling's participating in an event at the group home," Ben said. He leaned in. "Her mam thought volunteering with children less fortunate would do her a world of good." Dimpna agreed, and although Aisling was from a wealthy and connected family, she'd also lost a father and a grandfather, so she needed a little boost.

"That's wonderful," Dimpna said, reaching down to touch Aisling's shoulder.

"Are you still mad at my da?" Aisling asked her, looking up at her with big eyes.

Dimpna felt her stomach clench. "I'm not mad at anyone, luv." Dimpna felt the lie rolling around inside her, poisoning her. Then again, she wasn't *mad*. She was livid. Just thinking of Sean filled her with rage.

Ben took Aisling's hand. "We should get going. We don't want to miss the presentation, do we?"

"Presentation?" Dimpna asked. "Is Paul presenting?"

"Someone from the Irish Society for Prevention of Cruelty to Animals," Ben said.

"Charlie Meade?" Dimpna asked.

Ben frowned. "I don't have a clue."

"What time is the presentation?" Maybe Dimpna would help Cupid out. Let Niamh take a long lunch.

"Starts in twenty minutes, which is why we have to get our legs under us," Ben said.

Dimpna nodded. "Save a seat for Niamh." *Tell him about the letters.* "Can you stop by the clinic later? Alone?"

"Why?" Ben was already suspicious.

"Does a mother need a reason to see her son?"

He glanced at Aisling. "We have a party to plan for."

"It's my birthday," Aisling said. "In five days."

"Happy birthday, pet," Dimpna said. She glanced at Donnecha. "I'm sure my brother wouldn't mind some time alone; you could even spend the night."

Donnecha looked away. Uh-oh. Now what? "Donnecha lives alone," Aisling said.

Dimpna smiled. "Donnecha and Ben live together, pet."

"No, silly," Aisling said. "Ben lives with me."

"With you?" She looked at Ben with a grin, expecting it to be a joke. One look at Ben's face, and she knew it was not.

"In my daddy's room." Aisling flashed a bright smile. "It was Granny's idea."

"Was it now?" She could not believe what she was hearing. She wasn't going to cry. Not in front of Aisling. "Ben. We need to have a chat."

"Mam," Ben said, his tone a warning. "Not here. Not now."

The letters from Sean flashed in front of her once again. *He knew.* Sean knew Ben was living at his home, and yet he sent the letters to Dimpna. In fact, that's *why* he sent them to her. He probably also knew that Ben had kept Dimpna in the dark and he was rubbing her nose in it. She thought for sure she was done with the O'Reillys forever. She'd even withdrawn as their veterinarian, which came at a financial cost. Was she doomed to be betrayed by those she loved the most? She would not lose her son to that family. She would not. "Benjamin."

Ben held his hand up. "Another time, Mam. We don't want to be late for the presentation." He sounded calm. Which made her feel untethered. Didn't he realize this was like sticking a knife in her back? Ben chose *her*. He did the right thing and chose her. Now he was supposed to stay on her side of the fence.

"Does he know?" she asked. "Does *he* know you're living there?"

Ben stared at her, a look of disappointment stamped on his handsome face. Was he disappointed in her? He took Aisling's hand and walked away from her. Dimpna soon realized her hands were clenched into fists; her jaw was locked. She wanted to run after him. She wanted to hold his hand. She wanted to be the one he was worried about. She found herself yelling something after him she never thought she'd say in a million years. "You've only got one mother!"

Donnecha lingered for a moment. "Don't do this to yourself."

"Don't do what?"

"He's in the past, Dimp. He's never going to hurt you again."

"Funny," Dimpna said, "because it feels like he's doing it right now."

"Ben just wants to get to know his half sister."

"You're an expert on my son now, are you?"

"Jesus, Dimp. Don't kill the messenger."

Dimpna clenched her fist. She had never imaged there would be a day when Donnecha was the voice of reason. "I can't stand the thought of him living under their roof."

"You can't blame Ben," Donnecha said. "He spent his entire life in the dark about his father."

"I had no choice."

"I'm not saying he should have known about Sean. But now he does. And he wants a relationship with his half sister."

Dimpna knew he was right, but she couldn't help how she felt. She should be free of this. Free of her secret, free of Sean, free of the entire O'Reilly clan. But how could she if her son was living with the madman's family? In Sean's room? Ben wasn't after their money, was he? Their money was tainted. She glared at Donnecha. "You should have told me."

Donnecha shook his head. "I'm not a middleman. He's an adult. You're an adult. You want to know what's going on his life? Ask him."

"You think I haven't?"

"You can't blame this on me."

"Life's so simple for you, isn't it?"

"It can be." He looked as if he wanted to touch her, then thought better of it. "You should try it sometime." In the distance, Ben and Aisling had stopped. They were waiting for Donnecha to catch up. "I'll talk to him." With that, Donnecha turned and walked away. A gull cried overhead. She wished she was riding on the gull's back, circling in the wind. She would steer him out over the ocean, and fly far, far away from here. Far, far away from home.

CHAPTER 35

"I know you're at lunch . . ." It was Niamh; she had just phoned Dimpna, and she sounded worried.

Dimpna was walking back to the clinic, trying to clear her mind of the walkabout that was supposed to have cleared her mind. Trying to rid her body of the anger coursing through it. Writing hateful letters to Sean O'Reilly in her mind. "I'm on my way back. In fact, there's a little event I thought you might like to attend."

"An event?" Niamh perked up.

"Charlie Meade is giving a talk at the group home. I thought you might like to pop in."

"Oh," Niamh said. "I'd love to go, but it's jammers here."

"I'm almost there. I can hold down the ark for a few hours. I insist you go." It was always jammers at the clinic.

"Paul Byrne is here."

"Paul?" She hadn't heard from him since the drop-in with Cormac. She doubted he was there for a social call. "Is it King?"

"Spot-on. His paw was caught in a trap. He's in with Patrick now, but I assumed you'd want to be here."

"Tell Paul I'm on my way."

* * *

The first thing Dimpna noticed was that both of Paul Byrne's hands were bandaged. He made eye contact with Dimpna as she rushed in. He had that haunted look of someone waiting to hear how a loved one will fare. "I will do everything I can," she said to him as she ran past. He nodded, his eyes filling with tears. She couldn't think of that now.

"Exam Room 2," Niamh said.

"Go to the event," Dimpna called as she went past. "I've got this."

Patrick didn't look up as Dimpna entered. King lay on the examination table, and Patrick was stroking King's head.

"Poor love," Dimpna said. "Poor, poor love."

"His leg is bruised, swollen, and cut," Patrick said. "But Mr. Byrne got the trap off within minutes of King stepping in it." He paused. "But he's lost a few teeth as well."

"Teeth?"

"He tried to bite the trap off himself."

Dimpna swallowed and found tears coming to her eyes. Leg-hold traps were illegal and barbaric. Chris Henderson had been on a rampage against the continued use of them by some to catch fox going after chickens. "Thank God Paul was right there," Dimpna said.

"I think he needs a doctor himself, but he refused to go." That's why his hands were bandaged, from prying open the trap. Dimpna knew that Paul Byrne would have given his life for King and vice versa. The bond was just as strong as any love bond a human could form. Those who weren't animal lovers would never understand.

"Did you give King meds?"

Patrick nodded. "Antibiotics and painkillers. He's all bandaged. But it's going to be a challenge getting him to keep his weight off the foot for a while."

"The owner is a very old friend of mine."

"Niamh said as much."

"I'm only saying it so you'll know why I'm doing what I'm about to do."

"Okay." Patrick waited.

"I'm assuming King could go home right now?"

Patrick nodded. "I think this is all we can do for him."

"I'm going to tell Paul that we need to keep King overnight, although I'll make sure he's not charged."

"Okay." Patrick waited once more.

"He won't go the doctor if we release King. He'd take him home and fuss over him all night." Dimpna would do the same. But Paul needed those cuts on his hands looked after.

"Got it." He glanced at the vents.

"Sound only flows this way. What's on your mind?"

"Nothing. No harm done. It's just . . . it's not like you to be dishonest with a client."

He was right. She was always blunt with clients. "Paul isn't a client. He's family." And as history would attest, it was family she lied to. "I need to make a call first. Can you stay out of the waiting room until I speak with Paul?"

"I can go to the kennels for a bit," he said.

"Thank you."

Patrick nodded, although his forehead remained creased. The minute he was gone, Dimpna took out her mobile phone. She called the one number she thought she'd never use again.

Dimpna was still arguing with Paul when Sheila Maguire walked into the clinic. Paul was trying to talk Dimpna into letting him see King, even though Dimpna had sworn on her life that he was going to be fine. Paul had still refused to let Dimpna see his hands. She could only imagine his reaction when he found out that she'd called in reinforcements. And here she was, standing in front of Paul, then kneeling in front of him, speaking in a low, soothing voice, a voice filled with love. Paul stiffened at first, and then at Sheila's touch and voice, he started to sob. Dimpna felt it in her solar plexus but stood aside.

"King is going to be just fine," she told Sheila. "But Paul needs to see a doctor."

"I don't need you managing me," Paul said.

"Yes, you do," Sheila said.

Paul shook his head. "Now the two of you are in agreement?"

"I'd rather you mad than dead," Dimpna said cheerfully.

"We're going straightaway," Sheila said. "Can he leave his truck parked here for a spell?"

"Absolutely," Dimpna said. She touched Paul's shoulder. "Is the trap in the truck?"

He nodded. He still couldn't speak. "I'm going to call the guards and report this. Where was the trap?" Dimpna asked.

He looked up, his face red, his eyes angry and alert. "It was a few meters from my cottage," he said. "Any chance your lover set the trap?"

"My lover?"

"That detective inspector."

She took a step back, shaking her head. "He's not my lover. And no. Not a chance."

"He isn't exactly an animal lover," Sheila said.

"He has a phobia," Dimpna said. "But he's not a monster."

How could the divide be so great between them? She knew these two like the back of her hand. They were a part of her. They were all a part of Dingle. And yet it was as if they were all caught in steel traps, unable to move.

"Just promise me you'll report this to Sergeant Neely. Not him."

"Not a bother," Dimpna said. "But she won't keep it from him." Especially if they thought this had anything to do with the murder.

"Why would Neely bother an inspector with a report of an animal trap?" Sheila asked.

Dimpna hesitated. She didn't want to lie again. She'd had enough lying. "Because this incident could be related to the recent murders."

Paul's head shot up. "Explain."

"You walk around your property as much as King. You could have stepped in it."

"You're saying the trap was purposefully set to catch me?"

"I don't know," Dimpna said. "But what if the person who set the trap is the same person who stole your book?"

Paul dropped his mouth open, then shook his head. "Impossible," he said.

"How do you know?"

"Because I told that inspector a little white lie."

She knew it. She could always tell when Paul Byrne was lying. She felt a strange flush of satisfaction. She caught Sheila's gaze and prayed Sheila wasn't picking up on Dimpna's glee. "What lie?" She kept her voice light; she had to know.

"I know who stole my book," Paul said. "And if she found a way to set that trap, we've got even bigger problems in Dingle."

"Seriously," Sheila said off Dimpna's perplexed look. "We're going to need an exorcist."

Paul made eye contact with Dimpna. "The book thief couldn't have set the trap," he said. "Because the one who stole my book is Brigid Sweeney."

Cormac stood in Neely's office, staring at his phone with a somber expression. He'd just hung up from a call.

"What is it?" Neely asked. "Wait. Do I want to know?"

"That was Dimpna. Paul Byrne just told her that it was Brigid Sweeney who stole his book."

"How does he know that?"

"Apparently, he saw her near his property with a book in her hand. Didn't put two and two together until after my little visit."

"And now he suddenly decided to tell the truth?" Neely frowned. "If Brigid stole the book, what does that do to our theory that the killer used the Bella case as his inspiration?"

"It means . . . he or she was inspired *after* Brigid took that book to the caravan."

"Eve, Alan, or Billy then, is it?"

Cormac nodded. "They definitely had access to it."

"Should we bring Paul Byrne in for questioning?"

"It will have to wait. Someone set an illegal animal trap on his property. Paul and his dog are injured."

"Paul's a good man. Former detective."

"I'm aware."

"A bit like you."

"Me? We're nothing alike."

"Paul didn't always follow the rules. A rogue cowboy. Just like you."

"I made a colossal mistake. Wouldn't call myself a cowboy."

"Misfit then. Will that do?" Before Cormac could reply, Neely held up a finger. She pressed a button on her phone. "Heya, Ann. Can you get me a report on petty thefts—trespassers, any kind of activity like that in Dingle and Camp in the past month? Thanks a million." She hung up and leaned back in her chair.

Cormac knew she wanted him to sit, but he was too hyper. McGraw had lost the plot when Cormac had confessed to having sex with Eve Murray before this whole mess began. Cormac and Neely had delivered the confession together, and the next hour had been excruciating. McGraw had yelled, stomped, and even lobbed a stapler at Cormac's head. Luckily, Cormac had ducked, and instead it hit a light switch behind him, plunging them into darkness. Then McGraw stormed out, but not before announcing that the official story would be that Cormac was off the case on bereavement leave. Unofficially, he was on team Neely or team catch this bastard. Cormac brought his thoughts back to the present moment and turned to Neely. "What are you thinking?"

"I'm thinking the four of them were acting the maggot. Stealing bits here and there. Maybe they messed with the wrong household."

Neely's phone rang, making them both jump.

"Doctor Helen Fielding, the state pathologist, is on the line for you, Sergeant," Ann said.

"Put her through." Neely nodded for Cormac to stay as she took the call in her office and put it on speaker.

"I have initial findings for the Brigid Sweeney case," she said straightaway.

"Fantastic," Neely said. Cormac took the chair across from her as she grabbed a notebook and biro and slid it over to him. "I have Inspector O'Brien here as well, and we're ready."

"This is a grim case you've been saddled with," Dr. Fielding said. "We need this perp off the street now."

"We're putting everyone we have on it," Neely said. "Hoping your findings can help steer us in the right direction."

"Ketamine was found in Brigid's system. She has no defensive wounds anywhere on her. She has some bruises, but they're older and fading, so I don't believe they were a result of her murder. I believe she was unconscious from the drug when she was tied to the tree, and all indications point to her hand being purposefully severed. Exsanguination is the official cause of death."

Cormac scribbled a note and turned it around for Neely to read.

"Can you tell us anything about the killer from the severing of her hand?"

There was a pause. "Although there could be exceptions, it's most likely the killer is male. It was a clean job, although it took three strikes. I believe you're either looking at someone with a background in a butcher's shop or at the least a little anatomy background. Medical knowledge, that type of person." She sighed. "Then again, anyone with determination and YouTube could probably figure it out."

"YouTube aside, why do you think it's a male with that kind of background?" Cormac asked.

"It's not easy to cut through the radial artery. And doing so while the victim was still alive? I shudder to think of who this killer is, and I know it's not my job to say so, but we're all sending our prayers that you'll find him sooner rather than later."

Even though it was still horrific, there was some small comfort in knowing she wasn't awake for the barbaric end. "How long would you say it took for her to die?"

"She could have bled to death within fifteen minutes. I'd put the time of death between midnight and three in the morning. The wee hours, there's no doubt about that. There were no objects in her mouth, no signs of a struggle, and no indication of sexual assault."

"Can you tell us anything about the murder weapon?" Cormac asked.

"Sharp blade. A cleaver is my best guess. But, as I mentioned, it wasn't a precise cut. Looks as if it took at least three attempts."

"How could someone have drugged her with ketamine without a struggle?" Cormac had his guesses, but he wanted an expert's opinion.

"We found an injection mark. Either she was a willing participant, or she was taken by surprise and injected quickly enough that she didn't struggle."

"Ketamine is used in veterinarian practices, is it not?" Neely asked.

Cormac found his hands tightening into fists. This again. He thought they were past it.

"Absolutely." There was a pause. "Is there a reason you ask?"

"The caravaners have two large dogs and a parrot," Cormac said before Neely said anything else.

"That doesn't give them access to ketamine," Fielding said.

"A local veterinarian found the body," Neely said.

"Is she a suspect?" Fielding asked.

"No," Cormac said. He seared Barbara with a look, and although her eyebrow shot up, she didn't say anything further. "But the victim visited the veterinarian clinic before she passed, and the reason for her visit was a bit strange, to say the least, so we were wondering if she was there to distract the veterinarian while one of the others in the group stole their ketamine."

"Was there a theft of ketamine reported by this local vet?" Dr. Fielding asked. "Who is this vet?" They heard the rustling of papers. "Is it Doctor Dimpna Wilde who found the body?"

Cormac squeezed his eyes shut. What was Neely trying to accomplish here? "That's her," Cormac said. "But no. We have no reports about any break-ins at her clinic." Christ, that better be the end of it. Neely couldn't really suspect Dimpna, could she? Neely took the pad and furiously scribbled something on it: *Medical knowledge. Last to see victim. Access to ketamine.*

Cormac added his own note: *Cop on!*

Neely tore the note out, balled it up, and lobbed it at Cormac's head. He didn't bother to duck, and it bounced off his forehead and onto the floor.

"It's pretty easy to score ketamine these days," Fielding said. "My guess is they bought it from a dealer. That would attract a lot less attention than breaking into a veterinarian clinic."

Cormac turned to Neely. "Let's round up the local dealers."

"Consider it done," Neely said.

"Is there anything else, Doctor?" Cormac asked.

"Her dress did not have any pockets, and we did not find any jewelry on her," Dr. Fielding said.

Cormac nodded, even though she couldn't see him. His instincts had been spot-on. The book had been a red herring. The killer must have noticed it while he was in the caravan. Perhaps when he was waiting for Brigid? Did he read about Bella and the wych elm and plan the murder accordingly? Then he staged the book, wanting them to find it. Wanting hysteria to grow, and hoping the guards would chase their own tails trying to connect the murders of long ago with the one today.

"Are you ready for the biggest news?" Fielding asked.

"Yes," Neely and Cormac said in unison.

"The jacket we received, the one with blood on it . . ."

"Yes," Cormac said. "Is it rabbit blood?"

"Hare's blood," Neely corrected. Cormac retrieved the balled-up paper and tossed it back at her. She moved out of the way, and it hit the dirty window behind her.

"No," Dr. Fielding said. "It's human."

"Human?" Cormac and Neely leaned forward.

"We wouldn't have known whose blood it is, except that from the parallel investigation, we already had plenty of samples." Neely and Cormac stared at each other as they listened. He had no idea where she was going with this. "The blood on the jacket matches our blood samples for Chris Henderson."

"You're joking me," Cormac said.

"This is why I like to meet in person, Detective. If you could see my face right now, you would clearly see I am not joking." Cormac was saving time where he could, and he always hated visiting morgues. With his own mam recently deceased, he was happy to avoid it altogether, and she had agreed to a phone call.

"He knows that," Neely said. "We're just a bit in shock."

"We were too. I ran the test twice."

"Is there any way of determining *when* the blood got on the jacket?" Cormac asked.

"I can get close," Fielding said. "It must have been shortly after the accident." They heard the rustling of papers. "Do you have your crime-scene photos handy?"

"I can pull them up," Neely said. She held up a finger and ran out of the room.

"She'll be back in a minute with a laptop," Cormac said. "How's your day going other than this?"

Dr. Fielding laughed. "It's a typical day, Inspector. Living the dream."

Neely returned. "I'm back. Just give me a second to pull them up." Neely tapped on the keyboard, and soon the photo of Chris Henderson's murder scene filled the screen. "Got them."

"Look at the fifth picture, the one showing the body from a bit of a distance."

Neely clicked until she reached the photo and then enlarged it. "We're looking at it."

"Can you see what appears to be a smear in the blood?" Fielding asked. Toward the upper left. It didn't take long to see it. There was a path through the blood as if something had been dragged over it. A jacket. Who would do that?

"This looks like someone deliberately dragged the jacket through the blood," Cormac said. It sounded like their killer alright. *Psychopath.* He didn't use the term lightly. But why? And it was Brigid who wore the bloody jacket into the clinic. Did that mean she was working with the killer at one point? Was it Billy or Alan? Did the foursome accidentally kill Chris Henderson, and were they trying to pin it on someone else? Perhaps Brigid felt remorse, and it was her way of confessing?

Cormac jotted down a note and showed it to Neely. *Alan's truck.*

Neely nodded, then jotted down a note of her own to Garda Lennon and hurried out to take it to him.

"We found bits of dirt and asphalt in the jacket as well, and it's not a typical pattern of spatter," Fielding said. "So, yes, I believe the jacket was smeared through the blood on the road sometime after Chris Henderson was struck."

"It had to have been before the guards arrived and cordoned off the scene," Neely said.

Cormac nodded. It could mean the four of them were involved in the murder. But why would Brigid smear the jacket through blood? It wasn't her jacket. Whose was it? Chris Henderson's? "Even though I don't know what any of this means yet, I can't thank you enough," Cormac asked. "Could you make out the wording on the jacket?"

"We scrubbed until we could almost read them," Fielding said. "Our best guess: Hidden Valley."

Shortly after the call with Dr. Fielding, Neely called the team back into the incident room. McGraw had returned to Dublin for a briefing, so Cormac attended but kept to the back of the room. They were eager to share the recent developments and strategize what it meant for the case. Neely assigned a few guards to check into Hidden Valley Caravan Park and look into any problems that may have been reported there going back to last year. Another guard was assigned to speak with Paul Byrne about the trap on his property and the stolen book. Cormac wanted them to get their hands on Alan's truck pronto. If there was any evidence that it had struck Chris Henderson, he would arrest them. Garda Lennon was way ahead of him.

"I just phoned the mechanic, and he said that Alan's truck had no signs of striking anyone. There are no splatters of blood, no weapons in the car . . . nothing that sets off any alarm bells per se."

"Per se?"

"He did find a set of chains in the bed of the truck."

"The dog chains." That was something. But was it enough? Cormac wanted to slap handcuffs on one of those lads. They were hiding *something.* "Next?" Cormac asked. They'd given Lennon a list of tasks to accomplish.

"We heard back from Coillte," Garda Lennon said, referring to a state-owned forestry-management group. "It turns out the map of Glanteenassig Forest Park isn't their official map."

This was interesting. "It looked official," Cormac said.

"Get this. It was one of a dozen entries in a contest to redo the park map," Neely said.

"Who is the artist?" Cormac could see that they knew the answer.

Lennon glanced at Neely before answering. "George O'Malley."

The mute. The donkey man. The caricature artist. And the collector of lucky rabbits' feet. *Interesting.* "Looks like it's time I meet Mr. O'Malley."

"I would suggest bringing Dimpna Wilde," Neely said.

Cormac's stomach did a little flip. He hadn't told Neely that she was browned off with him because he took her along on his little visit to Paul Byrne. He couldn't do it to her again. "That won't be necessary."

Neely frowned. "He likes her. And he's comfortable with her, and she seems to get him."

"I see," he said. "Thank you, but I will visit him solo." Back to Lennon. "Any new updates on our three caravaners?"

"We had a man on them. They spent a good portion of the day at the harbor. They seemed to be arguing."

Cormac felt panic belly-crawling up his spine. "Bring Eve Murray back in for questioning," he said to Neely.

Neely frowned again. "The pathologist was pretty certain that our killer is a man."

"Eve knows something," Cormac said. "And we have her

dead to rights on the chalk drawings in town. That's enough leverage."

Neely checked her notes, then addressed Lennon. "Have any of our house-to-house inquiries revealed anything?"

Garda Lennon shook his head. "Nothing but speculations."

"What kind of speculations?" Neely pressed.

"There have been a few folks who reported *feeling* like things were missing and then spotting one of the four nearby," Lennon said. "One woman was convinced one of them broke into her place and *rearranged* her things."

Cormac thought of the book. Paul Byrne seemed genuinely shocked it had turned up in their caravan. "How many folks?"

"At least five," Neely said.

Once again, Cormac felt behind the eight ball. "You haven't mentioned this until now?"

"We've had bigger things to deal with than someone 'breaking in' to rearrange furniture and take a knickknack or two," Neely pointed out.

"But if it's our caravaners, then we could at least arrest them on theft and keep them here," Cormac said. "We only need one of them to turn on the other two."

"True." She sighed. "I suppose we can go through the list of what people are missing and compare it to the caravan inventory."

Cormac snapped his fingers. "Which means we cannot yet release the caravan."

Lennon groaned. "That will take some paperwork."

"Better get cracking," Cormac said. "How soon can we get our threesome back in for questions?"

"We?" Neely said.

"I could sit in." He grinned. "*Unofficially.*"

"Before or after you *unofficially* visit George O'Malley?" Neely asked.

Once again, Cormac felt a sense of panic. This killer was getting away.

"Sergeant Neely and I are paying a visit to Robert Brannigan as soon as we conclude here," Lennon said. "We're expecting a warrant to search his residence and his vehicle any moment now."

"Perfect," Cormac said to Neely, as he mentally ditched all other plans. "I'll drive you."

CHAPTER 36

Robert Brannigan and his wife lived in a newly built house in Tralee. A rental car was in the driveway, this time a white BMW. Cormac stood back by the squad car as Neely knocked loudly on Robert Brannigan's door, warrant in hand. Brannigan was expecting a friendly chat, but that's not what he was going to get. Six guards stood behind Sergeant Neely. A curtain twitched upstairs, and a woman's gaunt face appeared. "That's Lorraine," Neely said. "The missus." Seconds later, the door opened. Robert Brannigan stood on the other side, dressed in a suit, his tie hanging loose as if he was just about to unwind. He was tall and hefty, and north of sixty.

"Barb," Robert Brannigan said. "Is this about the Audi?"

"May we come in?" Neely said.

"I thought we were meeting at the station." He was starting to sweat under his collar, and his eyes suddenly seemed to protrude.

"I have a warrant to search your premises and your vehicle," Neely said.

A look of annoyance flicked across his face. "My sister-in-law can tell you all about my Audi. I parked it at Vera's, and according to her, it must have been stolen." He leaned in. "I was in Dublin on business."

"And your sister-in-law went with you?"

"With me?" Brannigan glanced back into the house, no doubt looking for his wife. "She wanted to tag along. Change of scenery, do some shopping. But no, she wasn't with me. She drove herself, and I caught a ride with an associate of mine."

"We'll need the name and number of this associate," Neely said. They already had it, but he was sweating, and they needed to keep the pressure on.

"Not a bother."

"We need you and Lorraine to step out of the house," Neely said. She gestured to the van that was pulling in, which had GARDA TECHNICAL BUREAU written on the side.

"For Christ's sake." Brannigan opened the door. "Lorraine?" he yelled into the house. From where Cormac stood, he could see a bit into the house. White tile floors, white walls, white furniture. But nothing like heaven. More like a hospital. Cutting off someone's hand was messy. Was it all because of Lorraine, or was Robert Brannigan *not* their guy?

"You could have given us some warning," Robert said, clearly aggrieved.

"That's not how this works," Neely said.

"You're not going to take my laptop, are ye?" Cormac heard Robert yell.

"We are, so," she said.

"This should be illegal! I have work to do."

"You do know what happened to Chris Henderson, don't you?" Neely asked. "And Brigid Sweeney?"

"I had nothing to do with that! I can't help it if my car was stolen." They heard footsteps on the stairs, and minutes later, Lorraine Brannigan appeared in the doorway. Cormac had to force himself not to stare. She was rail thin; he suspected she was anorexic. Was there major trauma in this marriage? "They're going to search the house," Robert said to his wife. "Get your shoes on."

"My shoes?"

"We can't be in the house; we'll go for a drive."

"I'm afraid you'll need to wait on the property," Neely said. "You'll know exactly what we removed, and it will all be returned in good time."

"My husband would never hurt anyone," Lorraine said. "This isn't right. Barb. Please. This isn't right."

"You'll address her as Detective Sergeant Neely," Garda Lennon said.

Good for him. He was a fine lad.

"We have an elderly man who's been murdered, as well as a young girl," Neely said. "The sooner we eliminate Robert, the better."

Lorraine chewed on her lip. "Get your shoes," Robert said.

Cormac cringed at his tone. It was like Robert thought he was speaking to a child.

Lorraine scurried out the door, a pair of heels dangling from her hand. This tidy and unblemished home was probably all Robert's doing.

"Are you a bird-watcher?" Cormac asked.

Robert frowned. "I'm a bird-watcher like you're a fisherman."

Cormac tilted his head. "Explain that."

"You're fishing right now, aren't ya?" Robert suddenly grinned, then looped his arm around his wife's shoulder as she returned to his side.

"According to that analogy, you do watch birds, just not the feathered kind?"

Robert grinned, then seemed to think it through, and the grin disappeared.

"You're also a bit of a photographer, aren't ya?"

Neely exited and gave Cormac the side-eye. He was overstepping. "Let's do this at the station."

Cormac removed the envelope from inside his jacket pocket. "Did you take these photos, Mr. Brannigan?" He slid the photos of Brigid out of the envelope and began holding them up one by one.

"Cormac," Neely hissed, "what are you doing with those?"

"They're copies of copies," he said.

"What are those?" Lorraine asked. "Why would you think Robert took them?" She shrugged off her husband's arm.

Cormac reached the last one, the one of Robert standing by his Audi with a pair of binoculars. "Doing a little bird-watching here, were you?"

Robert whirled around. Cormac crossed his arms and leaned against the squad car.

"There's nothing wrong with those photos," Robert said. "No harm admiring a pretty girl."

"Chris Henderson thought there was something wrong with it, though, didn't he? Is that why you ran him down?"

"What?" Robert shook his head. "I did no such thing."

"When did you take these photos?" Neely asked.

"I don't know. Shortly after they arrived. A few weeks ago?"

"You're lying," Cormac said. "You took these the day before she was murdered."

"They're in here," Robert said, digging out his mobile phone and handing it over. "Check the dates."

Neely put on a glove before touching the phone. "Our forensics team is going to have a look at this."

"Come on," Robert said. "It's not against the law to take a few photos. You can see she liked the attention."

"Why?" his wife wailed. "Why would you take these?"

"They're innocent," he said.

"Her lips, her cleavage, her thighs? That's what you call innocent?"

"It's normal." He wiped sweat off his upper lip, then gestured to Cormac.

"Tell them it's normal."

Cormac simply stared.

"What? You never look? If you say that, you're a damn liar."

"I don't take intimate photographs of twenty-somethings," Cormac said. Even though the statement was factually correct, Cormac knew his actions made him a hypocrite. By God, he'd learned his lesson. But Brannigan wasn't his priest, and there'd be no confessing today.

"Intimate! She's out in plain view."

"And where were you?"

"Excuse me?"

"Were you in plain view when you were having a gawk and taking photos, or were you hiding behind a tree?"

Robert's face was now turning red. Cormac was starting to guess the kind of things they were going to find on his laptop. Robert suddenly dashed. Cormac was on his heels, but Robert was already jumping into the BMW. The car revved up and peeled out. Was that why he always kept his keys in the car? Was he expecting to be chased? Cormac ran for the squad car.

"Wait!" Neely shouted, running to catch up.

"Let him go," the wife said. "He'll come back."

Cormac nodded to a guard. "Take her to the station. Now."

"That's not fair," she shouted. "Barb?"

"You'll be fine," Neely said. "Make sure she's comfortable."

Cormac didn't give a rat's arse about her comfort, but he kept his gob shut. "Hurry," he said. He jumped into the driver's seat and started the car.

"I cannot believe he'd be so stupid," Neely muttered as she took the passenger seat and they scrambled to buckle up.

Cormac peeled out, but seconds later he faced a fork in the road. "Left or right?" he shouted. He couldn't see Robert's car.

"Right," Neely said, pointing to faint tire marks. Cormac took the right and put on his lights and siren.

"How well do you know this man?" Cormac asked as he increased his speed. In the distance, he caught the back end of a white car turning left.

"I know the wife better. He's in Dublin a lot."

"Hidden Valley Caravan Park is in Dublin," Cormac said. "He's fat, and he was creeping on Brigid, but wouldn't she have recognized him as the yoke who was bothering her a year ago?"

"Maybe she did," Neely said. "Maybe it's his jacket. Maybe Brigid dragged it through Henderson's blood because she saw Brannigan run Henderson down in cold blood. Maybe she stole Robert's coat and dragged it through Henderson's blood as a way of proving it was him."

"In this scenario, does he then kill Brigid because she's a witness?"

"It's a strong motive."

"It is. But why go through all that? Why not just come forward and tell us what she saw?"

"Because we weren't very friendly with her, now were we?"

"That doesn't mean we wouldn't have believed her."

"I know that. And you know that. But she didn't know that."

"Or maybe she had something else to hide. Something that ended up costing her her life." Ahead, Cormac saw the back end of a white car take a left. He sped up and took the left.

"Wait," Neely said. "This is heading toward the agricultural show."

He'd heard mention of that. Farmers came from all over Ireland with their livestock. "I saw a white car turn here."

"Don't do it. It's a trick. Turn around."

"But he's just ahead of us; it had to be him."

"Turn around."

"I can't." He sped up.

Neely gripped her side door. "You mean you won't."

"He's just ahead of us." Was she worried about crowds? He had his lights and siren on; they'd have to move aside. The road curved, and although he wanted to catch up to the bastard, he was forced to slow down a tad. Robert had the advantage of knowing these roads better than he did. He spotted the white car in the distance, just beyond a curve. "See? That's him." He sped up again.

"Sheep!" Neely said. Cormac heard her, but it didn't quite register. Sheep were everywhere in Ireland. He took another curve, and she said it again, this time at top volume, this time she was yelling. "Sheep!"

And there they were, standing in the middle of the road, a huge flock of sheep. Beyond them, the white car honked and zoomed away. "Fuck!" Cormac slammed on his brakes and laid on his horn as his heart hammered away at his chest. The sheep looked equally traumatized as they froze in place; there must have been twenty of them, all big-eyed and slack-jawed and not moving a single hoof. Neely was breathing so hard she was panting, her hand firmly over her chest. Cormac cursed and looked for a spot to go around, but they were hedged in by a dip in the field on one end and a stone wall on the other.

"He took this route on purpose," Cormac said.

"You don't say."

"Son of a bitch."

Neely radioed in to the station; soon other squad cars would be after the BMW, but Cormac knew they'd been beat. Despite manpower on it, they still hadn't located the black Audi. Robert Brannigan had a good hiding place, and he'd taken Cormac and Neely on his version of a wild goose chase. Only these were domestic and, he was starting to think, very dumb sheep. A chorus of "Baa," greeted him when the sheep finally started to move again, but there were so many it looked as if they were well and truly stuck.

Cormac, furious, got out of the car. "Shoo!" he yelled. "Shoo!" They stopped again, and stared. Not a single sheep moved its wooly arse.

Neely got out and leaned against the car. "Could have taken the other road," she said. "Headed him off from the front."

The sheep baaed. They agreed. It would have been funny if a pervert, and maybe a killer, hadn't just disappeared around the bend.

CHAPTER 37

It was the lightest sound that woke Dimpna up. A creak of a floorboard. She knew that creak. It was the first step leading up to her flat. Was someone upstairs? Why wasn't her four-pack barking? Had something happened to them? Spike would sleep through an intruder, but E.T., Guinness, and Pickles would not. Not ever. Her stomach lurched. Something was wrong. "Hello?" Dimpna called, as if it were perfectly reasonable to have a discussion with someone violating your home at night. Or was it just the wind? A storm had whipped up, rattling the windows, plunging the temperature.

"Grow," a male voice in the dark said.

Dimpna screamed and fumbled for the light beside her bed, heart thudding, adrenaline rising, and mind desperately trying to make sense of the nonsensical. A man was in her room. "Go away." She hated the sound of the fear in her own voice. The light would not switch on. Why weren't her dogs barking? *This is something that's been planned.* The thought of her fur-babies being harmed filled her with rage. "Who are you? What have you done with my pets?"

"Transform," the voice said. It was hard to tell exactly where in her room the voice was coming from.

"Help!" Dimpna yelled. Hearing the helpless terror in her

own voice scared her more than anything. Was there anything on the bedside table she could throw? She did not recognize the voice; it was deep and warbled, as if someone was purposefully trying to make it unidentifiable.

"Change," it said.

What the hell was going on? Did Brigid Sweeney hear these very words before she was brutally murdered? Where was her phone? Had he taken that too? "E.T.," she yelled. "Pickles!" Guinness wouldn't be much of a fighter. *Please let them be okay. I'll do anything.*

The floorboard creaked again, and then came the sound of heavy footsteps going down. *Retreating.* To do what? Wait for her at the bottom of the steps? The only window in her flat was below the pitched roof. She couldn't climb up to it, and it was too high to jump down. She'd never felt so helpless. *Be brave.* She got out of bed and steadied her vision until her desk came into view. There was a letter opener in the drawer, underneath the pile of sealed letters from Sean. From below came the sound of the front door banging shut. She ran to the window in time to see a dark figure hurrying out of the courtyard; then she heard a vehicle rev up. She dashed over to the desk and turned on the light. "Guinness!" she yelled. "Pickles! E.T.!" Their dog beds were empty. *Grow. Transform. Change.* They were the mutterings of a psychopath. Dimpna grabbed the letter opener and crept down the stairs. Darkness greeted her, and a heavy silence. "E.T., Pickles, Guinness!"

Something rubbed against her leg, making her jump and scream. She pawed along the wall until she found a switch. *Spike.* She breathed a sigh of relief as he yowled at her. "Where are the others?"

She headed for the front door first, locking it shut. Then she turned on every light she could find, looking for any kind of disturbance, footprints, anything. She needed to call 999, but she wanted to find her dogs first. She went down the hall and threw open the doors to the exam rooms. Nothing had been disturbed.

She headed for the kennels. The minute she opened the door, E.T., Guinness, and Pickles tripped over each other to get to her. "Thank God." She knelt, allowing all three of them to jump on her. It was only after a few seconds of cuddles that it hit her. Were the mastiffs still across the street? What if the intruder had been Alan Flynn or Billy Sheedy? Given that this was not a break-in for money or drugs, nor had they touched her, apart from frightening her to death, what if one was coming back for the dogs? Perhaps the two of them were in it together and one had wandered upstairs; perhaps he didn't realize she lived up there. Then again, someone had lured the dogs into the kennel without a single bark. How? She was going to have to give them a full examination. But first she was going to have to check on the mastiffs and then call the guards.

The minute Dimpna stepped into the courtyard, she knew that Hell and Fire were gone. The boarding facility across the street used to be a mechanic's shop, and the garage doors yawned wide open. Dimpna hurried over, fury rising as she faced how vulnerable they were. Not just her, but the lovely animals under her care. Her watch. And her loyal employees. Work was stressful enough without having to worry about one's own safety. She'd nearly reached the gate at the end of the courtyard when she stopped cold. Where was Tiernan? The old black Lab *never* left the courtyard. It was his safe place. Dimpna even had to build an overhang so he would have a place outside of the rain because nothing ever coaxed the old lad inside. Dimpna turned around and scanned the courtyard. "Tiernan?" she called. "Tiernan?" It was possible he had passed away, but he would have never left the courtyard to do it. Dimpna turned back to look at the gate: *open*. Of course. As if the thugs who had broken in would close the gate on their way out. Had they taken Tiernan, or had he wandered off on his own? It was just then that Dimpna thought of her mother out there in her caravan. Where were the guards? Worries were piling up one after the other. Dimpna ran through the gate and over to the boarding facility. She entered directly through the open garage doors, but—no surprise—the dogs were gone. If it wasn't Billy Sheedy, she would have to deal with him when he found out they were missing. She wasn't sure which was worse.

A red Toyota screeched up. *Cormac.* As soon as he got out of the car, she pointed to the field where her mother had parked her caravan. "I have to check on Mam."

"Are you hurt?"

Dimpna shook her head. "Traumatized, but physically okay."

"Traumatized?" Concern radiated from Cormac.

"It was so startling, a man in my room, talking to me in the dark—"

"That's terrifying," he said. "Did you recognize the voice?"

"No. I think he was disguising it." Did that mean she knew him? Then again, she could barely hear him over the thumping of her heart.

"Is there any chance it was Robert Brannigan?"

"It could have been anyone," Dimpna said. "Why do you ask?"

"He's on the run again," Cormac said.

"Can we go over this later? The mastiffs are gone as well as Tiernan, the black Lab from my courtyard. He also may have drugged Pickles, Guinness, and E.T. But right now, I have to make sure my mam is alright."

"Let's go," Cormac said. "More guards are on the way." They both headed for the caravan. "Stay back when we get to the door," Cormac said. "Let me go first."

"I'll kill them," Dimpna said. "If anything has happened to my mam, I'll kill them."

* * *

Cormac stepped up to the caravan door and banged on it. Immediately, a sound was heard, that of something clattering to the floor. "Mrs. Wilde?" Cormac yelled. "It's Detective Inspector O'Brien." Cursing was heard.

"That's Mam," Dimpna said. She was alive. Relief prickled her skin.

A light came on above the door before it creaked open. Her mother appeared, uncharacteristically unkempt. Her hair was tousled, and without makeup, she seemed softer, more vulnerable. Was someone with her?

"Hey, Mam," Dimpna said. "We're sorry to bother you."

"Who's there?" a male voice called out.

"Are you . . . ?" Dimpna said. "Is there . . . someone in there?"

Seconds later, a figure appeared behind her mother, his features unreadable in the dark. Fur, a pointed nose, and ears seemed to be growing out of him. Was he holding a dog? Cormac stumbled back, nearly tripping down the few steps that led up to the caravan door. "What the hell?" he said.

The figure stepped forward, under the light. It was her father. And he was holding a fox. It took Dimpna a minute to understand what she was seeing. The mama fox from the hit-and-run. It was sitting upright, its eyes glassy and unblinking. "He had it stuffed?" Dimpna said.

"He insisted," Maeve said. "He carries it around everywhere."

At least one mystery had been solved. No wonder Donnecha and Ben had been so gleeful about her father having a "new friend."

"Who are you?" Eamon demanded. "This is private property."

Cormac was bent over, breathing hard. Dimpna was still angry with him, but she didn't want him to have a heart attack. "Are you alright?" she asked.

"That put the heart in me crossways," he said.

"My folks will do that to you," Dimpna replied.

"I'm going to sic Harriet on you if you don't leave," her father said.

"Harriet?" Dimpna asked.

"That's what he's been calling her." Maeve shrugged. "I don't know where he gets his ideas." Guard cars were approaching the clinic, their lights and sirens sounding.

"We had a break-in," Dimpna said. "We wanted to make sure you were okay."

"I won't let them take Harriet," her father said. "She's my girl." He clutched the fox to his chest.

"Is that . . ." Cormac asked, "the mother fox from the hit-and-run?"

"It is," Dimpna said. "I hope he doesn't bring it around the pup."

Cormac shook his head, then scratched his nose, then brought out an inhaler and took a hit.

"Did either of you hear or see anything unusual this evening?" Dimpna asked.

"You're joking me," Cormac said, pointing to the fox.

Dimpna laughed. "You'll get used to it," she said. "Mam? Did you hear noises or see anyone?"

"In the dark?" Maeve asked. "With my eyes closed?"

Eamon Wilde suddenly dropped the fox, and it tumbled down the steps, making Cormac shriek. Dimpna would have laughed, had it not been for the horrified look on her father's face. "My clinic," he said. "What's happening at my clinic?"

Guard cars were pulling up, creating a light and sound show.

"It's okay, Da," Dimpna said, her throat pulsing. Her father loved Tiernan like a child. So did she. But due to his condition, he may not even remember in the next hour that he was missing, so there was no point in upsetting him further. "We had a break-in, but everyone is okay. All the animals are okay." *Liar. Sweet old Tiernan is missing.*

"Did they break into the medicine cabinet?"

"No," she said. "It was just a few lads acting the maggot." A deranged person. *Grow . . . transform . . . change.* A person with that kind of mind might just be unstable enough to stage a murder like poor Brigid Sweeney's. She would have to remember to tell Cormac about the strange utterances, but first she needed to find Tiernan.

Cormac, Sergeant Neely, and Dimpna stood in the waiting room of the clinic, trying to piece together the frightening evening. Given that a typical break-in wouldn't have summoned Neely, Dimpna realized they were treating this as part of their murder inquiry. Had the voice in her room belonged to the sadistic killer? Why had he spared her?

"You said you heard a vehicle?" Neely asked.

Dimpna nodded. "I heard it tear out."

"But you didn't catch a glimpse?"

"No. By the time I came down, I only heard it screeching away."

Cormac wanted to debrief her, and then he wanted her to go through the clinic to make sure nothing else was stolen, but she would not be deterred from looking for Tiernan. She put on her wellies and examined her pack. The dogs were not showing any signs of having been drugged. They must have brought treats instead. Most likely, the intruders had scared the poor old Lab, and he was hiding somewhere.

"I really can't have you running off until we go through everything that happened," Cormac said.

"They didn't take anything but their dogs," Dimpna said. "But I have to find Tiernan."

"Take me through the break-in," Cormac said.

"I heard a creak on the first step. Then a man was in my

room. It was dark. He spoke to me, but I think he was trying to disguise his voice."

"What did he say?" Neely asked.

"Something very bizarre. *Grow. Transform. Change.*"

"What?" Cormac asked. "What does that mean?"

"I don't know. He sounded like a madman."

Neely was busy thumbing through her phone. "Are we boring you?" Cormac asked.

"No," Neely said, turning the screen toward them. "*Grow. Transform. Change.* It's the motto of Coillte."

"Who?" Dimpna asked.

"They manage Glanteenassig Forest Park," Neely said.

"Looks like I'm going to get to see that forest after all," Cormac added.

"I'm coming with you," Dimpna said.

"No," Neely said.

"I think . . . he wants me along . . . he broke into my room . . . I think he's taken Hell and Fire there. Maybe even Tiernan."

"Tiernan?" Neely asked.

"He's an old black Lab that never leaves the courtyard. He's the sweetest boy, but he's shy. If he's taken him there, Tiernan won't come to you. Please."

"The intruder has involved her in this for whatever reason," Cormac said. "And since I'm not officially on this case—"

"What do you mean?" Dimpna asked. "You're not on this case?"

"Long story." Cormac held up a finger and turned back to Neely. "There's no law that says Dimpna and I can't take a drive to the forest in the early hours of the morning, now is there?"

"I knew you'd go rogue," Neely said covering her ears.

Dimpna didn't have the brain space to decipher whatever was going on with Cormac and this case. She had to find Tiernan. "It could have been Billy, Alan, and Eve," Dimpna said.

"Hell and Fire are gone." The more Dimpna thought about it, the more convinced she was that this was the work of Billy and Alan. Probably both. One must have been freeing Hell and Fire, while the other crept into her room. She shared her theory.

"We've been keeping close tabs on them, but Robert Brannigan threw us out of alignment," Cormac said.

"Maybe you should count sheep," Neely said. "That might sort you out."

Dimpna didn't have time to figure out whatever that comment was about. She couldn't believe she'd forgotten all about Bette Davis. "One second." She ran to the reception desk and whipped the cover off the birdcage. *Gone.* She turned back to Cormac and Neely. "It was all three of them," she said. "Bette Davis is gone too."

"To the park we go," Cormac said. "I just wish I knew what's waiting there."

"Or who," Neely added. "Or who."

CHAPTER 38

It was dawn when they finally pulled into the base of the Slieve Mish Mountains. Glanteenassig Forest Park consisted of 450 hectares of natural beauty. Its two lakes were nestled within a dense forest, framed by mountains. The early-morning light seeped through the trees and bounced off the lake in front of them, making it glow. Cormac and Dimpna arrived first in his Toyota, with Neely and Lennon right behind them in her squad car. Dimpna could feel the tension in Cormac, but she somehow managed not to ask him what the hell was going on with him. When he was ready to tell her, he would tell her. In the distance, Sitka spruces beckoned. Dimpna hadn't been prepared for the sight of Eve, Billy, and Alan's caravan when they pulled into the first car park, but there it was, parked alone in the farthest corner of the lot. "Why would they want us to follow them out here?" Cormac said as they all emerged from their vehicles and stared at it.

Neely shook her head. "I was wondering the same thing."

Cormac turned to Dimpna. "Can you do me a favor and stay in the vehicle while we check this out?" Technically, it was a question, but from the tone of his voice, Cormac wouldn't accept no as an answer. Dimpna nodded, got back in the car, and rolled down her window. She gazed out at the lake, trying to calm her mind. Something dark and metallic protruded from the surface. She scrambled out again.

"Two seconds," Cormac said. "Are you joking me?"

"What's that in the lake?" she said. "Just a ways out."

Cormac, Neely, and Lennon whirled around to look at the shiny, dome-like surface piercing the lake like a submarine coming to the surface.

"It's a car," Neely cried out.

"Jaysus," Cormac, Neely, and Lennon ran to the edge of the lake. Dimpna followed suit; they couldn't keep her away now.

There was no doubt they were looking at the hood of a car. The rest of the vehicle was submerged. "Do you think someone's in there?" Neely's voice betrayed her fear.

"Call for backup and divers," Cormac shouted.

"On it," Lennon said hurrying back to the squad car.

"They're not going to be quick," Neely said. They were too far out.

The car wasn't too far from shore. Dimpna knew she could swim to it. "I can help," she said.

"You?" Neely sounded annoyed.

"I'm a strong swimmer, and if there's a window cracked in the vehicle, I'm your best bet for going through it."

"I don't like it," Cormac said.

"We have to let her try," Neely said.

"Give me a minute to think." Cormac ran over to the caravan and pounded on the door.

The door finally swung open. Alan Flynn stood on the other side. "We can't get a bit of peace, can we?" A chorus of barks erupted behind him.

"If those dogs charge out, I'm shooting," Cormac said. He'd deal with the fact that they broke them out of Dimpna's boarding facility later.

"They won't," Alan said.

"Did you drive a car into the lake?" Cormac asked.

"What?" Alan said. His gaze flicked toward the partially submerged vehicle. "Oh my God. I had nothing to do with that."

Dimpna had already stripped down to her bra and panties. Before Cormac could try and stop her, she waded into the lake and began to swim to the car.

"Damn it," Cormac called. "Be careful."

She ignored all the slimy bits rubbing against her skin, and the ice-cold water piercing her like needles, and concentrated on her strokes. The car was only a few meters from the shore. She reached it and took a moment before taking a breath and diving under. It took time for her eyes to adjust to the bits of dirt that she had churned up, but she pushed through until she reached the vehicle. It was white and fancy-looking. She hit the surface, took a deep breath, and dove under once more. She reached out until she felt a door handle. She waited, then peered into the window. A grotesque blob greeted her. A bloated face pressed up against the glass. Dimpna swam up to the surface and screamed. "Someone's in there. A man. I think he's dead."

She dove back down. The windows were all closed. She found the handle of the driver's side door and pulled. Purplish-blue lips open in a scream and bulging dead eyes stared back at her as she tugged on the door. *Our Father, who are in heaven . . .*

Locked. She swam to the back door. It too wouldn't budge. By the time she checked the other two, she was exhausted, her adrenaline pumping. She swam to the surface. Cormac was swimming toward her. "Is it the black Audi?"

"No," Dimpna said. "White. Fancy."

"BMW?"

"I think so; it's hard to see. Looks like the driver was a large, white male."

"Robert Brannigan," Cormac said. "My God." He reached Dimpna's side. "Stay here." He dove under.

"I had nothing to do with that," Alan yelled. "I never even saw it."

"Step out of the caravan, and hands where I can see them," Neely could be heard saying. The water was like ice, and Dimpna's teeth were chattering. She dove under; it was better than being half-submerged. There was something else down there. *Beneath* the white car. Why was she seeing even more tires? It was a second vehicle, submerged even deeper, flipped on its back like a turtle.

Dimpna used all her strength to swim to the surface, and when she broke through, Cormac was swimming toward her.

"There's another vehicle below the white one," she said. "On its back."

"The Audi," Cormac said. "My God. Good catch. We've got diving teams and cranes on the way." Cormac's arms were suddenly around her. "Let's get you to shore and get you dry."

They swam. Cormac was faster than Dimpna, but she concentrated on her strokes and breathing. Every time that bloated face rose to mind, she tried to shove it away. When she reached the shore, Neely hurried toward them with blankets.

"Got them from the caravan," she explained as she handed one to Cormac and placed the other around Dimpna. "It's Robert Brannigan, is it?"

"It is," Cormac said. "It certainly is."

"But it's not the black Audi?"

"No. It's the white BMW, but Dimpna just spotted a second car below it."

A watery dumping grave. In the midst of all this beauty. Then again, taking a human life was much worse, so what did they expect from this monster? It was so easy to call him a monster, pretend he was not part of the human race. But he was. And that made it even more terrifying. He could be the man standing in front of you in SuperValu who sees you have fewer items and smiles at you as he insists you go ahead of him. It could be your neighbor. Or the man you sleep next to at night. A monster in plain sight.

Eve Murray stepped out of the caravan, followed by Alan and Billy.

"We never saw that car," Eve said. "We swear."

"How is that possible?" Neely said.

"We came in last night," Billy said. "It was dark."

"We were asleep when you pounded on our door," Alan added.

"Are you saying someone drove this car into the lake with your caravan only a few meters away, and you didn't hear a thing?" Cormac's tone made it clear he didn't believe it.

"The car could have already been in the lake," Eve said. "But, like Alan said, it was dark."

Billy stuck a cigarette in his mouth and lit it. "I told you someone was following us."

"What do you mean?" Cormac said.

"Someone knows where we are at all times. I don't know how. But they do."

"I told you how," Eve said. She pointed at Dimpna. "She put a tracking device on Bette Davis."

"What?" Dimpna said. "Show me."

Eve whirled around and went back into the caravan.

"Where is the black Lab that was in the courtyard of my clinic?" Dimpna called to Billy and Alan. Billy blew a long chain of smoke out of his nose.

"What black Lab?" Alan said. "We didn't take a black Lab."

"Shut up," Billy hissed.

"I believe they just admitted to breaking and entering," Cormac said.

Sirens wailed in the distance. "Where's Tiernan?" Dimpna asked again. "You see your dogs have been well taken care of."

"They were kidnapped," Billy said.

"Dognapped," Alan added.

Billy silenced her with a glare before turning back to the detectives. "We were just taking back what's ours."

"You came into my room and terrified me," Dimpna said.

Billy shook his head violently and looked at Cormac. "We didn't. I swear. We only went into the old garage to get the dogs and the first floor of the clinic to get the bird."

"Oh," Dimpna said. "Is that all?" Fury pulsed through her. First, they were the closest people to Brigid, who was found not far from their caravan. Now they were only meters away from another body. She wasn't in charge of the investigation, but if she was, she'd be hauling them into the station.

"How did you know that's where she was keeping your dogs?" Neely said.

"Because I called out for them and they barked," Billy said.

"They broke a window in the garage to gain entry," Eve said, as she emerged from the caravan with the parrot. "But the door to the clinic was unlocked. And I didn't go beyond the first floor. I *swear.*"

Dimpna didn't answer right away; she was chewing on the revelation that Eve had just heard *everything* they'd said from inside the caravan. They'd been speaking in a normal tone. If Brigid had been in that caravan with her killer and anyone had been around, they would have heard them. Were they telling the truth? Was the killer stalking them, or was one of them the killer?

Eve approached with Bette Davis and pointed to her parrot's left claw. Around it was a tracker. "Can you take it off?"

"I didn't do that," Dimpna said. "But she's right. It's a tracker."

"I told you we were being followed!" Billy said. He began bouncing around, as if gearing himself up for a boxing match.

Cormac motioned for Dimpna to have a private chat with him and Neely. When she reached them, she spoke first, already knowing his question. "I've seen them on wildlife shows," Dimpna said. "They're used to track migration patterns."

"How did one end up on the parrot?" Cormac asked.

"I honestly have no idea."

"You said Paul Byrne is a bird-watcher."

Dimpna cringed. She'd walked herself into this one. "And?"

"Does he track them?"

"He might."

"Could someone track these lads using it?"

"If the parrot is with them, then yes."

"And you're sure the parrot didn't have that tracker when she was brought to your clinic?"

"I'll have to ask Niamh," Dimpna said. "But we don't even have trackers, let alone place them on animals."

"Would anyone who walked into your clinic have had access to the parrot?" Cormac asked.

"Yes," Dimpna admitted. "Bette Davis was quite popular with our clients. She wasn't caged when she was in the reception area with Niamh."

"Can we track the tracker?" Neely asked.

"It's not my expertise," Dimpna said. "You'd need to contact the Irish Wildlife Trust."

"We're out of here," Billy yelled across the car lot.

"Like hell you are," Cormac said. "You'll be going back to the garda station."

"You already released us," Billy said.

"Breaking and entering is a crime," Neely said. "We can arrest and detain you."

"Not to mention we have CCTV footage that proves at least one of you knows a lot more about this case than you pretended. And lying to the guards during a murder probe does not sit well with judges." Cormac made intense eye contact with Eve Murray.

"Don't let them rattle you," Alan said. "We keep our mouths shut."

Cormac strode over to the threesome and glared at them. "I'm beginning to think none of you have the sense you were born with." Eve was jittery now and looking as if she was going to bolt.

The sound of approaching vehicles got their attention. An ambulance, three police cars, and a truck with a crane were pulling into the car park.

"Help," Bette Davis said. "Get a record!!"

"Get a record?" Cormac said.

"She says it periodically," Dimpna said. Cormac looked to Eve. She swallowed hard.

"Would you please take her bracelet off her?" Eve begged. "What if he's coming?"

"Who is he?" Cormac asked.

Eve ignored him and advanced on Dimpna. "Please take her bracelet off. I'm begging you."

"It's a tracker, not a bracelet. I could take it off back at the clinic, but I don't have any tools on me." Dimpna knew wrapping duct tape around it could disturb the signal, but it could also interfere with the investigation. She would have to let Cormac handle it.

"Please don't press charges," Eve said. "We just needed our babies back. You, of all people, should understand. They're family."

"I want to know which one of you came up into my flat," Dimpna said.

"I swear," Eve said, "I found Bette Davis in the reception area. Lovely cage, thank you for taking good care of her." She looked at Cormac. "How can you treat me like this when I kept our dirty little secret?"

"You think I don't know what that was all about?" Cormac said. "How you crippled me so I couldn't investigate Brigid's murder?"

"What?" Eve said. "That's not why I did it."

He'd slept with her. It hit Dimpna between the eyes, as a strange jealousy pulsed through her. It explained a lot. She didn't know how to process it in the moment, but it explained a lot.

"If you're telling the truth about that, then tell me the truth about everything," Cormac said. "You're not going to get another chance."

"I'll tell you everything," she said. "I swear."

The truck with the crane beeped as it backed up to the shoreline. Divers emerged and began preparing the chains.

Bette Davis imitated the sound of a siren. "Woo, woo, woo."

Eve was eyeing Dimpna. "Brigid's clothes might be a little big, but you can borrow track pants and a shirt from me, and she has a cardigan that would keep you warm," Eve said. "And Alan's would fit you, Inspector. You two are going to freeze to death if you stay in those wet clothes."

"She's right," Cormac said, as he approached. "We'll take you up on those clothes."

The white BMW hovered over the lake, water gushing as the chains creaked and groaned under the weight. Slowly, it moved toward the shore, a flying, dripping car. Dimpna wanted to see the car, but not the bloated body inside. Had he driven himself into the lake? Crime-scene tape emerged, and guards began placing a perimeter around the car. "The coroner is on the way," Neely said. "Hopefully, he won't have to sit here too long."

"Search the boot," Cormac said to Lennon. Neely and Lennon donned gloves and booties and approached the boot of the car with crowbars. Minutes later, Neely reached inside and soon held up a butcher's knife. The blade glinted in the sun. The divers and cranes went back to the lake for the second vehicle.

Cormac turned to Dimpna and jerked his head to the knife. "Does that look familiar?"

Dimpna nodded. "I mean, I can't swear by it, but that looks just like the one Brigid brought to the clinic."

"Oh my God," Eve said. "Did he do it? Did that fat pervert murder Brigid?"

Billy charged the car, screaming obscenities and breaking through the crime-scene tape. It took three guards to pull him off.

"Enough," Cormac said as Billy thrashed in their arms. It took another minute, but Billy finally stopped struggling. A sob was heard, and they whirled around to see Alan bent over, huge gulps coming from him.

"That fat fuck," he said. "If he wasn't already dead, I'd kill him." Neely and Lennon hurried over to keep them calm. There was acting, and there was *this*. Cormac was starting to think that none of these three had anything to do with Brigid's murder. But they knew something. Whatever they were hiding might be the key to unlock the identity of the killer.

"Inspector?" a guard at the boot of the car called. "You're going to want to see this."

Cormac headed over. Dimpna hugged the cardigan around her and couldn't help but follow. One look at the guard's face as he held something wrapped in bandages in his gloved hand, and she knew it was bad.

"It's a hand," the guard said, shock evident in his voice.

Dimpna's own hand flew to her mouth, and she backed away.

"Lower your voice," Cormac said. "Keep it out of sight."

A car pulled into the lot, and the next thing Cormac knew, a reporter was headed his way with a camera rolling.

"Turn that off," Cormac shouted.

"We're live," the reporter said. "We're on public property."

"Detective Sergeant," yet another guard yelled over to Neely. "A hand—we have Brigid Sweeney's hand."

"Did he say, 'We have her hand'?" the reporter asked, shoving his way through.

"No comment," Cormac said. "Now back up."

The guard holding the bandaged hand seemed frozen in place. Or maybe he thought the public should know.

"That's a human hand," the reporter yelled. "Whose hand is that?"

"Brigid Sweeney," Eve yelled. "It's Brigid's hand." She pointed to the menacing knife, which was also still in plain sight. "That's how she died. Some psychopath tied her to a tree and cut off her hand!" She whirled on Cormac. "Why didn't you tell us? We had a right to know."

"Neely," Cormac yelled. He wanted to strangle this reporter, stomp on the camera—neither of which would help this case.

Neely, looking a bit green, tried to take the reporter and cameraman aside. Cormac turned to the caravaners. Eve had her hands over her mouth, and the lads looked as if they were going to lose their last meal in short order. Everyone had seen the hand.

"Did you know?" Billy yelled. "*Is* that Brigid's hand?"

"That's why he was asking us about her rings and tattoos," Alan said. "I think I'm going to be sick."

"Tell me what you're doing here," Cormac said to Eve, the

only one of the three who was relatively calm. "And if you lie to me again, I swear I'll lock you up myself."

Eve's eyes widened. She nodded. "We came here because we found part of a map in Brigid's things," she said. The lads' heads whipped in her direction. "Enough," Eve said, holding up her hands. "I'm sick of lying." She stared at Cormac. "I'll tell you everything. I just hope you believe the truth when you hear it."

CHAPTER 39

Hidden Valley Caravan Park, Dublin, Ireland—one year ago

"Soft stealing?" Eve said. "What is soft stealing?" They stood around the campfire at Hidden Valley Caravan Park. Brigid was holding court yet again with one of her hare-brained ideas. That gross man from the neighboring caravan was staring at Brigid, his flabby white stomach hanging out of his wifebeater. Although from the enraged look on the wife's face, who knew who was beating whom. Brigid, either oblivious to the attention or ignoring it, grinned, one of her signature "Wait until you hear this" grins.

"It's sneaking into a place and stealing something so small they don't even know they've had anything nicked." Her gaze landed on the loser across the way.

"What would be the point of that?" Eve looked to Alan and Billy to see if they were just as confused. But Billy was smoking and staring at her chest, and Alan seemed lost in one of his meditative trances.

Brigid grinned. "If no one realizes anything has been stolen, you never get reported to the guards, and you get away with it."

"Once again," Eve said. "What's the point? If you're not stealing much, then there isn't really anything to gain, is there?"

"It's all about the adrenaline rush. It makes you feel alive." She twirled a strand of dark hair around her finger and thrust out her bottom lip. "Besides, if you do it enough times, you might find something good."

"Eventually, your luck would run out, and you'd get caught," Eve said. Why weren't the lads saying anything? Brigid was vapid; couldn't they see that?

Brigid whirled on Eve, anger swimming in her eyes as if she could read her mind. "Haven't you ever heard of the thrill of the chase?"

"I'm getting a thrill just listening to you," Billy said.

"We're surrounded by caravans here," Eve said. "There's no way to just sneak in. Someone is always watching." The fatso and his wife had finally gone inside.

"I didn't say it would be easy," Brigid said. "But if it were easy, it wouldn't be thrilling."

Eve rolled her eyes. She was going to have to figure out a way to ditch Brigid. She was better off alone with the lads.

"There is the potluck coming up," Alan said. "Most folks will be out of their caravans for that."

"Now you're thinking," Brigid said.

"And what?" Eve said. "All four of us traipse into a caravan and somehow no one notices?"

"No," Billy said. "We each take a caravan. Then meet up and see who scored the best item."

"Interesting," Alan said. "A competition."

"Yes!" Brigid said. They turned to Eve. She shook her head.

"That means four chances of getting caught. Or bit by a dog. Or attacked by a sleeping resident."

"If you're too afraid, you can stay out of it," Brigid said, looping her hands around the lads. "It'll be us three."

"You're mental," Eve said. She glared at Billy and Alan. "And shame on you two for encouraging her."

"We go during the potluck," Brigid said. "And I have dibs

on our neighbor's caravan." She turned and stared at the creeper's caravan. "That pervert's been leering at me since we arrived. I can't wait to see what he's hiding."

"That was the start of it," Eve said. "We've been competing ever since."

"Competing," Neely said. "You mean stealing."

Eve shrugged.

"Did one of you steal a book from Paul Byrne?" Cormac asked.

"*Murderous Tales and Talismans*," Alan said. "That was Brigid."

"We should have stopped after Brigid nicked a sketchbook from that creeper," Eve said.

"A sketchbook?" Cormac felt a tingle up his spine.

"It was terrifying," Eve said.

"Do you still have this sketchbook?" Cormac asked.

"No," Billy said. "We tossed it out the window as we peeled the hell outta there."

Cormac felt a headache looming. "Give me the gist."

"Graphic illustrations of women being tortured," Alan said. "I had to teach everyone to meditate after looking through it."

Cormac had heard enough to know one thing. This was their man. Not the local poet. Not the three caravaners in front of him. Not George O'Malley or the hiker with the past. Could Robert Brannigan be the creeper at Hidden Valley? Wasn't he too fancy for that? Or was that his "disguise"?

"Hold on," he said to the three as he pulled his mobile phone up. It took him a minute, but he finally found a business site with Brannigan's photo. He showed it to them. "Could this be the creeper?"

"No," Eve said. "He was younger than that." Brannigan was in his sixties.

"How much younger?"

"I'd say he was in his forties," Billy said. "But that was a year ago. Do you really think he followed Brigid here?"

"She certainly thought he did," Alan said. "We all thought she was messing." Eve and Billy shot him a look. "Come on. It was your idea to come clean, Eve. We have to tell them."

"You're damn right you have to tell us," Cormac said. "We're talking about a very sadistic killer."

Eve nodded. "The day of the media shower, George O'Malley drew a picture that freaked her out. We're not sure why. She said something about turning the tables. She changed into that blue dress, said it ought to bring him out of hiding."

"Him?" Cormac said. "O'Malley?"

"She didn't say," Billy said. "But she was worked up. Just like she was over that creeper."

"She insisted he was in Camp," Eve said. "And she had a plan." Billy kicked a rock, and Alan closed his eyes. "She said we couldn't go to the guards without irrefutable evidence of a crime."

They were interrupted by the creak of the cranes as they struggled to lift the submerged vehicle. Suddenly a woosh of water sounded as the black Audi emerged from the lake. Cheers rose from the crew.

"Go on, so," Cormac said to Eve.

"She started following this creeper without telling us," Eve said.

"She took my truck without asking," Alan said. He shrugged. "Doesn't matter now."

Eve jumped back in. "She came back a few hours later with a man's jacket. It did have 'Hidden Valley' written on it. That's the first inkling we had that she might be telling the truth."

"Brigid had a habit of being dramatic," Billy said. "She was a tornado of drama."

"She said the jacket belonged to the creeper from Hidden

Valley last year," Eve said. "And she was going to make sure he went down."

"Where did she get his jacket?" Neely asked.

Eve shook her head. "All I know is she was following him."

"And the chalk scribbles?" Cormac said.

"What chalk scribbles?" Billy's face scrunched in confusion.

Eve took a deep breath. "Brigid wanted this story to have weight. From the book she stole, she read all about the Bella murder. She said if we started with the chalk scribblings it would be more proof that we had a maniac running around. She wanted him put away for good."

"Why the hell didn't you say any of this before?" Cormac asked.

"We had no idea what was going to happen," Alan said.

"And when it did happen, we were treated like suspects," Billy added.

"And then there was the hit-and-run," Eve said.

"Henderson?" Neely edged in. "What about him?"

"Brigid heard some hikers talking about a poor old man getting struck down." Eve chewed on her lip. "They said there was blood everywhere. She said it was him. It was the creeper. She said that Henderson had come to her, telling her about a pervert watching her with binoculars. We all thought it was Robert Brannigan. She said it wasn't. I think that's really when her plan started to emerge."

"She took the creeper's jacket, went to the scene of the crime before the guards had arrived, and managed to drag the jacket through Chris Henderson's blood," Cormac said, filling in the rest. How had she managed it with so many people looking on? That was the problem with people. They often made assumptions without really looking.

"It was the craziest plan I'd ever heard of," Eve said. "But Brigid was almost giddy."

"I stole that butcher's knife," Billy said. "From the kitchen of a shop. A big one." He wiped tears away from his eyes. "She asked me to steal it for her, but I did it. This is all my fault."

"No," Eve said. "We've all kept quiet because we blamed ourselves. It's the killer's fault. We have to get him."

"How did she plan on connecting the butcher's knife to this killer?" Cormac asked.

"She said he was following her and she would set a trap so he would pick it up," Alan said.

"Someone stole it from my clinic courtyard," Dimpna said. "The person could have worn gloves, but that has to be the murder weapon."

"I don't think Brigid planned on him getting his hands on that knife," Eve said, whirling on Dimpna. "She thought you'd take all the evidence that she brought you to the guards."

"That's why she pretended there was an injured hare and a psychopath," Dimpna said.

Cormac's fists clenched. "She should have come directly to me." He glanced at Eve. "Or you should have."

"You weren't exactly following up with me after our little encounter," Eve said.

"What encounter?" Billy asked, narrowing his eyes at Cormac.

"What does any of this have to do with George O'Malley's drawing?" Neely asked.

Silence fell on the group. "Fat," Dimpna said. Heads swiveled her way. "O'Malley draws everyone a bit chunky. The man from Hidden Valley last year. He was?"

"Fat," Eve said.

"Maybe he isn't anymore," Dimpna said. "Maybe Brigid didn't recognize him until she saw him rendered in George's drawing."

"My God," Cormac said. "Who else was in that drawing, barring this group?"

"Brendan Keyes," Neely said.

"Jaysus," Cormac said. "You're right."

"Who is that?" Eve asked.

"He's a hiker," Neely said. "He was in that caravan drawing."

"Peter Nosh saw him annoying a young woman at the Village Pub," Cormac said.

"And he has a record," Lennon piped in.

"I dismissed him too fast," Cormac said.

"That's on me," Neely said. "This is my case."

"We need eyes on him," Cormac said.

"Cormac." Neely motioned with her head, and he joined her for a private chat. In the distance, the wind made ripples on the surface of the lake, and the giant Sitka spruces leaned to one side. "I can see your wheels turning," Neely said. "But once McGraw knows that Brannigan drove his BMW into the lake with the murder weapon, not to mention Brigid's severed hand in the boot, he's going to close this case down."

Cormac was already shaking his head. "We don't know that he drove it into the lake himself. Or his cause of death."

"I'd say drowning is a good guess."

Cormac glanced back at the three: Eve, Billy, and Alan. "You cannot let McGraw shut us down. Brannigan is a loser. An adulterer. Probably a bit of a pervert. But he's not a sadist. He's not our killer."

"Brendan Keyes checked out of his hotel ages ago," Neely said. "He could be long gone."

"He's not," Cormac said pointing to the white BMW. "He murdered Brannigan and drove him into the lake," he said. "He was just in Dimpna's room whispering to her in the dark, and he took her black Lab. He's here. He's sticking around for the show."

"Then how do we find him?"

"We don't," Cormac said. "He finds us."

"What?"

"We've been approaching this all wrong. He wants a spotlight. Let's give him one." It was time to feed the beast. Spill all the lurid details to the media and lure Brendan Keyes into a trap like the crispy chicken lured the fox. Dangle the tasty little morsel in front of him. Then they would have to step back and pray that the sadistic killer would take a bite.

CHAPTER 40

The media wasted no time in spreading the salacious details of Brigid's murder:

GARDAÍ KEPT MACABRE MURDER SCENE A SECRET.
GOTTA HAND IT TO 'EM.
BEAUTY AND THE BUSINESSMAN. KILLER'S CAR
PULLED FROM THE LOUGH.
DISMEMBERED BEAUTY—WHO TIED BRIGID TO THE
OAK TREE?

Furious that they had been left in the dark, a large crowd had gathered in front of the Tralee Garda Station to protest the investigation. When Daniel and Emma Sweeney arrived, they were swept up in the hysteria. Buoyed by the fever pitch that the guards were lying to them, they demanded justice.

"My daughter deserved better," Daniel Sweeney yelled beside his sobbing wife. "I want answers! I demand to know why we were left in the dark."

"They didn't want us to see her body," Emma said. "Now we know why."

"Look at the mess the pair of ye caused," McGraw said.

"Cormac isn't on the case," Neely said. "This is on me."

"The pair of ye are lucky we have our killer," McGraw said.

Cormac shook his head. "We don't. Please do not tell them we do."

"Give us a little more time," Neely said. "Twenty-four hours."

"Go home," McGraw said, turning to Cormac, "before I tell everyone you slept with one of our suspects."

Neely and Cormac stood by helplessly as Superintendent McGraw approached the podium.

"Any word on Brendan Keyes?" Cormac asked Neely.

She shook her head. They scanned the crowd. Was he out there? Gloating? McGraw was at the podium now, adjusting the microphone.

"Thank you for attending," he began. "This morning, in Glanteenassig Forest Park, we found a submerged vehicle containing the body of local resident Robert Brannigan. In the boot of his car, we found a butcher's knife and Brigid Sweeney's severed hand. That detail was kept from the public not to keep you in the dark, but as leverage over this brutal killer. Sergeant Barbara Neely brilliantly put pressure on this brute until he cracked. We are all safer today because of the efforts of Sergeant Neely and her team."

"Are you sure he's the killer?" a reporter shouted.

"We will have to wait until all the evidence is processed," McGraw said. "But I can assure you—we have our man."

Dr. Dimpna Wilde was in the middle of stitching up a cat when the door to the exam room flew open and her father barged in.

"I couldn't stop him," Niamh said, hurrying behind him. "He's in a state."

Her father was opening drawers and rifling through them. "Da?" Dimpna said.

"You can't come to work with me today, Dew," her father said. "I have a surgery."

"Patrick?" Dimpna called.

"He's in Exam Room 2 with a patient," Niamh said. "Charlie's here; he wonders if he can grab his crate?"

"Absolutely. It's in the back kennel. Please pass along my thanks."

"Will do."

"How are things going with you two?"

Niamh's grin said it all. "We're taking it slow. Rather, *he's* taking it slow. But I think he's into me."

"And why wouldn't he be," Dimpna said.

"My fox!" Eamon said, running for the door. "He cannot have her."

"What do I do?" Niamh said. Dimpna had to concentrate on finishing up the stitches. This was the worst possible moment.

"Call my mam. If she doesn't answer, keep ringing her until she picks up."

"And if she doesn't?"

"I'll be there as soon as I can," Dimpna said. "Almost through here." The people in the waiting room were going to have to do just that . . . wait. Dimpna could hear her father ranting and literally rattling cages in the back. The dogs who were kenneled began to bark. Dimpna had to shut it out and focus on the poor wee cat in front of her. She finished the stitches and gently placed her in a crate with soft bedding. "It's on you now, little one," Dimpna said stroking her soft head. "Get some rest and heal." She quickly removed her gloves and apron, tossed them in the sanitary bin, and hurried out the back door to the kennel. She wasn't prepared for the chaos. Her father stood in the middle of the kennel. Every dog had been let loose. Charlie Meade was pinned against the wall, guarded by a growling King. Her father was standing in the middle of the space with the stuffed fox tucked under his arm, grinning and thoroughly enjoying the show. Thank God, the baby fox had been picked up by a wildlife volunteer this morning. He would be rehabilitated and hopefully returned to the wild to roam free.

"A little help here?" Charlie Meade said.

"King," Dimpna called. Paul's dog turned his head in her direction. "Heel." For a second, the dog wavered, then it turned around and trotted to her side. "Good boy," she said. She guided him back to his kennel and then one by one sorted out the rest of the dogs.

She turned to Charlie. "Are you alright?"

"I won't lie," he said. "That got the blood pumping."

"I'm sorry," she said. "My father has dementia."

"No need to apologize," Charlie said. "I would have let you keep it, only the agency keeps tabs on the crates."

"As they should."

"That belongs to Harriet!" her father shouted as Dimpna approached the cage.

"I can come back for it," Charlie said.

"He'll lose interest soon," Dimpna said. "I can leave it in the courtyard and text you when it's ready to pick up."

"That works," Charlie said.

"Lock him up!" her father shouted, pointing at Charlie as he sidestepped out of the room. "Lock him up!"

It took hours to calm her father down. Maeve never did answer the phone; she simply showed up at half past five to pick him up as if Dimpna was a child minder who had agreed to take care of him for the afternoon. By this point, her father was drinking tea and laughing with Niamh.

"I thought you said he was causing a bother," Maeve said. "I finished early because you were in hysterics."

"He's calmed down," Dimpna said. "But we can't have him barging in here all worked up ever again. It puts our patients at risk."

"He almost gave Charlie Meade a heart attack," Niamh said.

Maeve frowned. "Who?"

Dimpna sighed. "He's with ISPCA. He owns the crate we used to house the mama fox, and every time he tried to get it back, Da said he's the one who should be locked up."

"He also went up to your flat for quite a spell," Niamh said.

"Charlie Meade?" Dimpna asked, her sense of alarm rising.

"No, luv," Niamh said. "Your father."

Dimpna's shoulders settled. She was on edge, jumping to conclusions. "That makes more sense."

Niamh threw her a concerned look. "Ever since the other Doctor Wilde's come down from your flat, he's been asking everyone for forgiveness."

"What?" Dimpna could hardly blame her father for going up to her flat. It used to be his. All of this used to be his. His clinic, his flat, his kennel, his furry patients. He hadn't made a decision to retire; his dementia had forced him out. Now he was an interloper. She couldn't imagine how strange that must be for someone like Eamon Wilde. Someone who was used to being in control and had been very, very good at it. Her heart squeezed for him.

"Forgive me," her father said. "Forgive me."

"Forgive you for what, Da?" He pointed to the ceiling. Was he referencing her flat?

"Forgive me," he said.

She felt like the worst daughter on the planet. Even though he'd never been demonstrably affectionate, she threw herself into his arms and squeezed him. "There's nothing to forgive," she said. "Thank you for helping out today." He stiffened at her touch. When she finally pulled away, he patted her on top of the head awkwardly.

"You're not much bigger than my daughter," he said. "She's a doctor of veterinarian medicine in Dublin."

"I bet she learned everything from you," Dimpna said. "I bet she's very grateful."

He frowned as if he couldn't imagine her that way. "She's in trouble," he said. "She's in so much trouble."

Before Dimpna could ask her father what he meant, a familiar figure was coming toward the clinic. Ben.

Dimpna threw the door open. "I'm so happy to see you."

Ben grinned. "I'm here, Mam." He threw his arms open. "If you want to have that chat, I'm here."

Dimpna waited for him to enter, then ambushed him in a hug. She could feel the others staring at her. "Let's go up to my flat," she said. "I'll make us a cup of tea."

Ben followed her upstairs. If only she'd suggested somewhere outside of the clinic. Pieces of paper covered her walls. Letters. "What in the world?" Ben said. Confused, Dimpna approached the nearest wall. They all said the same thing. *Forgive me, forgive me, forgive me.* The words covered each letter, all handwritten in loopy black or block letters. Some were dainty, others shouting:

Forgive me

FORGIVE ME

Forgive me

"Mam," Ben said. "What is this?"

"It has to be my father," Dimpna said.

"He taped this up?" Ben said. "Forgive him for what?"

"I don't know." It had to have been her father who taped

these letters up but . . . it wasn't his handwriting. And then she saw the envelopes all ripped open and discarded on her bed. Sean O'Reilly's letters. Her father must have found them in the drawer, then opened them and taped every single one to the wall. FORGIVE ME. Sean must have written it hundreds of times. The envelopes. Dimpna whirled around, her brain scrambling for a reason Ben needed to go downstairs. But it was too late. He was shifting through the envelopes on the bed.

"Are these from Sean?" he said. "They're addressed to *me*."

"Ben," she said.

"And to think I came here to apologize." He marched over to the wall and began ripping the letters off the wall. "I can't believe you."

"Think about it, Ben. Sean sent them *here*. In care of me. When you're the one under his roof."

"Is that what this is all about? You're jealous?"

"Jealous? What are you on about?"

"Admit it. You don't even want me to have a relationship with my own sister."

"Half sister."

"I never knew you to be so petty. But then again, maybe I did."

"Ben, listen to me. I was going to give them to you. I didn't even open them; my father did."

"Now you're blaming him? Why can't you ever take responsibility?"

"I didn't open them."

"You didn't tell me about them either, and you obviously left them unprotected."

"Unprotected? Why would the letters from that man need to be protected?" Ben shook his head. He'd snatched up every letter, every envelope.

"I like Aisling. I'm happy you're in her life," Dimpna said.

"Is that right?"

"Yes. I even bought her a birthday present." Thank God, she had. It was a lovely doll, from a career-doll series. This one was dressed as a veterinarian. Aisling loved animals, and it was the perfect time to encourage her. "Just hold on." She went to the desk and headed for the box. "I haven't wrapped it yet." She opened the box and lifted out the doll. She held it up. Ben stared at it, his facing morphing into disgust.

"What did you do?" He pointed at the doll. She turned it around. She didn't see what he was on about at first. "Her hand."

Dimpna looked. The doll was missing her left hand. It looked like a clean break, like it had been cut off. "Oh my God. I didn't do this." The two of them stared open-mouthed.

"Do you think Eamon did that?" Ben asked.

"He must have. After he saw it on the news . . ." She dropped the doll. "I have to call the guards."

"Why are you always mixed up with these things?" Ben asked.

"I'm sorry," she said. "I'm sorry."

"I don't think you should come to her birthday party," Ben said. "And I just can't talk to you right now."

He turned and left. They had so much to work through, but right now she needed to think.

Dimpna turned to the coatrack and grabbed a cardigan. The one Eve let her borrow. She stuck her hand in the pocket as she headed for the door. There was something in the pocket. A piece of paper. She brought it out and unfolded it. It was one of George O'Malley's drawings. Dimpna opened it. As always, George was talented, apart from making everyone look heavier. She recognized the foursome. Then she thought she recognized Brannigan, who actually looked about the same weight, but there was something else. A man standing off to the side, nearly hidden beneath a tree, but his round face was sticking out, and his tongue was hanging out. He was staring at Brigid. He looked familiar, but she couldn't quite place him.

"What's that?" Niamh said. She was standing near Charlie, her face glowing.

"I don't know," Dimpna said. "A George O'Malley drawing." She put it back in the pocket of the cardigan.

"That jumper is a little big on you," Niamh said. "Is it a love drawing?"

"It's not mine," Dimpna said. "And no. It's definitely not a love drawing."

"Let's have a look," Niamh said.

"Actually," Dimpna said, pressing her hand against the pocket, "it belonged to Brigid. I'd rather hand it over to the guards."

"I'd better load the cage while I can," Charlie said. He stepped away.

"Here," Dimpna said, showing the sketch to Niamh. "Don't tell anyone I showed you."

"Why is it a secret?" Niamh took in the drawing of the caravan scene. "I would hate for him to sketch me," she said.

"Does this man look familiar to you?" Dimpna started to point to the man hidden by the tree, but Charlie was coming back in. Dimpna quickly folded the sketch and stashed it in her pocket. Niamh gave her a funny look but didn't say a word.

"You loaded the cage already?" Niamh asked.

"No," Charlie said. "I just got a call about a black Lab tied up and crying just outside of Camp."

"Oh my God," Dimpna said. "It could be Tiernan."

"Looks like that crate will come in handy right about now,"

Charlie said. "I can't be sure it's Tiernan, but the neighbor said they've never seen this dog next door before. Would you like to go with me?"

"Try and stop me," Dimpna said. After the horrible day she'd had, she needed something good. And getting Tiernan back was definitely something good.

CHAPTER 41

The last thing Cormac expected when he and Neely walked into the station after the press conference was to see Chief Superintendent McGraw grinning like a Cheshire cat and holding up a bottle of champagne. He popped the cork and hooted as the cork hit the popcorn ceiling. "Solved, solved, solved, solved!" Cormac shook his head, and McGraw's face darkened. McGraw then looked to Neely.

"We can't be sure," she said. "We still have some dots to connect."

"He drove himself into a lake with the murder weapon and the victim's hand," McGraw said. "The pair of ye were on to him. You chased him. You found him. This. Case. Is. Solved." He approached and thrust the bottle of champagne at Cormac. "Take a drink. Accept the victory. When Cormac didn't take the bottle of champagne, he offered it to Neely, who shunned it as well. McGraw shook his head and took a swig out of the bottle. "I'm glad the public doesn't know what milquetoasts the pair of ye are." He set the bottle down. "I'm closing this case. Daniel and Emma Sweeney are going to join me for the candlelight vigil, then we'll all be attending the Mass for the poor young woman, and like it or not, you're going to wear your hero hats and tell anyone who asks that all is right as rain on the Dingle Peninsula."

"Even if it's a lie?" Cormac knew better than to push Mc-Graw, but he wasn't going to be bullied into solving a case too soon.

Neely held up her hand and stepped forward. "What he means is, we had a lot of suspects. What if Brannigan didn't drive himself into the lake?"

"Our other victim was drugged with ketamine," Cormac said. "The killer could have done the same with Brannigan."

"Then placed the knife and the hand in the boot of his car," Neely said. "Alan, Eve, and Billy were right there at the lake."

"It's not them," Cormac said. "There was a man stalking her about a year ago. The lads said Brigid thought he was here. In Camp. Watching her."

"You need to keep your gob shut," McGraw said. "This case is closed."

"Help us find Brendan Keyes," Cormac said. "He's our killer."

"I know you're grieving your mother," McGraw said. "That's understandable. You did a great job, and hell if I know why you can't take praise where praise is due. But that's it. You're done, and I insist you take bereavement time."

"And if I say no?"

"Depends. Do you want bereavement time, or do you want to push pencils back in Killarney?"

Cormac was ready to retort when he felt Neely's hand squeezing his arm. He closed his eyes and said nothing.

"That's settled," McGraw said. "More champagne for me."

Cormac had just parked near his flat. He'd stopped at the off-license for a bottle of whiskey. Maybe he'd hit a pub up first and save the bottle for a nightcap. The Village Pub came to mind. It was the pub where Brendan Keyes had hung out. Maybe he'd get lucky. Maybe he'd be there and Cormac would wring a confession out of him. Neely pulled up in her squad car. If she was here to cheer him up, she could turn around and go home. He was done.

"I've got nothing for you," he said.

She eyed the bottle. "Daniel Sweeney wants to talk to you."

"What good would that do?"

"He wants to hear it from you that we've got the killer."

"That's not going to happen."

"He's a father desperate for answers."

"Nobody wants to hear the answer. Because it means there's a killer still out there. It means another father is going to lose his daughter."

"I'm listening, Cormac. I'm listening."

"I know. I know you are. And I appreciate it. You're a good sergeant. The best. This was my fuckup."

Neely waved away his comments. "What if McGraw is right? What if Brannigan is our killer? It's possible, isn't it?"

"He's a lightweight compared to our killer," Cormac said. "The kind of sicko who makes sketches so graphic they disturbed the likes of Billy Sheedy. *That's* my killer."

"Your killer. Listen to you."

"You know what I mean."

"McGraw wants you at this candlelight vigil. He's demanding it."

"He can fuck off." Cormac lifted the bottle. "I'm going to hit a pub and then hit this."

Neely narrowed her eyes. "You won't find any answers at the bottom of that bottle."

"Maybe I don't want answers. Maybe I just want it all to go away."

"Lorraine Brannigan came to the station. She said there's proof that her husband was in Dublin during the murders. McGraw is going to have to come around."

"By then, it might be too late for the next young woman."

"Then we'll save the one after her."

"Goodnight, Sergeant," Cormac said. "I'm taking the night off."

"Grief is a bitch, Inspector. Don't help it along by drowning your sorrows. They'll come back tenfold."

"I'll jump off that bridge when I come to it."

"Where are you going? Just so I know."

He sighed. "The Village Pub," he said.

"Get some food in you too."

"Defeats the purpose," he said. "But thank you."

Cormac was on his fourth pint. "I'm missing something," he said to the publican. He'd just learned that Brendan Keyes hadn't been in for days. All evidence pointed to him having left town. That was very unlike the killer. Had he simply gone into hiding? "What am I missing?" He pushed his empty glass up to the publican.

"How about a little food to soak up the alcohol," the publican said.

"Like your famous crispy chicken?" Cormac said. "Save it for the foxes."

"Crispy chicken?" the publican said. "We don't serve crispy chicken."

"No?"

The publican shook his head. "We only serve burgers and chips, or toasties," the publican said. "Makes life easy."

"Nice of you to make an exception for a fox," Cormac said. He finished his pint. "Another and a shot of whiskey."

The publican poured the shot with a shake of his head. "What's this about a fox?" he asked.

Niamh answered the phone straightaway, but the man calling sounded drunk. It took her a few minutes to understand him. "Doctor Wilde is with Charlie Meade," she said. "He got a lead on Tiernan." She heard a click and a dial tone, then stared at the phone. "Rude," she said to the phone. What was that all about?

Charlie's truck bumped along the old narrow road, toward Glanteenassig Forest Park, where they had found Brannigan's body and the caravaners. "Are we going to Glanteenassig?" Dimpna asked. Had Tiernan been there after all and they'd missed him?

"The location is a house. But it seems to be in that direction."

"I was just out here. If only I had known."

Charlie squinted as it started to rain, pummeling his windshield. "Tiernan did not run away on his own free will, I take it?"

"Tiernan never leaves the courtyard. He was taken." She swallowed hard. "Maybe we shouldn't do this without backup."

Charlie swerved at something in the road, throwing Dimpna hard against the passenger door. "You're worried this could be the killer?"

She straightened herself up and glanced at his speedometer. Why did men always have to drive so fast in the rain? "It's a distinct possibility." Although what would some madman after young women want with her?

"I'll make sure we proceed with caution. If I sense any danger, we can call it in."

Dimpna glanced at her phone. "I barely have reception."

"I can turn around if you want, but I need to make sure this dog is alright."

"Of course." A text pinged on her phone. It was from Cormac.

The Village Pub doesn't serve crispy chicken.

What in the world? Why would he be texting her this? Another came in.

Where are you?

The Village Pub doesn't serve crispy chicken.

"Something wrong?" Charlie asked.

"Just struggling to understand a text." The phone dinged again.

He lied. Get away from him.

She slid the sketch out and opened it. Then she looked at Charlie's profile. He didn't turn his head toward her, but his grip on the wheel tightened. It was him. A fat Charlie Meade. She swallowed and looked out the window. *Think. Stay calm.* Charlie was wearing his red ISPCA shirt. The rain was tapering off, and there was still a bit of daylight left. She would need every last bit of it. How good was Cujo's eyesight? Was he in the field? Was he still alive? Dimpna glanced at the back seat. There sat a thick coil of rope. She'd missed it. She'd been so concerned about Tiernan, she hadn't even looked. Soon they were coming up on the familiar field with its famous sign:

DO NOT CROSS THIS FIELD UNLESS YOU CAN DO IT IN 9 SECONDS
BECAUSE THE BULL CAN DO IT IN 10

She took a photo of the sign and texted it to Cormac. Cormac would have no idea what she meant. But Neely or any other local would. It was now or never. She undid her seat belt.

"What are you doing?" His voice was low now, and not at all friendly. She lunged for the steering wheel, and while she had the element of surprise, she jerked the wheel hard to the left, steering the truck into Donie's fence.

"Fuck!" Charlie yelled. "Stupid bitch." She threw herself at the passenger door, fumbling for the handle. He reached for her just as the shoved open the door and jumped out. She could hear him right behind her as she mounted the fence.

"I guess there's no bull," Charlie said, barreling after her.

"There is," Dimpna said as she reached the top of the fence. "I promise you."

Charlie was climbing after her. "What gave me away? The doll?"

He'd been the one in her room. He was the killer. He was a sadist. Dimpna jumped down into the field, and as she landed, she felt her ankle twisting. She had no choice. She scurried up and began tearing across the field toward the rusty tractor. Beside it was the old burial chamber where the young lad had hid from the bull. It was a tiny space, but she could fit. "Cujo!" she yelled. "Cujo!" *Please let the bull be in the field today. Please.*

"It didn't have to be this way," he said. "A drawing doesn't prove anything."

The Village Pub didn't serve crispy chicken. Such a little thing to lie about. But he couldn't tell them the real reason he had both a cage and crispy chicken; he must have used them to lure a perfectly healthy mama fox and one of her pups into the cage. Just so he could set them loose in front of Chris Henderson and run him down. Somehow, Chris had figured out that Charlie wasn't who he purported himself to be. Somehow, Henderson knew he was evil.

And once Brigid Sweeney saw George O'Malley's sketch, she knew it too.

"You can't outrun me," Charlie yelled, gaining on her. Dimpna picked up speed and screamed. She saw a flash of white and brown fur racing toward them.

"Watch out," Dimpna said. She felt a tug on her cardigan. Charlie was on her.

"You want to play, is that it?"

She struggled out of the sleeves, leaving it with him.

The bull was close. "Fuck," Charlie said. "Help!"

Dimpna saw the hole in the ground and crawled into the chamber as a loud grunt sounded behind her followed by a scream. "Help!" Charlie yelled. "Help!"

Dimpna scrunched into a ball and heard another grunt as the cry of the bull mixed with Charlie's. She peered out to see Charlie being flung into the air. For a moment, he seemed suspended in time, as he hovered midair and the bull pawed the ground. He landed with a thud facedown, and Cujo moved in to stomp him. Dimpna covered her ears and thought of Brigid tied to that tree. Her hand severed. Poor Mr. Henderson lured to the middle of the road and mowed down. Charlie, a true psychopath, pretending to be a do-gooder, moving freely among them.

"Bitch," she heard him gurgle.

Those were his last words. There was no need to point out that the bull was a male.

CHAPTER 42

Charlie Meade's truck held more evidence. Photos of Brigid, hundreds of them, from the time at Hidden Valley Caravan Park. There were also photos of Charlie from a year ago and four stones heavier. He'd been fired from ISPCA after he was reported by the owner of Hidden Valley Caravan Park for harassing women. A trove of images of women being tortured had been discovered as well. Lennon had finally received this info, but, of course, it was too late. After the incident, Meade's wife divorced him. He lost custody of his kids. And he started planning his revenge. Brigid posted everywhere they went on Instagram. She wasn't hard to follow. He stalked her for an entire year while losing weight and gaining muscle.

By the time the field was cleared and paramedics could arrive, Charlie Meade was already dead. In his pocket they found a list:

Doctor Dimpna Wilde
Detective Sergeant Barbara Neely
Vera Brannigan
Eve Murray

Apparently, he'd planned on sticking around. ISPCA confirmed that Charlie had been fired last year. They then reported that a man by the name of Chris Henderson had called them, asking about Charlie Meade. Cormac traced the call back to the same morning Henderson left the Tralee Garda Station. The front-desk clerk had given Henderson the business card for Charlie Meade. Henderson, always one for due diligence, had called ISPCA about him. He'd been told that Charlie had been fired. Shortly after that, he'd called Neely. *A wolf in sheep's clothing.* A man purportedly trying to help animals, when he was an animal himself. If only Neely had been able to understand his cryptic message. When he laid eyes on Charlie, he recognized him as the pervert staring at Brigid through the pair of binoculars left in Vera Brannigan's car.

They also found a new stack of extremely disturbing sketches. One of them Cormac wanted to burn. In it, Dimpna was tied up. The point of a knife glimmered near her throat.

Charlie had tracked the caravaners using the tag on the parrot, thus tracking Brigid, and he had access to several facilities that used ketamine. It would take a while to sort out all the details, but they had their man.

Keys and a rental agreement were found in the truck, which led them to the small cottage he was renting just outside of Camp. There they found Tiernan chained outside. He was unharmed, save for being hungry and thirsty. Dimpna dropped to the ground and threw her arms around Tiernan. He licked her ear and thumped his tail. The owner of the cottage lived in Spain, and the rental had taken place online. Inside the cottage, one entire wall was covered with photos of Brigid. Another sported photos of Dimpna, Neely, and Vera.

They held candles in the dark. The procession began at the car park where the caravan used to be parked and ended near the old oak tree where Brigid had been tied. In addition to Brigid, they were saying their prayers for Chris Henderson. It was unknown at this point if there were other victims, apart from all the women who had accused Charlie Meade of stalking them. Dimpna held hands with Aisling O'Reilly, as her family rallied behind her. Her father insisted on carrying the fox, but given that they were also honoring Chris Henderson, Dimpna found it appropriate. Ben had barely left her side, and this was the first time she could remember being surrounded by them all—her mam and da, Donnecha, and Ben. And now Aisling. She was as much a part of this family as the rest of them. Sean O'Reilly had no power over her now.

The vigil was filled with song and tears. When it was over, Dimpna made her way over to Niamh. Her eyes were red and swollen.

"How did I not know?"

Dimpna hugged her. "This is not your fault," she said. "He fooled me too."

"The thought of losing you," Niamh said, choking on her words.

"I feel the same when I think of him alone with you," Dimpna said. "We will put this behind us. We're better than our worst memories."

"I guess it's a good thing they hadn't put down that bull," Niamh said.

"Funny how life works," Dimpna said. Cujo had saved her life. He had already been put down, but he'd performed one last good deed.

She found Cormac waiting for her by her VW bus. Before she could say a word, he advanced and drew her into him. He held her tight. She felt his entire body shaking. She began to rub his back. "It's okay," she said. "It's going to be okay."

"I don't know what to do," he said. He pulled back. "I slept with Eve Murray."

"I know."

"How? How do you always know?"

She shrugged.

"It's unforgivable."

"It's not."

"I don't know what comes next."

"You grieve for your mother."

"I don't know how."

"You keep breathing. You keep living. Watch the sun rise. Howl at the moon. Bathe in the stars."

"Sounds like something my mam would say."

"Get in." She gestured to the bus.

"Where are we going?"

"I don't know," Dimpna said. "We'll find out when we get there."

ACKNOWLEDGMENTS

I had some help on the other side of the pond for this one. I'd like to thank Fiona Dwyer for providing me with videos and photos of the area around the village of Camp, and Tom with Tom's Tours Ireland for additional videos, photos, and location suggestions. And as with the first book, I'd like to thank the brilliant veterinarian/writer Austin Donnelly for patiently answering all my animal-related questions. All mistakes are my own. And back here in the States thanks as usual to my agent Evan Marshall, my editor John Scognamiglio, my publicist Larissa Ackerman, Robin Cook, and the entire hardworking team at Kensington Publishing.

Visit our website at
KensingtonBooks.com
to sign up for our newsletters, read
more from your favorite authors, see
books by series, view reading group
guides, and more!

Become a Part of Our
Between the Chapters Book Club
Community and Join the Conversation

Submit your book review for a chance to win exclusive
Between the Chapters swag you can't get anywhere else!
https://www.kensingtonbooks.com/pages/review/